Assassin

Assassin

Published by The Conrad Press Ltd. in the United Kingdom 2021

Tel: +44(0)1227 472 874
www.theconradpress.com
info@theconradpress.com

ISBN 978-1-914913-43-3

Printed and bound in Great Britain by Clays Ltd, Elcograf S.p.A

Typesetting and Cover Design by The Book Typesetters
www.thebooktypesetters.com

The Conrad Press logo was designed by Maria Priestley.

Assassin

A Hunter & Selitto Thriller

Robin Nye

By the same author

For my sister Lindsay

Prologue

September 2019

Pale light framed the square hole in the wall directly in front of him. He blinked, trying to get proper focus. The light was fuzzy. Sometimes bright. Sometimes the brightness was diminished. At other times, there was no light at all.

His head throbbed. His whole body ached. The wrist and ankle manacles had rubbed the skin raw where he had tried to free his hands and feet. He could feel the sores which had formed on the open wounds. His strength had all but deserted him. He had remained constrained by the heavy chains which only allowed him within a metre's radius of the bed. Long enough to allow him to stagger to a bucket and to a table on which meagre portions of bread and water would appear at times when he was asleep.

How long had he been in here? It was a question he had spent hours trying to answer. He remembered being at the pub over the road from the yacht club. He was hanging out with a few of the crew from one of the ocean racers which occasionally dropped anchor in the harbour. He'd crewed with some of them in the past, and had been enjoying an evening reminiscing about journeys and races they had been on together.

They'd started on the Goddards Starboard ale before moving up a gear to the Fuggle Dee Dum – nutty, hoppy and strong! The beer was so good that it just kept on sliding down his throat.

As the evening wore on, he recalled that he had started to

make eyes at an attractive woman who had been sitting with another woman on the periphery of the group. They seemed to have been enjoying listening to the nautical banter, and had laughed along with the best of the jokes. The woman had shoulder length fair hair which had pink streaks running through it. She had a rosy complexion and eyes that truly sparkled.

When 'last orders' was called, the crew had decided to return to their boat to carry on the party. He had declined an invitation to join them instead preferring to chance his luck with the woman.

She was definitely giving him a 'come-and-get-me' look. Wasn't she? He could tell that she had the hots for him. Didn't she? Yessss! He was definitely in here, no problem. He was going to score tonight.

But, as he started to move across the bar towards her, everything started to get a bit hazy. Suddenly, he was in her car, laughing as she drove through the lanes. Let's go down to the beach, she had suggested. A midnight swim would be fun, he had added. She had laughed and then proposed some skinny dipping. He was becoming aroused. He couldn't believe his luck.

He remembers arriving at a secluded area of the beach. She leans across and starts kissing him on the mouth, her tongue darting in and out of his open lips, his tongue clashing with hers as he tries to explore her sensuous mouth. Her hand drops into his lap and starts to lazily rub him through his trousers. He remembers the sensation – he is now very aroused. He's proud of his erection despite all the beer he has had to drink.

As she forces her tongue further into his mouth, he suddenly feels a sharp scratch on his neck. He tries to pull away from her but she has him in a vice-like grip. He suddenly feels all the energy drain out of him, curtains closing across his eyes as he succumbs to a deep and dreamless sleep.

Since then, he has remained on a narrow ledge which runs between consciousness and unconsciousness. He edges along the ledge and eats hungrily of the bread because he is starving. He drinks greedily of the water because he is so thirsty. But then he loses his footing and tumbles into the abyss of unconsciousness until the next time.

When he is aware of his surroundings, he spends time hallucinating. He has long conversations with his history teacher at school who sits on a chair in the corner of the room. Sometimes someone else from his past drops in to see him. A light occasionally shines down on the bed from the ceiling, and he is able to look around the room with its bare walls. He can see the two cameras which are trained directly on the bed. When the light is on, he looks at his increasingly emaciated body. He notices that his arms are bruised at the elbow joints but he doesn't know why.

His brain is struggling. He is tiring. The light is still fuzzy around the square black hole. The rest of the room is in darkness apart from the two red lights which blink above the cameras. He is lying on his side looking at the square hole. His heavy eyelids are slowly moving across his eyeballs. The uncluttered world of unconsciousness beckons once more.

1

Sunday 19 November

A white sphere of phenolic resin careered across the green baize before crashing into an identically constructed ball, this one painted in black. Enlivened by the encounter, the black ball sped towards one of the six openings on the flat slab of slate which stood exactly eighty-seven centimetres above the floor. There was an audible intake of collective breath in the darkened auditorium as the black ball juddered in the jaws of the opening before being spat out like a gobbet of well-chewed gum. It had lost all momentum and could only roll to a halt along a strip of vulcanised rubber, all life extinguished.

A cacophony of noise suddenly erupted within the amphitheatre that surrounded the heptagonal playing area – the centre of the stylishly-appointed Prism Theatre which had recently been opened in the centre of Tonbridge, a bustling market town which straddles the River Medway in the west of Kent. Spectators were vying with each other for screaming rights as they tried to make themselves heard by their heroes, one of whom was now bending towards the green baize, studiously working out angles like a modern-day Archimedes.

A tall woman in a black trouser suit and starched white blouse was trying to quieten the crowd, raising and lowering her white-gloved hands as if in an act of supplication, her impassioned expressions of 'Quiet Please!' falling on deaf ears. Finally, Archimedes seemed to have decided on his shot strategy and had chalked his cue tip to within an inch of its life. He bent to the table, his posture presenting a perfect right angle to the floor, left foot in front of right, chin resting on the cue, his eyes bearing down on the white ball before refocusing on the black ball a short distance away.

He had played this shot a thousand times. He knew the drill.

The white ball had to hit the cushion at the same time as it hit the black ball so that the black ball was nudged along the cushion to the far corner pocket.

He knew the drill.

White ball to hit the cushion at the same time it hits the black object ball. He knew the drill.

He picked his spot on the cushion, cast a couple more nervous glances between the white ball and the black ball, gently pulled the cue back and struck the white ball.

It was at moments like these that he could swear he felt his heart actually stop. He had been in these situations before but each time it became more difficult as the expectation from his adoring fans had grown to the extent that he could not let them down. This burden of expectation was getting progressively harder to bear – but he couldn't let them down. He simply couldn't!

The white ball hit the cushion in the perfect spot, lightly kissing the black ball which started sauntering along the cushion like a cheeky schoolboy bunking off classes. It had a look at the pocket. Could it be bothered to drop in? Did it fancy another few minutes of being propelled around the table? Nah! Not today! Let's get this done! The pocket looked so inviting as the ball passed the jaws and sank into the comfort of the cotton netting where it sat in splendid isolation.

The crowd was on its feet, shouting, screaming. Grown men were crying as wave after wave of emotion drained out of their bodies. It had been a gruelling session. Four hours of nip and tuck snooker. Three all, four/three, four all, five/four, five all. The eleventh and last frame with everything to play for. A few points ahead, a few points behind. Then it had become a black-ball frame with the tension rising to fever pitch. The victor waving his cue around like a crusader's battle axe, the vanquished sitting in his corner draining the last drops of a bottle of Highland Spring and mournfully wiping his cue with an old cloth which had seen better days.

Davie Monroe had been playing snooker professionally since he was eighteen years old. Ten years on and he was a regular player on the UK League circuit, mainly appearing for teams in his local Essex league. He also spent a lot of his time trying to qualify for the larger global tournaments but kept finding the competition was just too much for him. On a couple of occasions, he had scraped into the last sixty-four of a ranking tournament only to be despatched in the first round. On one occasion, he had drawn Ronnie O'Sullivan who had certainly given him a lesson he would never forget having spent most of the match sitting in his chair watching the maestro at work.

He had been thrilled to receive an invitation to take part in the inaugural event to be held at the new Prism Theatre in Tonbridge. Thirty-two professionals from Kent, Sussex and Essex had been invited with a good pot of prize money for the winner. He knew most of the other pros and had certainly fancied his chances so he had spent even more time than usual practicing in advance of the tournament. Now, a week after he had first ventured over the Queen Elizabeth II bridge, he was about to receive a smart silver trophy and a cheque for £40,000. The gods were indeed smiling on him.

But he had allegiances to his adoring fans, most of whom had also made the journey from Essex-side to west Kent and were now still screaming his name to the rafters. Davie rolled his cue under the cushion on the table and went over to a particularly boisterous group he recognised as being some of his mates from Southend. He grabbed hands, he shook hands, he high-fived, he punched knuckles, right hand, left hand, it didn't matter – everyone wanted a piece of Davie Monroe, even the fan who grabbed his left hand and gave it a congratulatory squeeze. The men around him were still singing Davie's praises as the fan stepped back, slowly turned away, climbed the steps away from the playing area, and headed for the exit.

2

Two years earlier

At a noisy and acrimonious meeting of the Tonbridge & Malling Council's Planning Committee, approval had finally been granted for the erection of a new civic centre to be built principally on the site of the Sovereign Way North car park in the centre of Tonbridge. The building was to be known as 'The Prism' and would feature a heptagonal auditorium which would attract prime indoor sports events as well as theatre and music in the round.

The idea had been the brainchild of Reggie Lemon who, along with his business partner, Jasper Lime, had formed Lemon & Lime Promotions in the early 1990s. The company had been so successful in its early years that Reggie and Jasper had moved its base to the Channel Island of Guernsey where they were able to benefit from some more favourable banking and taxation arrangements. The two men had also taken up residence on the island, and had grafted their way to riches which would have been unthinkable when they had left school at sixteen.

Both were Tonbridge born and bred but had lost their way in their early teens and had, individually, become well known to Kent Police. Time spent in the cells on Friday or Saturday nights normally preceded a visit to the Magistrates Court on a Monday morning with more and more cautions being heaped on their young shoulders.

At one of these hearings, an exasperated magistrate asked Reggie why he didn't go and do something useful like gardening instead of slobbing about in the town centre causing trouble. He even went as far as slipping Reggie a note of the name and phone number of someone who was looking for a handyman to do odd jobs around an estate out in the country near Bewl Water. Against his better judgment, Reggie decided to give it a try and, after finally managing to find a phone box that worked, he got the address and went over to Bewl on the bus to see what it was all about.

To his enormous surprise, he was greeted by someone he vaguely recognised. A fit-looking man with well-developed biceps, coiffured hair, dark glasses, gold medallions around his neck, rings on his fingers, gold bracelets on each wrist. But where had he seen him before? That Thursday, he was having a few drinks with his mates in The Chequers in Tonbridge when he nearly choked on his beer. The TV set perched precariously on a table in the corner of the pub was showing *Top of the Pops* and, there on the screen, large as life, was the man who had offered him a job earlier in the week.

Baz Biondi was the epitome of a 1980s pop superstar. Smooth talking, mean looking, fit as anything. A snappy dresser who wore shades permanently no matter what the time of day or night. And he was possessed of a very good singing voice. Reggie couldn't wait to get back to work to check out that he really was employed by Biondi, and he wasn't disappointed.

Over the next few months, Reggie and Biondi hit it off. Baz got him involved in a number of little projects which were all mainly to do with entertaining the numerous groups of people who would descend on Biondi's huge estate almost on a weekly basis. There were lakes full of fish, a nine-hole pitch & putt course, a go-karting track and a couple of tennis courts. The main swimming pool was in its own building but there was also an outside pool with water slide and a jacuzzi at one end. There was even a helter-skelter ride complete with its own ornately coloured tower.

When one of Biondi's party planners had fallen ill, Reggie had been drafted in to help with organising Baz's annual mid-summer party. This was always a major date in the social calendar when all Baz's mates from the music industry descended on the Kent countryside for what was basically a weekend thrash. Plenty of food, drink, and music-making on two stages which were set up within the grounds. In between impromptu concerts, the guests could engage in fishing, go-karting, pitch & putt – or they could simply relax in the jacuzzi with glasses of Bolly seemingly on tap. Some wanted to get back to nature and brought multi-roomed tents with them, others drove their expensive motor homes into the grounds. And, for those who couldn't spend one night without their customary luxury living, Baz provided sumptuous accommodation inside his sprawling mansion.

Reggie was captivated by the whole thing. The amount of planning that went into putting together an event like this, the detail which had to be thought through, the ordering of stocks, the contractors who had to be found for the catering and for the music systems. Were there enough toilets? How was the rubbish to be collected? Was there enough lighting? What about medical treatment facilities on site? Health & safety? Wow! He had never had to think of so many things all at the same time.

But it also sowed a seed in his head and, over the next few

months, he hatched an idea. He could sell a party planning service to the rich and famous!

He always remembered the day he finally told Biondi about his plans. For days beforehand, he had worried about how his boss would take the news that he was leaving. As it turned out, Baz couldn't have been nicer. He also told Reggie that, once he was established, he could perhaps take on the organising of one of the summer bashes. Finally, he suggested that Reggie should contact another young man who was starting to make a bit of a name for himself in the architectural world.

Reggie hadn't been too sure about how party planning and architecture went together but, if Baz Biondi had suggested that they did, then the introduction was certainly worth pursuing. So, Reggie got in touch with Jasper Lime.

Reggie and Jasper immediately sparked off each other. They both found that they had been young layabouts in the West Kent area at about the same time but, strangely, had never bumped into each other. They had, however, both come to the notice of Baz Biondi. Jasper had been a young student architect working in his father's practice in Sevenoaks. Biondi and Jackson Lime had been drinking buddies for years, and Baz had watched as Jasper had grown up, gone off the rails, got back on board again and had then started to produce some really inventive ideas for development projects. When Jackson Lime had become ill with liver disease, Jasper had taken over the small practice and was largely responsible for establishing it as one of the go-to practices in the niche entertainment sector.

Reggie soon realised that Jasper had a real talent for designing temporary structures which could be used as backdrops for the sort of events which Reggie had set his heart on organising, and the two of them started to cooperate on providing what they marketed as the ultimate party experience. And so Lemon & Lime Promotions had been born.

Over the years, Lemon & Lime had grown exponentially and had branched out into the design and build of sports and entertainment centres. The move to the Channel Islands had helped them to exercise greater financial control on the complex projects they were now engaged in, and they also enjoyed the lifestyle on the island of Guernsey.

Reggie had heard on the grapevine that Tonbridge & Malling Borough Council had become strapped for cash, and were desperately looking for ways in which they could get an injection of income without having to raid the pockets of the long-suffering council tax payers. He and Jasper had paid a visit to their old hunting ground and were amazed to find most of the pubs they used to frequent were still in business. Although there was probably now a greater choice of eateries, very little had changed.

Having spent a day wandering around Tonbridge eyeing up potential sites for development, they had turned up at the Council's Planning Department offices in Kings Hill with an outline proposition for developing the site of the car park at Sovereign Way in the centre of the town.

Surprisingly, their proposition did not fall on deaf ears and, having been encouraged to work up a more detailed plan, they quickly found that the planners were keen to press ahead

– albeit that the final decision would depend on the support of a majority of the Council Chamber. And, after many acrimonious meetings, the Council eventually gave the project the go-ahead with the Mayor of Tonbridge laying the foundation stone at a ceremony in May 2017. Thereafter, and despite a few delays, The Prism was gradually erected on the old car park area, and the people of Tonbridge had a new entertainment centre in the middle of their town.

3

Sunday 19 November

Reggie Lemon followed the Mayor of Tonbridge into the playing arena as the still boisterous crowd started to retake their seats in readiness for the presentation ceremony. Lemon & Lime Promotions had sponsored the event as a gesture of thanks to the Council, and Reggie was there to present the winner with his cheque for £40,000. The mayor would hand over the trophy.

A Master of Ceremonies had appeared from the depths of the auditorium and was now introducing the presentation party. Davie Monroe sat in his chair, beaming at his adoring fans in the audience, pushing his fingers through his thick mane of hair, scratching the back of his left hand. Johnnie 'Westie' West sat a few feet to Monroe's right, still forlornly wiping his cue with the oily-looking cloth. Davie looked across at him – why couldn't he be more cheerful? He was getting a cheque for £15,000 after all. Come on mate, cheer up!

After the introductions had been made, Westie was called up to collect his cheque. He monosyllabically answered the moronic questions asked by an increasingly excited MC before sloping back to his seat. He eyed up the cue and the cloth but then appeared to think better of having another lengthy wiping session so just stood by his chair.

The MC was now in overdrive, his voice reaching a crescendo as he announced the winner. The audience erupted again as Davie Monroe stepped forward to receive the trophy from the mayor. Reggie Lemon was pleased with the design of the trophy as he had wanted it to look like the Ryder Cup except that it was in silver instead of gold. He watched as Monroe first kissed the trophy and then held it high above his head. A small phalanx of photographers had been positioned at the other end of the snooker table and they were now merrily snapping away. Davie's victory might just make it into one of the monthly snooker magazines, and probably onto the front page of the Tonbridge Courier.

Monroe had now placed the trophy on the table and was squatting down with his face to the left of it, a smile from ear to ear, beads of perspiration forming on his brow, a sheen of sweat above his top lip. Had those lights above the table become even hotter? Meanwhile, the audience had ceased its collective caterwauling and was now engaged in voluble discussion about the match they had just witnessed. Of greater importance appeared to be a question of what was open at this time of the evening? Will the traffic have eased off yet? Who's driving? Let's get going before they close!

Reggie Lemon and the mayor had left the auditorium closely followed by Westie West, and they were now standing in the Lemon & Lime hospitality suite enjoying a glass of champagne and some of the substantial canapes which Reggie always provided at functions like this. He had a favoured supplier down in Horsmonden, and had arranged for them to do the catering for this tournament. He was not disappointed. Other local dignitaries were similarly enjoying the spread which Reggie had put on, and there was a gentle air of satisfaction that the tournament had gone well. The

Prism had been put on the map as a great venue for snooker.

Eventually, the photographers had left and Monroe was ushered out of the auditorium by the MC, and shown to his dressing room. He walked into the darkened room, the only light coming from the bulbs which surrounded a huge mirror on the wall behind the make-up table. He placed the trophy on the table and sat down on the chair – staring at the reflection of himself with the trophy. At last, he had really achieved something after all these years.

The door to the dressing room opened quietly, and a figure slipped into the room. Davie kept staring at his image in the mirror as a face he knew as well as any other swam into view on the other side of the trophy. She was still as beautiful as the day he had first met her, Davie thought. She smiled at him, her eyes bright, sparkling – genuine happiness seemed to be painted on her face. They turned towards each other and shared a momentary kiss before turning back to the mirror.

Jacqui Anderson had been Monroe's manager since the early days when he had turned professional. She was the brains behind his progress up the rankings and, over the years, she had driven him on to a level of success he could only have dreamed of. She had pushed him hard and had given him the self-belief to be successful.

She had ambitious plans for him to break into the UK's top fifty players, although she accepted that would be a hell of a challenge. But Jacqui thrived on challenges. She was also good at spotting talent, and her Anderson Sports agency was very much an up-and-coming business in the world of sports management.

Although Jacqui and Davie had been occasional lovers over the years since she had first started to manage him, their liaisons had become few and far between of late. Unless he was strutting his stuff around a snooker table, Monroe was essentially an introvert. He could be moronic and very difficult to communicate with. And, as time had gone by, he had started to become depressed with the time it was taking to break into the big time.

On the other hand, Anderson was the complete opposite. She was vivacious, outgoing, and definitely preferred life in the fast lane. She was also becoming more well-known and had an expanding number of business commitments to the extent that she found it difficult being around Monroe when he was suffering with his mood swings.

She was also increasingly concerned that Davie had been connecting with some of the low-life drug distributors in his Essex homeland, and that they were gradually reeling him in to help them get increased distribution amongst his fellow players and those who hung around at snooker clubs. She detested anything to do with drugs – especially in sport – and had lectured Monroe about how crazy he was to even think about getting involved.

But he had refused to listen to her wise counsel so these days she kept their business on a strictly 'manger & client' basis.

She now moved away and then appeared behind him, placing her hands on his shoulders, resting her chin on the top of his head, both of them staring at their image in the mirror. A grin spread across Monroe's face.

'We did it, Jacs! We bloody well did it!' he whispered.

'You certainly did, Davie!' she purred. 'The way you held it together in that last frame was sensational. I'm so proud of you!'

She watched as a rivulet of sweat made its way down the side of his face until it eventually plunged off the edge of his chin and splashed onto his black waistcoat. She also noticed droplets of perspiration cascading into his bushy eyebrows.

'Are you a bit hot, Davie?' she enquired, feeling that it wasn't that warm in the room.

'Aye, the heat from the lights over the table was getting to me during the presentation. I'll cool down in a moment.' He absent-mindedly wiped the back of his hand across his top lip, and winced as the salty perspiration seemed to agitate a small skin abrasion. He scrutinised the skin on the back of his hand and noticed a slight scratch. So many people had been maniacally shaking both his hands that he'd obviously got a nick from a long fingernail or maybe a ring or a watchstrap. He thought nothing more of it.

'We'd better join the party, Davie,' Jacqui said as she stood up and adjusted her skirt. She bent down for a quick look in the mirror but was happy with her appearance.

'You go on ahead, Jacs,' Davie said as he got up from his seat. 'I'm just getting a quick shower and a new shirt then I'll be through. Champagne all the way tonight, eh?' He smiled and winked at her. He put his arms around her and they embraced. She was somewhat alarmed to feel that the back of his waistcoat was soaked with sweat and pulled away from him.

'You sure you're OK?' she asked, giving him a steely look.

'Never better!' He smiled, and gave her a playful slap on

the bottom. 'Now, off you go and hobnob with the great and the good of Tonbridge – and get the champers organised!' With that, he slunk off to the shower room.

Jacqui stared after him before having one last look at herself in the mirror. You'll do, she thought, and then left the room on her way to the hospitality suite.

4

Sunday 19 November

The sideburns had been a mistake. Never again!

On the long, circuitous walk back to the house, there was a burning desire to rip them off but that might damage the skin underneath. Better to do things properly – avoid mistakes.

The house was in darkness. Not a glimmer of light to show that anyone was at home. A biometric access control panel at the rear of the extended double garage had been activated allowing entry to a secret apartment, and now its occupant sat in a luxurious bedroom in front of an ornate dressing table which was laden with bottles of liquids, tubes of creams, general make-up paraphernalia, boxes of tissues, brushes and combs. It was all here!

Staring at the mirror, both hands rose up to lift the quiff of hair which hung over the forehead. The wig cap was then gently peeled back to reveal long tresses of hair which had been meticulously pinned into place. Elegant fingers extracted the hairclips which were placed in a container on the dressing table. A shake of the head releasing a cascade of long copper red hair, the tresses dancing seductively over the neck and shoulders of the beautiful woman who still stared intently at her reflection in the mirror.

Eventually coming out of her reverie, she reached for one of the bottles on the table in front of her and extracted a cotton bud from a jar next to it. Undoing the bottle and dipping the cotton bud into the liquid, she gently swabbed the area around the sideburns. As she did so, the woman gingerly released the sticky material from her cheeks, all the time trying to avoid doing anything that would leave a mark. The sideburns followed the wig into the black sack which was on the floor by her feet. She gently rubbed some cream on her cheeks which were still stinging from the effects of the removal of the sideburns. That was definitely the last time she would wear sideburns. Anyway, they were now out of fashion – weren't they? Passé even?

She got up from the dressing table and moved over to a wardrobe which covered the length of one of the walls in the room. Each of its six door panels had a floor to ceiling mirror on it, and she now opened two of the doors and stood between them looking at her image in one of the other doors in front of her.

She slowly began to undress, removing the male clothing she was wearing. Most of it had been bought in the plethora of charity shops on Tonbridge High Street. The old Ted Baker bomber jacket, the Pringle V-neck jumper, an old pair of M&S cord jeans, the Charles Tyrwhitt checked 'weekend' shirt. She had certainly blended in well with all the snooker afficionados in the audience.

She loved watching herself getting undressed. She spent time removing each item of clothing, looking at herself from every angle as she slowly bared more and more of her body. This was a ritual to be savoured. Her eyes swivelled from mirror to mirror, intoxicated by her own beauty, her head gently tossing her silken hair from side to side so that it caressed the skin on her naked back.

Her toned arms crossed each other and reached around her

body, her fingers searching for a firm grip on her sports bra which always made a good job of flattening her chest. She gently manoeuvred the garment up and over her head and then watched, mesmerised, as her soft pale breasts sprang back into their natural shape. She now stood there in her panties, drinking in the heady beauty of her own naked body.

Giving herself one last lingering look in the mirrors, she turned and headed to the wet room which adjoined the bedroom. There, she stood in front of another huge mirror and threaded her hair into a shower cap, gently tucking her copper red tresses into the plastic covering. She turned to a small control panel on the wall and pressed one of the buttons.

Behind a glass screen, over one hundred jets pumped needles of water from a square shower head which was recessed into the ceiling. She leant into the shower to make sure that the temperature of the water was just right and then removed her panties. She walked into the centre of the waterfall, closing her eyes, letting the water run off her body onto the floor, turning her face up, feeling gentle pinpricks of water on her cheeks and eyelids. She was in heaven!

5

Sunday 19 November

Detective Chief Inspector Alan Iversen was enjoying a rare evening out with his wife, Jenny. An invitation to the final night of the inaugural snooker tournament at the new Prism theatre had dropped onto the desk of the head of CID at Tonbridge police station, and Iversen had decided that he was long overdue a freebie at a local event. Besides, he liked snooker and often watched the late-night highlights of tournaments shown on television.

He was now enjoying the hospitality in the Lemon & Lime Suite although he had been collared by a couple of zealous local councillors who were trying to have a discussion about crime figures in the local area. Iversen was having nothing of it and kept batting their questions away with placatory remarks until they moved away to annoy some other poor unsuspecting local dignitary. He wanted to have a word with Reggie Lemon whose collar he was sure he had felt back in the dim and distant days when he was a lowly police constable in uniform. He could see Jenny on the other side of the room deep in conversation with a woman who he knew to be the headmistress of one of the local schools. It was good that she had met someone she knew.

He sidled up to Lemon and was just about to tap him on the elbow when he noticed a commotion taking place at one of the entrances to the hospitality suite. A woman appeared to be haranguing one of the security personnel, waving her arms in a clearly agitated manner. He veered away from

Reggie Lemon and threaded his way through the milling crowd in the room until he got to the doorway. By this time, the security guard had managed to get the woman out of the room and into the corridor. Iversen followed and quickly realised that the woman was in a distressed state.

'Anything I can do to help?' he asked as he caught up with them. 'I'm a police officer,' he added in case that might help the woman.

She immediately spun round to face him. Iversen recognised her as someone he had seen sitting in the audience, in the front row looking directly across to where the players had been taking their seats between shots.

'Are you really the police?' she exclaimed breathlessly. 'Something terrible has happened. He's collapsed – I can't get him to wake up. He's just lying there!'

'Who's just lying where?' Iversen asked, taking her elbow and indicating that she should take him to wherever it was that whoever it was was lying.

At the end of the corridor there were two doors with crude cardboard cut-outs of stars stuck on them. The woman pushed through the door on the left, and Iversen found himself in what was clearly one of the dressing rooms. On one side of the room, there was a classic theatrical make-up table with a wall mirror surrounded by lightbulbs. The trophy he had seen presented earlier was sitting on the table which gave him a clue as to who he would probably be seeing next.

The woman pushed through another door at the end of the room, and Iversen could hear the sound of running water – most probably a shower. He stepped into the room, and his eyes were immediately drawn to a body lying on the floor of a huge shower cubicle. He pushed past the woman who appeared to have frozen with panic, and pulled the cubicle door open. He reached across the jets of steaming water and pushed the 'off' button.

The body was clearly that of a male and looked as if it had simply crumpled to the floor. Iversen knelt down on the wet floor of the shower and urgently felt for a pulse before turning the head and the upper body. As the shoulders came round, the sightless eyes of Davie Monroe stared back at the head of Tonbridge CID.

Iversen stared back at the man who he had been enthusiastically applauding only some sixty minutes earlier, a deep frown creasing his forehead as he noticed a pool of vomit which was now spreading across the floor from underneath the body.

He stood up and stepped back from the shower, almost tripping over the woman who he had forgotten was also in the room with him.

Iversen turned to her, apologising profusely as he hurried her out of the shower room. 'I'm afraid that I'm going to have to ask you to leave these rooms until I can get a team here,' he said as he gently ushered her across the dressing room to the doorway back into the corridor. The security guard led the way and, once all three of them were out of the room, Iversen shut the door and turned to the guard.

'You stay here and don't let anyone into this room until I get one of my team here,' he instructed. 'Shouldn't take too long.' The guard nodded.

Iversen then crossed to the other starred door and, on

opening it, found that the room was empty. He flicked the light switch and then gently guided the woman into the room and across to one of the two settees arranged along the wall. She sat down rubbing her eyes which were still streaming with tears. Iversen spotted a box of tissues on the make-up table and took them over to the woman.

'Here,' he said. She took a couple of the tissues and started wiping her eyes and face. 'Could you just tell me who you are and how you know the man in the shower.'

'Yes, sorry,' the woman whispered between sobs, 'I'm Jacqui Anderson and I'm also Davie Monroe's manager. Have been all his professional life. And now he's… he's….' Another huge sob engulfed her whole body, tears rolling down her cheeks, black mascara starting to darken the cheeks underneath her eyes.

'Okay,' Iversen said, reaching into his jacket pocket for his phone. 'I'll just have to make a couple of calls and then we can have a chat. You just wait here and I'll be straight back.'

Iversen crossed the corridor and entered the other dressing room, making sure he closed the door properly once he was inside. He then made his way into the shower room where the body of Davie Monroe was still on the floor of the shower. He held up his phone and quickly fired off some shots of the body to make sure that he had a record of the scene as he had left it. He also crouched down and took a couple of shots of the area of vomit which was still visible on the floor of the shower cubicle.

As he exited the shower room, he heard voices in the corridor so he strode across the dressing room and opened the door just as a couple of paramedics arrived, one of whom he thought he recognised.

'Through here,' he said pointing towards the shower room. 'On the floor in the shower.' The medics barrelled through the door into the dressing room, their bags of medical paraphernalia scraping against the newly-painted door frame. Iversen followed and took up a position just to the inside the shower room and watched as the medics went to work on the body. He wasn't surprised when, after a couple of minutes, they looked up at each other and then back at him.

'Looks like we're too late here,' one of them said. 'Can't find a pulse or any sign of cardio activity.' They both got up from the floor and took off protective gloves. Iversen stepped back into the dressing room and waited for the medics to emerge.

'Any initial thoughts?' he asked as the medics started to punch information into their tablets so that it could be relayed back to HQ.

'Difficult to say.' It was the medic that Iversen thought he recognised. He now saw her name badge – Sharon Weston – but just couldn't remember under what circumstances the two had met in the past. 'It looks as if he may have suffered some sort of catastrophic trauma which closed his organs down in a short period of time. He's probably been dying for the last couple of hours, but didn't realise it. I'll be interested to hear what the cause of death is.'

'Okay! Thanks Sharon – the CSIs should be here soon so we'll get the place locked down,' Iversen said as he followed the medics out of the room. 'I'll try and get you a copy of the autopsy report.' With a wave, the medics wandered off down the corridor with their heavy bags as Iversen scrolled through his list of contacts and then hit the call button.

Detective Inspector Sarah Hunter was just finishing a week as on-call Senior Investigating Officer for the West Kent sector this week and, as was her preference during those weeks when she was on-call, she chose to spend most evenings in the Operations Room at the Tonbridge police station. Sarah and her team were still working hard on clearing up a complex case involving the trafficking of young girls for the sex trade which they had busted a few months earlier so she was grateful for the quiet time that these evenings offered. That was until her phone sprang into life on the desk beside her.

'Good evening, sir,' she answered, recognising the caller ID.

'Hi, Sarah. Are you in Tonbridge?' Iversen was straight to the point – no pleasantries. Sensing something was up, Sarah got up from the desk and walked stiffly over to the window, looking down on the trail of red brake lights which was still encircling the roundabout beneath the office window.

'Yes, sir. In the Ops Room,' she replied. 'Everything okay?'

'Afraid not,' Iversen continued. 'I'm at that snooker event at The Prism. Without going into too much detail, we've got an IC-One male who has died on the premises in what could be suspicious circumstances. Can you get up here with some uniforms and take charge of the scene so that I can get to work on making sure that no one leaves the building? When you get here, I'm upstairs and will be in the hospitality suite. You should be able to find it quite easily.'

'Right!' She was already across the room, gathering her coat as she went. 'On my way!'

6

Sunday 19 November

Wrapping herself in a giant Egyptian cotton bath sheet, the woman returned to the bedroom. Shaking her head from side to side to loosen her hair after freeing it from the confines of the shower cap, she walked over to a small fridge which sat on top of a storage unit just to one side of the dressing table.

Opening the door, she reached into the fridge and extracted a bottle of Bacchus white wine from the Bolney Estate vineyard in Sussex which she had recently visited. Bending down to open a small cupboard in the storage unit, she selected one of her expensive Zalto Denk'Art wine glasses and poured a measure of the opaque chilled liquid into it. Drawing the thin lip of the glass to her nose so that she could smell the exquisite bouquet of elderflower and gooseberry, she took a sip of the wine before heading over to the bed.

Sitting on the edge of the bed, she opened the drawer in the bedside cabinet and released a mobile phone from its secret compartment. This phone very rarely left the apartment and only one other person knew its number. Not surprisingly there were no messages. He would be unlikely to have called her unless there was a real problem, she told herself.

She scrolled through a couple of news channels on the small screen but they wouldn't yet have the news of Monroe's demise. So, she whiled away her time by looking at exotic locations for her next trip abroad. Once the cash hit the account in Bermuda following her latest escapade, she would disappear overseas for a while if for no other reason than to get away from another British winter. But where to go?

Her glass of wine was soon finished and she carefully put it down on the bedside cabinet. Looking at the clock in the top right corner of the screen, she thought that it was time to make a call. Better ring the old bastard before he starts getting twitchy, she reasoned. He'd once held back five grand from her fee because she hadn't called him within an hour of a hit. They had had a monumental bust up over that but he eventually settled the matter. She liked to think that he had agreed to pay because he was worried that she might come after him!

She dialled up a number she knew by heart, and then lay back on the bed while the call was connected. It was answered on the third ring.

'Tinx!' He always called her Tinx. It was his shortened version of Tinkerbelle, the name she had given herself. They had joked that he should be Peter Pan, but she knew exactly who he was. He had a divine husky voice which she would recognise anywhere. Was it due to an earlier addiction to nicotine or had he had some sort of problem with his vocal cords? She had no idea but she had to admit that she found the sound of his voice mildly arousing.

'What you got for me?' he continued.

She told him all about the hit on Davie Monroe and, although she hadn't been able to yet find out if he had been confirmed dead, she knew that it was highly unlikely that he could survive. There was no antidote to the toxin she had dispensed.

'Great news, Tinx!' he growled. 'Send me a signal when you get confirmation. I'll then organise the usual charitable donation to Bermuda without any deductions!' She heard him chuckle – a little joke! She raised her eyes to the ceiling, focusing on a point beyond the mirror tiles. She was in her own little world. Wonder when I'll get rid of this jerk, she speculated.

She was just thinking of hanging up when he was back on the line, an unusual sense of urgency now in his voice.

'I've got another project for you!' She frowned and swung her legs off the bed, sitting up now, paying attention. 'You still there, Tinx?'

'Yeah!' she said, reaching into the drawer to get hold of her Bluetooth call recorder. She didn't use the recording device on the phone as she didn't want Peter Pan knowing that he was being recorded.

She listened as the man described the target for her next hit. Unusually, it was to be a woman, and she found herself frowning at her reflection in the mirror on one of the wardrobe doors. But she kept listening.

'That's about all the information I can give you,' he eventually concluded. 'You'll probably need to take a bit of time setting this up but do watch out! She is very – and I mean very – smart. The slightest indication that something's not right and you'll get rumbled. And that, my dear Tinx, will be *sayonara* for you!'

A slight shiver made its way down her spine. She wasn't normally spooked when he gave her warnings about a target but, in this instance, he had just sowed the tiniest seed of uncertainty in her mind. She shook her mane of hair as if trying to rid herself of any self-doubt.

The man droned on. 'If you need any advice, I'd say that you'll probably be better to play the long game. But I'll leave that up to you. That's why I'm paying you!' She could hear him chuckling at his own joke.

'And you say she lives completely alone? No partners, pets, maids, gardeners, other hangers on?' she asked.

'Affirmative!' That voice again. Almost melodious. Mid-Atlantic perhaps? She'd probably be disappointed if she could see the face. Better to dream.

'Okay! No time limit but soon. And the fee will be higher.' She did a quick calculation in her head and then gave him the numbers.

'Hey, Tinx, you're one expensive lady!' he scoffed.

'You'd better believe it!' she responded. Silence hung in the air, both parties weighing up their options. 'Are we go for this or not?' she pushed.

Eventually he replied with a sigh. 'How could I ever refuse you, Tinx, but you do drive a hard bargain!'

'Take it or leave it!' She had the upper hand and she knew it. He would never find anyone better than her.

'Yeah! Yeah! Yeah!' he finally conceded. 'You got me! Let's do it. I'll get back to you with a couple more details but let's just do it!'

The next thing she heard was a click followed by an empty silence. He'd hung up on her. Bloody tosser!

7

Sunday 19 November

S arah Hunter would normally have power-walked her way
to The Prism from the Tonbridge police station but her
legs and ankles were still recovering from the beating she had
received at the hands of a Romanian madman who had been
involved in the trafficking case. So, she drove her car round
to The Prism and took the lift to the first floor.

Coming out of the lift, she immediately took in the layout
of the floor. The hospitality suite was behind the two sets of
doors immediately to her left and she could hear the steady
drone of conversation coming from within. Peering into the
distance, she could see someone in a security uniform
standing uneasily at the end of the corridor. She was just
contemplating whether to go and speak to the guard first
when one of the doors to the hospitality suite opened and her
boss peered out.

'Ah, Sarah, you made it!' Iversen exclaimed. 'Hang on
there!' He then disappeared back into the suite before
reappearing through the other door. He ushered her back
towards the lift so that they could talk without being
overheard by the guard.

'Right! I've managed to keep everyone in the hospitality
area so that we can at least get a short statement from each of
them. Are uniforms on the way?'

Sarah nodded. 'I left orders for half a dozen PCs to be
deployed to The Prism before I left the station.'

'Good!' Iversen looked relieved. 'What about the Crime

Scene gang?'

Iversen always referred to the Crime Scene Investigation unit as a 'gang' which in some ways annoyed Sarah Hunter as it sounded unprofessional. However, she did find the description quite amusing as, on occasion, they acted like a bunch of naughty kids on a school outing.

'I spoke to Beth Dench and she's sending the boys along to get things started. Once they've scoped the scene, they'll report back to her and decide whether to put in an all-nighter or wait for the morning.' Anticipating Iversen's next question, she carried on. 'Pathologist's also on his way – we've got Norman this weekend so he'll be glad of something to do. Should be here soon.'

As if on cue, the lift pinged behind them and the doors opened to reveal six PCs who all filed out to stand awkwardly with Iversen and Hunter.

While Iversen briefed the constables, Hunter sauntered off down the corridor towards the security guard who still stood between the two dressing rooms. She showed her warrant card which the guard studied before appearing to finally satisfy himself that he was, indeed, talking to DI Sarah Hunter.

'That's where they found the body,' he told Hunter, pointing to the door on her left, 'and there's a witness in there.' He pointed to the other door. Hunter took the door on the left first.

The room was dimly lit by the lightbulbs surrounding a large mirror which was attached to a make-up table and cupboard unit. A silver trophy had been positioned in front of the mirror, the lights setting off caustic reflections across the darkened ceiling and walls of the room. Her eyes were drawn to a pale light coming from a doorway to her left. After crossing the room and pushing the door open, she found herself in a well-appointed bathroom which boasted two washbasins, a toilet unit and a large shower cubicle which took up most of the available space.

Lying on the floor of the shower was the body of a man. She crouched down and instinctively felt for a pulse on the man's neck even though she knew that the medics had confirmed that the man was dead. Old habits die hard and she was immediately aware of how cold and clammy the skin had already become. She peered at the small pool of vomit which had now congealed beside the body, and eased her phone out of her back pocket so that she could take a couple of shots of the position of the body. It would be very important for her to be able to recall its position at a later stage.

A sharp pain suddenly jagged its way up her leg from her left ankle and she quickly got to her feet and backed away from the shower. That bloody ankle's going to be the death of me, she cursed to herself. Stuffing her phone into her back pocket, she retraced her steps across the dressing room and back to the corridor. She stared at the guard.

'Do not, repeat do not let anyone into that room unless I say so!'

The guard looked a bit sheepish but didn't respond so Hunter entered the other dressing room.

A woman was sitting on a sofa with a box of tissues by her side and a pile of used tissues next to that. Hunter looked around and, spotting a small waste bin by the make-up table, took it over to the sofa. She then got hold of a chair and sat in front of the woman. She was well-dressed, probably in her late thirties with shoulder length auburn hair. She seemed intent on making no eye contact with Hunter, her gaze fixed firmly on the floor in front of her. Eventually, she plucked another tissue from the box.

'I'm Detective Inspector Sarah Hunter from Tonbridge CID. Perhaps you could just tell me who you are?'

The woman suddenly looked up at Sarah, tears streaming down her face, curtains of mascara now accentuating the rivulets of salty water, her eye make-up all over the place. 'I'm Jacqui Anderson,' she said in a faltering voice.

'And you know the man in the other room?' Hunter pressed on.

Jacqui Anderson nodded and then let out a sob, trying desperately to control herself in front of this police officer. 'He's Davie Monroe, the snooker player. I'm his manager.'

Monroe's name didn't mean anything to Hunter. She wasn't really into sport, and snooker had certainly never interested her. A game of pool in the pub after a few drinks perhaps but that was the limit of her knowledge.

Hunter waited while Jacqui Anderson took another tissue and blew her nose before continuing. 'Can you just give me an idea of the events of the last hour or two so I can understand the sequence of events?'

In a faltering voice, Anderson gave her the bare details of Monroe's victory, the presentation, their chat in the dressing room, her attendance at the hospitality event and then her growing concern when Monroe didn't appear at the sponsor's party. She had gone back to the room and found him on the floor of the shower. That was all she knew. There had been another policeman here who had told her to sit in this room. So here she had stayed.

Sarah asked a few supplementary questions to get a better idea of timings but Anderson was so distraught that she had difficulty articulating any specific details. Eventually, she decided that she would leave Jacqui Anderson to her own thoughts while she went off to find out how things were going with processing the guests in the hospitality suite.

She exited the dressing room and was halfway along the corridor when she heard the ping of the lift which heralded the arrival of the Crime Scenes Investigation team.

'Hello, boys!' Hunter greeted them as they lurched down the corridor towards her, huge cases of equipment in tow. 'This way,' she beckoned as she turned and headed back to the dressing rooms.

'Evening, ma'am,' Jim Carrigan, the taller of the two CSI officers, said as they reached the end of the corridor. The other, Donny Campbell, nodded a greeting as they came to a halt in front of the dressing rooms.

Hunter pushed her way into the room on the left and signalled for the CSIs to follow her. Once they were all inside and the door had been closed, she gave them as much information as she had so far managed to gather and then showed them into the shower room. Carrigan quickly opened one of the heavy cases and took out a small portable light panel which he set up so that they could get a better view of the body.

Davie Monroe lay prostrate in front of them, his skin already a deathly shade of white, water and vomit pooled around him. The two CSI officers had squatted down beside the body for a closer look, exchanging knowing glances with each other.

'Probably best if I leave you to it?' It was more of a question than Hunter had intended but she wanted to get back to Jacqui Anderson and get a better idea of the events which had led up to Monroe's death. There was a chorus of 'Okay!' from the CSIs so she turned to leave the bathroom. And walked straight into Norman Partington.

'My dear Sarah!' the pathologist enthused as he offered his hand by way of a greeting. 'How lovely to see you again!'

Hunter shook him warmly by the hand. 'And you, Norman. I hear that we've been keeping you away from the golf course!'

He smiled back at her. 'Don't you worry about that. Silly game was frustrating the hell out of me so it's been good to get back to doing something I know that I'm not bad at!'

As a retired Home Office pathologist of some distinction, Norman Partington was a well-respected member of the pathology team at Tunbridge Wells. His genial nature and the care he took when informing those attending his post mortems made visits to the mortuary almost bearable for Hunter and her team. Sarah herself had learnt a huge amount from Partington, and they had become firm friends although she seemed to rarely get to see him these days. So, tonight was a bonus.

She moved aside and indicated the door into the bathroom. 'There's an IC-One male in there all ready for your kind attention, Norman. And I'll look forward to hearing what you make of the cause of death. Might even put in an appearance at the PM if I have the time.'

Partington smiled, a customary twinkle in his eyes. 'It's always a pleasure to welcome you to a post mortem in my lair, Sarah. You know that. But you so very rarely make the journey!' he exclaimed.

Hunter smiled. 'This could just be the opportunity I've been looking for!' And with that she turned and headed out of the dressing room.

Outside in the corridor, she checked her phone to see if there were any new messages before pushing her way into the other dressing room to see how Jacqui Anderson was getting on.

But the room was empty. No sign of Anderson. An eerie silence. Perhaps she was in the bathroom cleaning up her face. She crossed the dressing area and stuck her head through the bathroom door.

Empty!

'What the fuck's going on here?' she murmured under her breath, her eyes roaming the empty spaces. She re-crossed the room and nearly wrenched the door off its hinges before striding out into the corridor, almost knocking the security guard over.

'Where's that woman gone? Did you let her leave the room?' Hunter was trying to keep her voice down and her temper in check.

'Said she needed to get to a toilet,' the guard replied, beginning to look somewhat alarmed as Hunter's eyes bored into him, 'so I directed her to the female toilets which are just down past the hospitality suite.'

'God's sake! There's a toilet in the bloody dressing room

you idiot!' she exploded. 'Didn't you think that it was a strange request considering that each of these rooms has a bathroom?' Sarcasm wasn't normally in Hunter's make up but, in this instance, she couldn't help ladling it on. She was furious.

'You wait here while I take a look in the toilets,' she ordered. 'Do not let anyone, repeat *anyone*, into these two rooms until I come back. And if that woman does reappear, keep her under lock and key until I get back. Got it?' The guard was cowering away from her but nodded and then watched as Hunter stalked back up the corridor, a perceptible limp in her step.

As expected, there was no one in the female toilets. Just for good measure, Hunter also took a quick look in the male toilets but there was no one in there either. She then crossed the corridor and poked her head into the hospitality suite. Everything appeared to be under control with the guests having been split into six groups. One PC had been assigned to each group, and they were busily taking names and addresses as well as making a note of any other information which might assist Hunter's investigation.

She noticed that Iversen was talking to the Mayor of Tonbridge. He spotted her and excused himself before crossing the room to speak to her.

'I'm trying to get everyone processed as quickly as possible,' he told her whilst taking a furtive look around the room. 'Taking a bit of time as you can see, but everyone seems to be very cooperative. Probably to do with the lovely canapes on offer. Have you tried any of the food? It's really very good!'

Hunter cast her mind back to the M&S cheese & pickle sandwich she had consumed about five hours beforehand but decided that now was not the time to get stuck into the undoubtedly excellent buffet which was on offer here.

'Think I'll give it a miss if you don't mind,' she said by way of excusing herself from any further discussion about food. 'We've got a bit of a problem down the other end of the corridor which needs sorting.'

Iversen raised an eyebrow and looked inquisitively at her. Instinctively, they both moved closer to the door as Hunter briefed her boss on developments.

'CSIs are here,' she started, 'and Norman has arrived to take a first look. And then there's the woman sitting in the other dressing room saying she's Jacqui Anderson and that she's the snooker player's manager. Only she's now no longer sitting in the dressing room!'

Iversen stared at Sarah, a look of incomprehension on his face, his jaw slightly dropping. 'Not there? What? She's done a runner? Is that what you're telling me?'

As Iversen was speaking, Hunter backed away to the door of the suite and glanced down the corridor to make sure that the guard was still maintaining his position at the other end of the corridor.

'Looks like our Ms Anderson has indeed done a runner - disappeared! Just walked straight out past that dozy security guard.' Hunter was still seething.

'Jeez!' Iversen exclaimed. 'What the hell's she up to? You would have thought that she might have wanted to stay around until her protégé had been zipped into a black bag!'

Hunter gave her boss a quizzical look. He didn't usually use such flippant language but perhaps he had been emboldened by the glass of red wine which he was still clutching in one hand. There was, however, something that Sarah really needed to know.

'Did you give her to believe that you thought Monroe was dead?'

Iversen gave this question some thought, going back over his discovery of the body on the floor of the shower, the little pool of vomit, turning the water off, feeling for a pulse. Had he ever actually said that he thought that Monroe was dead? Eventually, he told Hunter that he couldn't specifically recall making such a statement to the woman.

'Well, I didn't mention he was dead either,' Hunter explained.

Iversen stared at her. 'Bloody hell! You don't think *she* killed him do you?'

Hunter hadn't got quite that far in her reckoning – but it was certainly a possibility. But how?

'No idea, sir,' she concluded. 'No immediate sign of cause of death so we'll have to leave that to Norman Partington.'

Sarah could see a dark cloud developing over her boss's face, the deep furrows of a frown spreading across his forehead.

'So, can we just confirm that it is definitely the snooker player we've got on the floor in the shower,' Iversen sighed. Hunter nodded. Of that there was no doubt.

'Hell!' he continued. 'That's going to attract an army of scribblers! They'll be all over this like wasps on a jam tart! And you say the woman's gone as well? God! This'll be in the nationals!'

Hunter could only nod sagely in agreement. 'Which makes finding this bloody woman our number one priority!'

8

Sunday 19 November

Tinx had been dozing, running through the events of the evening, checking for anything that might have given her away.

The new glove had been a revelation. She had worked so hard on that, trying to get maximum delivery without endangering herself. It had been easy to put on and disposal afterwards had been quick so as to avoid detection. The glove was now in a secure container in her laboratory where it would stay until she had a chance to properly assess whether it could be used again. But there were other ways of dispensing the deadly poisons which she had created so there was no rush. She already had other ingenious ideas about how to deliver her brand of instant death but she would take her time to assess the risks and rewards of each idea. Then she would start development.

She pulled the duvet a little further up the bed until it was tucked under her chin. She could make out the vague outline of the room around her through the subdued lighting which was recessed into the walls at floor level. The electrician who had installed this had called it 'floor washing' which he told her was a method of skimming light across the floor. As her room had no windows, the skimmed light at least allowed her the sort of ambient light which she might have got from moonlight coming through a window. She could also dim the level of light right down which is how she now had it set.

She had just turned over to get more comfortable when the

phone buzzed and a tiny red light flashed on the screen. She opened one eye and looked across at the code at the bottom of the screen. Good! Visitors to her secret bunker entered through an elaborate security system involving iris recognition. Once the system was activated, the identity of the person seeking entry was established by a detailed image of the iris being transmitted to this phone. If it matched the image which was already stored on the phone, a photo of the visitor would appear on the screen. Tinx would then activate the locking system and the visitor could gain entry. Having now confirmed the identity of the visitor, she transmitted the unlocking signal. Eventually, a thin edge of light appeared around the outline of the door into the bathroom.

She heard the shower powering up and could picture her visitor standing naked under the hot jets of water. For a moment, she thought of joining in but then decided to wait – anticipation was so much more rewarding. She shivered at the thought of what was to come. She turned over just as the light in the bathroom was extinguished and watched in the mirrors of the wardrobe as a figure made its way across the darkened bedroom and crawled under the duvet beside her.

Tinx felt soft breasts caressing her back as an arm came over and very gently massaged her own nipples. She felt her bum being caressed by a delicate area of pubic hair as a pair of legs followed the contours of her own legs in a classic spooning embrace. The nerve endings on her skin were fully aroused, pulses of sheer pleasure coursing through her body. The hand left her breasts and slowly caressed the flat of her stomach, stopping to embrace the jewel which adorned her belly button. Tinx was so aroused by now that she grabbed the hand and thrust it into the deepest recesses of her body. She heard the other woman let out a contented sigh, her tongue now exploring the nape of Tinx's neck.

All of a sudden, Tinx's whole body tensed as wave after wave of pleasure washed over her. She let out a low satisfied moan as her limbs seemed to go weak and her breathing became ragged as she came down from the dizzy heights of delight. The two women lay there entwined, fingers still gently exploring and caressing the soft skin of each other's bodies.

After a while, she untangled herself from the embrace of the other woman. They both lay on their backs, breathing heavily. Tinx turned onto her side and allowed her hand to caress ample but firm breasts. She looked at the woman's face in the dim glow thrown up by the floor lighting.

The woman opened her mouth as if to say something.

'Shhh!' Tinx dabbed a finger across the woman's soft lips.

She was just pleased that the woman was here and that they would have the opportunity for one more night together. This woman could take her to places very few others could get anywhere near. There was something about her body and the way she used it that simply blew Tinx's mind. And the heights of arousal that she reached under the command of those hands were truly amazing.

Indeed, Tinx could feel herself becoming aroused again and, suddenly straddling the other woman, she plunged her body downwards, her small pert breasts nestling against their fuller counterparts, her tongue urgently exploring the darkest recesses of the woman's open mouth.

They made love shamelessly for what seemed like an

eternity until, utterly exhausted, they fell asleep in each other's arms with Tinx feeling her whole body gradually subsiding from the absolute height of pleasure. She knew it would never happen again – but at least the last time had been positively memorable.

9

Monday 20 November

Both hands on the clock in the hospitality suite were nudging the number twelve at the top of the dial as Sunday slipped into Monday. The last of the guests had finished giving their statements, and were now being ushered to the lift by an increasingly exasperated DCI Alan Iversen. The whole process had taken far longer than he had intended but at least everyone had been both patient and cooperative.

Sarah Hunter had flitted between the hospitality suite and the dressing rooms in order to keep an eye on any progress being made by the CSIs. Norman Partington had left earlier with a smile, a wave of his hand and a promise to reveal all once he had got Davie Monroe on the table down at Tunbridge Wells mortuary. And the security guard had been sent packing with a rather large flea in his ear. Even though Hunter felt that she was probably wasting her time, it was good for her soul to have given him such a severe bollocking that he couldn't wait to get out of the building.

Jimbo Carrigan and Donny Campbell had made good progress. They had arranged for the body to be removed by a couple of grumpy porters from the Coroner's Office who had grumbled about having their Sunday evenings interrupted. Hunter had told them not to be so wet and had stressed that the body was to be on the table ready for the post-mortem by 08.00 a.m. the following day or else. That hadn't helped relations between them but, by then, she was past caring.

In the hospitality suite, all the local dignitaries had left a long time ago. Reggie Lemon and his entourage had also departed leaving the Lemon & Lime catering team to pack up all their gear. They were moving on to their next venue with a quick pit stop at their local kitchens to stock up on supplies for another event that was taking place the following day over in Surrey. A caretaker had appeared at some point in the late evening and was now fussing around the room making sure all the furniture had been returned to its rightful spot.

Sarah Hunter had obtained keys to the dressing rooms from the caretaker, and had impressed on him that these were crime scenes. Under no circumstances was anyone to be allowed into the rooms. The CSIs had taken the keys and, after locking up the rooms, they had covered the doors with an intricate pattern of yellow and black tape bearing the motif 'Crime Scene – Do Not Enter'.

Iversen had sent his wife home earlier and he was now in conversation with the last of the uniformed constables. Hunter watched them chatting easily to each other. This was typical Iversen, very much a copper's copper. He had joined as a constable on the beat and, by sheer hard work, had risen through the ranks to DCI. Now in his mid-fifties, he was probably not destined to go much further but he was always looking out for talented youngsters who, in his opinion, had the potential for making an impact in the Kent force. The young constable to whom he was now talking had obviously done something of note to attract Iversen's attention this evening.

Hunter now moved her position so that she was in Iversen's line of sight behind the constable and raised her wrist to point at an imaginary watch. He got the message and quickly brought his conversation with the young man to an end before crossing the room to stand next to Hunter. They both observed the caretaker repositioning the tables and chairs with such precision.

'Time to go,' she said. 'Are you looking for a lift?'

'No, I've got the car thanks. Jenny went home with one of her friends who she discovered was here as a guest of the mayor.'

Iversen put his coat on and pulled up the collar. 'What about the Anderson woman?'

Hunter shrugged her shoulders. 'I'll get back to the nick and get all that started. At least we know who she is so it shouldn't be too difficult to trace her. However, I might put out an All-Ports Warning on her just in case she is thinking of skipping the country. Funny really – she didn't come across as anything other than deeply upset.'

'Clearly a good actress,' Iversen mused, 'but, yes, an APW would be a good idea.'

Then, looking around the room one more time, he instinctively pulled at the collar of his coat again and started making for the door. 'Let's catch up late afternoon. I should be back from Maidstone by then.' And, with that, he was gone.

After one last look round the room, Hunter followed him out into the corridor and then couldn't resist one last look in the female toilets. After pushing open the doors of all the cubicles, she suddenly caught sight of herself in the mirror.

'What on earth are you hoping to find in here, you silly woman?' she berated her reflection. It had been a long day. Time to get on home.

10

Monday 20 November

She entered a pin number into her phone and then held the screen to her left eye for iris recognition. There was a click as the wall panel in front of her moved ever so slightly. She pushed it just as far as she needed to get through into the secret room beyond before turning and firmly closing the door behind her. Strategically placed LED lighting immediately flooded the work surfaces which wound their way around the four walls of the room.

A sterile atmosphere pervaded the whole room, and there was a low hum from two small refrigerators which sat next to each other under the work surfaces. There were two defined workstations, each with its own upholstered pneumatic chair and an array of laboratory-standard equipment which had been placed within easy reach of each work area. There were analytical balances, centrifuge tubes and trays, orbital shakers, and vial racks. Other equipment was stored in drawers under the workbenches, each drawer marked with a single letter of the alphabet.

She plucked a white lab coat from a peg beside the door and, quickly pulling it on, she shuffled across the room to sit at one of the workstations. From the drawer in front of her, she removed a face mask and a pair of nitrile gloves both of which she put on. She quickly pinned her hair up and pulled on a plain floppy cap before putting on a pair of safety glasses which she had fished out of the drawer.

Now that she was fully kitted up, she reached to her right

and slid the mesh door across the front of a cabinet before carefully extracting a couple of petri dishes. She then opened a small microbiological incubator which was located on the workbench in front of her and, carefully extracting a tissue culture dish, she placed this next to the petri dishes.

Reaching down to open a drawer to her left, she took out a single-channel pipette and carefully drew clear liquid from one of the petri dishes. She transferred this to a vial which she had plucked from the rack in front of her and gently allowed the liquid to flow into the vial. She then transferred two drops of liquid from each of the petri dishes into the vial and placed the cap on it.

She got up from the workbench and walked over to the other side of the room where she placed the vial into a benchtop biological shaker. She switched it on and then bent down to open the small refrigerator. A blast of cool air tumbled out around her legs and caused her to give an involuntary shiver. She reached in and extracted a small tray of vials, each containing more clear liquid. Returning to the workstation, she opened another drawer and took out a hypodermic syringe which she carefully unwrapped from its sterilised packaging.

She flicked a switch on the shaker and the machine came to a stop. Extracting the vial from the shaker, she slid it into one of the holders on the rack in front of her. Picking up the syringe, she drew off some of the liquid in the shaken vial and then dipped the needle into one of the vials she had taken out of the refrigerator, carefully drawing off some of its contents. She examined the clear liquid now encased in the tube of the hypodermic and judged this to be exactly what she needed.

Sliding the cap over the needle, she smiled at the instrument of death which she now held in her hand.

She bent down and returned the vials to the refrigerator and the petri dishes to the cabinet before removing all her protective equipment and returning it to the drawer. She hooked the lab coat over its peg, and then let herself out of the room. As soon as the door had clicked shut, the lights were automatically extinguished. Outside the room, the wall panel slid back into place – everything was normal.

She made her way back to the secret apartment and entered the bedroom. The woman lay motionless on the bed, the dim lighting giving her skin a sallow complexion. Trusting that she had not administered too heavy a dose of chloroform, she sat on the bed and checked the woman's neck for a pulse. She then reached over to manoeuvre the woman on to her back, making sure that her head was turned to the side.

She allowed her hand to momentarily drift down over the woman's naked body, gently playing with one of her nipples, drawing imaginary circles across her stomach. But she knew that time was marching on.

Getting up off the bed, she activated the bedside light and turned the beam so that it lit up the woman's body. Carefully removing the cap from the hypodermic syringe, she flicked at the flesh surrounding a small, colourful tattoo of an elephant which nestled in the crook of the woman's right arm.

Once she had agitated the vein so that she could see it through the intricate tattoo, she carefully guided the tip of the needle to the selected landing site and exerted pressure until the needle had punctured the skin and entered the vein. She gripped the barrel of the hypodermic and deftly depressed the plunger. The clear liquid flowed effortlessly into the woman's bloodstream and started its inexorable journey towards her heart.

11

Monday 20 November

'Morning, Miss Frobisher!' A cheery greeting from the security guard as he operated the barrier of the secure parking lot which surrounded a modern three storey building located in the Kings Hill business park just on the fringes of West Malling in Kent.

The driver of the black Audi TT Roadster waved back as she turned to the left and drove around to the north side of the building. She easily found a parking space and, after a quick check in the mirror, she got out of the car and made her way towards the entrance to the building. Swiping her pass through the card reader beside the automatic doors, she passed through another set of glass doors before arriving in the spacious reception area.

'Morning, Samantha!' the receptionist called over as the woman made her way to the lift.

'Hi, Christa! How're you doing?' she replied as she approached the lift and entered a security code into another reader on the wall. As there was no response to her enquiry, she turned to look back at the reception desk and realised that the receptionist was now on the phone. She turned back to the lift just as the doors opened, and she got in.

Exiting the lift on the third floor, she went through an intricate biometric security process involving iris and fingerprint recognition before she finally entered her work area and headed for the female locker room. She walked round the room until she came to her locker and, after unlocking it, she hung up her coat and scarf and put her bag on the top shelf. She then bent down and grabbed a package from the floor of the locker before tearing it open and shaking out a newly-laundered white lab coat.

She never dressed smartly for work and today was no exception. She was in an old pair of jeans, and a thick round-neck jumper which covered a t-shirt and a vest. She reasoned that there was no point dressing smartly when she spent all her day wearing a lab coat which only offered a view of her neck and the bottom third of her legs.

In the washroom area, she soaped her hands in warm water and gave her nails a quick clean with one of the nail brushes which were chained to each sink unit. She then gathered her long hair into a bunch before clipping it loosely to the back of her head. She opened a sterilised cabinet on the wall beside her and extracted a white cap which she put on whilst at the same time pushing loose strands of hair under the brim.

One final mirror-check. Something was missing! She retraced her steps to the locker and reached up to the top shelf to retrieve her name badge with 'Samantha Frobisher VV17' emblazoned on it. She locked the locker, crossed the room and swiped her card through yet another reader. Hearing the reassuring click as the door came off its latch to allow her entry into her working environment, she eased through into the laboratory.

'Hey, Frobes! How's it going?' The Texas drawl filtered across the room as Samantha reached her workbench. Gregory Zeltenbloc III was the very epitome of the proverbial pain in the arse, and would not command a single milli-second of

Samantha's time if it wasn't for the fact that he was a brilliant scientist. He, therefore, had to be credited with some respect which she managed to give him on a daily basis through gritted teeth.

'All A-OK with me, Greg,' she replied. 'How's life in the Zeltenbloc world on this cold and damp morning?' She knew she had to humour him if she was going to get anything done today – and she had a mountain of stuff to get through if she was going to make it home in time to have the early night she had promised herself.

Zeltenbloc looked across at Samantha and started a detailed dissemination of everything he had done at the weekend. As he droned on, Samantha tuned him out and busied herself by logging on to her desktop computer. She also fired up the tablet that each of the scientists were given so that they could work away from their benches in other parts of the lab. She opened one of the drawers under the bench and took out her safety glasses and looped the neck cord over her head before tucking the glasses into the top pocket of her lab coat. She also removed a box of sterile nitrile gloves which she placed on the bench in front of her. She clipped a pen into her top pocket and removed a ring-bound notebook from the drawer. She looked around her to make sure she had everything she needed before reluctantly tuning back into Zeltenbloc's tedious account of his weekend.

'Sounds great, Greg,' she said as he drew breath. She just hoped that he had, in fact, had a good weekend and that she hadn't missed reports of any deaths in the family simply because she hadn't been listening.

'And you,' he asked.

Bastard! Don't be so bloody nosey!

'Oh! You know me, Greg – life in the fast lane. Partied until I dropped. Men falling at my feet! Eating at the best restaurants! Just another weekend in the life of a high society gal.' She smiled demurely at him before turning back to her bench and tapping some commands into the computer. Thankfully, Zeltenbloc took the hint and turned his attention back to his own workbench.

Samantha looked around her to see who else was in today. There were quite a lot of empty workbenches but then she remembered that there was a one-day seminar in London that many of her colleagues had decided to attend. No doubt with the intention of getting some early Christmas shopping done, she thought. Anyway, with a minimum number of staff in today, it would seem the ideal time to put the next part of her plan into action. She was just taking that idea on board when she was aware of a figure approaching from her left.

She spun round on her lab chair and stared into the green eyes of Alicia Gabriel, her boss and the tormentor-in-chief of all scientists working on research into toxins on the third floor of Drummond House on the Kings Hill Business Park.

'Morning, Frobes!' Alicia chortled before parking her ample backside on a chair which she had wheeled over from one of the deserted workbenches. Samantha noticed that her boss had taken the precaution of planting her feet on the floor in front of her to avoid careering off into the darkest recesses of the lab.

Samantha knew that there were never any pleasantries with Alicia who she considered to be the quintessential epitome of a jolly-hockey-sticks snob. Public school educated before reading biochemistry at Cambridge, she had had the silver spoon inserted so far down her throat that it had almost made a reappearance in the nether regions of her fulsome body. She could be both rude and gregarious at the same time, and she certainly didn't suffer fools gladly – in fact, she didn't suffer them at all. That didn't mean that she was a bad boss but Samantha just knew that the best tactic was to sit quietly, smile, and wait for the woman to start giving orders. Never poke the wasps' nest!

'Just got notice from on high that HSE want to do yet another bloody spot check on your pets and, for good measure, they're going to bring along their very own herpetologist. Can you believe it?'

Samantha raised her eyebrows and was now looking quizzically at her boss.

'A bloody herpetologist for Christ's sake,' Gabriel continued. 'What the hell do they think we're running here? Zoology classes for 5-year-olds?' She looked over at Samantha as if for some reaction but then just carried on.

'Anyway, they're coming tomorrow morning which doesn't give you long to make sure that each of your vivariums actually contains what it says on the label – and that the contents are alive and in good health. Don't want any repetition of their last visit when one of your little darlings was in someone else's vivarium.' Samantha winced at the memory, and still couldn't fathom how that had happened.

Gabriel steamed on. 'So, can you get on to that pronto, Frobes? Get that tosspot to give you a hand to speed things up,' she said, hooking her thumb over her shoulder in the direction of Zeltenbloc.

'I heard that!'

'You were meant to, Gregory dearest!' Gabriel smiled, all the while training her eyes on Samantha. 'It's a term of endearment which we Brits like to use when referring to you Yanks!' She laughed.

'Bollocks!' came the response.

'Okay! Okay! Keep your hair on – or what's left of it!'

There was more laughter as she slid off the chair and turned around to look at Zeltenbloc who was tapping away on his keyboard. She then turned back so that she was facing Samantha.

'Just get it done, Frobes, there's a good girl. I know the HSE are a pain in the arse and I'm sure that the herpetologist will be an even bigger pain. All we need to do is make sure that they can't find any reason to close our research down otherwise we'll all be in the queue at the Job Centre!'

With that, Alicia Gabriel marched past Samantha and took a twirl around the lab before returning to her corner office and slamming the door shut. Samantha watched her go and then turned her gaze back to her computer screen.

An audit? By a herpetologist? Shit!

12

Monday 20 November

'Found by the groundsman when he arrived for work at around 09.00 a.m. this morning.'

Detective Constable Elaine Jennings was reading from her notes and pointing towards a silver BMW 520i that was parked on the edge of the driveway which encircled the chapel at Southborough Cemetery.

DI Sarah Hunter had been in a meeting with the Serious & Organised Crime unit at Tenterden, and had dropped in to Southborough on her way back to the Pembury Road nick at Tonbridge. The two detectives now walked towards the car which was partially covered by a forensic speed tent. Hunter could see that all the car's doors were open whilst the white-suited and booted Crime Scene Investigators did their best to unravel the last 12 hours in the life of the vehicle.

A bitterly cold northerly wind had sprung up during the night, and there was a light dusting of powdery snow on some of the flowerbeds. Both detectives were trying to keep their backs into the wind in order to avoid its icy blast. The CSI team appeared frozen and wouldn't have looked out of place at the North Pole in their white suits. But they stoically continued with their work, hunting for clues which might help to establish what exactly had happened here.

'The body?' Hunter asked whilst bending down to take a long-range look through the front passenger door although her view was partially blocked by one of the CSI team.

'IC-One female,' Jennings replied. 'Dr Swartzman

reckoned mid-to-late thirties but wouldn't commit any further. Also reckoned that she hadn't been dead for very long as rigor mortis hadn't set in. They've taken her off to the Wells mortuary and he said that he might get the post-mortem done this afternoon.'

Hunter moved to the back of the car and squatted down so that she could see the length of rubber piping which had been crudely stuffed into the exhaust pipe of the car. She had already noticed that the window of the rear door was slightly open although the other end of the piping now lay on the ground in front of her.

'Are we thinking that this is a straightforward suicide?' Hunter asked as she straightened her legs and stamped her feet to get the circulation going.

'Looks like it,' Jennings replied. 'The guy who found her is the groundsman here. He'd just popped over to make sure that a grave had been dug and properly laid out for a funeral later today. He says that there are quite often cars parked here what with relatives visiting the graves of their loved ones, putting fresh flowers on the graves, giving headstones a brush up – that sort of thing.'

Hunter suddenly focused on the gravestones which were all around her and thought about the amount of upkeep which was probably needed to keep the cemetery looking its best.

'Groundsman thought he could hear a car engine running but thought nothing of it as he went about his business. But, when he got back to the chapel, he could still hear an engine idling and assumed it must be the BMW so he came over to have a look. Saw the driver was slumped against the door and called it in. Luckily, there was a patrol car just passing the

Hand & Sceptre so they diverted down Victoria Road and were here in about five minutes.'

'Presumably she was dead by the time they got the door open?' Hunter looked back at the car.

'Yes, ma'am although the PC from Traffic noted that she had been sick which he said was unusual in his experience of suicides like this.'

Hunter was now rubbing her hands together as well as stamping her feet. It was damned cold! At least Jennings had a thick winter coat, a woollen scarf which seemed to have been wound round her neck two or three times, and a bobble hat pulled down over her ears. In contrast, Sarah Hunter was completely under-dressed for the conditions and was now bitterly regretting not having tried to at least look at a weather forecast before leaving home that morning.

'How about ID?' Hunter asked as she walked round the car to look in at the driver's seat.

'Nothing on her,' Jennings replied. 'Absolutely nothing in the car, not even the manufacturer's manuals or a road atlas of the UK. No personal effects, no mobile phone, not even an empty coffee cup or sweetie paper! Zilch!'

'Car registration?'

'Passed that over to Grace.'

DS Grace Kendall was a highly-rated desk investigator and researcher who always seemed to be able to dig up nuggets of intelligence which often lay hidden amongst the masses of information which flooded in during complex investigations. Hunter rated her work highly, and was eternally grateful to have Grace with her at Tonbridge.

'Okay, good!' Hunter said, looking at her watch. 'Think I

better get back to base and catch up with developments on the incident at The Prism last night. Have you heard anything further on that?'

Jennings shook her head. 'Nothing more than the snooker player died and his manager did a runner. Sounds as if it was all a bit chaotic with the DCI in charge of things!' She allowed herself a smirk which didn't go unnoticed.

'You may well laugh but I can assure you it was frustrating as hell at the time,' Hunter replied as she turned and started walking back towards her car. 'Any idea of when they're planning on doing the post-mortem on the snooker player?'

Jennings was trying to keep up with her boss who had almost reached her car. 'DS Selitto mentioned that he hoped it was being done today by Norman Partington. As far as I'm aware, The Prism's still shut down and the CSIs are all over it. Not expecting any sort of report from them until at least tomorrow.'

'Okay,' Hunter said as she opened the door to her car. 'You staying on here?'

Jennings nodded. 'I'm just going to wait until the car is lifted and then I'll get back to the station.'

'Right! See you later.'

Hunter got into her car, started the engine, threaded her way around the chapel and back down the driveway until she reached Victoria Road. She turned left and then took another left onto Constitution Hill Road so that she could skirt around Southborough Common before joining London Road and heading north to Tonbridge.

13

Monday 20 November

Situated at the junction of Pembury Road and Quarry Hill Road, and a short walk from the town's railway station, Tonbridge Police Station was a modern brick-built building boasting distinctive blue window frames and two Kent Police shields which adorned the walls that are visible from the road. An old blue 'Police' lamp hung next to the main door into the building. There were three floors above ground as well as a lower ground floor and an underground car park.

Sarah Hunter slowly climbed the stairs to the first floor where the main Operations Room was situated, and almost immediately bumped into Detective Sergeant Ted Selitto who was sauntering back from another trip to the kitchen area, a cup of steaming coffee in hand.

'Boss?' Selitto seemed surprised to see her. 'Wasn't expecting you for a while yet.'

Hunter smiled. 'Managed to get away a bit early and then had a quick look at Southborough on my way in.' They walked along the corridor towards the Ops Room.

'Good! I sent Elaine down there to see if she could get an update from the CSIs.' Selitto got to the room first and held the door open for Hunter. The large open-plan operations area was fairly buzzing today as she made her way across to the far corner of the room where the diminutive figure of DS Grace Kendall was almost completely hidden by two huge screens which were set up on the desk in front of her.

'Hi, Grace, what you got for us?' Hunter bustled as she

gratefully installed herself on the chair next to Kendall's desk. It was good to get the weight off her legs after the walk up the stairs from the car park. Selitto manoeuvred himself to the other side of Grace's desk and took up his familiar position next to the window.

'Probably not much more than you already know, Sarah,' she said, tapping the keyboard in front of her. 'The deceased would appear to be the snooker player, Davie Monroe, but we'll have to wait for final confirmation once Dr Swartzman and his team have finished with him. Monroe has been knocking on the door of the top echelon of players in world snooker for a couple of years. Never quite able to make it into the really big time, but his death will probably command a few column inches in the snooker press.'

Selitto grunted. 'Saw him playing a game on TV once. Odd flashes of brilliance but when it came down to the wire, he seemed to bottle it. Couldn't quite get over the line. It's a mental thing with these guys. You've either got the mental strength like a Steve Davis or a Stephen Hendry, or you're destined for a life in the second division.'

'Hmm!' Hunter ruminated on this. 'But a second division player wouldn't necessarily expect to end up dead on the floor of a shower room at the moment of what was probably his biggest achievement.'

They sat in silence for a moment.

'And no sign of the manager yet?' Hunter said to no one in particular. Selitto just shook his head. Kendall zapped a few more keys before also shaking her head. 'No sightings anywhere.'

'What about her car? Surely she must have driven to

Tonbridge?' Hunter was beginning to get impatient.

More key-tapping. 'Well, we've managed to find out that she lives near Brasted. Someone's been round to check up on the house but it doesn't look as if anyone's been there in the last twenty-four hours. I checked with the DVLA but there are no vehicles registered to Jacqui Anderson at that address.'

Hunter stared idly at the screens; Selitto looked out of the window at the never-ending traffic circling the roundabout below him. God, this was going nowhere fast, he thought, just like the traffic.

'Okay! Let's move on to the car at the cemetery.'

Kendall's fingers flew over the keyboard as the screens changed to reveal information about the registration of the car found at Southborough Cemetery.

'DVLA's got this registered to a company at an address on the Isle of Wight,' she eventually announced.

'Good grief!' exclaimed Hunter. 'Don't tell me someone drove it all the way from the Isle of Wight to sunny Southborough just to conduct their own last rites?' That got a smirk from Selitto but Kendall kept her eyes on the screens.

'An address just outside Bembridge near the airport,' she said, pointing at the information on the screen. 'Company by the name of Prospero Inks.'

'Airport? The Isle of Wight's got an airport? Hunter sounded incredulous.

'It's got two airports actually,' Kendall informed her.

'*Two*!' She stared at Grace. 'You'll be telling me the island's got a NATO air base next!'

Grace Kendall slipped a sideways glance at Selitto and raised her eyebrows. She was clearly starting to wind her trusted colleague up, but these were the facts that she had so far uncovered. Selitto pushed himself away from the wall.

'I seem to recall that Bembridge was quite a famous airport at one time,' he informed them. 'I'm sure it's where they used to build those little Islander planes. Couple of propellors, about 10 passengers, good for hopping from island to island. Did what it said on the tin – an islander!'

'So, it's a fully functioning airport is it?' Hunter wanted to know. Kendall attacked the keyboard again.

'Er, no,' replied Kendall looking at the screen. 'It no longer seems to have a CAA licence for flights carrying passengers, and gliding seems to have ceased as well. So, I'd say that it is probably a non-functioning airfield. The other airfield further down the coast at Sandown looks as if it's used by small private planes.'

They lapsed into silence again, all staring at the screens.

Eventually, Hunter found her voice. 'What does Prospero Inks do?'

Kendall turned her attention back to the keyboard. Hunter watched as the screens changed to a rainbow of colours, overlaid with designs of flowers, animals, and other abstract art. 'Looks like they supply inks for tattooists,' she ventured. 'There's also a note to say the website's under construction.'

She stroked a few more keys and the left-hand screen changed to show a printed document.

'Prospero Inks is registered at Companies House at that address on the Isle of Wight. Let's have a look.' And Grace started scrolling through the documents on the Companies House website.

'Small business,' she commented as she read through the

information. 'One registered director at the moment – Lulu Harrison. Her address is also given as the Isle of Wight address. Looks like there might have been a change of ownership a few years ago. Previous directors were Lucinda Lemon and Gustav Holmes. It's only filing micro-entity accounts because its turnover is so low that it's entitled to exemption under section 477 of the Companies Act 2006. It could, in fact, be dormant.'

The detectives looked gloomily at the screens. Not many clues there, Hunter mused to herself.

As if on cue, her phone started buzzing on the desk in front of her. She swiped the screen. 'DI Hunter!'

Selitto and Kendall watched as Sarah slowly got up from the chair and started pacing around the area beside the desk, subconsciously twirling strands of hair through her fingers.

'Okay, I'm on my way!' she eventually announced and disconnected the call. The other two detectives stared at her.

'That was Norman Partington.' She then filled them in on the call. It seemed that the vastly experienced pathologist was having difficulty establishing a cause of death and had asked Sarah if she could drop by so that he could bounce some ideas off her.

'Ted, you're with me on this one. Two brains will be better than one if something's outsmarted Partington!' And with that, she launched herself in the direction of the door. 'See you later, Grace,' she called over her shoulder.

14

Monday 20 November

As a young girl, Samantha Frobisher never really saw the attraction of dolls or teddy bears. They were inanimate objects which her parents kept giving her. They didn't speak; they didn't move. They had no personality. They didn't respond when she touched them. She couldn't love them. They didn't give her the sort of love she craved, the sort of love her ultimately broken family was totally incapable of providing.

By the time Samantha reached the age of five, her mother had started taking recreational drugs and her father was drinking heavily. He eventually lost his job after getting into a drunken brawl in the warehouse following a three-hour session in the local pub. After that, he would sit around the house all day drinking super strength lager while her mother smoked whatever type of weed she could lay her hands on.

About a month after Samantha's sixth birthday, her father had gone out to the local pub and never returned. Years later she discovered that he had run off with some floozy he had met in another local boozer, and they had both gone to live in Margate. Meanwhile, her mother had progressed on to harder drugs and was using all her benefits money to feed her increasingly desperate habit. By this time, alarm bells were ringing in Social Services circles, and Samantha was moved out of what was left of the family home and into the care of an older couple who lived near Crowhurst on the Kent border with East Sussex.

Samantha had liked her new surroundings – lovely house, lovely gardens, loads of space to indulge her increasingly independent thought processes. Esther and Simon were a loving couple who looked after her very well. They didn't exactly spoil her, but their inclusive approach gave her the love and security which she had craved in the darkest days of living with an alcohol-dependent father and a mother who was now a hopeless drug addict.

But it was Simon's hobby which really attracted her attention, and gave her an interest in life which just kept on giving, year after year.

She had lived with Esther and Simon for about three months when she started to notice that Simon always disappeared for an hour or two in the evenings. At first, she had assumed that he was going out for a drink because she had been so used to her father spending all his evenings in the local pub. But one evening she was coming downstairs from her room when she caught sight of Simon going through a door which she hadn't noticed before.

The following day, she decided to see what was on the other side of this mysterious door but, when she tried the handle, she found that it was locked. Disappointed, she turned and walked straight into Simon who had crept up behind her.

'And what, young lady, do you think you are doing?' he had asked her with just a hint of annoyance in his voice.

She told him that she had seen him going through the door and she wanted to see what was on the other side. Simon had given her request some thought and had then made her promise that she would never tell anyone what was inside the room – it was to be their little secret. And then, with her heart racing inside her little chest, Simon pulled a key out of his pocket and unlocked the door.

Samantha had stood in the middle of the room and just stared, her mouth hanging open, her eyes swivelling around as if on stalks. Spread around the room were wooden shelves on which stood glass cabinets of all shapes and sizes. She peered at them in wonderment but with a frown beginning to crease her brow. As far as she could see, all the cabinets contained plants or other greenery with some of the bigger ones having small trees growing in them. She couldn't work it out.

Then Simon beckoned her over to a cabinet at the far side of the room which had a very dim light on inside it. She crept over to stand beside him, her heart still trying to explode out of her chest. And then she saw it – a creature of such beauty that her whole life changed in that moment.

Simon squatted down beside her so that his head was at the same height as hers, and they both stared at the cabinet.

Samantha's mouth hung open as she feasted her eyes on the creature. It was dark brown with light brown blotches on its back and sides, and its cream belly was scattered with black markings. It looked quite stocky with a relatively small head, and she was mesmerised by the little tongue which kept darting in and out of the front of its head.

'Meet Pyrus!' Simon whispered.

After what seemed an age but was probably less than a minute, Samantha managed a strangulated reply. 'Wow!' she stammered. 'Wha…what is it?'

'My dear Samantha, Pyrus is a snake. More precisely, he is a Ball Python and is not poisonous. He would originally have come from West Africa so he's a long way from home. What else can I tell you?'

Simon thought for a moment. 'Oh! And he's called a Ball Python because he tends to curl up into a ball if he is stressed or frightened.'

Samantha nodded, her brain hoovering up the information, her eyes never losing sight of Pyrus. 'Wow!' she repeated.

After a few more minutes spent looking at Pyrus, Simon introduced her to all the other snakes which lived in the serpentarium which he had created in his house. Samantha was agog and begged Simon to be allowed back into the room soon so that she could look at all its inhabitants again.

And that is how Samantha's interest in, and obsession with, snakes began. She became fascinated with the creatures and was constantly studying the breeds which Simon kept in his serpentarium. In fact, she became so knowledgeable that Simon would often take her with him if he was visiting a dealer so that she could give an opinion on the specimen that he was thinking of acquiring.

At school, she only had time for the sciences and maths achieving A-star grades in her chemistry, physics, biology and applied maths 'A' levels. Shunning an opportunity for an Oxbridge education, Samantha attended University College in London where she obtained a first-class degree in chemistry & biology with mathematics.

She then managed to get signed up for a research project where she could combine her interests in bio-chemistry and the wider subject of reptiles. And it was during this project that she first encountered the practice of milking snakes. This opened up a whole new area of interest for her as she came face-to-face with the development of antivenoms designed to neutralise the effects of snake venom toxins.

In the latter stages of her project work, she had visited a pharmacological company in Kent which specialised in research into antivenoms. After a short discussion and a look around the facilities, Samantha accepted an offer to join them so that she could further her interest in the development of antivenoms.

Now, some three years later, she sat in her own serpentarium surrounded by various glass cabinets and vivariums, trying to get to grips with the prospect of an audit of all the snakes she had gathered together in this one serene and peaceful room. The only sound in the room was the very faint hum of the equipment she had recently installed to monitor the humidity in the cabinets. Otherwise, you could hear the proverbial pin drop.

Samantha had decided against asking Gregory Zeltenbloc to help her prepare for the audit. As far as she was concerned, he was an oaf of the first order; someone to be tolerated, not encouraged. In any case, he was not remotely interested in snakes as his research was more to do with amphibians from Australasia which was a whole different ball game as he kept telling her.

She got up from the little desk she had squeezed into the corner of the room. This was where she kept all the stats about the snakes in her care, and made copious notes about the smallest thing she had noticed about their behavioural patterns. It was also where she kept other coded information which was for her eyes only.

Resuming her meticulous review of each cabinet, Samantha now approached the case which housed the Gaboon Viper. This was one of her favourites, not only because it was mainly a docile and sluggish reptile but also because its venom glands produce the largest quantities of venom of any of the venomous snakes known to man. It also boasts the longest fangs of any venomous snake and, along with its enormous venom glands, this was Samantha's 'go-to' snake for her antivenom research.

She checked on the heating pads underneath the cabinet as well as the basking spot light, making sure that the viper was getting enough 'daylight' every day. She also checked the hygrometer to make sure that there was sufficient moisture in the air inside the cabinet. Lastly, she took readings from thermometers attached to the sides of the cabinet which monitored the warm and cool areas so that the viper had a choice of microclimates.

Next, she checked on the Cascavel which was one of the most valued snakes in the collection. Also known as the Neotropical Rattlesnake, its importance was due to its venom toxicity and the presence of neurotoxins in its venom. She was well aware that these neurotoxins cause progressive paralysis leading to eventual life-threatening respiratory collapse, and she had to be extremely careful when handling this species. Having taken readings from all the monitors, and having eyeballed the snake resting on the sand and gravel at the bottom of the cabinet, Samantha was happy that this would satisfy the herpetologist.

Finally, she looked in on the Caspian Cobra, the most venomous species of cobra in the world. She was lucky to have been able to obtain one of this species from the Central Asian region, and had to beg Alicia to agree to the budget-busting deal she had got from the supplier. The importance of this cobra was that its venom has a potent composition of toxins made up of highly potent neurotoxins and cardiotoxins. Samantha was well aware that the severity of its neurotoxicity could kill a human being in less than one hour. But it was central to her current research work so she lavished just a little more attention to this species than she did to some of the others in her care.

Returning to her little desk, she stopped to put together a few handwritten notes which she locked in the drawer to her left. She then spun round on the chair and looked across to the small workbench which was jammed into the opposite corner of the room. The ring stand with its utility ring clamp stood erect in the middle of the bench, a couple of crystallising basins and a beaker standing ready to collect venom at a moment's notice. She had intended to do some milking today but wanted all her charges to be in tip top condition for the visit by the herpetologist so she decided against it.

There would be time for that after the visit tomorrow.

15

Monday 20 November

Ted Selitto parked his black Megane close to the door which led into the mortuary so that his boss didn't have too far to walk. It had also started to drizzle and he wasn't sure whether the slope down to the entrance was going to be slippery. The last thing he wanted was a visit to A&E – even if it was just around the corner!

Having tested the surface to make sure that it was only a sheen of rain and not a treacherous sheet of ice, he scuttled round to the passenger's side in order to help Hunter out of the car. But she had already untangled herself from the seatbelt and was wandering off in the direction of the mortuary. He caught up with her and almost took hold of her elbow – like he was used to doing if he saw an elderly person trying to cross the road.

'I'm not old and infirm yet!' Hunter growled as she shoved her hands ever deeper into her pockets. Selitto immediately backed off and was mightily relieved when they made it to the portico at the front of the building. Hunter slid her ID card into the reader and faced the camera. After a couple of seconds, the door clicked open. She entered and then had to let the door close before Selitto could go through the same process to also gain entry to the building.

They walked along the corridor until they came to the pathology office. The door was open and Hunter could see Partington sitting at one of the desks peering intently at a computer screen. He was still in his scrubs but had removed his cap and face mask which sat on the desk beside him. She rapped on the door frame. 'Can we come in?'

The old pathologist looked round and a broad smile creased his face as he realised that Sarah Hunter had actually come to see him.

'My dear Sarah,' he exclaimed, getting up from the desk. 'Come in! Come in! Make yourself comfortable! And you, Ted!' He indicated a couple of chairs which Hunter reckoned had seen better days but she was pleased to have any opportunity to take the weight off her legs.

'Fancy you coming to visit me in my lair!' he gushed. 'Haven't seen you down here for years.' He did look genuinely pleased to see her, and Hunter was quite touched by his sincerity. 'I see quite a lot of Ted and some of your DCs but very little of you!'

'You know how it is Norman, monkey and organ grinder and all that,' she smiled back at him. 'Anyway, now I'm here, what have you got for me?'

Partington returned to his position behind the desk, casting a glance through a small rectangular window which gave him a view of the examination room, almost as if he was making sure that none of the inmates were escaping. He sat heavily in the chair and placed both his elbows on the desk, fingers steepled under his chin, bushy eyebrows knotting together in a pronounced frown.

'I seem to have hit a bit of a brick wall with your Mr Monroe,' he began. 'The cause of death would seem to be due to the fact that his heart simply stopped functioning. But I cannot for the life of me find any reason why that should have happened in an otherwise perfectly healthy young man. The heart seems to be fully functioning, I cannot find any evidence of blood clotting, and his other organs all seem to be in good shape. Stomach contents were minimal which you would probably have expected – I doubt he would have eaten much either before or during a big match. Anyway, there was nothing that attracted my attention.'

Hunter was now also frowning and twirling fingers through her hair. Selitto was busily making notes in his pocket book.

'So, I'm wondering whether he might have suffered from some sort of neurological catastrophe which paralysed his heart to the extent that it simply stopped working.' Partington paused to give the detectives a chance to take in the hypothesis he was putting forward. He sat back in his chair. 'The other puzzling factor is that he must have vomited just before his heart stopped. I've sent a sample of this away for a tox report but my analysis showed it to be much the same as the stomach contents. I've also sent bloods and other samples off for urgent tox reports in the hope that we may get a better idea of what caused his heart to stop.'

They all sat in silence, the only sound being the endless hum of the chillers and mortuary fridges which permeated the walls of the little office.

'Hmm!' Hunter finally sighed. She blew her breath out through tight lips. Selitto looked up as it sounded as if she was blowing a raspberry.

'Presumably there are no marks on the body, Norman?' he enquired.

'None that are obvious,' the genial pathologist replied, pushing his glasses further up his nose so that the DS came into focus. 'But there is something that you could usefully look at and take into consideration in your investigations.'

That got Hunter's attention, and she sat up straighter in her chair.

'Have you got time to take a look?' Partington asked, noticing Hunter's heightened level of interest.

'Right now, we need all the help we can get!' she replied. 'Do you want us to get gowned up?'

'Afraid so. You'll find loads of sterilised gear in the scrubs room. Just had a delivery this morning so you should be able to find something that fits. Come through when you're ready.'

Ten minutes later, the three of them were standing around one of the stainless-steel autopsy tables which were spread across the centre of the examination room. Harsh overhead lighting contributed to the eeriness of the shadowless environment they were standing in. Workbenches and washing units were arranged around the room, and various dispensers hung from the walls. The hum of the mortuary fridges was more noticeable now they were in the room, and the sound of an endless trickle of water was coming from the sluicing system which was embedded in the floor around them.

Sarah Hunter was standing next to the pathologist who signalled for Selitto to come and stand on his other side. In front of them lay the body of Davie Monroe which thankfully, as far as Selitto was concerned, was covered by a body sheet.

Partington addressed the two detectives. 'I have carried out a thorough examination of the deceased's body and can find no puncture wounds. No sign that he was in the habit of injecting himself, or that he had recently been injected. I also couldn't detect any sign of anything having been inserted into any of his bodily orifices. However, I did notice a small scratch on the back of his left hand.'

With that, Partington pushed back the sheet in front of him to reveal Monroe's left arm which lay lifeless on the table. The skin appeared almost translucent under the harsh lighting. The pathologist picked up the dead man's left hand and held it in his own, making sure that the detectives could clearly see the back of the hand.

'The rigor mortis has started to dissipate so the hand is more malleable to the touch. If I turn it to the light, can you see the little scratch there?'

The two detectives bent in to take a closer look at what Partington was pointing to. As they did so, he dropped the hand back onto the table and ambled over to one of the cabinets near the door. He returned with a huge magnifying glass.

'Have a look at it through this,' he invited. Sarah Hunter took the glass and held it over the hand. The translucency of the skin meant that she could clearly see all the little veins immediately under the skin. And there was no doubting the fact that something had scratched the skin. But had the skin actually been broken?

She passed the magnifier to Selitto who carefully scrutinised Monroe's left hand.

'Well?' Partington eventually asked. 'Any observations?'

Hunter was still staring at the hand. 'Certainly looks like he's got a nick there but has it actually broken the skin, Norman?'

The pathologist took the glass from Selitto and had a prolonged look at the scratch. 'Difficult to say, Sarah, but there is one thing I am certain of and that is that this scratch occurred very close to the time of death. See here,' he pointed to the hand, 'the skin has had no time to start its own healing process. There's no crustiness around the wound. And there's something else.'

He rummaged in the pocket of his gown and fished out a small LED torch which emitted a surprisingly strong beam of light. He shone the beam onto the back of Monroe's hand.

'See the marks around the site of the abrasion? They look like nail scratches to me – as if he had been scratching himself. I've taken scrapings from under the nails on his right hand, or what's left of them, and the general detritus looks as if it includes tiny fragments of skin. So, perhaps the skin on the back of his left hand had become itchy. I don't know about you but some of the scratches I get when I'm gardening are very itchy to start with.'

The two detectives looked across at each other, neither daring to admit that gardening was anathema to them.

'Are you saying that the main scratch could have been caused by a fingernail?' Selitto asked, still looking down at Monroe's left hand, 'From what we know, there was a bit of a scrum going on around him when he went over to the audience; lots of people trying to shake his hand.'

'That's certainly possible, Ted, but I couldn't guarantee that he acquired the scratch during that melee,' the pathologist replied. 'However, I do think that the other smaller scratches are self-inflicted.'

Hunter couldn't disagree that the pathologist had a point,

and that the scratch on the back of the hand was something to take note of, particularly as there were virtually no other clues to be had from the post-mortem. Or, at least, not until the results of the toxicology reports were in.

She eased herself away from the table and stood upright just as there was a clatter of metal on metal behind her. She turned to see two of the porters wheeling in a steel gurney closely followed by Dr Toby Swartzman who headed up the pathology unit at Tunbridge Wells.

'Hello, Sarah!' he called over, an element of incredulity in his tone of voice. 'We really must be honoured to have a visit from you to our humble abode here amongst the dead souls!'

'Ha! Ha! Toby,' she replied. 'Just checking up on you to make sure that you've recovered from all that work I created for you a few months back!' She was referring to the trafficking case when a number of bodies were discovered in body bags at the bottom of a lake. It had, indeed, been a grim episode for Swartzman's team which had been overwhelmed to start with until more pathologists had been drafted in to help with the complex issue of dealing with unidentified immigrants.

'Jolly good!' Swartzman replied, swaggering over to stand at the end of the table on which Davie Monroe still rested. 'All OK here, Norman?'

'Yes, Toby. Just trying to give my learned friends a few meagre clues as to what might have befallen our friend Mr Monroe.' He turned to watch as the porters removed another body from the gurney and placed it carefully on the third autopsy table, the body sheet obscuring any sight of the deceased. 'And you?'

Swartzman looked over to the table. 'I'm going to get started on the poor woman who decided to end it all in her car at the cemetery this morning. Hopefully, won't take too long.'

Hunter turned away from looking at Davie Monroe's body and wandered over towards the newly-arrived corpse. 'Any chance of a quick look at the face, Toby?'

'Sure! Be my guest,' he said, addressing one of the porters. 'Joe, can you just lower the sheet so that DI Hunter can have a look at the face.'

The porter did as he was asked and peeled the sheet back so that it was folded underneath the chin of what had undoubtedly been a beautiful woman.

Hunter looked down at the face and then froze as if she had seen a ghost. Even though the paleness brought about by death was now eroding her features, Sarah had no doubt about the identity of the woman who lay on the table in front of her.

'For fuck's sake!' she blurted out. 'That's the manager! That's Monroe's manager!' She moved around the table so that she could get a better perspective of the attractive face of the dead woman.

'That's Jacqui Anderson!'

16

Monday 20 November

On the way back to Tonbridge, Hunter took a call from DCI Iversen who was still in a budget meeting at HQ in Maidstone. They agreed to meet in his office at 5.30 p.m. so that she could bring him up to date on the Davie Monroe case. She decided against telling him about her identification of Jacqui Anderson until she had had a chance to at least consider the sequence of events which had led to the deaths of a well-known snooker player and his manager.

On arrival in the Operations Room, Hunter and Selitto made straight for Grace Kendall's corner desk and resumed their positions either side of her.

Sarah quickly filled Grace in on developments at the mortuary, and the identification of Jacqui Anderson as the body in the car at the cemetery.

'Well, that's interesting isn't it?' Grace observed. 'Anderson doesn't have a car registered in her name but she's found dead in the driving seat of a car registered to Prospero Inks with an address on the Isle of Wight.'

'Unless she and the car are not related at all,' Selitto said, leaning down to look at the registration document which Grace had put up on one of her screens.

'What, you mean she was put in the car to make it look like it was her vehicle?' Hunter asked although she somehow doubted that this was the case.

'Probably not,' he accepted, 'but worth retaining as a possibility.'

'Okay! Let's park that idea for the moment if you'll excuse the pun.' As usual, Hunter was keen to get on and, in her mind, the ownership of the car was not the number one issue here. She shifted in her chair to get comfortable.

'Right, Grace. CCTV. In the theatre, in the cemetery car park. Any ANPR tracking?' She looked across at Kendall hoping that she had at least made a start on these important methods of detection.

Kendall consulted some notes which she had written out on a pad. 'Well, as you can imagine, The Prism has a modern CCTV system in prime working order. There is good coverage in the auditorium and in the hospitality suite and other areas of the building. I've also discovered that the final was filmed for one of the snooker subscription channels so I've asked for a copy of their coverage. I haven't really thought about how useful ANPR is going to be but we can try and see if the Prospero Inks car comes up. The only blank I've drawn so far is the cemetery which doesn't seem to have any CCTV at all. However, there is some ANPR on the A26 road so we might get lucky with a hit on the car travelling towards the cemetery.'

Hunter mulled all this over in her mind. 'Good work, Grace,' she eventually said, tucking a loose strand of hair behind one ear. But Kendall wasn't finished.

'I've also been onto HantsPol on the Isle of Wight,' she told her colleagues, reading from another page on her pad. 'Detective Sergeant Jack Jones is part of their CID team operating out of the Ryde nick.'

'Thought he was a singer!' Hunter sniggered at her own witticism; the others took no notice.

'DS Jones hadn't heard of Prospero Inks but knew roughly the location of the registered address. Said he'd try and do a drive-by and get back to me. Nice guy; very co-operative.'

'Excellent!' Hunter enthused. She looked over to the clock on the wall above the door. Once she realised that it couldn't possibly be 9.50 either morning or evening, she took her phone out and swiped the screen. Still thirty minutes before her meeting with Iversen.

'Okay, Grace!' she said, rising to her feet. 'Good work! Let me know as soon as you get the CCTV stuff. Ted – with me!' With that, she marched across the room and out through the door. Selitto followed her and they met up in the corridor. They walked slowly towards the kitchen area.

'Who've we got available at the moment, Ted? You know, if we had to put a team together tomorrow, who's around?'

Selitto normally kept a close eye on who was doing what in CID so he had a good handle on which detectives would be available to make up a new team.

'I'm pretty sure that we could get Azzar and Elaine,' Selitto replied. Azzar Mishraz and Elaine Jennings were both detective constables and had been part of Hunter's team involved with the international people trafficking case. She would be more than happy to have them on board again.

'Stuart Crosby's at Canterbury,' Selitto continued, 'and is working with the Serious & Organised team on the flood of illegal immigrants pitching up almost daily on the Kent coast. Carolyn Pennant's now back but still struggling after the surgery she's had on her jaw. She's also still having nightmares after her ordeal in the lighthouse so she may not be ready for any serious field work. But there are a couple of others I've had my eye on.'

'OK,' Hunter said as they reached the kitchen. She doubted that they would need more than four for the time being and she could always call on Grace's services as a central information resource whenever required. 'Who are the two you've had your eye on?'

Selitto busied himself getting two coffees while Hunter leant against the corner of the kitchen unit and bunched her hair behind her head before threading it through a scrunchie band to create a pony tail. She then pushed a couple of loose strands of hair behind her ears and gratefully took the coffee offered by Selitto.

'There's good reports on a young DC who came on board last year by the name of Jed Crowther,' Selitto said, taking a sip of his coffee. 'Certainly showing promise and not frightened to get stuck in. Works long hours, too. Word on the vine is that he needs to be challenged.'

Hunter nodded, wrapping her hands around the mug of coffee and holding it under her chin.

'I'd also like to see how Carina Morgan shapes up under pressure,' Selitto continued. 'Unfortunately, there's a few around here who think she's difficult to manage so she seems to get left back at base most of the time. Might be good to give her some room to see what she really can do.'

Hunter considered what he was telling her. 'Yep! Interesting, Ted,' she eventually said. 'So, we won't be short if and when the time comes.'

At that moment, her phone started vibrating in her pocket. Looking at the screen, she realised that it was a call from the mortuary. 'DI Hunter!'

'Hi, Sarah,' came the reassuring tones of Toby Swartzman. 'Have you got a minute? Only we've got another problem down here.'

Hunter looked at Selitto and frowned. 'Okay Toby, what've you got?'

'Well,' the head pathologist started, 'it's more about what I haven't got than anything else. And what I haven't got is any sign of carbon monoxide in the lungs of the body identified by you as Jacqui Anderson.'

Hunter stared wide-eyed at Selitto who was struggling to understand what was going on.

'Jeez, Toby,' she began slowly, 'that...means...'

Swartzman finished the sentence for her. 'That means she was dead when she was put in the car! Correct!'

17

Monday 20 November

'Christ! It must be something serious if that fucking psycho Hennenbont's turning up here! And he's coming by boat!'

Jasper Lime turned away from the balcony and stepped back through the huge glass sliding doors leading into the vast kitchen which took up much of the second floor of his three-storey apartment in the sought-after area of Fort George in St Peter Port, the main town on the Channel Island of Guernsey. The balcony provided a panoramic view over the main harbour and, during daylight hours, he could clearly see the islands of Herm, Sark and, very occasionally, Alderney.

He had been watching the night slowly take hold as the lights began to twinkle brightly along the esplanade, the last of the day's ferries dashing into the safety of the South Quay, others departing for one final journey before the engines would be allowed to cool. But there was a fresh easterly wind getting up so he activated the remote and watched as the doors slid to a close in front of him.

A fully-equipped bar took up almost the entire length of one wall just to the right of the glass doors, and he now slipped behind the counter and placed his empty glass under the optic for the Tanqueray Gin. After releasing two measures, he coaxed some ice cubes into the glass before splashing in a meagre amount of tonic water. Finally, a slice of lemon joined the ice cubes floating in the glass.

'You're right there, Jas, he hardly ever leaves Bréhat and

hardly ever by sea. He's a dreadful sailor by all accounts. Goes green at the mere sight of a wave!'

Reggie Lemon had only recently arrived off an Aurigny Airlines flight from London Gatwick which had been badly delayed by a bank of fog that had obstinately enshrouded the western side of the island for much of the day. He had headed straight for Jasper Lime's apartment and was now sitting up at an enormous cooking island in the middle of the kitchen where Jasper Lime did most of his entertaining. Reggie was enjoying a pleasantly chilled glass of Pecherenc from the South-West Region of France.

His observation about Hennenbont amused Lime. 'Very good, Reggie, but he'll be wanting to see us once he's got his land legs back so you'd better give me the SP from the homeland?'

Lemon took a mouthful of the cold wine and then set his glass back on the island's marble top. He had been dreading the moment when he had to report back on the happenings of the last twenty-four hours. 'Not good, I'm afraid.'

Jasper could see that Reggie was trying to avoid eye contact with his old friend and business partner, and this started alarm bells ringing. Reggie was never normally backward in coming forward.

'Someone got to Monroe before I had a chance to make him the offer,' he said, eyes darting around the room.

'What d'you mean *got to him*?' Lime asked, a look of incredulity spreading over his face.

'Well, you know, got to him!' Reggie exploded. 'He's fucking dead, Jas.'

Jasper Lime just stared at Lemon. He was having difficulty

fully comprehending the consequences of what his old mate had just told him. He carefully placed his glass on the bar, scrubbed his hands over his trademark stubbly beard and covered his mouth with steepled fingers nestling under his nose.

'You mean all that time and effort – not to mention money – we put in to getting him into the winner's enclosure has been fucking wasted?' Jasper was trying to control himself. This was bloody serious in the great scheme of things. Not least because he knew that Hennenbont would be asking some awkward questions when they met later that evening.

'What the fuck happened, Reggie?' Lime demanded.

'God knows, Jas,' Lemon almost whispered the words. 'One minute we're all waiting to welcome the new champ into hospitality and the next I'm being told by the old bill that there's been an incident. Eventually, I heard from one of the cops that Monroe had been found dead in the shower. Managed to get out of there after providing ID and then hightailed it back to Gatwick – would have been here sooner if it hadn't been for that bastard fog this morning.' He sipped some more of his wine, feeling its iciness gently permeating his body.

'So, you didn't get to do the business with Monroe?' Jasper asked although, knowing the answer he was going to get, he just ploughed on. 'So, we haven't got access to any of his gear, we haven't got the intel he had been promising, and we haven't got the forty-odd grand he was paid for winning a tournament which he couldn't lose because it had been fixed in his favour. *Brilliant!*'

Reggie Lemon rested his arms on the island either side of his glass, and this time he looked straight at Jasper Lime.

'We've got a big fucking problem here, Jas,' he started, never taking his eyes off his business partner. 'Not only have we lost part of our supply chain but we were relying on Monroe to open up other opportunities. Hennenbont's so pig ignorant that he'll be expecting it all to come gift-wrapped whereas, in reality, there's nothing in the fucking gift box. The big problem is that there is obviously someone on our trail who has decided that it would be better to have Monroe out of the way.'

Lime thought about this for a moment. 'What about that tart of a manager of his? Is she involved?'

'Well, she was there, Jas, floating around like Lady Macbeth with her dagger. All ready to dice up anyone who said anything negative about dear Davie. Seemed to disappear once news got out about the incident. Probably helping the cops with their enquiries. But she doesn't know much, does she?'

'Doubt it. He never had much time for her so it's unlikely that there's ever been any pillow talk. Anyway, these days she's always fannying around with those golfers she's got on her books. That gets her around the world in first class which is much more than poor old Davie could ever give her.'

They lapsed into silence, both pondering the fact that they had failed to complete a deal which they had invested so much in. Their thoughts were interrupted by the sound of a police siren as Jasper Lime's phone burst into life. He scooped it off the bar and stared at the screen – Hennenbont! He swiped his thumb across the bottom of the screen.

'*Pascal,*' he gushed, '*vous êtes arrivés dans Guernsey, n'est ce pas?*'

There was a pause before Hennenbont replied. 'We agreed to always speak *Anglais* because your *Français* is so shit!' he growled.

'OK, Pascal, whatever!' Lime looked over at Reggie and raised his eyebrows. The French bear seemed to have brought his sore head with him. Or perhaps he'd spent the last hour spilling his guts as his hydrofoil bounced across the water from Bréhat.

'Anyway, no talk now.' Hennenbont seemed keen to get on with things. 'We meet at eight – Ship pub, at back.' The next sound Jasper Lime heard was a click which told him that the call was ended.

18

Monday 20 November

There was a crack as one of the logs spat a burning ember onto the hearth in front of the inglenook fireplace. Tentacles of heat radiating out from the fire spread to every corner of the pub creating a warm and cosy atmosphere as Sarah Hunter and Ted Selitto settled into The Kentish Rifleman at Dunks Green.

There had been little more that they could achieve at Pembury Road this evening so Hunter suggested that they stop for some refreshment on the way home. There were a few early evening drinkers in the main bar, but the cold weather was probably keeping others at home with temperatures due to plummet overnight. So, they had the smaller of the two bars to themselves.

Sitting at one of the tables close to the fire, Hunter was enjoying the pint of Guinness which she had greedily glugged as soon as it was placed in front of her. This had given her an impressive white moustache along her top lip which she had then studiously licked off. Selitto soon made a similar impression on his foaming pint of Harveys bitter, licking his lips to ensure he didn't miss a drop.

'Grace has made some progress on the CCTV and has secured a feed from the company that filmed the final. Should be here by the morning,' Selitto was saying as Hunter attacked a packet of salt & vinegar crisps. 'We should also have the feed from The Prism to look at.' He had another mouthful of the Harveys. 'Anyway, how did you get on with Iversen?'

Hunter delayed answering until she had managed to get a huge mouthful of crisps under control. She hadn't realised quite how hungry she was so the crisps had all but disappeared by the time Selitto had got his hands on the packet.

'We just went over our recollections of last night at The Prism to make sure that we hadn't missed anything. As he was the first to get to the body of Davie Monroe, he was interested to hear that dear old Norman is stumped for a cause of death. He was also very surprised to hear about the Anderson woman as she seemed to be distraught by the whole thing. Even when I saw her, she was having trouble keeping it together. Hard to think that she might have been faking it.'

Selitto had another mouthful of his beer. 'I agree! Even if she was faking it, it's hard to understand why she would bugger off like that when she'd just discovered her protégé was dead. People normally only run away if they have something to hide.'

'Well, she obviously didn't run very far,' Hunter mused, 'and whoever she ran to clearly had no intention of looking after her!'

They sat in silence for a moment, Hunter hoovering up the remaining crumbs at the bottom of the crisp bag. She then washed these down with the last mouthful of Guinness and plonked her glass back on the table. Selitto didn't need any further prompting and made his way back to the bar.

Sarah Hunter was restless; she always needed to feel as if she was making progress. Instead, she felt as if she was swimming around in a thick gloopy sludge. Two suspicious deaths and an increasing number of unanswered questions.

Selitto returned with two half-pint glasses and another packet of crisps.

'At what point is Anderson's death going to be considered as murder?' he asked, retaking his seat.

'Not yet, according to Iversen.' Hunter was wrestling her way into the next packet of salt & vinegar. 'Says we've got to be positive about cause of death so I'll need to get onto Swartzman first thing in the morning.' She took a mouthful of the half of Guinness and got a smaller moustache for her troubles. 'Have we got anything from the CSIs yet?'

'I'll get on to them in the morning,' Selitto promised as a fusillade of embers crackled in the fireplace. He backed his chair further away from the fire just in case.

'The question that's going round in my head is whether Anderson had anything to do with Monroe's death.' Hunter was back to twirling a strand of hair through her fingers which, Selitto knew, meant she was concentrating. 'If she didn't, then it's difficult to understand why she should turn up dead within twelve hours of his death. If she did somehow manage to kill him then her death might make more sense. But if it definitely isn't suicide, then someone seems to have really wanted them both out of the way – and quickly!'

Selitto stared into the pile of burning logs which were very gradually being reduced to ash on the fire basket in the inglenook.

'Agreed,' he finally commented. 'At the moment, it's difficult to see how she could have killed him. But, if she did actually carry out the killing, then she may well have been disposed of to keep her quiet for whatever reason. So, it could be possible that the same person killed them both.'

Hunter was nodding. 'Makes sense,' she commented. 'I think we need to know a bit more about Miss Anderson and her relationship with Monroe which may be more than just on a business level. Where did Grace say she lived?'

'She mentioned somewhere near Brasted,' Selitto replied. 'Could probably get out there tomorrow to have a look around. Probably take Jennings with me. Won't need a warrant assuming no one else's there.'

'Yep, let's get that box ticked.' Hunter's level of enthusiasm was rising. 'I also think that we should find out a bit more about Prospero Inks on the Isle of Wight.'

'Also agreed!' Selitto had been thinking along similar lines. 'Grace got good vibes from the HantsPol DS in Ryde so we may be able to get along for the ride – if you see my meaning!' Selitto looked pleased with himself for using a couple of homonyms; Hunter's arched eyebrow indicated that she was less impressed.

'He said he'd do a drive-by,' Hunter recalled, 'so let's get on to him again and see if he's been out there yet. Near an airport Grace thought, or what used to be an airport.'

They both stared at the fire, deep in thought. Eventually, Hunter sat back in her chair.

'By all accounts, this Anderson woman was a successful manager of young up-and-coming sportsmen and women. So, what the hell's the connection with a company dealing in inks for tattooists? Doesn't make sense! Should we be looking for another car? But, even if we found another vehicle which we could prove she had driven, that still wouldn't answer the main question – what was she doing lying dead in a car registered to an address on the Isle of Wight?'

'She could have taken a taxi to The Prism,' Selitto interjected, 'or she could have been given a lift by someone else.'

Hunter gave this some thought. 'OK. Fair point. Better touch base with the Tonbridge taxi companies tomorrow just in case. If she was given a lift, then we'll only be able to rely on CCTV.'

Her half-pint glass stood empty, some of the foamy head of the Guinness still sticking stubbornly to the sides of the glass. She flicked her phone to look at the clock, and decided that it was time to get home for some shut eye. Tomorrow looked like being a busy day.

She was just starting to get up from the table when Selitto's phone burst into life. He looked at the screen, opened up a new text message from his colleague, DS Rod Mason, and then sat back staring at the phone.

'*Shiiiit*!' he exclaimed, still staring at the screen. Slowly, he passed the phone over to Sarah Hunter who was by now wondering what she was going to see on the screen. Not in her wildest nightmares would she have guessed.

'For God's sake!' she started. 'How could…? Where did this…? For fuck's sake!'

Beneath a photograph of Davie Monroe lying dead amongst his own vomit on the shower room floor, Rod Mason had typed 'This has gone viral'.

19

Monday 20 November

Gavin Staunton eased his Ford Mondeo Zetec into the parking slot allocated for his two-bedroomed apartment situated in a gated development of two and three bedroomed properties on the outskirts of Edenbridge. He heaved himself out of the car and then retrieved two black aluminium snooker cue cases from the back seat before flicking the fob to lock the car.

He ambled up the path to his front door and was soon settling into the spartan surroundings of his bachelor pad. Not that he was a bachelor. He was still legally married to that money-grabbing bitch Lorraine. She with the solicitor father who was busily engaged in taking him for every penny he had. She with the mother who was something important in Social Services and who was engaged in a campaign to prevent him having any access to his little princess, Rosie. The fucking bitch!

Gavin had stayed late at the snooker club tonight. He was trying out a new cue and had wanted to get some practice with it before committing to buying it. Monday evening was also the time that he held two coaching sessions in the club and, this evening, he had coached twelve youngsters using the four tables available. Not ideal, but he had stayed beyond the 10.00 p.m. cut off time to ensure that everyone received an equal amount of his time.

His mates at the club had all wanted to hear about his semi-final match against Davie Monroe which had taken place at The Prism in Tonbridge a couple of days ago. More particularly, they were keen to know how he had let slip a three-frame lead which allowed Monroe to just get over the line to claim his spot in the final.

'Blimey, Gav! You must have thought you had him at that point!' his good friend, Tommy Regan, had said when he had joined a group of mates at the small bar at the back of the snooker hall. 'Was it the pressure, Gav?' another had asked. 'What's it like with all those cameras, and the lights, and all those people, Gav?' More questions. And more bland, non-committal answers. He wasn't good at answering such banal questions, and he wasn't good at swatting them away either. And, eventually, it seemed that all his mates were just talking to each other so he quietly slipped out of the bar and went back to doing what came naturally to him – cuing a snooker ball.

Staunton now sat in his lounge chair, feet gratefully resting on the footstool in front of him, and a glass of Rioja on the small table to his left. He took a decent glug of the wine and then sat back in the chair, idly scrolling through the channels on the TV in front of him. Although he could see what was on the screen, his mind was miles away as it analysed and re-analysed everything that had happened to him in the last seventy-two hours.

Gavin had always had a talent for snooker and, at a young age, his father had got him into a snooker club where he was coached by a man who had retired from the professional circuit and who was keen to help youngsters like himself. He had left school at sixteen and, although his father insisted that he must take up some work to pay the fees for the snooker hall, he spent as much of his time as he could on the green baize. Eventually, he started to win some amateur tournaments and then, at the age of twenty-two, he took the plunge and turned professional. He could still remember the first cheque he had received for being knocked out in the second round of a little tournament in Essex after getting a bye from the first round. He had photographed it and sent it round to all his mates. He was on the way!

As the years passed, Gavin played a lot of exhibition snooker and enjoyed some success in minor regional tournaments. He also enjoyed the trappings of fame within the snooker fraternity, and his weight ballooned out to nearly twenty stone helped by his consumption of copious amounts of beer and lager provided by sponsors and an increasing fan base. He had met Lorraine at one of the exhibition matches when she had got the job of looking after him for the day. They were married after a lengthy and, at times distant, romance, following which she gave up her job and accompanied him to all his snooker engagements.

Soon after Rosie was born, Lorraine started to suffer from severe post-natal depression which wasn't helped by the fact that Gavin was now drinking heavily in order to help him get through an increasingly hectic schedule. One night, he returned from a lengthy drinking session following an exhibition match and found that the locks on their house had been changed. After sleeping in the car overnight, he pleaded with Lorraine to let him back into the house but she refused. Instead, she invited him to retrieve all his belongs which had been bagged up and left in the lane which ran along the end of the back garden.

Since that time, he had largely given up drinking at functions although he still enjoyed a glass or two of wine in the evenings. He had found this two-bed flat by chance which suited him as it was close to London Gatwick airport and to the motorway system. And, although he was now engaged in a legal wrangle to get access to Rosie, his career had taken a turn for the better. He was now nosing back towards the top sixty-four and had set himself an ambitious goal of breaking into the top fifty in about a year's time.

Gavin Staunton had been surprised and elated to get an invite to the tournament at The Prism, and had practised hard to give himself every chance of getting to the later stages of the tournament. He had played well in the early rounds, recording straightforward victories over his opponents. By Friday, he knew that he would be up against Davie Monroe in the first semi-final, and he definitely fancied his chances. Monroe was doing well in the Essex League but Staunton had heard that his mental health was beginning to affect him when push came to shove in the pressure-cooker environment of a big match venue.

That was before Staunton received the call which he was now replaying in his head.

He slid out of the lounge chair and went over to the dresser. He bent down and pulled out the bottom drawer and, after removing a couple of boxes and a pile of old *Private Eye* magazines, his hands alighted on a bottle gift bag which he had hidden in the drawer. He carried it back to the chair and sat down again before gently easing the neck of the bag open. He then pulled out a bundle of bank notes followed by another bundle and then yet another. He flipped through the notes in each bundle – a mixture of five pound, ten pound and twenty pound notes – all used and untraceable, just as the man had told him. He had already checked the amount and knew that he had £15,000 sitting in his lap.

Someone had really wanted Davie Monroe to win this tournament, and a guaranteed fifteen grand had seemed to be a reasonable exchange for helping him to do so. Added to his winnings for reaching the semi-finals, it had been a good pay day for Gavin Staunton which would help him fund further legal representation against that fucking bitch so that he could see and hold his beloved Rosie again.

A trill sound from his phone alerted him to an incoming text. He grabbed the phone from the table next to his chair and scrolled to the messages screen. At first, he couldn't quite comprehend what he was looking at. But, as he twisted the phone around in his hands to get a clearer view of the message, he felt as if his heart had jumped into his throat as he suddenly realised what was on the screen.

His hands began to shake as he looked down at a photograph of a naked man lying on a wet floor, a small pool of vomit clearly visible beside the body. Staunton looked closely at the picture but had no doubt as to the identity of the man. Underneath the photograph were two words '*Who's Next?*'

20

Tuesday 21 November

Sarah Hunter hadn't slept much, and had spent much of the night trying to make sense of what had happened over the last twenty-four hours. She was now prowling around the Operations Room like a bear with a sore head. There were so many things she wanted to get on with but she couldn't get started unless there were people around to do her bidding. She looked up at the clock on the wall – still 9.50 either morning or evening. She raised her eyebrows in despair and swiped the screen of her phone. At least it was getting on towards 07.00 a.m. so Grace should be here soon.

After leaving the pub the previous evening, Selitto had said that he was heading straight back to Pembury Road to mobilise the techies to get on to the source of the Twitter feed showing Monroe's body on the floor of the shower room. Hunter could only think it was the dozy guard who had let Anderson leave the room. He would have certainly had the opportunity to slip into the dressing room and take a couple of shots of the body. But was he colluding with Anderson? Or had Anderson, herself, snapped the body on her phone before she had gone for help?

Hunter had given a lot of thought as to how or why Anderson might have done this but, in the end, she had dismissed her as a suspect when she received confirmation that the Twitter feed had been uploaded after Anderson had been discovered dead in the car. Apart from the paramedics, no one else had seen the body so it surely had to be the guard.

It was, therefore, a top priority today to bring him in for questioning. Hopefully, Selitto would be in early so that he could get on with organising that line of enquiry.

As if on cue, Grace crept through the door and sidled over to her corner desk clutching a beaker of coffee which bore the name of the shop over the road from the station. She pulled off her woolly bobble hat and Hunter watched, mesmerised, as her friend unwound a woollen scarf which must have been at least two metres long. She then slipped out of a huge woollen coat underneath which she wore a padded gilet which she unbuttoned but left it hanging loosely over a dark sapphire cowl neck jumper. Hunter wasn't sure that it was quite that cold outside but knew that Grace had an aversion to the sort of weather they were having to endure.

'Morning, Grace,' she said as she slid into the chair next to Kendall's desk. 'Sorry to be on to it so early today but we've got a stack of stuff to get through. Can we do CCTV first?'

'No problem, Sarah. I'll just get this lot fired up. Have you had a coffee yet?' she enquired.

'I've had two,' Hunter replied, 'so better not have any more for the moment! Don't want to look any more maniacal than I already do!'

Grace gave her a sideways glance and smiled. 'Okay! Here we are. What do you want to start on?'

'What's the TV feed like?'

'Not bad; a bit amateurish but clear pictures.' Kendall spun the mouse around the screen and, after a couple of clicks, a picture appeared showing the balls spread around the snooker table with one of the players standing beside the table chalking the tip of his cue. She froze the picture.

'That's Davie Monroe,' she pointed out, 'always wears light coloured trousers and a black waistcoat apparently. This is the penultimate frame, the one that Johnnie West wins to draw level.'

They watched as Monroe took his time assessing his shot options, prowling around the table like a cat stalking its prey. Once he was ready, he bent to the table and placed his cue across the bridge he had made with the thumb and forefinger of his left hand. The rest of his fingers were splayed across the baize, his middle finger involuntarily tapping the table. Hunter was intrigued.

'Stop it there, Grace!' she whispered.

Kendall did as she was asked, and they both stared at the screen.

'Can you enlarge the hand in some way?' Hunter asked.

Grace sped the mouse across the top of the screen, clicking on a couple of icons along the way before the picture was enlarged. She then zoomed in on Davie Monroe's left hand.

'Jeez!' Hunter exhaled, staring at the screen.

Kendall also stared at the image in front of her. 'No scratch,' she observed. She unfroze the screen and they watched as Monroe took the shot, missed the opportunity to pot a red and then stood away from the table chalking his cue. Grace froze the screen again. This time Monroe's left hand was gripping the top of the cue whilst he mercilessly chalked the tip. The back of Monroe's left hand was clearly visible, and the two detectives turned to look at each other.

'Well, that's fairly conclusive,' Hunter observed. 'Let's go forward to the end of the match.'

The DS fast-forwarded the action through the final frame

until the only colours left on the table were the pink and black. She had found another sequence showing Monroe standing near the table chalking his cue, and she froze the screen once more. The skin on the back of his left hand was clearly unmarked. She took a screenshot which showed the date and time in the bottom left-hand corner of the screen, and filed it. She then turned back to Sarah Hunter.

'Okay, let's just run it on – see if we can get any clues,' Hunter suggested. They watched in silence as Monroe eventually won the frame, waved his cue around above his head, put it on the table and then went over to his fans, shaking hands, high fiving, getting thumped on the back. At this point, the TV feed cut to the programme host who was presumably in the commentary box, and there followed a dialogue between her and a man who may well have been the commentator. Eventually, the TV director cut back to the auditorium just as the presentation ceremony started.

Hunter and Kendall watched as West received his cheque and then Monroe stepped forward to receive the trophy. He lifted it up in triumph but the camera angle was such that they could only see his right hand. Finally, he turned to face another section of the crowd, and the left hand came into view. Kendall froze the screen. The angle wasn't perfect and the director had clearly not zoomed in on the trophy, preferring a wider angle to provide more atmosphere of the occasion.

They carried on watching until, eventually, Monroe placed the trophy on the table and started posing for the cameras. Again, the camera angle was such that they were unable to clearly see his left hand. Hunter was just beginning to get exasperated with the director's shot selection when Monroe suddenly moved the trophy further up the table and placed his hands either side of it. Kendall froze the screen and then enlarged the area around his left hand.

'Well, well, well,' Hunter said under her breath. 'What have we here?'

They both continued staring at the screen. Although the enlargement had created a slightly fuzzy picture, there was no doubting that there was now a mark on the back of Monroe's left hand. Kendall took another screenshot and filed it. Hunter sat back in her chair.

'Okay, Grace, I'm going to have to leave that with you for the time being,' she said, making as if to get up from the chair. 'You'll obviously have to get on to the CCTV in the auditorium and find out what Monroe did between the time he moved away from the table to talk to the audience and the time that he received the trophy. Also, find out from the TV company if they have any other feed to show what was happening in the auditorium at the time that they cut away to the commentary box. Perhaps there's some footage of Monroe going over to greet the audience or shaking hands with someone. Also, see if they can provide any clearer definition for his left hand during the presentation ceremony.'

'Will do, Sarah, I'll let you know how I get on.'

Hunter had just got to her feet when she thought of something else.

'Oh, and Grace, can you also get on with finding the security guard who was assigned to The Prism on Sunday. Presume he was hired by the promoters but perhaps it was a tie up with the Tonbridge Council. Not sure who is responsible for security at events like this – you got any ideas?'

'No idea I'm afraid but I can find out' Kendall said and made a note on her pad. 'Would you like me to get him in here for questioning?'

Hunter thought about this. 'Yep. Send some uniforms round to pick him up. Also get on with a background check - let's just find out who he is to start with and whether he's already on our radar. It may be that the only thing he is guilty of is being a particularly useless security guard in which case I'd rather limit the amount of time we might waste on this!' Grace Kendall smiled and scribbled another note on her pad.

21

Tuesday 21 November

T he Ops Room was filling up now, and Hunter spotted DS Selitto sitting on the corner of a desk talking to DC Elaine Jennings. She crossed the room, collecting a spare office chair on the way which she wheeled to the side of the desk.

'Morning you two,' she said as she approached. Selitto slid off the desk and Jennings started to get up from her chair. 'Stay where you are!' Hunter commanded. 'This isn't a formal visit!'

'Morning, Boss,' Selitto replied. 'Just bringing Elaine up to speed on the rogue photo of Monroe. Any further developments on that?'

'My view is that it can't be Anderson because she's unlikely to have had the time to put it on Twitter and, even if she had, then why would she then top herself? Doesn't make sense to me.' The two detectives nodded in agreement. 'But I still think it's worth following up. How much did she use social media? What sort of stuff is on her Twitter feed? Instagram? WhatsApp? Have we got her phone?'

Selitto and Jennings looked at each other. 'I'll check with the Crime Scene team to see if they picked anything up from the car,' Jennings said and scribbled herself a note on the pad on the desk in front of her.

'Okay, Ted, what's your plan for the day?'

'Either the CSIs or the mortuary,' he replied. 'Not sure that the CSIs would have got anything of interest from The Prism but we need to know more about how Anderson died. Her car's also a bit of a mystery.'

'I think I'll take the mortuary,' Hunter told them. 'Particularly as there seems to be a doubt about the suicide verdict. I want to make sure I understand what Swartzman's come up with.' She now shifted her attention to Jennings.

'Right, Elaine, you'd better go along with Ted and see what the CSIs have got to offer us.' Elaine nodded her head.

'Now, let's talk about...' but Hunter's voice trailed off as she noticed Selitto staring wide-eyed at her and nodding his head towards a point behind her. She looked round and saw Iversen standing in the doorway. He flicked his head to one side, inviting her to join him. She dutifully got up from her chair and followed him out into the corridor. He beckoned her into an empty office across from the Ops Room.

'In here and shut the door.'

She did as she was told.

'This picture on Twitter,' he said, getting straight to the point. 'There's all hell let loose at HQ. How on earth could this have possibly got out?'

Hunter had known that the Twitter feed would cause the shit to fly at HQ in Maidstone, so she had been prepared for Iversen's intervention.

'Looks like the security guard fancied himself as a latter-day David Bailey and thought it would be fun to post something particularly offensive on Twitter.'

'When would he have had the chance to do that?' Iversen frowned as if trying to picture the events of Sunday night in his mind.

'Probably between the time you first found the body and

the time I arrived. That would have been at least twenty minutes during which time you were getting the hospitality suite organised and Anderson was sitting in the other room. Wouldn't have taken him more than a couple of minutes to get in, fire off a few shots on his phone, and get back to his post in the corridor.'

'Do we know who he is?' Iversen was keen to know.

'No, but we're on to that. Should have him in for questioning by this afternoon,' she replied, subconsciously crossing her fingers as she spoke.

'Okay, but get him dealt with quickly. I've got that infernal woman from the press office chasing me. Apparently, her phone's ringing off the hook from journos, and the top brass are also giving her a hard time. The sooner we can say we've charged someone over the Twitter splurge, the better. It's difficult enough trying to keep the lid on the death of the snooker player, and heaven help us if they get a whiff of the fact that his manager has also died in suspicious circumstances.'

'I'll make sure that all communication with the press is embargoed for the time being,' Hunter said in order to try to placate a clearly stressed Iversen.

Sarah was acutely aware of the pitfalls of dealing with the press, and had often gone out of her way to avoid any interaction with journalists whatsoever. But it was a known fact that the press could come to the aid of the police during times when it was difficult to make progress in a case. Iversen had always encouraged her to be open-minded about the value of perhaps cultivating some sort of arms-length association with one or two journos. She hated the thought of doing as Iversen had suggested, but she could see the value in developing a connection if the case required it. Perhaps this was the opportunity for her to give it a try.

'Anyway, just keep me up to speed with developments,' Iversen continued. 'Once the snooker story hits the headlines, my masters will be demanding regular briefings so don't let me go into any meetings without being fully briefed about the latest developments.'

Hunter nodded to indicate that she had understood. 'I'm hoping to get an affirmative from the pathologists about causes of death later today so I'll let you know. Ted Selitto's also going to get on to the CSIs to see if they've got anything.'

'Not sure what they might have found at The Prism,' Iversen commented, 'unless there was something in that dressing room. But the car might reveal some evidence. Is anyone going to be helping Ted?'

Hunter hadn't been going to broach the subject of a small team at this stage but Iversen seemed keen so she thought she'd sound him out. 'I was going to put Ted with DC Jennings and then get another couple of DCs. And I'll still use Grace Kendall in the central office. Presumably you would sanction that if we've got a couple of murders on our hands.'

'Yes, that would seem appropriate in those circumstances but no more dedicated manpower until we absolutely know what this is all about.' Iversen suddenly looked at his watch. 'I've got to go! A call with Superintendent Eaves in about ten minutes and then a meeting over in Canterbury. Contact me if you need anything but proceed as just agreed for the time being.'

Iversen had left the room and was on his way down the corridor before Hunter even had a chance to mumble a 'thank-you'.

22

Tuesday 21 November

Samantha Frosbisher was at her workbench early to make sure that everything was ready for the inspection. She had already completed a quick tour of the cabinets in the serpentarium. All the inhabitants had been accounted for apart from the Boomslang which she couldn't see in the vivarium she had reserved for this venomous snake.

Although she thought it is was probably hiding inside the makeshift cave which took up most of one side of the vivarium, she had to be sure that it was still alive. Taking a stick with the shape of a T at one end, she lifted the lid of the cabinet and then gently poked the T into the front of the cave. Despite the fact that Samantha knew the Boomslang to be a relatively timid snake, she also knew that it could become aggressive if disturbed. It was also capable of delivering a highly potent venom from large fangs located in the back of its jaw. She knew better than to try to locate the snake with her bare hands, and she was relieved when it slithered out from the cave and made its way into the foliage which covered much of the remainder of the vivarium.

Sitting at the little desk, she made sure that all her reports were correctly filed and that all the information on feeding and temperature control for each snake was up-to-date. As a precaution, she removed the equipment she used for venom extraction as she didn't want a long discussion on this practice to develop with the herpetologist. There were several schools of thought on snake-milking, and she didn't want to get marked down just because the herpetologist didn't approve of her snake-milking technique.

She took another look around the cabinets before letting herself out of the serpentarium and returning to her workbench in the lab. All her colleagues were in this morning in anticipation of the inspection, and there was a hive of activity as everyone engaged in decluttering their workbenches. She never ceased to be amazed by the amount of surplus equipment which was always lying around simply because no one could be bothered to put it away after use. One of the scientists on the reptile section was now having a mild panic attack because she couldn't even remember where she had taken a piece of equipment from in the first place.

Strewth!

Samantha shook her head in disbelief. She always kept her workbench spotlessly clean and free from clutter. In her early teens, Esther had always impressed on her that an untidy room meant an untidy mind and that, if she really was going to be a scientist, she would need to have a tidy mind. She had never forgotten that piece of advice. So, today she could just sit back and await the arrival of the dreaded herpetologist.

In fact, she didn't have to wait long as the clock on the wall had barely ticked on to 09.15 a.m. when Alicia Gabriel ushered two people into the lab.

'Okay, everyone, listen up!' she commanded from her position in the centre of the floor. 'Let me introduce you to Gemma Pearcey from the HSE. She'll be carrying out the spot check today and will now tell you what this will involve.' Alicia then turned to Gemma and indicated that the floor was all hers.

Samantha thought that Pearcey was probably in her mid-forties, dark hair cut in a bob, quite petite, her white lab coat covering her clothes although she was clearly wearing trousers. She was pleased to see that the HSE inspector was also wearing sensible flatties on her feet – nothing worse than when these people turned up in ridiculous high heels.

The man standing next to Pearcey was a different proposition altogether. He towered over her and, in fact, he towered over everyone else in the lab. His olive skin betrayed Mediterranean origins, an angular face set off with short-cropped black hair and a full set of designer stubble. On closer inspection, Samantha detected a slight greying around the temples but, overall, she considered him to be a very handsome specimen.

Pearcey was now into her stride describing the way the inspection would work. She wanted to speak to everyone individually and observe an example of their workplace activities, conditions and practices. She may ask to see relevant documents and she would be closely scrutinising risk controls to check their effectiveness.

Samantha wondered how long all this was going to take. She really needed to extract some venom today if she was going to keep up with the programme of experimentation into neurotoxins which she had recently agreed with Alicia Gabriel.

At that moment, Gemma Pearcey seemed to finish her introduction and had turned to the swarthy gentleman at her side.

'Let me introduce Pablo Hernandez,' she said as she stood to one side. 'Pablo is on loan to us from the European Agency for Safety & Health at Work, and has particular responsibilities for monitoring the use of animals in the workplace. So, he'll be taking a look at your snakes and other reptiles while he's here.'

'That'll be with Frobes, then!' Alicia interrupted, pointing towards Samantha's workbench. She smiled demurely as his eyes met hers, a huge smile breaking out across his face. Could have been worse, she thought as she shifted her position to give the impression that she was in the habit of being introduced to a six foot something bronzed Adonis every day of the week.

Gemma Pearcey had now produced a notepad and was giving times for the short meetings with each of the scientists. Once that was done, she turned to Hernandez and suggested that he just fit in with whatever work Samantha had to complete that morning. She hoped that their presence wouldn't be a disruption, and she thought that she and her colleague would be finished by lunchtime.

With that, everyone went back to what they had been doing as Pablo Hernandez approached Samantha's workbench.

23

Tuesday 21 November

DS Ted Selitto and DC Elaine Jennings had arrived at the CSI headquarters in Maidstone, Selitto parking his Megane in the visitors' bay near the front door. As was his custom, he called the CSI office to announce his arrival. He always found that it was much easier to get through the labyrinthine security system if you had a CSI officer on the other side of the glass.

Once he and Jennings had swiped their ID cards through the reader to gain entry to the building, they had waited until Jimbo Carrigan appeared on the other side of the toughened security glass. He activated a panel which slid back allowing the detectives to enter a glass bubble one at a time. Once in the bubble, they were each photographed before another glass panel slid back in front of them allowing them to exit the bubble and join Carrigan.

'Morning, Jimbo!' Selitto shook Carrigan's hand as he waited for Jennings to be released from the bubble. 'See you've had a busy forty-eight hours!'

'You could say that!' Carrigan replied as he ushered them into the lift. It was a small lift and, with three of them in it, there was not much room for conversation as they rode up to the third floor. Once the doors opened, they stepped out into a small reception area. Carrigan walked across the room and then invited the detectives to look up at a camera on the wall just above the entrance to the CSI labs.

'New bit of kit,' he informed them. 'It's got to recognise

your faces from the pictures just taken downstairs otherwise you can't come in!' A couple of reassuring green lights lit up beside another reader on the wall. Carrigan bent down and looked into the reader whereupon a panel slid back in front of them. 'Iris recognition technology,' he informed them. 'Good when it works; a nightmare when it doesn't!'

They entered the spacious CSI laboratory which took up the entire area of the third floor. Selitto was always impressed when he came here as the range of equipment on view was just staggering. He looked off into the distance and waved to Beth Dench who was sitting with one of her team. She waved back. 'Two minutes!' she called across the lab before going back to talking to her colleague.

Carrigan steered them into a small meeting room, and invited them to sit at a semi-circular table facing a large screen mounted on the wall in front of them.

'Any teas, coffees, water, ice creams, soda pops?' he asked with a broad grin. The detectives both asked for coffee before taking their seats. Soon after Carrigan had left the room, Beth Dench arrived carrying a thickish file and a tablet which she put down on the table.

'Hi, guys! How are you both?' she enquired as she took her seat. 'Haven't seen you for ages, Ted. In fact, probably not since you gave me a lighthouse to look at.' She smiled as they all privately recalled the horrors which had been discovered in an abandoned lighthouse some two months earlier.

Bethany Dench was, in fact, a highly respected forensic scientist who was about halfway through a two-year secondment to Kent Police from the Home Office. She was acknowledged for her analytical approach to crime scene investigation, and had always been extremely helpful to Hunter and Selitto. They were both impressed with the way she always challenged the veracity of evidence whist still retaining a sense of humour, and she was good fun to work with.

Tucking some loose strands of unruly blonde hair behind her ears and pulling a pair of chunky round-eye glasses from her lab coat pocket, she pressed a few keys on her tablet and the screen in front of them came to life.

'Thought I'd just take you through the layout of the dressing room at The Prism,' she started, and then scrolled through a number of photographs of the room before getting into the shower room.

At that point, Carrigan returned with the coffees and then took up a seat next to Dench.

'I hear you've hit a spot of bother with a rogue picture of the deceased,' he said as his picture of the body of Davie Monroe came up on the screen.

'You could say that!' Selitto replied. 'Not ideal that it's gone viral but there's not much we can do about that.'

'Any news on cause of death?' Beth Dench asked.

'Not yet,' Selitto replied. 'All a bit of a puzzle at the moment. We're trying to establish when he got a scratch on the back of his left hand. At the moment, we think this happened when he went across to shake hands with a section of the audience.'

Beth scrolled through all the photos of the body she had but, in each one, the left hand was either obscured or not even in shot.

'Nothing here we can help you with I'm afraid,' she said,

leaving the last photo on the screen showing the body of Davie Monroe lying lifeless on the floor of the shower.

Selitto sat back in his chair.

'Anything else for us from the auditorium?' he asked, beginning to think that this was a bit of a wasted journey.

'Nothing in the auditorium, I'm afraid, but there is something for you that we picked up in the dressing room.' And, with that, Beth posted a photo of a snooker cue on the screen.

'This is Monroe's snooker cue,' she said, pointing at the screen. She clicked the mouse and another picture showed a cue carrying case which was open. An extension butt was lying inside the case.

'Not sure how much you know about the technology of snooker cues,' Carrigan started, 'but these days a cue is made up of two or three sections all jointed together. The butt is the biggest and heaviest part of the cue, and most professionals now use extension butts which give them extra control when taking a shot using a table rest.'

The next photo showed Monroe's cue split into two parts. Carrigan continued. 'Basically, the two components are the shaft and the butt. The shaft is a solid piece of wood although the butt has to be hollowed out at its base in order to facilitate the docking of the extension which is normally screwed in. So, you can see here that there is a hole in the butt of the main cue.' Dench activated the pointer on her tablet and dragged the arrow across the screen until it was positioned next to the end of the cue.

Selitto and Jennings were certainly interested to learn about how a snooker cue fitted together but were both wondering where this was going. They didn't have to wait long.

Dench took over. 'It was Donny who got us onto the cue. He's played a bit of snooker in his chequered career, and he reckoned that Monroe's cue was quite heavy. According to our research, a cue used by professionals would normally weigh around nineteen ounces. We put this one on the scales and it came out at twenty-five ounces. Donny also thought that the butt was a bit chunky – it was difficult to get his fingers round it in terms of getting control of the cue.'

'So, we had another look at it to see where the extra weight was, and discovered that the butt was indeed broader than the butts of standard professional cues which are normally around twenty-nine to thirty millimetres. We also discovered that it had been hollowed out behind the butt-end where the butt extension docks with the cue.'

The next photo was an x-ray of the butt section of the cue which clearly showed that a channel had been bored through the butt of the cue. There also appeared to be some obstructions in the channel which were indistinguishable.

'Once we'd seen these,' Beth continued, 'we had little option but to take a much closer look.'

The next photo showed the butt section of the cue on its own having been cut into two halves. They could now clearly see the channel which had been bored into the cue stretching almost the entire length of the butt section.

'Wow!' Jennings exclaimed. 'That would take some precision engineering to get that exactly in the middle of the butt and not alter the dynamics of the cue.' Selitto was impressed by her apparent knowledge of engineering but invited Dench to continue.

'After discovering this, we had another look at the butt extension and, hey presto, it had been subjected to the same treatment.' She put another photo up on the screen showing the butt extension after it had been cut in half. Again, a channel had been bored almost the entire length of the extension.

'Once we had cut up the cue and the extension, we knew exactly what we were looking at,' Beth continued, flicking to another photograph. The detectives were now looking at the two halves of the extension, but this time the channel had what looked like small tablets nestling along some of its length. The rest of the channel was coated in a thin film of white powder.

'Bloody hell!' Selitto exclaimed, trying to come to terms with what he was looking at. 'What are the tablets?'

'They're straightforward Es,' Carrigan stated. 'We're not 100% on the powder yet but should have an inkling by close of play today.'

'How much are we talking about?' Elaine Jennings wanted to know.

'Well, there was very little of the powder left although the cue butts had probably been full at some point,' Dench replied. 'There were also very few tablets left so we can only assume that a drop had been made.'

Selitto sat back in his chair, mind buzzing. This was the last thing they had expected but the drugs find probably now brought Monroe's death into clearer focus. He stared at the screen, intrigued by the simplicity of the subterfuge. No one would ever think…!

Carrigan's voice interrupted his thoughts. 'I'm afraid that's not all we found.' Dench tapped the screen of her tablet and a photograph of the cue carrying case came up on the screen. To Selitto's eyes, this was a photo they had already seen.

'This is another carrying case we found in the dressing room,' Carrigan continued. 'It clearly belongs to Monroe as it has his prints all over it. The cue it contained was similarly bored out so that it could carry tablets and powder.' Another couple of photos filled the screen so that the two detectives could see the cue's deadly cargo.

'Any idea of what we're looking at here in terms of weight or street value?' Jennings asked.

'Tricky!' Dench replied after some thought. 'We don't know how much the cues might have weighed when fully loaded so we are doing some tests on that now. We also think that the powders are different in each cue. So, using a bit of fag packet maths, we reckon about £15,000 per cue when fully loaded.'

'Blimey!' Selitto exhaled. 'So, you'd put your money on Monroe being a supplier wouldn't you?'

Dench and Carrigan both nodded in agreement.

'Okay! What about the car?' Selitto was keen to get on.

A photo of the car now filled the screen with the body of the woman slumped in the driver's seat. Jennings nodded as if confirming that was how she had found it when she first reached the cemetery.

'Now this is where it gets even more interesting!' Dench teased. The next photo was a close up showing the woman sitting with her hands in her lap, the steering wheel in front of her.

'So, here's a question for you! How do you hold a steering wheel?'

The two detectives both lifted their hands and curled their fingers as if they were gripping a steering wheel.

'Now,' Dench continued, 'where would you expect to find fingerprints?'

Selitto looked down at his hands and then at the photograph on the screen. 'Probably on the inside of the wheel or on the back of it?' he asked. Jennings nodded her head in agreement.

'That's right!' Dench continued. 'Only problem is that prints from the deceased were only found on the front of the steering wheel not on the underside. There were no other prints in the car. None on the door to indicate that she had got into the car, none on the gear stick to indicate that she had driven the car, and none on any of the controls. If she had driven the car, she could not have had control of it if she was only touching the front of the steering wheel. So, we have concluded that she did not drive the car to the cemetery. Which means that she was probably put into the car post mortem and that someone carefully applied her fingertips to the steering wheel in order to make it seem like suicide.'

Beth Dench waited for a moment to let this information sink in, again tucking loose strands of long blonde hair behind her ears. 'The only other prints in the car were a few smudged partials in the boot so we have had to conclude that the car had been wiped clean – probably before the deceased had been put into it.'

Selitto stared at the screen. 'Okay! That fits with what we're getting from the morgue. They think that the deceased died elsewhere – no carbon monoxide in the lungs. This evidence will help us progress with that suggestion.'

'Well, there you are!' Dench smiled at the detectives. 'We didn't find any other possessions in the car – no handbag, briefcase, overnight bag, mobile phone. Nothing. In fact, there was absolutely nothing in the car at all apart from the body. We did, however, find some traces of a white powder in the boot and it's gone for analysis so the results will be in our report.'

Selitto shifted in his seat, giving the impression that he wanted to be elsewhere. 'That's great, Beth, and you too, Jimbo,' he said, getting up from his chair. 'You've certainly set the hare running with your discoveries about the cue! There'll be a very excited DI once she hears about this!'

Beth Dench smiled again. She knew exactly what Selitto meant.

24

Tuesday 21 November

A wintery sun was slowly making its way into an otherwise clear blue sky above the Bordeaux Harbour area just to the north of St Peter Port on the island of Guernsey. It was another cold November day with a steady north easterly adding to the discomfort of those who were brave enough to be out in it.

Reggie Lemon painted a lonely figure as he trudged across the sand on Blakes Beach. It was low tide and all the small boats were lying at various angles across the waterless harbour. Some were almost right over on their sides, others were propped up by joists attached to their hulls. Ropes ran in a myriad of directions as boat owners had made sure that their prize possessions wouldn't float away once the tide returned. Gulls screeched overhead, using the wind as a buffer so that they could take a good look at the exposed seabed to see if there was anything worth swooping down for.

Reggie had a lot on his mind.

The meeting with Hennenbont had not gone well the previous evening. Jasper Lime should perhaps not have antagonised the Frenchman in quite the way he had done given their weak bargaining position. But, if Reggie knew nothing else about his mate and business partner, he knew that Jas always saw attack as the best line of defence. He also knew that the pair had a deep-seated dislike of each other – Lime because he couldn't stand having to communicate in Franglais and Hennenbont because, as far as Reggie could see, he didn't seem to like anyone at all irrespective of whether they were French or English.

Why had they got tied up with this guy? *How* had they got tied up with him? Reggie couldn't quite remember but he did know that it was one of Jasper's hare-brained schemes to make even more money than they were already making with their international events company. The idea that the two of them could open up conduits for the supply of Class A drugs to suppliers in the UK seemed a fairly straightforward proposition to start with. And Jasper had totally embraced the concept, telling Reggie to just get on with the events stuff.

The only problem was that when things went wrong, which they often did, it was always Reggie who was called on to scrape the shit off the fan.

The death of Davie Monroe was one of those nasty little problems which had engendered the wrath of Monsieur Hennenbont, and Reggie was somewhat concerned that he might be in the firing line if they were unable to sort out a new supply line in order to placate the furious Frenchman.

Reggie had done all that had been asked of him. He had made contact with Monroe and had put a business proposition to him which he seemed interested in. Davie had heard of Hennenbont which helped as he seemed to hold him in quite high esteem or, at least, he held the quality of his gear in high esteem and seemed to think that he would get top dollar for it on the streets of the UK.

He kicked aimlessly at some of the detritus which was scattered along the beach – small pebbles, sea shells, empty plastic bottles. The roar from a throaty motorbike caught his attention, and he watched as the rider turned up the Rue de

Bordeaux leading away from the harbour. He continued shuffling through the sand, watching as the high-speed ferry from Portsmouth slowed on its arrival into St Peter Port, the small island of Herm behind it in the distance.

How were they going to find another supplier in the same league as Davie Monroe?

He felt his phone thrumming in his pocket. He had to shade the screen so that he could read caller ID. It was Jasper Lime. Reggie thought of letting it ring out to voicemail but then decided that would be childish and probably counter-productive.

'Yes, Jas,' he said once the call had been connected.

'Where are you, Reggie?' His business partner sounded on edge.

'Just out for a stroll at Bordeaux. What are you up to?'

'Get your arse over here, pronto!' Lime told him. 'I think I've got a solution to our little problem.'

25

Tuesday 21 November

On arrival at the mortuary in Tunbridge Wells, Sarah Hunter had gone straight to the scrubs room and got gowned up, pinned her hair into an untidy bunch at the back of her head which she then tucked into a surgical cap, slipped nitrile overshoes over her flatties, and clipped a mask behind her ears. The mask was so big that it covered most of her face.

She had then listened as Dr Toby Swartzman had methodically gone through all the evidence he had collected from the post mortem. He had chosen to do this whilst they were standing around the autopsy table on which Jacqui Anderson was laid out.

Hunter had to agree that, even in death, she was an attractive woman and that her body appeared to have not a mark on it to provide any clue as to cause of death. Swartzman had put forward his view that she had not committed suicide because there was no sign that she had breathed in carbon monoxide at any stage. There was also no evidence of any barbiturates or other tablets in her digestive system. He would, therefore, have to rely on a comprehensive toxicology report to establish the cause of death.

Although she hadn't attended a post mortem for a long time, Sarah knew that the pathologist would have collected the samples he needed for the tox report including bloods and stomach contents although he had told her that there was virtually nothing of significance in the woman's stomach. He would have also taken samples from her organs and from inside her mouth, and he would have probably collected some of the vitreous humour from her eyes. Hunter was particularly thankful that she hadn't been present for that procedure. She found it especially difficult to look at eyeballs which had been deflated after the loss of the clear gel-like substance that filled the space behind the lens. Finally, Swartzman would have extracted hairs from her head making sure that the follicles were attached in order to enable successful DNA testing.

'There are a couple of things that puzzle me,' he said as he straightened up after making another close inspection of the body. Hunter, who was now on the opposite side of the table, looked across at Swartzman hoping for something which would help her investigation.

'First of all, my gut feeling is that she either died after a particularly lethal drug was administered intravenously or that she ingested a cocktail of drugs. But I can't find any needle puncture marks and there is nothing in her digestive system to suggest that she took any drugs orally.' Hunter nodded and unconsciously started her own hunt for needle marks, her eyes roving over the body in front of her.

'Secondly,' Swartzman continued, 'I'm pretty certain that there was some sexual activity close to the time of death although there are no traces of semen in or on her body or on her clothes. I have, however, sent these for analysis just to be sure. There is slight bruising around her vagina but nothing to suggest that she had been subjected to violent sex of any sort.'

'Are you saying that she had consensual rough sex at some time close to the time she died?' Hunter was frowning.

'Yes and no,' came the reply. 'Yes, I think that it was probably consensual and a bit rough but I'm pretty certain that it was non-penetrative.'

Hunter stared at Swartzman. 'What, you mean non-penetrative as in woman-on-woman type of sex?'

Swartzman was making another examination of the body, trying to avoid Hunter's stare. 'That was pretty much what I was thinking, yes.'

'Well, that's certainly interesting but, at this stage, I'm not sure why.' Hunter's voice trailed off as she continued her visual examination of the body in front of her even though she didn't really know what she was looking for.

'What's that on her arm?' Hunter's gaze had eventually been drawn to a small mark on the crease of the dead woman's right elbow.

'Got that down as a tattoo,' Swartzman replied distractedly as he continued his own examination of the woman's legs. 'A sort of flowery elephant,' he went on. 'Bit of a throwback to the sixties when the humble elephant symbolised prosperity and good luck although it also embodied power, strength, dignity and longevity if my memory serves me right.'

Hunter stared at the pathologist. 'Hmm! Doesn't seem to have done her much good! Anyway, I didn't know you were into all that mystic hippy stuff, Toby.'

He looked up at Hunter, slightly flustered. 'Not into it exactly but quite interested in the philosophy of it all and the symbolism carried by different animals.'

They continued with their own visual examinations of Jacqui Anderson in silence.

Eventually, Swartzman called one of the mortuary

assistants who came scurrying in from the refrigeration room.

'Here, Joe, give me a hand to turn this one.' And with that, the two of them carefully turned Jacqui Anderson over, Joe making sure that her head didn't get tangled with the headrest. The three of them stood looking at the body in front of them for a moment before Joe sloped away in the direction of the refrigeration room.

'I want you to just take a look at her back,' Swartzman said as he wandered over to one of the workbenches. Once he had found what he was looking for, he returned to the autopsy table and was now sweeping the rays from a UV lamp across Jacqui Anderson's pale back.

'Looks to me as if there are some scratch marks on her back,' he noted, 'although the skin doesn't seem to have been broken.'

Hunter followed his hand movements as he swept the UV light over areas of her back, but she couldn't really make out the scratch marks he was referring to. Anderson's skin appeared almost translucent under the strong overhead lights which made it even more difficult to see any of the scratch marks Swartzman was referring to. Instead, she was transfixed by the overall shape of the body. Even in death, it seemed to have retained its tantalising dimensions. Not for the first time she thought that Jacqui Anderson would have been a very attractive woman.

'I'm going to have to take a much closer look at her,' Swartzman was saying as he casually strolled around the table to stand next to Hunter. 'In my mind, something must have caused her body to shut down but I cannot see any evidence of the cause or how it manifested itself.'

Hunter felt a little uncomfortable with Swartzman standing quite so close to her so she moved to the top of the table.

'While I'm here, can I have another look at Monroe?' she asked. Swartzman gave her a questioning look. 'I would just like to take another look at the scratch on his left hand.'

'Yes, sure, no problem!' Swartzman replied.

'From the TV pictures we have, there seems to be no scratch whilst he was playing but, by the time he received the trophy, it looks as if there was a slight abrasion on his hand.' Hunter smiled at Swartzman. 'Only a quick look. No need to get the whole body out of the drawer.'

'Okay, follow me,' and Swartzman led her in the direction of the refrigeration room, calling for Joe once they were both standing in front of a wall bristling with cold cabinets. Joe seemed to know exactly who they wanted to look at, and he pulled out a drawer which was just to the left of where Hunter was standing.

Swartzman opened up the body bag and gently extracted the left arm. He then held it up to the light. They both looked at a very faint abrasion of the skin which appeared just under the knuckle joint of the middle finger.

'Hmm,' Swartzman sighed. 'Looks like it's close to a tributary of the cephalic vein. If a poison or toxin was administered here, it would travel fairly speedily through the body. What did you say was the time frame from the point when this scratch occurred and time of death?'

'As I said, we think the scratch occurred between the time the game finished and the time the trophy was presented. Time of death was close to ninety minutes later – two hours max.'

Swartzman gave this some thought, still holding on to the cold hand. 'Neurotoxins attack the central nervous system and the brain so that death can occur in a very short period of time depending on the strength of the dosage. So, that is probably what we're looking at here. The tox report will give us an idea of the strength of the toxin but, given the circumstances, it must have had a hell of a strength.'

They both stood there staring at the back of Monroe's hand before Swartzman eventually laid the arm down next to Monroe's body before zipping the bag up. Seeing Joe loitering in the background, he signalled that he could now close up the drawer. They then ambled back into the autopsy room before again gathering around the body of Jacqui Anderson.

'Well, we're obviously looking for something fast-acting for Monroe,' Hunter surmised, 'but could Anderson have also been despatched with the same toxin? It can only have been a matter of ten or eleven hours between the time I last saw her and the time the body was discovered.'

'Agreed!' Swartzman replied as they looked down on the pale body of Jacqui Anderson. 'Hemotoxins destroy the red blood cells and cause organ degeneration over a period of time depending on the strength of the toxin. But, as you saw her late on Sunday evening and she was dead by Monday morning, we are unlikely to be looking at hemotoxins as cause of death as they would take longer to close the body down.'

'So, probably the same toxin,' Hunter concluded before looking across the table at Swartzman. 'And the same killer?'

'The tox reports will be key to all this,' he replied cautiously, 'as there seems to be no other sensible suggestion as to how or why she died. The only thing I can be certain of is that her body just suddenly stopped working. Like someone took the plug out at the mains!'

26

Tuesday 21 November

Pablo Hernandez had certainly known his snakes! Samantha had been thrilled to find someone who was almost as fanatical about these cold-blooded vertebrates as she was. He was softly spoken with a lilting Hispanic accent which added to the enjoyment of the couple of hours she had spent in his company whilst he inspected her serpentarium.

As he looked into each cabinet and vivarium, he commented on the occupants and provided anecdotes about other experiences he had had with each species in the past. He handled each snake with immense care and appeared to be very pleased with the health of all of Samantha's entourage. He had quizzed her about her methods of temperature control which, she knew, was most important in respect of snakes being kept in captivity. He also wanted details of the feeding regimes, and was very impressed when she told him about how she controlled diet to ensure that they all had exactly the right quantity of food at the appropriate time.

Hernandez had made some suggestions about how she could improve the habitats in one or two of the cabinets, and they had had short discussions about his suggestions and Samantha's counter-suggestions. But, otherwise, she had hoovered up as much information as she could from this extremely knowledgeable expert.

He had also regaled her with tales of snake hunting in India and Australia, on the Malay peninsula and in Mozambique. He had only been bitten once and then by a less poisonous variety of snake for which there was a good supply of anti-venom medication. He kept some snakes at home as pets and never ceased to be in awe of the beauty of these creatures.

Samantha couldn't believe how quickly the time had flown by and, all too soon, they were back in the main laboratory where Gemma Pearcey gave a short summary of her findings to the assembled members of the team. A full written report would be produced at a later date but, for now, there didn't seem to be more than a few minor recommendations which were more to do with administration than anything else.

Pablo Hernandez had given Samantha his business card before he left with a conspiratorial wink of the eye. She reckoned that, if they had had another hour together, he would have definitely invited her out for dinner – but they hadn't, and he didn't.

Everyone seemed a bit deflated after the HSE circus had left town so Alicia slipped out to the local bakery and returned with a box of sticky doughnuts. Samantha collected hers from the box but, just as she got back to her workstation, she dropped the doughnut on the work surface. Amidst much swearing under her breath, she eventually completed a lengthy clean-up process and ended up angrily tossing the miscreant doughnut in the bin.

In order to restore her temperament, she took herself off to the serpentarium and started to implement some of the adjustments to habitats which Pablo Hernandez had suggested. He really was a bit of a dish, she thought, idly imagining the two of them lying together beside a swimming pool in the hot sun. Or perhaps lying together somewhere else, perhaps even in bed! 'Snap out of it, girl,' she chided herself. Dare to dream and all that. She had work to do!

Having done the best she could with the habitats Hernandez had mentioned, she went over and sat at her little desk. She reached down and unlocked the bottom drawer before pulling out the battered notebook which had seen better days. This book contained crucial and accurate information about her snake milking activities. True, she did have to account to Alicia for the amount of venom which she extracted from the snakes but what were a few micrograms between friends? It was, however, most important that she kept a record of exactly how much venom she was extracting in order to ensure the continued good health of each snake. Over-milking was definitely to be avoided.

Ideally, she needed help with the milking as it was sometimes difficult to control the snake when one hand was engaged in holding the head and squeezing the glands. A helper would hold the lower section of the snake's body so that it didn't gain momentum by thrashing about. Her partner of choice in this activity was Sophie because she was not only interested in snakes but she was also fascinated by the milking process. She had a great understanding of how to hold the snake which made life so much easier during the milking process. Sophie herself was an expert in scorpions and arachnids, and was never happier than when baiting a scorpion in order to entice the sting out of the tail.

She was sitting at her workbench when Samantha went looking for her, and they both retired to the serpentarium.

'Well, that was a bit of a waste of time!' Sophie exclaimed once the door of the serpentarium was closed. She was a bubbly blonde with a ridiculously good sense of humour, always chattering away, never frightened to give her views on anything and everything. Samantha liked her spontaneity and enjoyed her company in the laboratory although they never met outside mainly because Sophie was so much in demand on the local social scene.

They chatted for a moment about the events of that morning whilst Samantha assembled the equipment required for the milking. She brought out the ring stand and then a selection of small glass beakers. Next, she removed a box of latex from another drawer and spread sheets of the substance across the tops of the beakers before slipping tight elastic bands over the rims to make sure the latex stayed in place. She then slipped one of the beakers into the ring and tightened the screw holding it in place.

'What are we going to start with today?' Sophie asked, her eyes sparkling, a keen sense of anticipation in her voice.

Samantha was keen to extract a quantity of neurotoxin today, and she had already decided that she would be engaging with an Inland Taipan which she had always considered as possibly the most venomous land snake. The venom from the Inland Taipan was well known for its effects on its victim's nervous system along with its blood clotting properties.

She also wanted to extract some venom from the Caspian Cobra which was one of her most prized reptiles. It had a high-level delivery of neurotoxins and, although its size made it difficult to handle, she knew that Sophie would be able to keep the snake still while the milking took place.

They went over to the cupboard in the far corner of the

room and put on their safety clothing – heavy duty lab coats, thick gloves, safety glasses, masks and reinforced rubber knee-length boots. Samantha then led them to the cabinet which housed the Taipan. Fortunately, the snake seemed to be resting so it was quite easy to collect it before they moved back to where the ring stand was located.

Samantha now took off the glove on her right hand and gripped the snake's head using her finger and thumb. She expertly manipulated the jaws and soon persuaded the Taipan to open its mouth. Upon seeing its impressive fangs, she pushed the head down until the fangs punctured the latex covering on the beaker. She then continued to massage the venom glands on either side of the head, and watched in awe as the deadly yellow venom squirted into the beaker. She held the snake in position for a minute or two, continuing her gentle massaging of the jaws, coaxing the last drop of venom out of the snake's fangs.

The two women quickly returned the Taipan to its cabinet where it slithered away into the darkest recesses of its home. Samantha then sealed and labelled the beaker before depositing it in a small laboratory freezer which sat beside her desk. She looked across at Sophie.

'Ready for the next one?' she asked.

'Sure am!' her helper enthused.

Next up was the Caspian Cobra which they had a bit of trouble milking due to its generally aggressive and bad-tempered nature. Sophie had struggled to keep its body still while Samantha was performing her art at the business end of the reptile.

Just for good measure, Samantha decided to also milk the

Gaboon Viper and, as it was in a fairly placid mood, they had little difficulty in keeping it under control. Once the beakers were sealed and labelled, and had been placed in the freezer, Sophie returned to her workbench in the main lab while Samantha remained in the serpentarium and started writing up her notes.

She recorded the date, time and place, and the circumstances in which each snake had been milked. She also recorded Sophie's name as assistant. She reached down and took the beakers from the freezer and lined them up on her desk. She then removed three small 5ml vials from her coat pocket and lined them up alongside the beakers. Once everything was in place, she carefully transferred some of the venom from each of the three beakers to each of the three vials and then made sure that each vial was labelled correctly.

Next, she weighed the reduced contents of the beakers and recorded the weight of the venom in her notebook. The weight of the venom in the vials was not recorded. She then reached down and placed the beakers back in the freezer along with the vials.

Before she left that evening, Samantha would return to the serpentarium and remove the vials from the freezer. They fitted snugly into the little freezer box she carried in the rucksack which would be slung over one shoulder when she waved a casual goodnight to the security guard as she left the building.

27

Tuesday 21 November

Sarah Hunter arrived back at Pembury Road and hobbled up the stairs to the first floor. Stopping off at the kitchen area for a coffee, she found that Selitto and Jennings had beaten her to the last slice of a birthday cake which had been lying on the worksurface.

'Whose birthday?' she casually enquired, trying not to give the impression that she would have dearly loved to have had a slice of the cake – she was starving!

'No idea,' Selitto replied, wiping a few crumbs from the corner of his mouth, 'but it was a great cake. All gooey and tasted of walnuts.' Sarah poured herself a coffee and kept her own counsel, feeling her stomach rumbling as if it was admonishing her for not getting to the cake before it was finished.

'Okay, let's go and see what we've got.'

The Ops Room was busy but they managed to find a couple of chairs and gathered around Grace Kendall's desk, Selitto taking up his customary position leaning against the wall by the window.

Hunter took them through her visit to the mortuary and the fact that they would have to await the results of the toxicology reports. She told them that Dr Swartzman was of the view that the scratch on the hand was significant but he was less sure about how Jacqui Anderson had died.

'I may have something for you on Monroe,' Grace interrupted. 'I managed to get the CCTV from The Prism and I also have the TV feed. Having looked at it all a few times, it seems that the only time Monroe could have got the scratch on his hand was when he went over to his fans after the match had ended. Let me show you the TV feed for that.'

She keyed in a command and the screens on her desk both showed the scenes immediately following the winning shot. They watched again as Monroe went across to his fans, shaking hands, high fiving, generally basking in the adulation. The view was with his back to the camera so not ideal but it did serve as evidence of the general melee which Monroe had found himself in.

'That's about it for the TV feed,' Grace said as she keyed in another command, 'a bit one dimensional and we can't see where his hands are. But let's look at the CCTV.'

The screens changed to show the action from a sideways on angle so that the detectives could clearly see all the handshaking and high fiving. Grace suddenly froze the screen.

'This is where it gets interesting,' she said using her pencil as a pointer. 'See here, someone's grasped Monroe's left hand with a double-handed grip, doesn't really seem to shake it, then lets the hand go and backs away from the group of fans.'

'And out of shot,' Hunter observed.

'Yes, unfortunately,' Grace agreed, 'and there is no other CCTV of this person in the auditorium. However, we do pick up a lone person leaving The Prism almost immediately after the time recorded for the double handshake.' She ran the tape and the others watched as a figure crossed the foyer and exited the building. She ran the tape back until she got the best image of the figure and then froze the frame.

'OK,' Sarah started, leaning towards the screen, 'old bomber jacket, collar pulled right up, cap rammed down on the head, jeans, trainers. What else?'

'Sideburns?' Jennings asked.

The others came in for a closer look. 'Hmm! Yes, probably,' Hunter agreed, 'so we're looking for a white male. Anything else?'

'I'm going to try and get these images sharpened up but it looks to me as if he's also wearing gloves,' Grace pointed at the figure on the screen. 'So, I went back to the handshake. If it is the same person, I wanted to see if he was wearing gloves at the time he shook Monroe's hand.'

'What's the significance of that, Grace?' Hunter asked.

'I'm not really sure,' Kendall confessed. 'Would the glove help or hinder the process of scratching the back of Monroe's hand? Don't know about you lot but I can't do very much when I'm wearing gloves because they get in the way. I couldn't do anything that requires precision.'

'What sort of gloves are they?' Hunter asked. Grace rewound the tape so that they could look at the man crossing the foyer.

'Hard to tell,' Selitto summarised what the others were thinking, 'but is he wearing a glove on each hand? Can you enlarge the area around the right hand, Grace?'

A couple of clicks of the mouse brought the right hand into closer focus but it didn't seem to answer the question. 'I'll do some more work on that,' Grace said.

Jennings had been fiddling about with her hands, simulating handshakes. 'If the right hand gripped the back of Monroe's left hand, then there could have been something on or in the glove which caused the scratch. Perhaps he took it off after he left the venue.'

'Did the CSIs find a glove?' Hunter asked.

'Not that I'm aware, but we'll check that.' Selitto scribbled himself a note in his notebook.

Hunter's phone sprang into life on the desk in front of her. She swiped the screen to answer the call and then stepped away from the others. When she returned to her seat, she had a smile on her face.

'Looks like we could be onto something,' she said as she sat down. 'That was our friend Toby Swartzman. He thinks he's found a puncture mark buried in the elephant tattoo on Jacqui Anderson's right arm.'

Following the revelation about Jacqui Anderson's puncture mark, Selitto and Jennings briefed the others about the drugs found inside Davie Monroe's snooker cues. Hunter was particularly interested to learn that he could have stashed up to £15,000 of Class A drugs into each cue.

'What are we thinking?' she asked. 'Supplier or dealer? Or something a bit higher up the chain of command?'

'We had been thinking supplier,' Selitto replied, 'but we were wondering who he was supplying. He's an Essex boy but it seems that he may have offloaded a stash whilst he's been here in Kent for the tournament. So, he could be part of a bigger operation running Essex and Kent.'

Jennings had been looking around the huge Ops Room, trying to spot one of her fellow DCs. Once she had found who she was looking for, she explained to Hunter that DC Rory Easton had spent some time with the Kent & Essex

Serious Crime Directorate and that he should be able to give them some information about how drugs gangs are set up. Sarah agreed that that would be a good idea so Jennings persuaded DC Easton to join them and drew up another chair for herself.

Rory was a tall, well-built young man with dark hair and designer stubble. Hunter wondered why stubble seemed to be *de rigueur* for young men in CID; a puzzle which was never likely to be answered to her satisfaction. But DC Easton certainly had presence, and Sarah Hunter was immediately drawn to his good looks and deep blue eyes.

She explained what they knew about the case they were working on and asked Easton for his take on where Davie Monroe might have fitted into the chain of command of a drugs gang.

'You say this guy was carrying drugs stuffed into his snooker cues?' Easton sounded surprised.

Hunter nodded. 'But we don't know where he offloaded the contents,' she added.

'Well, he's probably not the leader of a mainline drug dealing group because leaders don't normally carry the drugs,' Easton started, 'although he could be the leader of a small group where the borders of responsibility become more blurred. Or he could simply be a supplier.'

The detectives were listening in rapt silence as Easton continued. 'A gang would normally have a leader and then a couple of what we call stockists who would package up the drugs for the street dealers to sell on. Then there'd be the marketers or call handlers who would drum up business or keep in contact with users. As I said, if your guy was the leader, it's unlikely that he would have been walking around with the gear on him. So, he was probably a supplier arranging for consignments of drugs to be delivered to stockists which means that he would have been getting orders from the gang leaders.'

Selitto wanted to know if Easton thought that Monroe could have been working on his own.

'He was probably working for one of the drug lords,' Easton continued, 'which means that he was quite a big fish. He was also probably well placed in the inner sanctum of the drug lord's organisation, and had easy access to plenty of good quality gear attracting high prices. It would have suited his cover to have a proper day job travelling around to snooker events, and he would have been able to supply to a wide geographical area.'

Kendall wanted clarification. 'So, you don't think he could have just been picking the gear up and then supplying to a small number of dealers he happened to know. Sort of like freelancing?'

'Doubtful if the amounts you are talking about are correct,' Easton replied. 'Problem with working on his own is that he's got far greater exposure to something going wrong with dealers, users, duff gear – you name it. If he's in thrall to a drug lord then he stands more chance of not having to deal with any problems so he can get on with his snooker. I mean, he'd have to spend time practising if he's going to maintain his professional ranking.'

'Could he be anything to do with something like one of these county lines gangs?' Jennings had recently attended a lecture on the increasing drug problem in Kent and had heard mention of county lines drug dealing.

'I doubt that your man's been involved in county lines,' Easton replied. 'That's more in the realms of organised crime where the criminals pressurise vulnerable adults and children to transport, store and sell drugs in smaller county towns. The county line refers to the mobile phone lines used to take the orders for drugs, and these practices are now leading to increased violence and weapons-related crime.'

There was a pause whilst the detectives took this information on board.

'Okay, thanks for that.' Hunter was keen to wrap things up here and move on. 'You must be busy trying to keep the lid on things in Kent *and* Essex!'

Easton smiled at her. 'Always going to be a problem, I'm afraid – particularly as it involves the exploitation of young people. Dealers will often target children to act as drug runners or move cash so that they can stay under our radar. But let me know how you get on. It may well be that your investigations overlap into what we're doing and vice versa – so let's share intelligence.'

28

Tuesday 21 November

As hare-brained schemes went, this one was right up there and straight out of the Jasper Lime book of crazy ideas.

Reggie Lemon had delayed going over to meet Lime at his apartment as he had just wanted to collect his thoughts before another session of ear bashing from his business partner.

On arrival, he'd had to listen as Jasper talked him through his plan for replacing Davie Monroe. He'd wandered out on to the balcony and watched boats entering and leaving the harbour while Lime droned on in the comfort of his own kitchen. And he'd sat on one of the chairs beside the kitchen island as Lime took time to convince himself that his plan was workable.

They had then started to have a discussion about the logistics of the plan when Jasper suddenly announced that he was hungry. Reggie knew that meant only one thing so they decamped from the apartment to Lime's favourite table next to the window at the Le Nautique Restaurant, a stone's throw from the harbour itself.

Looking out on a sea of twinkling lights across the harbour area, they had ordered half a dozen oysters each and had then decided to share a shellfish platter which always came with what Lime referred to as 'extras' as he was such a good customer. Extra lobster, extra king prawns, extra crab claws. A nice cold bottle of Chablis Grand Cru always seemed to complement the seafood nicely and, as they had left their cars at the apartment, a second bottle was now on the table as their fishy fingers were dunked in bowls of warm, lemony water before being dried on fluffy towels provided by the serving staff. Empty shells and other detritus from the meal had been cleared away, and they now sat facing each other across the table.

'Do you honestly think that she is going to go for it?' Reggie asked as a waiter topped up his glass with the refreshingly clean and crisp white wine from the Bourgogne region of France.

'Of course she is!' Lime replied. 'What's she not going to like about the plan? She's already keen to use that set up on the Isle of Wight. Thinks it'll be well away from prying eyes. And she helped us with registering all our mainland cars and other equipment to that address. Stroke of genius that was, using an uninhabited property as a registered address.' He paused to take a mouthful of wine. 'Is there any of Lucy's gear still in the house?'

'Don't be ridiculous! Her gear was very low class. Poor market for it and, in any case, it went off very quickly. All in all, it was a heap of shite. Anyway, Lucinda and I haven't spoken in years because, quite frankly, we haven't got anything to talk about!'

Jasper Lime hated Lucinda Lemon with a passion and had sung praises to the highest saints on the day that Reggie announced that Lucinda was no longer part of his life. He considered her to be a calculating and despicable enemy who was only interested in one thing – herself. Reggie had been slow to catch on to this, mainly because he had other more important matters on his mind, but he eventually came round to the realisation that she was screwing with his life – and also with the man she had set up a business with.

For a long time, Reggie had suspected that his wife was playing away with the ever-so-smart arse Gustav Holmes, and he eventually took matters into his own hands when he turned up at the Isle of Wight house, shotgun in hand. The sight of Gustav's hairy bum scuttling out through the patio doors as he discharged both barrels of the gun into the ceiling of the room would live long in his memory. He'd always thought Lucinda had been lucky that he hadn't brought any spare ammo with him. Anyway, she had got the message and scarpered before he could do any serious damage.

Soon after Reggie had closed the house down and had it all professionally sealed, Lulu Harrison had chanced into his life on a flight from Southampton to Guernsey. Space was so limited in the tiny aircraft that she was almost sitting on his lap for most of the short flight across the Channel. This hadn't been an unpleasant experience for Reggie and they had said their goodbyes at the airport. A couple of days later, he had bumped into Lulu as he was coming out of the NatWest International Bank in St Peter Port. They had a chat and a good laugh about the flight over from Southampton, and he was astonished when Lulu had suggested that they have dinner that night at Da Nello.

They had a great time at the restaurant, enjoying the superb Italian cuisine accompanied by a seemingly endless supply of Montepulciano. After a couple of Sambucas just to settle the stomach, Reggie had swiftly found himself between the sheets with an extremely active young lady, and surprised himself by managing to keep her entertained until about

04.00 a.m. when they both collapsed into a dreamless sleep.

A late breakfast on the balcony of Lulu's room with them both dressed in hotel dressing gowns and very little else had been the precursor to a further energetic session in the bedroom following which they realised that they had missed lunch. Not to be denied, Lulu had ordered something from the all-day room service menu plus a bottle of champagne, and they once again found themselves on the balcony in their dressing gowns.

It was at this point that Reggie had remembered some of the conversation from their time at Da Nello which he tried to pick up on. Lulu didn't seem keen at first but either his persistence or the effects of the champagne eventually managed to unlock the door to her inner soul. And she began to tell him about her life in the male-dominated world of international drug dealing. How she had developed her supply lines and how she managed her select band of dealers, always offering top grade gear for maximum profit. She'd also learnt to fly, gaining her Private Pilot's Licence in near record time. This allowed her greater opportunities for transporting gear, and she found that it gave her far more freedom when travelling around the UK and across the Channel. But she was strictly a one-woman show – no partners, associates, hangers-on. And that's the way she wanted to keep it.

Reggie was fascinated and so he told her a little about how he and Jasper Lime had got in with an unruly French drug baron. He had been surprised when Lulu said she had heard of Hennenbont although she hadn't actually had any dealings with him. She was impressed to learn about the operation they had set up in the UK in the shadows of their very successful events business, and she had reacted well when he had alluded to the fact that they might be able to do something together.

And so he had told her about Prospero Inks.

29

Tuesday 21 November

A cold north-easterly had been blowing across Mount Ephraim as Sarah Hunter made her way along the pathway leading down from the busy A26 towards the town centre of Tunbridge Wells. She was well wrapped up against the cold weather and had left her car in Royal Chase on the other side of the main road so that she could get some exercise by walking or, rather, hobbling to her destination.

She had arranged to meet DCI Jack Pennington for dinner at Thackeray's, very much her favourite restaurant in the town, and she was looking forward to catching up with him again. They had first met three months ago when he was assigned from Kent's Serious & Organised Crime squad to help her with the trafficking case. In the end, the case was cleared up without the need to involve SOC but they had kept in touch and had met up on a couple of occasions for a drink and a plate of pub grub in one of the many country inns which festooned the Kent countryside.

Tonight was Jack's treat as he had been given some sort of promotion but not in rank. Sarah hadn't really understood what he had been talking about when he called to tell her, but she was very pleased when he suggested celebrating at Thackeray's. She had rushed home from Pembury Road, had a quick shower and then ransacked her wardrobe, standing in front of her full-length mirror with items of clothing draped all over her. In the end, she settled on a blue polka dot blouse, a pair of dark washed flare jeans and an Italian check blazer.

She'd then wrapped herself in the biggest coat she could find before disappearing into the night to get to her dinner date.

Pennington had arranged a quiet table by the window and, although the restaurant was full, they had a decent amount of privacy which pleased Hunter as she hated having to listen to other people's conversations when she was trying to enjoy the one she was having. They had dined well with Sarah enjoying seared Orkney scallops followed by an excellent dish of Cornish turbot served with borlotti beans, heritage carrots and a coriander yoghurt. Jack had joined her in having the scallops but had then opted for Scottish sirloin of beef which was served with oxtail ravioli and other rich wonderments which Sarah didn't think she could have managed.

They had decided against a dessert but Pennington had then ordered a plate of local Kent cheeses so that they had something to nibble on whilst they continued talking. The conversation had been wide-ranging although Hunter had still not really understood how Jack's promotion had not included a step-up in rank. But she had smiled knowledgeably whilst he was telling her about it and then the matter was swept aside as they moved on to other topics.

Earlier in the evening, Sarah had been interested in something that Pennington had said about an ongoing drugs investigation in Kent. Now, as he helped himself to another morsel of cheese, she grabbed her opportunity and told him about the deaths of Monroe and his manager. Also, the discovery of drugs in the snooker cues and the possibility that both had been poisoned although they were still awaiting tox reports.

'Hmm! That's very interesting,' Pennington said as he

swallowed a last mouthful of red wine. 'Do you know anything else about this guy Monroe?'

'Not really,' she replied, 'apart from the fact that he's a travelling snooker pro as opposed to being in the top echelon of the sport. Travels extensively in the south of England so would have plenty of opportunity if he was a supplier.'

'What about the manager?'

'Even less about her. Name's Jacqui Anderson.' The name didn't seem to mean anything to Pennington. 'About the only thing we know about her is that she lives near Brasted. However, the car she was found in is registered to a company at an address on the Isle of Wight. There are no vehicles registered under her name as far as the DVLA is concerned so we have to assume that she has some tie up with this company.'

'And what line of business is the company in?'

'It's called Prospero Inks and seems to be something to do with tattoos – supplies inks to tattooists or something like that. They're located near Bembridge Airport.'

At this, Pennington suddenly tensed. 'An airport? On the Isle of Wight? You're kidding me!'

'No, it's legit. Not sure it's in use any more but has been there for many years. According to Grace, or perhaps it was Ted, they built those little Islander planes there. Company's defunct now but the airfield is still there – might just be used for gliders. Not sure.'

Pennington pushed the plate with the remnants of the cheese to one side, placed his forearms on the table and clasped his hands together. He bent in towards Hunter and lowered his voice.

'Off the record and for your ears only, this might be of interest,' he said, and then told her about an undercover operation being mounted by the SOC in conjunction with the Drugs Squad. He told her how Kent & Essex Police had managed to infiltrate a new-boys-on-the-block gang which was growing bigger by the day with operations extending well beyond the county borders. The police suspected that the drugs were either coming in by sea at any number of the uninhabited coves around the coastline – or they were being shipped by air with helicopter drops in untended fields. The other possibility they were investigating was the use of small planes and their intel was that Headcorn airfield was a potential landing site but, so far, they had not been able to prove this. The other problem they had was that they didn't know where the drugs were originating from.

Sarah listened intently, all the time wondering if the deaths she was investigating were in any way connected to the events that Jack Pennington was telling her about.

'So, how does your guy read the situation?' she asked, popping the last grape on the cheeseboard into her mouth.

Pennington sat back and had a look around the restaurant before resting his arms back on the table. 'Well, that's the problem. We've lost contact!'

Hunter stared at him. 'Shit!' she whispered.

'Shit, indeed,' Pennington nodded. 'Haven't heard from him for five days which is really exercising the minds of the powers-that-be at Maidstone as you can imagine. He's been gathering good intel and we were putting together a picture of the structure of the gang and some names of those involved. But this is a very sophisticated outfit and it's clearly not being run from within the UK. If we've learned nothing else it is that they are ruthless and they'll eliminate anyone who either crosses them or becomes surplus to requirements.'

He waited while a waiter poured two cups of coffee and then continued.

'The last time our guy reported in he mentioned something about a new, sophisticated ocean-going vessel which was all but invisible to radar. He thought that this was going to deliver drugs onto deserted beaches at night using illegals from Calais and the surrounding area as the couriers. We think that he must have thought that his cover was blown because the rest of his message was garbled and then he just stopped transmitting. So, we don't know how these couriers were going to operate.'

'Sounds like something out of James Bond,' Hunter commented, twirling a strand of hair around a couple of her fingers.

'In a previous report he mentioned something about air support being a key to getting the drugs dispersed from the landing area as quickly as possible so we have taken this to infer the use of helicopters. We've also looked at the possibility of using Lydd or Headcorn for distribution by fixed-wing but we don't see it as a viable option to support the beach landings. Having said that, we are keeping an eye on movements at airfields like Headcorn because there's no immigration or customs presence there, and landing fees are cheap. It's also the base for one of the most active parachute centres in the South-East, and our guy thinks that the gang might even try to get some of their gear in by parachute.'

'Blimey!' exclaimed Hunter. 'I can see why you think it's a

highly sophisticated operation. I suppose we're also talking about drones?'

'Again, we think that drones are involved but we haven't yet got any information about where they might be offloading.'

'So, Monroe's not been on your radar at all.'

Pennington shook his head. 'Not a name we've got. But, if he has been taken out, then he's obviously done something to annoy someone.'

'Or maybe he *hasn't* done something which has annoyed someone even more!' Hunter surmised. Pennington nodded, deep in thought.

Suddenly feeling very tired, Sarah politely excused herself and went in search of the toilets. Pennington took this as the cue to get the bill and their coats, and he helped Sarah into hers when she returned to the table.

'That was a lovely dinner, thank you so much,' she gushed as she pulled on her woollen gloves and gave her scarf another twist around her neck. They said their goodbyes to the restaurant staff and then stood outside the little wicket gate. It was cold and fresh but Hunter felt a warm glow inside her from the good food and good company. But now she needed to get home.

'Can I walk you to your car?' Pennington asked.

'No, I'll be okay on my own thanks,' she replied, immediately regretting that she had been a bit hasty in turning him down.

He leaned forward and put his hands on her shoulders. 'You take care of yourself,' he whispered before pulling her towards him in a tight embrace. As they parted, he brushed his lips across both her cheeks before sliding his hands down her arms and taking hold of both her hands.

'Let me know how your investigation goes because it sounds like we might have some overlap.'

'I will,' she replied, removing her hands from his grip and putting them firmly in her pockets. 'And next time it'll be my treat!'

He laughed as he took a step back from her. 'I'll look forward to that!' he called out as she turned to retrace her steps to Royal Chase, calling out a cheery 'goodnight' as she climbed the hill back up to Mount Ephraim.

30

Tuesday 21 November

S he allowed the door to click shut behind her, knowing that the lights would be automatically extinguished once she had exited her small laboratory. She then watched as the wall panel slid back into place. Feeling her way along the corridor in the dark, she turned into the small utility room and then opened the door into the back garden. Making sure that she locked it behind her, she took a couple of paces across the patio before activating the biometric access control panel at the rear of the extended double garage.

The door opened into the small but well-equipped kitchen. She was starving and hoped that she had enough food supplies for a snack meal before she collapsed into bed. Peering into the fridge, she spotted a carton of pea & ham soup. There was also an unfinished packet of farmhouse ham slices with an imminent sell-by date. After chopping up the remains of the ham and adding it to the soup, she put it on to simmer while she went in search of some bread.

After slathering marmite on to two slices of toasted sourdough, she poured the soup into a wide bowl and sat down at the kitchen table, activating the remote control for the TV as she started to sip the hot soup. Skipping through the channels, she realised that there was very little worth watching at this time of night. So, in between sips of the warming soup, she found a jazz channel on YouTube which was showing a concert by Sarah McKenzie, an Australian jazz musician who someone in the lab had been talking about recently. This was just the sort of music she needed at this time of night. The flavour of the soup had been enhanced with the addition of the ham, and the slices of marmite toast were the perfect accompaniment. As she ate, her feet started to tap out the jazz rhythms on the floor under the table. She started to relax.

Even after she had finished the soup, she found herself glued to the screen, mesmerised by Ms McKenzie's fingers flying over the black and white keys, still tapping her feet to the beat. But time was marching on and she was now feeling very tired so she dragged herself away from the comfort of the kitchen and stepped through the doorway into the bedroom.

She could see a light flashing on the bedside table and realised that she must have forgotten to return the burner phone to its secret compartment. *You stupid woman*! She continued to castigate herself as she walked across the room. One missed call was showing on the screen. She didn't need caller ID as only one person had the number for this phone. Nevertheless, she frowned at the thought that he had called her.

'What the fuck does he want now?' she muttered to herself. They had a tacit agreement that he would never call her and that, if he really did need to speak to her, he would send a coded text message to her so that she could contact him. She couldn't see that there were any text messages from him so what was going on? She stared at the screen and was just about to call him when the phone lit up with an incoming call. She angrily swiped her thumb across the screen and then rammed the phone onto her ear.

'I thought I told you never to call me on this number,' she snarled through gritted teeth. There was a long pause, in fact so long that she thought he had hung up on her. Or maybe it wasn't him after all. But then the usual soothing voice.

'Hey, Tinx, don't get all precious on me! Relax a bit!'

'But we've agreed that you don't call me!'

'Yeah, but you didn't call and I wanted to know about Monroe and his woman. Are they confirmed as being out of the picture? Looks like it from what I can see online. Someone even managed to get a shot of his dead body on social media. You know anything about that?'

She knew that Monroe's death had been revealed by the police after the photograph went viral. They couldn't really hush that up so they had just put out a press release confirming the death. But no word about Jacqui Anderson.

'Monroe's confirmed but no word on Anderson,' she told him

'Okay, okay! But we know she was dead when you put her in the car.'

'Affirmative.'

'Okay! So now we've got another problem, and this problem needs to be dealt with right away!'

She rolled her eyes up to the ceiling. Why did everything have to be dealt with as a matter of urgency?

'Is that the only reason you rang me? To tell me it's urgent? You could have just put it in the details you're going to send me. I can't get on to it until tomorrow anyway.'

There was another long pause before he spoke again.

'You know, Tinx, I really like it when you get angry!'

'Fuck off and send me the details!' she replied tersely,

disconnecting the call. She threw the phone down on the bed. Resting her elbows on her knees and her head in her hands, she stared at the floor.

God! What had he got a problem with now? Or, no doubt, *who* had he got a problem with? She was already concerned about the mission he had mentioned on Sunday evening, and the details he had subsequently sent her didn't fill her with confidence. Would she even be able to get anywhere near the target? And who was the 'String Girl' anyway? The details talked vaguely of her whereabouts but, reading between the lines, he hadn't got a clue. So, Tinx, as usual, it's pretty much up to you. Find her, trap her, kill her – and, if you survive, you collect the riches. Simple really!

She heard the phone ping with an incoming message. She swung her legs up onto the bed and propped herself up on the pillows, reaching for the phone at the same time. It was his email. She knew that it would only stay on the phone for thirty minutes so she reached over and fished her notepad out of the drawer in the bedside table.

The instructions were straightforward. She made a note of the name but committed the rest of the information to memory. Home location, work location, hang outs, habits. She knew that his research was always spot on which did make her life a bit easier. The only problem she had was the speed with which he wanted the hit completed. Friday! She read through the information one more time and then deleted the email.

She lay back on the pillows, thinking, scheming, plotting. Her mind engaging with the challenge she had been set. Her thoughts straying to the sun-kissed sands at East Whale Bay, lazing on the terrace at the Ocean Club with a Bermuda Sunset for company, watching the waves relentlessly lapping on to the white sandy beach below her, the blue sky meeting the deep blue ocean on the distant horizon. Her eyelids were heavy, her whole body succumbing to the need for sleep. The phone slipped out of her hand and slid onto the bed beside her as her breathing became measured and deep.

31

Wednesday 22 November

S arah Hunter pressed the button to activate her phone screen and saw that the time was 12.38 a.m. She was all snuggled up under the duvet. But she was alone in her warm bed, her brain whirring through the enjoyable evening which she had experienced with Jack Pennington. She forensically examined the information he had given her about the investigation he was coordinating from Maidstone, and the loss of contact with his undercover officer. She wondered if their investigations were going to collide at some point.

She was also cross with herself for not responding more to his advances. Why was she unable to let herself get more involved? When he had embraced her, she had just stood there, arms at her sides, not hugging him back or showing any sign of affection at all. Yet she was attracted to him and his lips caressing her cheeks had sent a little frisson of excitement through her body.

And now she was lying here all alone with just her thoughts for company, regrets coursing through her very being. Come on, girl, get a grip! She wasn't part of some restrictive religious order. She had feelings and needs just like any other woman but why did she find it so difficult to let herself go, to surrender to the passion which she always tried so hard to suppress within her? True, she was married to her job but that didn't preclude her from enjoying time with someone else away from work, someone like Jack Pennington. Although he was, of course, from the same working environment. But it wasn't as if they worked together.

She thought about this for a while. She had seen so many of her colleagues suffer relationship breakdowns with partners who were not in the job, and it had always worried her that she would suffer the same fate if she got into such a relationship. However, she reasoned that being with someone who was working the same long hours under the same levels of pressure and stress would make for a better relationship. Or at least a relationship in which each party understood what the other was going through.

She generally liked being on her own, and always looked forward to her 'me time'. However, just lately she had started to have a craving for company. She enjoyed stopping off at little country pubs on her way home when she and Ted Selitto would chat about the day's activities. But, when she got home and closed the door behind her, she had recently started to feel lonely and unloved. So, what did she want? Did she want to be loved? Did she know how to love? Was it the commitment she was worried about? Could she give up part of herself to someone else? Would she be able to welcome someone else into her life? Was she afraid of losing her independence?

These were questions she had been asking herself a lot recently and, hard as she tried, she just couldn't come up with answers which made any sense.

And then there was the little matter of the recent beginnings of some deep and complex feelings for another woman. Only Sarah knew about this, and she was at pains to supress these feelings as they were so alien to her. But, when they were in each other's company, she was starting to feel that there was some chemistry between them. A look here, a smile there, a flick of the hair, a casual pout. Could it be that the other woman had similar feelings for Sarah? She briefly pictured them together somewhere, the background blurred, everything blurred apart from a beautiful face looking at her and smiling.

She angrily wiped the picture from her mind and grumpily turned over so that she now looked out into the dark abyss of her bedroom. She felt a small tear escape from the corner of her eye and drop silently onto the pillow. A sob suddenly convulsed her body as the tears began to flow. Sleep would be a long time coming.

32

Wednesday 22 November

There were a few cars parked outside the Better Body Shop gym in Sevenoaks as Ted Selitto steered his Megane across the icy but surprisingly well gritted car park in front of the building. Thank goodness they always kept a good supply of rock salt for these cold mornings.

The clock on the Megane's dashboard showed 05.25 a.m. as he got out of the car, gingerly placing both feet on the ground. He hadn't bothered with tracksuit bottoms which he now regretted as a raw north-easterly caught his bare legs. He grimaced as he carefully picked his way across the tarmac to the entrance to the gym. Once inside, he gratefully immersed himself in the warmth of the building and all those comforting aromas which pervade even the darkest recesses of physical exercise emporia.

His trainer, George, was ready with a welcoming cup of coffee, and they had a five-minute chat in the lounge area before it was time to get down to a serious workout. Selitto could be a bit of a gym bore, happy to extol its virtues whereas he rarely enjoyed the pain of going through the exercise routines. But he also saw it as a test for his mental strength. He always pushed himself to the limit to see what he could achieve with a strong mindset.

George finished the session bang on 06.30 a.m. after which Selitto enjoyed a nice hot shower and a quick shave before piling back into the Megane and heading for the A21 road to Tonbridge.

'Morning, Ted!' The welcoming voice of the ever-reliable Sergeant Trevor Arnold greeted Selitto as he slid his card through the reader and then punched in the security code which opened the door to the inner sanctum of the police station. Sergeant Arnold was on the early shift at the Pembury Road nick today, and Selitto returned the greeting as he stepped through the entrance, the door slamming noisily behind him. Before he had a chance to climb the stairs to the Ops Room, Arnold stepped out into the corridor in front of him.

'Sorry to trouble you, Ted, but I've got a chap in IR2 who's desperate to speak to someone about the snooker player,' he said, lowering his voice in case he could be overheard. 'As her ladyship isn't in yet, thought you might just like to take a quick look. He's been here since about 05.00 a.m. and wasn't keen on leaving till he'd seen someone.'

Selitto frowned. 'Did he say anything more than just that it's about the snooker player?'

'Nope, apart from that his name's Gavin Staunton,' Arnold replied. 'No sign of him on the PNC records and, as he didn't look as if he was going to be any trouble, I just stuck him in IR 2 with last week's local paper for company.'

The fact that Staunton was not on the Police National Computer record system was a mixed blessing, mainly because it meant that Selitto would know absolutely nothing about him before they met.

'Okay, I'll take a look. Can you get someone down to keep an eye from the viewing room, and tell DI Hunter that I'm in there when she arrives.'

'No probs, Ted,' Arnold replied, retaking his position

behind the front desk before picking up the phone to make a call to the Ops Room.

Selitto wandered down the corridor and opened the door to Interview Room 2. A man sat facing away from the door, his back erect, his head slightly bent down as if he was indeed reading the paper on the table in front of him. Selitto closed the door quietly and walked round until he stood facing the man.

'Good morning, Mr Staunton,' he said as he took the seat on the other side of the table. 'I'm DS Selitto. My colleague tells me that you're keen to talk to someone about Davie Monroe?'

The man swivelled round in his seat to see if anyone else had come into the room and then set his eyes on Selitto. He was smartly dressed but looked as if he hadn't slept in an age. There was a dark hollowness around his eyes and Selitto noticed that he had an uneven growth of dark stubble. It also smelled as if he hadn't been near a toothbrush for a day or three.

'Well, yes, I mean...' Staunton stammered, his hands clasping the edge of the table, leaning in towards Selitto before regaining some control and pushing himself back in his chair – much to Selitto's relief.

'Sorry! Um...I want to...um...I want to...oh God!' Staunton slumped in the chair, giving the impression of a balloon which had just been popped.

'Okay, just take your time,' Selitto told him, trying to encourage a swift end to the interview so that he could get on with the mass of work which he knew was lined up for him today. 'Perhaps you could just tell me how you know Mr Monroe.'

Staunton seemed to pull himself together and sat up straight, forearms on the table in front of him, hands clasped together in a tight knot.

'He's a mate of mine on the snooker circuit. I'm not that far behind him in the rankings. We've played a lot together over the years.'

'Okay, so how can we help?' Selitto was wondering where this was leading.

'I've...I've been sent a text,' he stammered, scrabbling around in a coat pocket before retrieving his mobile phone and placing it on the table in front of him. He turned the phone on and then scrolled down the screen until he found what he was looking for. He then turned the phone so that Selitto could see a photograph.

'May I?' Selitto asked as he gently eased the phone out of Staunton's hands so that he could take a closer look at the photo. He immediately recognised that it was the rogue photograph of Davie Monroe lying on the floor in the shower at The Prism. But his eyes were inexorably drawn to the words underneath. '*Who's Next?*'

He looked up at Staunton who was doing all he could not to look at the phone. 'When did you get this?'

'Late Monday night,' Staunton replied, sounding a bit more in control. 'I'd been out at a small exhibition event and was just relaxing at home. Around midnight maybe.'

'And you immediately recognised who was in the picture?'

'Course I did. I've known Davie for a long time. I'd recognise him anywhere, even without his clothes on.'

Selitto's left eyebrow involuntarily raised itself at this remark but he let the remark hang in the air for the moment.

'Any idea who might have sent this?' he asked eventually, knowing full well what the answer was going to be.

'Not a clue! It just came up on my screen with no indication of sender or anything. It's scared the shit out of me, I can tell you. That's why I'm here.'

'Okay!' Selitto took another look at the picture of Davie Monroe and then looked up at Staunton. 'Can you think of anyone who might want to send you this, who might want to threaten you in this way?'

Staunton's hands pawed at the table, his eye's once again swivelling around the room. All of a sudden, he let out an enormous sigh and went back to looking like a burst balloon.

Staring down at his clasped hands which were now in his lap, Staunton whispered something which Selitto couldn't hear.

'I'm afraid you'll have to speak up, sir – can't hear what you're saying.'

'Sorry!' Staunton cleared his throat, and finally looked up at Selitto. 'It's just that I've done something that I'm not very proud of and I'm now beginning to regret it.' He paused, again looking down into his lap where he was busily clasping and unclasping his hands. Selitto was at a loss as to what was coming

next so just watched as Staunton went through the agony of unburdening himself.

'I took a bribe,' he finally whispered, although this time it was loud enough for Selitto to hear. 'I took a bribe,' he repeated, 'to throw my match against Davie so that he could get through to the final. I deliberately allowed Davie to win.'

There was silence in the room. Selitto was in two minds as

to whether to say something or wait for Staunton to continue. But, as the silence continued, he decided to get on with it.

'How much are we talking about?' he asked.

'Five grand,' Staunton said with a shrug of his shoulders.

'And how was it paid?'

'All used notes, packaged up and posted through my letterbox during the night after the game.' Staunton sat back in his chair. He looked spent.

Selitto just needed a bit more information and then he'd get Elaine Jennings to have a more in-depth session with Staunton.

'How did you get to hear about the bribe?' he asked.

'Phone call,' Staunton replied. 'Said my life wouldn't be worth living if I didn't take the bribe – I'd be finished, never invited to any other tournaments, would never see my little girl again. The sort of thing you see in the movies. Never thought that was for real.'

'And you just said okay and went and threw the match?'

'Yeah – pretty much!' Staunton was sounding a little more bullish. 'I've got some money troubles with the ex-wife bitch so an extra five grand would come in useful for legal fees. Anyway, I couldn't see myself winning the tournament, not with Westie playing so solid, so I thought I might just as well get out with what I could get.'

Selitto stared at Gavin Staunton, his mind trying to untangle what the man had just said. He knew that Westie had been beaten in the final by Monroe, but had Westie also thrown that match? Shit! This evidence was starting to take them in a completely different direction.

'Okay,' he announced. 'I'm going to talk to my colleagues and then someone will be back to take a statement from you. In the meantime, you just stay put.' Fielding a request for some water, Selitto then got up from his chair and left the room.

As he closed the door to IR2, the door to the viewing room opened and Sarah Hunter stepped out accompanied by Elaine Jennings.

'Bloody hell, Ted, what's that all about?' Hunter asked, as she started walking down the corridor towards the stairs.

'God knows!' he exhaled. 'Looks like someone was keen to get Davie Monroe's name on the trophy by fair means or foul – mainly foul. And, by the sounds of it, Gavin Staunton wasn't the only one involved.'

'What, you mean that Westie bloke too?' Sarah asked as they reached the stairs, one hand on the newel post.

'Sounds like it to me,' Selitto nodded, 'particularly as our friend here was inferring that Westie was playing so well. But there's just one thing that doesn't quite fit together in all this.'

Hunter and Jennings looked at Selitto, waiting for more. He didn't disappoint.

'Five grand's not enough,' he said. 'Not when there's ten grand on the table for winning the semi-final. Why accept a bribe for fifty percent of what you could get for winning? Doesn't make sense.'

Hunter nodded. 'I see where you're coming from.'

'So, you're thinking he's telling porky pies?' Jennings asked, looking back at the door to IR2.

'Well, it doesn't make sense does it?' Selitto reasoned. 'Now, if he'd been offered fifteen grand or even twenty grand then I could see the sense in throwing the match because he makes more than if he'd won it.'

'Yeah, but if he had won it then the worst he is going to get is the fifteen grand for losing the final.' Jennings was finding it increasingly difficult to understand why Staunton would have taken this bribe.

'Okay!' Hunter was keen to get on. 'Elaine, I want you to take a statement from our friend in IR2 and see if you can press him on how much he actually got. See if you can prise Azzar away from whatever he's doing so that he can accompany you. Ted, you and I can get a quick catch up with Grace and then we need to chase up those tox reports and anything else from the CSIs. We'll all meet up later.'

33

Wednesday 22 November

Reggie Lemon took the morning flight to Southampton and collected the company car from the long-term car park. When they first moved their operations to Guernsey, Reggie and Jasper had decided that Southampton would be the main entry point to England because it was much quieter than either Gatwick or Heathrow – not so many nosey parker entry control people. It was also a lot cheaper which always helped and, of equal importance on a day like today, it was close to the Isle of Wight.

He drove south from the airport, along the edges of the Cultural Quarter and through the city centre before arriving on Town Quay where the Red Funnel Line operated jet foil and car ferry services to East and West Cowes on the island. Today, he had a booking on a ferry to East Cowes and was in plenty of time so he parked up and went in search of a cup of coffee.

Sitting on a bench on the edge of the Mayflower Gardens, he looked out across the water towards the Marchwood industrial complex on the other side of the River Test. In the hazy sunlight, the complex was poorly defined but it still provided an interesting backdrop. A couple of yachts meandered across his field of vision, the crew on one of them energetically gathering in sails as it presumably headed towards its destination. To his left, he could see one of the Red Funnel ferries coming into port so he finished his coffee, tossed the cup into the nearest litter bin and went back to his car.

The short journey over to East Cowes had been uneventful. Reggie had been directed onto the upper deck of the ferry and, after getting out of the car, he had decided to stand outside on the top deck so that he could enjoy the view as the ferry crossed over to the island. He soon realised that this might have been a foolhardy thing to do as a fresh northerly breeze was blowing once they got into the Solent but, as the sun was shining brightly, he decided to stick it out for the short journey.

Once he had disembarked from the ferry, he drove south as far as Downend where he picked up the road heading east towards Brading. Skirting to the south of the town, he negotiated Yarbridge Cross and carried on along a winding road until the landscape flattened out and he saw the runway at Bembridge airport on his left-hand side. He passed the Propellor Inn which was attached to the old airport building and then just remembered in time to take the next right which would take him down towards Whitecliff Bay.

Reggie had a lot on his mind, and had been thinking through some of his plans on the drive across the island. He had been so lost in thought that he almost didn't register that there was a police car parked outside the old stone-built farmhouse as he rounded another bend in the road. His natural reaction was to slam on the brakes which got him a loud blast of the horn from the vehicle behind him. So, he drove on past the house and soon found a gateway into a field where he slewed the car off the road and parked up. The vehicle following him accelerated past with another serenade from the horn. Reggie gave the vehicle the finger which made him feel better even if it wouldn't have made the slightest bit of difference to the dickhead driving it.

He turned round in his seat and could just see the police car. He was frustrated at not being in quite the right position to see if there was someone sitting in it. Or was it empty? He looked at his watch and decided that he would have to find out what was going on as he didn't have any time to waste.

He walked back towards the house and quickly realised that there was no one in the police car. However, as he drew level with the house, he almost bumped into a uniformed police constable who was stepping through the tall wrought iron gate that filled the space between the hornbeam hedges at the front of the property.

Reggie stopped in front of the constable and cleared his throat. 'Ah, there you are,' he stammered, trying desperately to act calmly. He was also trying to look past the man to see if he was on his own or if there was someone with him.

'Perhaps you could just give a clue as to whether I'm on the right road for Bembridge,' Reggie continued, feeling his face getting hot despite the fact that it was bitterly cold. 'Seem to have taken a wrong turning somewhere,' he continued, spreading his arms wide, shrugging his shoulders, trying to give a bit more credibility to his question.

The constable looked him up and down and then adjusted his line of sight so that he could now see Reggie's car further up the road. 'Well, you won't get there by following this road,' he eventually said. 'You'll need to go back the way you've come, take a right and then right again once you get to the main road. Should see a sign pointing towards Bembridge. That'll be your best bet.'

'Oh, okay, thanks,' Reggie spluttered. He desperately

needed this cop to get in his noddy car and fuck off out of here pronto. 'Right! Well, I'd better call the guy I'm meeting and tell him I'm going to be a bit late.' He turned and headed off back towards his car whilst at the same time making a show of taking his phone out of his pocket and pretending to make a call. 'Thanks,' he called back over his shoulder as he got to the car and slid into the driver's seat. He rested his elbow on the window trim, phone clamped to his ear.

In the wing mirror, he watched as the constable got back in his car and was soon edging out into the road. As he passed Reggie, he turned and waved a friendly farewell as he continued around the bend further up the road and out of sight.

Reggie decided to give it a few minutes to make sure that the constable was not going to come back down the road to check that he had gone. He then reversed back to the farmhouse and parked in the small layby in front of the gate. He waited for a few more minutes before getting out of the car and pushing his way through the gate.

The building in front of him held so many memories – some good, many not so good. He seemed to have been here at important stages in his life, and his mind often returned to this house at Bembridge in idle moments.

An uneven cobbled path led across a small stretch of lawn to a wooden front door which had a huge wrought iron knocker as its centrepiece. The path then branched to the left and right before wrapping itself around the corners of the house and heading towards the rear of the property.

The windows either side of the front door were boarded up on the outside and, as he looked up, he checked that the interior shutters on the upstairs windows were also closed. After he had kicked Lucinda out of the house, he had appointed a company which specialised in securing empty properties to keep the house secure. He had no idea of how many times they came round each year but he was always pleased when he visited and found that the place was still secure.

Fishing a set of keys out of his coat pocket, he unlocked the door and stepped inside. Closing the door behind him, he flicked the light switch which he knew was on the wall to his right. A pale ceiling lamp lit up the hall as he crossed over to one of the reception rooms. A musty smell pervaded the room and, indeed, the other reception room was the same.

He took a quick look in the storeroom which was attached to the kitchen. Floor-to-ceiling cupboards were spread around the room, and he knew that they were full of jars containing powders and liquids as well as pigments and all the equipment required for making tattoo inks. Further storage was offered by way of large cardboard boxes which were piled up in the middle of the room.

In the kitchen itself, the cupboards around the work surfaces were also full of jars containing powders of many different colours. However, the problem here was that the contents could only be identified if one knew the meaning of the code on each of the jar labels. Which was probably why they looked as if they were unused.

Reggie skipped up the staircase and poked his nose into the two bedrooms at the front, then the bathroom, and then the two rooms at the back. However, he found that the door to the fourth bedroom was locked. He'd always known that all the doors had standard mortice locks but he'd never known them to ever be locked so he looked around to see if any of them had a key. Having searched in all the drawers in each bedroom and even in the bathroom cabinets, he drew a blank. So, what the hell was going on with bedroom four, he wondered.

Back downstairs in the kitchen, he unlocked the door leading out into the back garden, and walked across the huge patio which covered the entire area at the back of the house. An expanse of lush green grass lapped over the borders of the patio and stretched down to a small orchard of half a dozen apple trees, the hornbeam hedges sealing the borders of this rather lovely vista.

He stood there, taking in the view and feeling pleased that the old house hadn't been vandalised or occupied by squatters since he was last here. But there was something that was beginning to trouble him. Why was the bedroom at the back locked? And then he caught the first whiff of an unpleasant smell which pervaded the area at the back of the house. Where was it coming from? Smelled more like drains than anything else but there were hardly any other properties within at least half a mile of the house.

Pacing backwards and forwards across the patio, he couldn't quite place where the smell was at its strongest. He then spotted one of the drain covers which now had a two-seater garden bench positioned over it. Moving the bench to one side, he pulled up the cover and peered into the drain. No blockage down there and no odour apart from a smell of stale water. He walked to the edge of the patio and peered up the pathway on the other side of the house.

The smell was definitely stronger here and now he saw what might be the cause. A water butt stood next to the house on a base of bricks with a down pipe leading from the guttering above. Only the pipe was not now attached to the butt, and the connection was swaying gently in the breeze that was being funnelled into the area between the house and the hedge.

Reggie stepped off the patio and immediately noticed that the ground was softer here, his feet making squelching noises as he approached the water butt. Presumably this was because rain from the roof had been emptying straight on to the grass. The smell had now become a stench and Reggie was sure that the water butt was its source. Stale water could start to smell rancid like this, he told himself, more to allay some of his fears rather than for any scientific reason.

He felt around the rim of the lid and then simply lifted it off the top of the butt which had the effect of releasing an overpowering foul stench. Reggie instinctively ducked and turned away from the water butt while the first waves of nausea washed over him. He had always thought that he had a pretty good constitution for most things but even the strongest stomach couldn't have prepared him for this.

Pulling the lapel of his coat over his nose and mouth, he turned back towards the butt and then froze. A white face floated just below the surface of the water, the translucent bloated skin distorting the shape of its features, sunken eyes staring sightlessly towards the heavens, strands of hair floating on the surface. Reggie turned away from this monstrous sight and retched, thanking his lucky stars that he hadn't yet had anything to eat today.

When he felt more in control of his senses, he looked back at the face and realised that, to be in the position it was in, it was likely that the victim's neck had been broken. He was sure it was the face of a man but not someone he could recognise, particularly in this state. With trembling hands, he gently replaced the lid and squelched his way back to the patio and sat on the garden bench. After a moment to collect his thoughts, he called his business partner.

'Hey, Reggie, how's the good old Isle of Widget?' Jasper's voice sounded slightly slurred. Had he been drinking already?

'The good old Isle of Widget, as you call it, is fine. The only thing that isn't fine is that there is a very dead body at the Prospero house,' Reggie spluttered.

There was a pause at the other end of the call. 'Hey, Reggie, you're cracking up a bit – just run that by me again?'

So, Reggie repeated what he had said and sat back to wait for a response. He didn't have to wait long.

'What the fuck do you mean, Reggie,' Jasper's voice now sounding very wary. 'How can we have a dead body there? Where is it? *Who* is it?'

'Looks like someone's rammed it into the water butt down the side of the house. No idea who it is but it looks like they had to break the victim's neck to get the whole thing into the butt.'

'Fuck me! That sounds totally gross, Reggie.'

'And the old bill was here too,' Lemon interrupted.

'*What*?' Jasper shrieked.

'Okay, calm down. Looks like they were just passing and took a look at an empty property. Anyway, I thought we weren't using this place anymore.'

There was a long pause before Jasper Lime replied. 'Yeah, well I've let Looby have a set of keys because she needed somewhere to store a small consignment. Didn't think you'd mind as we haven't got a need for the property at the moment.'

For a moment, Lemon was stunned into silence. Jeez, this was getting worse by the minute, he thought. But he could feel a rage rising inside him.

'You've let Looby Lou use this place without even asking me?' Reggie exploded. 'You never mentioned this when we were talking about her last night! What the fuck's going on? What's this small consignment she's storing here?'

'Okay, Reggie, calm down – must have slipped my mind last night.' Jasper was trying desperately to appease his friend.

'Oh, come on Jas, I wasn't born under a toadstool.' Reggie was seething. 'She must have had the use of this place for quite a while bearing in mind all the gear that's stashed inside.'

'Well, her name's on all the paperwork for the property so I couldn't really refuse. Any case, we need to keep sweet with her - particularly if we're going to tap her up for the Hennenbont gig.'

'But we can't give her the run of the place if she's going to go round killing people and stuffing them into water butts!' Reggie was starting to wonder what exactly had been going on here. 'Anyway, do you know what this small or, in fact, rather large consignment is?'

'No idea. Said she was going to take it over to the island so she could do some cutting. Had a couple of dealers she was grooming in the Portsmouth area. And she was talking to some low-lifes in Southampton so the house was the ideal base.'

'When was this?' Reggie wanted to know.

'Oh, I don't know – about six months ago?'

'Six *months* ago?' Reggie was incredulous. 'How come you never mentioned this? Christ! I might have decided to stay here one night so I turn up and find Looby Lou walking around in her best negligee! God's sake, Jas, you are well out of order.'

'Does it look as if she's still using it?' Jasper asked, hoping to get a more civil response.

'Well, funny you should ask that because now one or two things are beginning to fall into place. One in particular is that the back bedroom is locked up. We don't have a key for it and, as far as I'm aware, there's never been keys for the rooms. So, presumably our dear friend Looby has got herself a key and has stashed God knows what in there.'

'Yeah, okay mate,' Jasper said, trying to calm matters and sound sincere, 'I should have let you know. But can't we just have a chat with her about this when we discuss the Hennenbont proposition with her? She'll just get the hump if we go in with all guns blazing about what she's been doing in the house and then that's us back up the *Swanee* with that French *chien de porc*.'

Reggie wasn't sure whether this was a term of endearment towards the Frenchman or something less flattering. What he did know was that Lime's use of the French language was bloody awful at the best of times. And, although he was furious, he felt that there was little to be gained right now by carrying on with this call. So, he told Jasper that they would continue the discussion when he was back in Guernsey.

Disconnecting the call, he sat back on the bench and stared down the garden towards the small orchard. Why the hell had Jasper let someone like Looby Lou have the run of this place? It was just asking for trouble and, boy, was she trouble! When Lime had first suggested doing a deal with Looby Lou, Reggie had had many misgivings but allowed himself to be talked round. Now, they had a real problem if she was going round killing people and stuffing the corpses of her victims into water butts on the property – particularly if the cops were now starting to take a closer interest in an otherwise empty house.

34

Wednesday 22 November

S arah Hunter and Ted Selitto sat across the table from each other in one of the small meeting rooms on the first floor at Pembury Road. Hunter had suggested that they have a short brainstorming session just to see if they could nudge the investigation on a bit. As usual, she was getting impatient and wanted to at least make some progress today.

'Is this all to do with drugs, Ted?' Hunter wanted to set her sights on what was the principal thread in their investigation.

'Well, it's certainly drug-related,' Selitto replied, 'but there's all sorts going on here. We've got two deaths, each unexplained via the normal post-mortem process. Both bodies have potential puncture sites where something could have been injected. We've got a car which is registered to an address on the Isle of Wight which is allegedly the headquarters of a company selling inks for tattooists. However, the person in the car appears to have no link with the company. And now we've got a snooker player saying that he's taken a bung for throwing a match in a snooker tournament.'

'And we've got a dead snooker player who was carrying drugs around in hollowed-out snooker cues,' Hunter continued. '*And* it looks as if this player was the one being set up to win the tournament. So, who would want him to win at all costs, why would they want him to win at all costs – and who wanted him dead?'

They sat and looked at each other, both seeking inspiration

from the other. Hunter knew that it only took a little spark for them both to start unravelling a seemingly impossible problem. What should she be concentrating on first?

'Let's see if there's any information from the tox labs yet,' she said, pulling her phone out of her pocket and selecting Dr Toby Swartzman's number. 'Can you just nip next door and check with Grace about that security guard. Surely we must have been able to find him by now.'

Selitto left the room while Hunter was waiting for Swartzman to answer. When he returned, Sarah was just finishing the call.

'Well, that confirms something,' she said, placing her phone on the table. 'No official tox reports yet but Toby's mate at the labs says that early tests have shown a high level of toxicity in both bodies. In fact, the guys at the lab are a bit concerned because it's not showing up as anything which they have ever seen before. Toby's saying that it seems to be an unusual combination of toxins which they are now analysing in order to try to identify the constituent parts.'

'Interesting!' exclaimed Selitto. 'No news on the security guard by the way. No one's clapped eyes on him since you last saw him at The Prism. Grace has checked with the agency employing him and he hasn't been paid for Sunday night because he hasn't sent in a timesheet yet so no idea what his game is.'

Sarah shifted in her chair, her leg starting to give her a bit of jip. *Try to keep moving*, the physio had told her but, as she had explained to the therapist who had hands the size of dinner plates, it was not always easy in her job to keep moving. Anyway, she decided to get up and walk around the room just so that she could give the leg some exercise.

'Is he a bit of a side show?' she asked. 'You know, Andy Warhol's prediction that everyone will be world famous for fifteen minutes? Just took the photo on the spur of the moment and then basked in the glory of getting a zillion hits on his Twitter or Facebook or whatever platform?'

'Yep, think I'm with you on that one,' Selitto replied. 'Can't really see what else he could get out of it. He's got no connection to Monroe as far as we can see. The press won't be interested, not even the red tops, especially without an inside story. So, there's no money to be made.'

'Presumably someone else downloaded the photo and then added the cryptic message to send to Staunton,' Hunter observed. 'Malicious? Or just someone trying to put the frighteners on the man for whatever reason. Ex-wife? Ex-wife's new bloke?'

'Hmm.' Selitto gave this some thought. 'Difficult to say. Unless Staunton's also carrying drugs around in his snooker equipment. But you're right, someone else has downloaded it – no way the guard could have sent it to Staunton. He probably doesn't even know who he is for a start.'

'Okay, let's just park the guard for the time being. I'll get Grace to keep on checking up with his employer in case he makes contact. Might as well knock on his door from time to time as well. Where is it he lives?'

'Think he's down near Lamberhurst. Hook Green? Somewhere like that. But I'll have to check with Grace.' Selitto scribbled himself a note on the pad that had been left on the table.

'Right. The car. Remind me who it's registered to?'

'Company by the name of Prospero Inks at an address in or near Bembridge on the Isle of Wight,' Selitto said, referring to his pocket notebook. 'Grace contacted the HantsPol boys at Ryde and was organising a drive-by so that we could get them to take a look. Nothing back from them so far, I'm afraid.'

'And no other information on this ink company?'

'Nope. Doesn't seem to be trading but hasn't been wound up either. No claims against it. No charges on the property. We're still trying to get some information on the registered directors – nothing about them on the PNC.'

Hunter had slowly perambulated around the room and was now leaning against the wall by the window, surveying the never-ending traffic as it snaked around the roundabout below her and off towards the High Street and the town centre shops. Selitto was pleased that she had come to a halt as his neck was beginning to ache with the effort of keeping his eyes on her.

'What about this Anderson woman?' she suddenly asked. 'Any more on her apart from the fact that she was Monroe's manager?'

'Not really. She ran her Anderson Sports agency which is very much an up-and-coming organisation as far as sports management agencies are concerned. She chose to specialise in signing up young talent of the future and, by all accounts, has been nibbling away at the market share of some of the big boys in this field. She and Monroe were in a bit of an on-off relationship but Anderson seems to have been out of the country a lot recently drumming up business with poorly managed young athletes from developing countries.'

Silence returned to the room as Hunter watched the traffic continue on its weary way towards shopping nirvana.

'At the risk of living to regret it,' she eventually said, 'I reckon that Anderson's a bit of a red herring in all this. She was probably in league with Monroe on the drugs so, if his death is drug-related, then she had to be despatched as well. I doubt that she had a clue about the fact that other players were being bunged to let her man win the tournament. I also can't see that her death is related to her business interests. No, whoever wanted Monroe out of the way obviously felt that she knew too much so she had to go as well. So, let's temper our interest in her.'

Selitto doodled on his pad. He liked it when Hunter was decisive like this. It helped them to cut through the crap of supposition and concentrate on the real issues.

Hunter pushed herself off the wall and started pacing again. 'Here's what's going round in my head. If we say that Monroe's death was drug-related, then could the fact that someone paid a lot of money to ensure that he won the tournament also be related in some way to his drug dealings?'

'Doubt it,' Selitto replied. 'If someone's paid up to get him into the winner's enclosure, they're hardly likely to then immediately top him. Doesn't make sense.'

'Perhaps he's done a dodgy deal, upset someone big time,' Hunter hypothesised, knowing deep down that she was arguing against herself.

'If you want my opinion,' Selitto replied, still doodling on his pad, 'these two scenarios aren't related.'

Hunter gave him a stare, arching one eyebrow.

'The bungers wouldn't have wanted him dead,' he stated

confidently. 'They were clearly setting him up for something – no idea what at the moment. Perhaps someone wanted to do a deal with him so giving him a win in this tournament might have been part of the plan to get him on board.'

Selitto sat back and stared at the ceiling.

'And perhaps, just perhaps,' he continued, 'someone else didn't want him to do the deal so took him out before he could get into bed with the others.'

Sarah retook her seat and put her elbows on the table, resting her chin on her steepled fingers. 'Hmm! Now that's an interesting proposition, Ted. So, you reckon that going after the bungers won't lead us to the person who killed Monroe and Anderson – and vice versa.'

'That's about the measure of it,' he replied.

There was a knock on the door and DC Elaine Jennings stepped into the room. 'Quick word?' she asked. Hunter nodded.

'We've pretty much finished with Staunton,' she said as she took a couple of steps into the room. 'He's absolutely determined to keep to the £5,000 story and says that he has no idea who was behind it. Also thinks this Westie bloke must have got bunged as well because he can't see how he would have lost to Monroe in the final otherwise. That picture on his phone has really spooked him and he's shit scared about what might happen next.'

'Okay, Elaine,' Hunter said, turning to face her DC, 'there's nothing we can charge him with and we can't give him protection because he hasn't been directly threatened so you might as well let him go. But suggest you tell him to keep a look out for anything suspicious – give him a card with your contact details. Also, find out where we can find this Westie – probably need to pay him a visit and see how much he's sitting on. No point in getting a warrant for Staunton's gaffe as he'll have moved the cash by the time we get there.'

'Right, ma'am, I'll get all that organised,' Jennings replied, turning and leaving the room.

'Looks like you're right, Ted,' Sarah said, getting up from the chair. 'The bunging is a distraction!'

35

Wednesday 22 November

Reggie Lemon had been sitting on the bench for rather longer than he had intended. Despite everything, he still liked to think of the house as being his house which made the discovery of the dead body even harder to bear. It somehow defiled his memories of the place.

He eventually got up from the bench and went back inside the house, making sure he locked the back door properly. He then carried out a careful inspection of the kitchen cupboards. There were a myriad of different storage jars containing all sorts of powders each with a label showing a number. He knew that the numbers were codes which related to the contents and that he could access the codes right now if he wanted to – but he couldn't be bothered at the moment.

He wandered out of the kitchen and into the store room. This is where they stored most of the tattoo equipment and all the inks. When they had first decided on the alias of Prospero Inks, they had bought the complete stock of a small chain of tattoo parlours which had gone bust. They then dumped the stock in the house and registered Prospero Inks as a supplier at Companies House. Jasper Lime had been keen to have a legitimate identity for the property even if the goings on inside it were anything but legitimate.

Returning to the top of the stairs, Reggie decided to make a closer inspection of the bedrooms and the bathroom. All the upstairs windows had been fitted with steel security screens on the inside because Jasper had thought that it looked better if a casual observer could see glass in the upstairs windows rather than having the whole thing boarded up. In any case, the boarded-up windows on the ground floor couldn't be seen from the road because of the hedge.

Reggie flicked the light switch in one of the front bedrooms and a dim yellow light filtered down from a bare bulb hanging off-centre from the ceiling. He looked around at the sparse collection of furniture – single bed, dressing table, chest of drawers, bedside table. He wandered over to the built-in wardrobe, opened the double doors and found himself staring at various items of female clothing which were hanging from a rail spanning the width of the wardrobe. A number of shoe boxes were stacked up underneath the clothing, so he squatted down to take a closer look.

The first thing he noticed was that all the boxes bore the names of well-known brands of expensive footwear. It looked like there were in excess of thirty pairs of shoes here so he reached out and pulled one of the boxes towards him. He was surprised to find that it was quite heavy, particularly after reading the labelling on the box which indicated that it contained a pair of slingbacks.

He stood up and took the box over to the bedside table. Flicking on the bedside light, he sat on the bed so that he could get a better look at the contents of the box. Once he had removed the lid, he sat back and simply stared at the contents.

'Well, well, well, what *have* we got here?' he muttered to himself.

Rather than a nice brightly coloured pair of slingbacks, the box was rammed full of what, to the casual observer, might have been the contents of a tin of Quality Street. But Reggie knew better. And he also knew that he was looking at around £5,000 worth of what was probably cocaine which had already been cut and packaged up for sale on the streets of the UK.

He got up from the bed and returned to the wardrobe where he selected another box from the bottom of one of the piles. Taking it over to the bedside table, he noticed that its contents should be a pair of evening shoes. Removing the lid, he found that the box contained bundles of bank notes all held together with elastic bands. He flipped through one bundle of twenty-pound notes and gave up counting when he got to £3,000. He couldn't even imagine how much money was stashed in this box.

Reggie sat back on the bed, staring at the opened boxes. What on earth was going on here? He knew that Jasper used the house for storage of gear but even Reggie knew that they would never have this amount of gear all packaged up and ready for distribution. In any event, they didn't do street dealing. And the money! Jas would never keep money in a shoebox. A bomb-proof safe perhaps, but never a shoebox.

He wandered back over to the wardrobe and started to look in some of the other shoeboxes. More drugs, some already wrapped up and some glass bottles all carefully marked in code. There were also boxes containing more cash – some with ten-pound notes, some with fifties or fivers. All carefully bundled up and secured with elastic bands.

After calling Jasper and getting his infernal voicemail message, he returned all the boxes to the wardrobe and shut the door. Crossing the hall towards the back of the house, he tried the door to the locked bedroom again but it still held fast. There was a big window at the end of the hall which would normally look out onto the back garden but was now boarded up. At this moment in time, it would have suited him to be standing there looking out onto the little orchard, trying to work out what was going on in this house.

He went into the bathroom and flushed the toilet to make sure it was still in working order. He was just on his way out of the bathroom when he caught sight of a wooden cabinet on the wall behind the door. He couldn't remember seeing that before, certainly not when he was living here all those years ago.

Pushing the door to one side, he stood in front of the cabinet and opened one of the doors. Inside, the narrow shelves were stacked with small glass jars containing powders and glass phials with clear liquid in them. He took one of the phials out and held it up to the light. No indication what the liquid was, no label on the bottle.

He put the phial back on the shelf and then froze as he felt the cold steel of a gun barrel pressing into the back of his neck. He instinctively raised his arms and stepped back from the cabinet so that he was now in the centre of the bathroom. The gun pressed urgently against the nape of his neck and a hand shoved him in the back as he was hustled out into the hallway.

Before he had a chance to turn around, a hand had grabbed his coat collar and the gun barrel was now nestled under his right ear. His assailant then pushed him along the hall towards the back bedroom with the locked door. Only the door now stood open and he was roughly propelled into the darkened room. Tripping over his feet, he stumbled across the floor and eventually crashed onto a bed. He turned just in time to see the door slam after which he heard the sound of a key turning in the lock. He peered unseeingly into the darkness.

36

Wednesday 22 November

B y late morning, Sarah Hunter was getting frustrated. They didn't seem to have made any progress and were in that no-man's land stage of an investigation where they were waiting for others to provide them with fresh information. She was particularly frustrated at not having the tox reports which meant that she still didn't have accurate causes of death for Monroe and Anderson.

She had taken a call from DC Elaine Jennings who, together with DC Azzar Mishraz, had gone off to take a look at Jacqui Anderson's house near Brasted. Nothing of note to report. The woman seemed to have lived a fairly frugal life but perhaps that was because she spent so much of her time on the road. Her passport apparently bore testament to a hectic schedule with immigration stamps from countries some people would never have heard of. They had found a couple of mobile phones and a laptop which had been bagged up ready for the IT tech team. The only other observation was that a man had either been living there or stayed from time to time. Given that they suspected there was some connection between Anderson and Monroe, the detectives had bagged up a razor, a toothbrush and a comb so that they could check the DNA. It would be another box ticked.

DS Grace Kendall had been working on another case but had been able to give some time to again reviewing all the CCTV footage they had collected from The Prism and the surrounding area. She had managed to find footage which showed the security guard leaving his post and entering the dressing room so that clearly implicated him in obtaining the photograph of Monroe. She then turned to the figure seen leaving the venue almost immediately after the melee around Monroe following his win.

'I've done some work to sharpen up the images we have of the man leaving the theatre.' She clicked a couple of commands on the toolbar at the top of the screen.

'You see here,' she said, pointing to the image, 'the man is holding something in his left hand. I've done a bit of work on this and I think that he's holding something which looks like a glove.' She flicked her mouse and a close-up of the man's left hand filled the screen. The detectives leant in to take a closer look – it did, indeed, look like a glove.

'He then goes outside,' Grace continued, 'and we can see the glove more clearly on the cameras covering the porch area. He's making no move to put the glove on which is odd as it was a very cold night. And look at the way he's holding the glove – almost as if he was evicting a nasty creepy-crawly from behind the sofa!' That got a snigger from Selitto.

'And then?' Hunter wanted to know where their suspect went.

'And then he pretty much disappears,' Grace replied. 'Obviously knows Tonbridge well and particularly the location of our CCTV gear. He goes across the Waitrose car park and then disappears into the alleyways behind Cornflower Court. Tried to see if we could pick him up around the Angel Centre but my guess is that he headed up to the High Street and then straight across into the area around the skatepark and the playground. Remember, it was pitch dark and the area's not very well lit so there would have been little chance of picking him up there.'

They all sat staring at the frozen image of the man with the glove. Eventually, Hunter broke the silence.

'Curiouser and curiouser! When I take one glove off, I normally take the other one off as well – it's a natural sequence. So, it seems strange that our man has left the other glove on. Why would he do that?' No one volunteered an answer.

'Perhaps there's something about the glove which he's not happy about,' Selitto suggested.

'Or is he just being really careful with it until he can get to somewhere he can dispose of it?' Kendall wondered.

'Presume we're far too late to start looking in bins now.' It wasn't really a question, more of a statement from Hunter. 'In any case, it doesn't look to me as if he was planning on just jettisoning it as he walked through the town.'

They lapsed into silence again, Hunter getting restless in her chair.

'Wind it back to the handshake please, Grace,' she asked. 'Let's have another look at that.'

Grace rewound the CCTV feed and they watched as the man came into shot on the left of the screen. He had to push his way through some of the fans until he got into a position where he could make a grab for Monroe's left hand. By this stage, Monroe wasn't caring about who was shaking his hands, he was totally immersed in the adulation.

They watched as the man took hold of Monroe's hand, his left palm grasping Monroe's left palm. Then his right hand covered the back of the snooker player's left hand, its palm seeming to caress the back of Monroe's hand before the man withdrew both his hands and turned to leave the auditorium.

'One more time please, Grace.' Hunter was increasingly certain that she was watching the killing of Davie Monroe.

Kendall rewound the tape and they watched it in slow motion until they got to the point where the man's right hand grasped the back of Monroe's hand.

'There,' Hunter exclaimed. 'Run it through frame by frame.' Grace did as she was asked while Hunter took up commentary on what she was seeing on the screen.

'See how the man grasps the back of the hand – looks as if he has applied some pressure and then he drags the palm of his hand across the back of Monroe's hand before withdrawing both his own hands. That's how he scratches Monroe.'

All eyes were glued to the screen as Hunter continued. 'So, the reason he's being careful with the glove is because there must be a device fitted to it which not only scratches the skin but injects a poison.'

'And without altering the recipient to the danger,' Grace added.

'Quite!' Hunter agreed. 'A bit like some of those nasty insects you find in foreign places. All sweetness and light to look at but with deadly intentions when they alight on your skin.'

She paused as if trying to remember something else she wanted to say but then shaking her head when it wouldn't come to her.

'Okay, Grace, thanks for that. So, now we've got probable cause of death, method, weapon, but no motive and no clue as to the identity of the assassin.'

Selitto raised his eyebrows at the mention of the word 'assassin' but then thought it adequately described what he had just seen.

The deadly assassin.

37

Wednesday 22 November

A thin band of partial daylight crept into the room around the metal screen which obscured all but the very edges of the window.

Once his eyes had grown accustomed to the darkness all around him, Reggie had been able to make out the general layout of the room and was now sitting on the edge of the bed. There was an underlying putrid smell in the room; a mixture of body odour, urine and faeces. Where was it coming from?

Then he noticed the two red lights high up in the ceiling to either side of the window. Unless he was very much mistaken, these would signify the presence of cameras so it was likely that he was being watched.

His phone had somehow slipped out of his pocket when he crashed into the bed but, thankfully, he had found it on the floor by his feet. He now activated the torch and swung the beam around the room looking for a light switch. There was one by the door but, on investigation, he realised that the switch had been removed and the wall-mount had been taped up. There were no other light switches in the room although he noticed that there was one light directly above the bed and one mounted on the wall over the door.

His first instinct had been to call Jasper Lime but once again all he got was the infernal voicemail message. Why wasn't he answering? Where the hell was he? There was very little point leaving a message because Lime hardly ever listened to his messages. However, Reggie had left him a curt 'call-me-back' message just in case Jasper changed his habit of a lifetime and actually listened to his voicemail.

He now used the torchlight to take a closer look at his surroundings. The room was similarly furnished to the front bedroom where he had found the drugs and cash about half an hour ago. So, he went over to the wardrobe and opened the doors in the expectation of finding more shoeboxes. Instead, he found that it was completely empty and had a musty smell – probably hadn't been used in a long time. There was nothing in the chest of drawers apart from some very old paper liners which were yellowing at the edges. The drawers of the dressing table were similarly empty.

As he returned to the bed, he noticed a chain hanging from the bottom of the iron frame. Pulling the chain out from under the bed, he was shocked to see a pair of manacles on the end of it. Laying them on the bed so that he could take a closer look, he was even more shocked when he realised that dry shavings of skin were stuck to the metalwork along with smears of dried blood.

Instinctively, he moved to the head of the bed and discovered another chain hanging down to the floor. Pulling the chain up onto the bed, he viewed another pair of manacles which also had scrapings of skin attached to them.

'God's sake! What the hell's going on here?' he muttered to himself as he fired off a couple of shots of the manacles so that he could confront Jasper with them.

Sitting back on the bed, he let the torchlight play around the walls of the room. Between where he was sitting and the door, there was a plain table with nothing on it. The light caught on a shiny object under the table and, bending down to get a better look, he saw that there was a bucket which had been pushed right up against the wall. He also realised that it was the source of the putrid smell, and decided to not even bother getting in for a closer look.

His mind was whirring, trying to understand what was going on. Of more concern was the increasingly likely scenario that the man in the water butt had spent his last hours or days or even weeks here in this room. And, if that was the case, who had been keeping him a prisoner here? And, more importantly, why?

At that moment, he heard a key turn in the lock and the door swung open. A shaft of pale light fell across the floor between the bed and the hallway. He couldn't see the person who had opened the door but he welcomed the opportunity to leave the room. The light was brighter in the hall but there didn't seem to be anyone waiting for him. He passed the bathroom and took a cursory glance inside before getting to the top of the stairs. The doors to all the other rooms were closed and he decided that it would probably be in his best interests to get out of the house and back to his car as soon as he could.

As he crept down the stairs, he began to hear voices coming from the kitchen. Female voices. Sounding conversational. One with a pronounced eastern European accent. Did he recognise the other voice? He picked his way across the hall and stood at the kitchen door.

'Come on in Reggie, I know you're there!'

He froze. He knew that voice, of course. He couldn't have failed to recognise it straightaway. But how on earth had

Looby Lou got into the house without him hearing her?

Reggie edged into the kitchen and eventually saw two women sitting up at the breakfast bar, two cans of cheap lager in front of them. He immediately recognised Looby Lou by her flowing blonde hair which had been streaked with shades of pink and light turquoise. She was wearing a black bandana, and a Nike baseball cap sat on the bar in front of her. Dark eyes peered at him through a huge pair of horn-rimmed spectacles and heavy circular earrings hung from each ear. Reggie felt a stirring inside him as he recalled the first time he had met her – she was still the most alluring woman he had ever met, and highly desirable.

The woman sitting next to her was a different proposition altogether and was unknown to him. She was well built with an undercut hairstyle which gave her a fearsome aura. A chunky ring hung from the bottom of her nose, and she had a scaffold piercing at the top of each of her ears. There were also a number of other piercings in the lobes of her ears, some of which looked extremely painful to Reggie. Further items of ironmongery stuck out of various parts of her face and nose, and she had piercings in each eyebrow. Her black hair matched her all-black attire and a gun sat on the table in front of her. Reggie wondered if she had had a sense of humour bypass as her face showed no sign of emotion whatsoever. Perhaps the weight of the ironmongery was preventing any movement of her facial muscles.

'Well, Reggie, this is a treat meeting up with you again! And on another island! God, how many years ago is it that you introduced me to the delights of Guernsey?'

Lulu Harrison was smiling at him, teasing him with a

reminder of their days and nights of passion. How could he ever forget?

He took up a position with his back to one of the worksurfaces, arms folded, waiting for some sort of introduction to the vision in black. When none seemed to be forthcoming, he took matters into his own hands.

'Okay, Lulu, what the fuck are you doing here?'

For a split second, he thought that she did look genuinely surprised by his question but she remained composed and simply stared at him.

'Can't help it if dear old Jas doesn't keep you up to date with what's going on, Reggie,' she taunted him. 'Any case, you haven't been properly introduced to Pranvera yet. Sorry if she roughed you up a bit but we didn't expect to find anyone here – particularly as Jas had said we could store some gear here.'

'*Some* gear?' Reggie spluttered. 'How much gear is *some* gear? There's loads of stuff upstairs in wardrobes and cabinets, there's goodness only knows how much cash up there, and there's one room looks like it's been turned into a torture chamber. Oh, and there's a dead body in the garden. So, what the fuck's going on?'

The two women glanced at each other. 'Okay, Reggie, the guy in the garden was a mistake. He wasn't supposed to die. We were just experimenting with some new stuff we've got our hands on.'

'Is that what's in the bathroom cabinet?' Reggie wanted to know.

'Yeah, some of it,' Lulu replied, idly scrolling down the screen on her phone. 'Presume you've heard of Fentanyl?'

Reggie nodded. He had heard of the synthetic opioid and knew that it was wreaking havoc among drug addicts in large swathes of America. He also knew that Fentanyl was far more potent when mixed with heroin or cocaine which greatly increased the risk of overdosing, particularly where the person using the drug was unaware that the powder or pill contained fentanyl.

'Pranvera here has managed to get her hands on some of this gear coming in from China and we've been doing a bit of experimenting.' Lulu suddenly looked pleased with herself. 'Nothing like using a human guinea pig, and we found one quite quickly. They're easy to find round here – the loud-mouths in any of the pubs frequented by sailors. So gullible.'

Reggie could picture Lulu in action, having had personal experience of falling for her irresistible charms in the past.

'To start with, we tried mixing it with the usual cutting agents such as mannitol, lactose and paracetamol,' she continued. 'The effects on the guy were a mixture of euphoria, drowsiness and confusion which was okay. But then we tried mixing it with heroin and other opioids to see if that made any difference.'

Pranvera's eyes had now dropped and she was gently shaking her head, perhaps at the memory of what had happened next.

'Well, that's when the trouble started,' Lulu continued. 'The guy went into respiratory arrest which rendered him unconscious. Thankfully, we got to him in time and managed to revive him but he then seemed to slip into a coma. And, before we knew what was going on, he had stopped breathing.'

There was silence in the room, Reggie seething with Jasper Lime for allowing these amateur bio-chemists to carry out experiments on live humans in what was, after all, his house. What the hell was in that bathroom cabinet? If that was stuff mixed or cut with a base of Fentanyl then they probably had enough there to wipe out the entire population of the Isle of Wight!

'Couldn't believe how quickly he went. Never seen anything like it. As I said, he hadn't suffered much apart from a mixture of euphoria and confusion when we mixed it with the usual cutting agents. It was when we cut a tiny amount of it with heroin that things really started to change.'

Lulu paused, her mind perhaps revisiting the scene as they crammed the body into the butt. 'We just put him in the water because we couldn't think what else to do with him,' she said.

'Yeah, and he's still there!' Reggie exclaimed.

At that moment, his phone thrummed on the work surface beside him, the screen lit up with caller identity. Jasper Lime.

He angrily picked the phone up and rammed it against his ear. 'Where the fuck have you been?' he rasped.

'Sorry, matey, affairs of state to deal with,' Lime replied. 'Anyway, I hear that you've got company there.'

'How do you know that?' Reggie seemed surprised.

'News travels fast when you're banged up in a dark room.'

Reggie looked across at the two women, the realisation dawning that they had probably called Jasper after they had incarcerated him in the bedroom.

'Anyway, Reggie,' Lime continued, 'now that you're there and have the attention of two gorgeous girls, why don't you make yourself useful and put our proposition to Looby Lou?'

To say that Reggie was pissed off with this suggestion would be an understatement. He seethed at the bare-faced cheek that Jasper had in asking him to discuss the proposition which Jasper had, himself, formulated.

'No chance, *matey*!' Reggie slung the insincere greeting back at his business partner. 'You talk to her. She's sitting right in front of me, waiting for your call. And don't keep her too long because she's got a dead body to deal with!'

He angrily disconnected the call.

38

Wednesday 22 November

Hunter cursed herself for looking up at the clock on the wall in the Ops Room. How many more days was time going to stand still at 9.50 either morning or evening? Couldn't someone use their initiative and go out and buy some batteries? Can't be that difficult!

Looking around the room, she couldn't see Selitto so she wandered out into the corridor and headed off to the kitchen, knowing that this was about coffee o'clock for her DS. Sure enough, he had got himself a steaming mug-full and was in conversation with DC Carolyn Pennant.

'Hi, Carolyn, great to see you!' Hunter exclaimed. She was genuinely pleased to see the woman who had stood by her in their desperate battle with a man mountain in the lantern room of an abandoned lighthouse. It was an experience neither of them would ever forget, and it had forged an unwritten bond between them which both women respected. 'How are you getting on with the recovery process?'

'Every day's an improvement, ma'am,' Pennant replied. 'Sleeping a bit better now that I don't have quite so many nightmares. And the jaw's feeling less stiff – almost back to eating solids!' She managed a weak smile. 'I'm desperate to get back into action and hope to be back up to full-time in a couple of weeks.'

'What are you up to at the moment?' Hunter asked.

'Just came in for the afternoon to see if anyone needed any help but no takers at the moment.' Pennant looked genuinely sad that no one had any work for her.

'Well, Ted and I might just have something for you – haven't we Ted?' Selitto frowned.

'Have we, boss?'

'Yes, Ted. I've been thinking about Jacqui Anderson's death and wondering if we've missed something which might help us with the Monroe case. Anderson's body was discovered in a car at the cemetery but we don't seem to have thought much about how it got there. I'd like to take another look at where the car was found – see if the location can tell us anything.'

Hunter turned and stepped out of the kitchen. 'I'm sure there's room for another one in the trusty Megane, Carolyn.'

Forty minutes later, they were standing at the spot where the BMW had been discovered on Monday morning. Sarah Hunter was well prepared this time and had dug out her thermal padded parka which came down to her knees. She had also found an old knitted scarf which was now wound round her neck and her head was topped off with a woolly bobble hat. The others were similarly attired which was just as well as the cold wind seemed even more vicious than on Sarah's last visit.

On their way over to the cemetery, Hunter and Selitto had given Carolyn Pennant a quick briefing about the discovery of the BMW and what they knew about its occupant. 'We're not a hundred percent sure why Jacqui Anderson was killed,' Hunter said, as she looked back at the little chapel in the middle of the cemetery. 'Her swift departure from The Prism is still puzzling me unless she knew the killer and wanted to get away before we started asking questions. So, I just wondered if we could come up with some other clues by returning to where her body was found.'

There was an air of tranquillity about the place and, even though the wind was doing its best to distract the detectives, they were able to immerse themselves in the peaceful surroundings.

Gravestones adorned the gently undulating grassy slopes that caressed the edges of the tarmacked drive surrounding the chapel. Some were huge slabs of stone, their ornate carvings having been eroded over the years, lichen and moss sticking to them like barnacles on a boat. There was also a proliferation of stone and marble crosses, each on a plinth of two or three granite blocks, nearly all of them standing sentry-like over a marked plot. Conifers of all shapes and sizes were sprinkled around the grounds adding to the eeriness of the place.

'So, the car was parked here all neat and tidy, no wheel marks on the grass. Unfortunately, no CCTV either and Grace hasn't been able to pick it up on ANPR either because there was a fault early Monday morning – something to do with weekend maintenance.'

Hunter was pacing up and down as she was speaking, trying to keep the circulation going in her feet. It really was very cold.

'One thing that's puzzling me,' Pennant started, 'is how the car got here in the first place. I mean, if this Anderson woman didn't die of carbon monoxide poisoning, then she can't have driven here because she was presumably already dead.'

'And she couldn't have driven herself here and then injected herself because we didn't find evidence such as a discarded syringe,' Selitto followed up, just confirming what the others were thinking. 'So, she must have been brought here and then placed in the car with the engine running.'

'But that would require two cars, wouldn't it?' Pennant asked.

'Unless the killer had another way of either transporting the body here or making their escape,' Hunter observed.

'Is there another way out of here rather than by way of the drive we came along?' Selitto asked, looking around him.

Hunter pointed to a path behind them. 'This path leads off to lots of different areas of consecrated ground – there are hundreds if not thousands of graves here. At the far end, the cemetery borders agricultural land. I presume you could eventually get to a road by going across the fields – it's reasonably well built-up round here.'

'So, no alternative vehicle access and a pretty long walk,' Pennant summarised.

Selitto wandered off towards the chapel, clapping his gloved hands to keep warm. He then turned to face his colleagues. 'If it was a one car job, the killer has to drive up here, and then position the dead woman in the driving seat. They then have to wipe the car clean and make their getaway. Forensics didn't find anything in the boot which indicates that the woman probably hadn't been stored in there so perhaps she was just propped up in the passenger seat. Or she could have been lying across the back seat.'

'And your point is?' Hunter enquired, not quite sure where Selitto was going with his thinking.

'Well, wherever she was when the car was driven here, she would have had to be moved. Don't forget, she's going to be a dead weight. So, it'll have to be someone who is strong enough to lift a dead body and place it in the driver's seat. There were no signs that the body had touched the ground or had been in contact with any other surface apart from the interior of the car.'

'Perhaps the car was towed here with Anderson already in the driving seat,' Carolyn Pennant suggested.

Hunter gave her a nod. 'Possibly, but you're really drawing attention to yourself by doing that. No, I fancy the one car approach. The killer drove here, moved the body, then legged it – perhaps with an accomplice waiting somewhere nearby or they had already placed a getaway car somewhere.'

'Or they had another means of getting away like a bicycle,' Selitto suggested. 'Could have packed one of those Moulton bikes into the boot of the car and then just cycled off. Completely negates the threat of ANPR, even if it had been working.'

'Did you say it had been snowing?' Pennant asked

'Yes, there was a dusting on the grass and in the flowerbeds,' Hunter said, casting her mind back. 'But I don't think it had settled on the drive so no chance of footprints or wheel tracks if there had been another car.'

'Or bicycle tracks!' Selitto smiled, still pleased with his suggestion that the killer could have made his escape on two wheels.

They lapsed into silence again, each pondering the sequence of events. Pennant went over to look inside the chapel but found that the door was locked. Not surprising really as it was only used for funerals.

'Okay,' Hunter said, 'so we're all agreed that the killer is likely to be male and that there was only one car involved. And that he left here either on foot over a couple of fields or by bicycle or some other form of non-motorised transport which can fit into the boot of a car.'

That seemed to be the sum total of what they had gleaned from this outing which probably wasn't much. However, to Hunter, the visit to the cemetery had proved something.

Carolyn Pennant was back.

39

Thursday 23 November

It had been at about 03.45 a.m. that Sarah Hunter had decided they should also take another look at The Prism to see if there was anything they were missing. She had tried to have an early night and, although she had quickly gone off to sleep, it hadn't taken long for the cogwheels in her brain to start churning information about the killing of a snooker player and his manager.

There were questions which she just couldn't seem to find an answer for. Why did someone so desperately want Monroe to win the tournament by offering huge bribes to his opponents? Having got him into the winner's enclosure, why had he then been killed? Was Monroe a supplier of Class A drugs or just a mule? And why was his manager also killed? Did she know anything about the drugs? Was she, perhaps, the person organising the bribes? Why was she found in a car registered to an obsolete company on the Isle of Wight?

None of it seemed to make sense to Sarah as she turned over in her bed, trying to get into a position where her leg was more comfortable.

She continued to wrestle with all these questions until they started to fragment in her mind as tiredness eventually took over again, and she had a fitful dalliance with sleep which was only brought to an end when her alarm clock heralded the start of a new day.

It was another frosty morning, and Hunter had called Selitto as she scraped the ice off the windscreen of her car – a job she hated doing. He was stuck in traffic on Riverhill, the road heading south from Sevenoaks. There was an extensive patch of ice on the bend outside Riverhill House which had already claimed two cars. The other drivers were tiptoeing their way around the problem and, although he was moving, Selitto's progress was very slow.

Having decided that she wanted to take another look at The Prism, Hunter instructed Selitto to go straight there when he got to Tonbridge. In particular, she wanted to spend some time in the auditorium to review the route the killer took in and out of the building. How did he manage to get close to Monroe? Who else might he have come into contact with? Could he have got in and out without anyone seeing him?

She had got to the theatre first and wandered into the well-appointed foyer. A couple of box office windows were located along the right-hand side of the area and a kiosk selling soft drinks and confectionery took up much of the left-hand side. A series of doors ran across the wall directly in front of her and there was a semi-circular desk to her right just past the box office windows. A woman was sitting at this desk staring at a computer screen whilst her fingers clattered away on a keyboard. She looked up as Hunter approached.

'Can I help you?' she asked, smiling. Good customer relations so far, Sarah thought, as she checked the woman's name badge which identified her as Diane Marshall. She always liked to know who she was showing her warrant card to.

'Hello, Diane. I'm just here to have a little look around

following the unfortunate incident on Sunday evening.'

'Oh, that was *terrible*! Just awful. That poor man.' Diane Marshall exclaimed, subconsciously reaching up and grasping her throat. 'We've only just been able to reopen, and we had to cancel a sell-out concert on Tuesday night. Not a very good start for this lovely theatre.'

Hunter looked around the foyer, trying to spot the CCTV. One camera was over the entrance into the theatre and there was another to the back of the foyer. Both would give a general view of people coming into and leaving the theatre. She just couldn't remember seeing this desk when she had been here on Sunday evening. So, she asked Diane if the desk stayed here all the time.

'Well, that's a bit of a bone of contention I'm afraid,' came the reply. 'I am supposed to sit here when I'm at work but, once I've gone home, the desk gets moved all over the place. Each morning, I have to go and fetch it from wherever it last came to rest the night before. You'll see that it's on wheels so it's easy for me to move it back here.'

'So, who moves it around at night?' Hunter wanted to know.

'Mainly the security people, sometimes FOH,' Diane replied. Hunter looked puzzled. 'Front of House,' Diane clarified. 'Think they own the place!'

Sarah was trying to remember where the desk was on Sunday evening but it just wouldn't come to her. If the security guard had been sitting behind the desk and it had been positioned where it was now, then he would only see the backs of people leaving the theatre. However, if it had been positioned just inside the front door, then he would have had a frontal view of everyone leaving the building. That's if the guard was actually sitting at the desk when their suspect left the theatre. Perhaps she needed to have a look at the CCTV again.

At that moment, Selitto came through the door, raising his eyes to the ceiling. 'The traffic! Nightmare!' he exclaimed.

'Okay, not to worry,' Hunter reassured him before turning to Diane Marshall. 'Would you mind if we take a look around inside the auditorium?' she asked.

That was fine with Ms Marshall so they made their way into the auditorium and sat down in seats that Hunter reckoned were exactly where all the handshaking had taken place. In fact, it was quite easy to picture the scene in her mind as the snooker table was still set up in the middle of the sunken stage.

'So, the killer comes down this aisle from the exit,' she started, turning in her seat to look towards the back of the auditorium, 'probably shuffles along this front row and then grabs Monroe's left hand when it becomes free. Then legs it out of the theatre via the corridor we've just come along and across the foyer.'

Selitto was thoughtful. 'There's just one problem with that hypothesis,' he said after looking along the row in which they were sitting. 'People would still be sitting in these seats.'

'Well spotted!' she smiled. 'So, we've got three options. Either he pushed his way along the row making everyone stand up to give him access to Monroe. Or everyone in this row was already standing and shaking Monroe's hand so he just tagged on the end and nudged his way in. Or...' her voice trailed off as she looked across the auditorium.

'Or he had been sitting here for the duration of the snooker,' Selitto finished the sentence for her. 'Which means that he must be on camera.'

'Certainly a possibility, Ted,' Hunter conceded, 'but how could he guarantee that Monroe would pick this exact spot for the handshakes? And how could he keep the murder weapon secure? Especially if it was a deadly toxin that had somehow been concealed in a glove.'

They sat in silence, staring at the snooker table which had a huge green cloth draped over it. Eventually Sarah broke the silence.

'You know, this whole bribery thing just doesn't make sense to me,' she said, getting up from her seat and moving further along the row of empty seats. 'Yes, I can understand that match-fixing does happen but there wasn't a significant amount of cash involved. Even if we say that Staunton lied to us and got, say, another five grand, it's still not much of a bung bearing in mind what he might have been able to earn had he beaten Monroe and gone on.'

'And it's unlikely that whoever organised the bribes would then top Monroe,' Selitto surmised, remaining in his seat. 'As you say, it just doesn't make sense.'

'So, there's someone out there who hasn't got any value for their investment and someone – perhaps a sworn enemy – who has thrown a huge spanner in the works.' Hunter had now propped her bum on the little wall which separated the seats from the playing area. 'Have our colleagues at Essex taken a look at Monroe's pad?'

'Sure have,' Selitto replied. 'Not much to report although there's quite a lot of evidence that he had drugs on the premises and was probably into cutting and mixing. No cash found so far although they haven't taken up all the floorboards yet. Car in the garage so maybe Ms Anderson drove him down here and put him up at her pad.'

Hunter changed tack. 'What about the promoters of the tournament. What do we know about them?'

'Not much, boss,' Selitto replied, consulting his notebook. 'Guernsey based operation. Two areas of business. Development of facilities such as theatres and public buildings. The other is high-end corporate entertainment for organisations which really do have money to splash and want to make an impression. The two directors are local boys come good. One of them was here on Sunday. Reggie Lemon. I heard that Iversen remembered feeling his collar once or twice back in the day!'

Hunter smiled. Yes, she recalled that Iversen had said that. 'Could either of them possibly have anything to do with this?'

'Can't see it myself,' Selitto admitted. 'Jasper Lime designed the building and project managed its construction. Lemon organised the snooker tournament as its first big function and laid on all the corporate entertainment. He might have known some of the players or their managers but his main interest would have been in promoting a flagship event to put The Prism on the map in the South-East.'

With her back to the arena, Hunter was looking up at the symmetrical rows of seats which gently rose up towards the back of the auditorium. There was something niggling her. What was it they were overlooking? What was familiar about these names – Lemon and Lime? And then she remembered.

'Ted, can you remember anything about that tattoo place on the Isle of Wight?' she asked.

'Not much apart from the fact it was called Prospero Inks,' he replied. 'What are you thinking?'

'There's a name that rings a bell,' she said, retrieving her phone from her coat pocket and punching in a command.

'Hi Grace! How's it going?' she said, turning to face Selitto. 'Good...yes...I'm with Ted at The Prism. What were the names of the previous owners of Prospero Inks who were registered at that address on the Isle of Wight?'

'Yes, there were two of them weren't there,' Kendall replied. 'Hold on, let me just get it up on the screen...ah, here we are. Two previous directors were Gustav Holmes and Lucinda Lemon. They resigned in 2015 and were replaced by Lulu Harrison.'

'Anything else on any of them?' Hunter asked but she was already feeling a little frisson of excitement. Kendall didn't have any other information apart from the registration documents.

'Right, Grace. I'm going to need all you can find on Lucinda Lemon – past, present and even future if there's anything coming up that we should know about. Quick as you like. Call me back.' Hunter ended the call before stuffing the phone back in her pocket.

'Lucinda Lemon,' she repeated, turning to look out across the playing area. 'Is it too much of a coincidence, Ted?'

'Sounds promising,' Selitto replied, taking out his notebook and adding Lucinda Lemon's name to a short list of people of interest. 'So, is your thinking that, if Lucinda is something to do with Reggie, we should perhaps be talking to Mr Lemon himself? Particularly as the car Anderson was found in is registered to Prospero Inks.'

'Let's think about it logically.' Hunter was now twiddling a strand of hair which she had released from behind her ear. 'Lemon possibly has some connection with a house on the Isle of Wight that is the registered address for a car in which is found a woman who has died in suspicious circumstances. Her protégé is similarly killed in a building which has a connection to the Lemon & Lime Group and was hosting a function sponsored by the very same Lemon & Lime organisation.'

Her phone was vibrating in her pocket. Kendall was back in double quick time.

'Yes, Grace, what've you got?' Hunter stopped twiddling her hair and listened. Selitto watched her, sensing that their investigation might be about to take a step forward. 'Great! Thanks, Grace. I'll be back soon.'

'Right,' Hunter declared as she slipped the phone back into her pocket. 'Let's change that *possibly* to a *probably* or even a *definitely* – Reggie and Lucinda Lemon used to be married.'

40

Thursday 23 November

'Afternoon, Grace,' Hunter called as she made her way across the busy Ops Room, collecting an office chair that actually had a full set of wheels as she went. DS Grace Kendall had sent Sarah a short text message earlier to say that she had received some interesting news from her contact at Ryde police station on the Isle of Wight.

After leaving The Prism, Hunter had spent the rest of the morning with Crime Scenes Manager Beth Dench over at Maidstone. They had been looking again at the car in which Jacqui Anderson had been found. Following her visit to the cemetery with Selitto and Pennant, she was determined to make sure that they had wrung every last piece of evidence from the car.

After a couple of hours of minute inspection, Beth Dench was fairly convinced that something had been stored in the boot of the car which could have been a bicycle. Dench had even suggested that it could have been one of the new E-Scooters which were now on the market. Hunter wasn't sure if she had seen any of these – there seemed to be so many kids on scooters and skateboards these days, blighting the lives of pedestrians. But Beth thought that they were the bee's knees and could speedily get you from A to B.

Of more importance, one of the technicians had found a couple of partial prints on the driver's seat sliding mechanism. This indicated that whoever drove the car to the cemetery may have had to either adjust the seat so that it was closer to the steering wheel or, alternatively, so that it was further back. There were other things Beth's team were working on, and she had hoped to be able to unearth more clues in the next few days.

Sarah Hunter was now sitting beside Kendall, eager to see what she had been up to.

'Remember I told you that I had been speaking to a DS on the Isle of Wight when we asked if someone could do us a drive-by for that address in Bembridge?'

Hunter nodded. 'He was a singer wasn't he?' she asked.

'No! He wasn't a singer – he had a singer's name,' Kendall replied, gently admonishing her colleague. 'Jack Jones.'

'Okay. And your point is?' Hunter was becoming impatient.

'Well, DS Jones got one of the traffic cops to do the drive by,' Kendall continued. 'This guy actually stopped outside the house and took a look inside the grounds because the house is surrounded by a high hedge and he couldn't see it from the road. All the windows are boarded up – a professional security job it looked like. He had a quick look round the back but the house obviously hasn't been lived in for a while. Thought it had one of those drain smells so the owners will probably have to sort that out whenever they return.'

'Hmm,' Hunter sighed. 'Interesting that it's professionally secured. Those firms charge a fortune.'

'Anyway, when the officer came back out to his car, there was a bloke in the road asking directions to Bembridge.'

'I thought they were in Bembridge,' Hunter remarked.

'On the outskirts by the airport. So, the officer gave him directions whereupon the guy walks back to his car and sits in it. The officer then drives off, passing the car and noting that the guy is now on the phone. He thought that was strange because, if he was meeting someone in Bembridge, then he would presumably have called the person he was meeting to ask for directions. So, the officer drove on and stopped further up the road. When the guy's car didn't appear, he turned back and did another drive by. This time the guy's car was parked right outside the house with no one in it. The gate was open whereas the officer had shut it when he left.'

'Interesting!' exclaimed Hunter. 'Why would someone be visiting a derelict boarded up house? Owner perhaps? Estate Agent? God, it could be anyone – bailiff, solicitor, local authority, meter reader.'

'The traffic cop took the registration of the car which is where it gets really interesting,' Grace teased, looking at Hunter to see if she was going to have a guess as to ownership. But she was just staring blankly across the room.

'The car is owned by Prospero Inks,' Grace continued, 'and, of course, registered at that property.

'Bloody hell!' Hunter exclaimed, turning back to look at her DS.

Kendall continued. 'The traffic cop was understandably confused by the behaviour of the driver – if he was something to do with the house, why was he asking directions for getting to Bembridge? So, he returned to Ryde and reported in to DS Jones.'

'Okay – it seems that all roads lead to Prospero Inks,' Hunter muttered. 'Used to be run by Reggie Lemon's ex until she was replaced by another singer whose surname has slipped my memory – Lulu someone?'

'Harrison,' Kendall interjected.

'That's right. Small company selling inks for tattooists – one director. No information on whether it's trading; could be dormant. Have we got anything on Lulu Harrison?'

'Nothing on the PNC, and her name doesn't come up in any other searches,' Kendall read out from her notes.

'What does your mate, DS Jones, make of it all?'

'Well, we can talk to him if you've got time. He's standing by to take a call on Zoom. It's a video conferencing platform.'

Sarah Hunter wasn't a great fan of video conferencing because the picture never seemed to be in sync with the voice which made it difficult to concentrate, but she was keen to see if this house on the Isle of Wight had anything to do with her investigation.

'Okay, when do we do it?'

'Well, I said you and I would be talking at about this time so he's waiting to see if you want to speak with him now.'

Hunter said that was fine and Grace made the connection. DS Jones appeared on the screen in front of them and, once all the introductions had been made, Hunter took him through her current investigation into the discovery of a body in a car registered to an address in Bembridge. It also now appeared that one of his traffic cops had come across another car registered to the same address.

Jones looked as if he was sitting in an interview room judging by his stark surroundings. It also seemed that the room wasn't heated as he had a woollen scarf wrapped around his neck. He stared at the two Kent detectives as he reiterated what he had told Kendall earlier.

'We haven't got a marker on this house,' he continued. 'It's in a semi-rural location on the outskirts of Bembridge, quite close to the airport. Gets busy round that area in the summer months. There's a couple of nice sandy beaches not too far away.'

Hunter wanted to know about the car. 'Is there any other information about the car? It seems that, if it is legitimately registered to that address, then it presumably has a right to be there.'

'Agreed on that, ma'am,' Jones replied. 'But we ran some checks anyway and found that it came across from Southampton to East Cowes yesterday morning and went back on the early evening crossing. No other information I'm afraid.'

Sarah Hunter wanted to be at the house, breathing in the sea air, using her own eyes to hunt for clues. But that wasn't a practical use of her time so she would have to use DS Jones as her eyes and ears – and hope that he came up to her high standards of observation and detection.

'That's all very useful information, DS Jones, so thank you for that,' she said, trying to smooth talk him into doing some more of her bidding. 'As we have reason to believe that the house or its occupants or its contents may be connected to a homicide here in Kent, what would you have to do to gain entry to have a quick look around on our behalf?'

'Well, we should really have a warrant. I could probably get that quite easily but I'll tell you what I'll do first. I'll shoot over there and just have a quick look at the property from the outside and then I'll apply for the warrant. Just gives me a bit more background in case anyone starts asking difficult questions.'

'You'd better send them to me if they do,' Hunter interjected.

Jones smirked. 'I'll remember that!' he replied.

'OK, that's a plan then.' Hunter had done with this video conference now and was keen to get on. 'How quickly can you get over there to take a look?'

'Could probably do that tomorrow and then send you a quick email report if you like.'

'Yep, that'll be fine. So, I'll wait to hear from you,' Hunter said, starting to wind up the meeting but then having another thought.

'Just one more thing before we go,' she said. 'Does the name Lulu Harrison mean anything to you?'

Jones looked thoughtful but then started shaking his head. 'No, ma'am, that's not a name that I'm aware of but I'll check it out with my colleagues. That's presumably L-U-L-U not L-O-U?'

Hunter frowned. 'Yes, Lulu as in the singer. Little Scots woman, big voice.' Jones looked blankly at her. No matter, she was now done with this meeting. 'Okay, Jack, thanks for your help so far and I'll look forward to hearing any news you have.'

Kendall also thanked DS Jones for his time and said she'd be in touch. A few clicks of the mouse and Jones disappeared into the ether.

'We've got to get inside that house,' Hunter was saying as Kendall saved and catalogued the video call. 'What did you make of Jones?'

'Yes, seems to be on the ball,' Grace said, turning to face

Hunter. 'Good that he'll take a look at the house first. That'll save a bit of time.'

'Sure will,' Hunter agreed. 'Shame he hasn't got a clue about Sixties pop music.'

41

Thursday 23 November

The call had been like a bolt out of the blue. So completely unexpected that she had almost been struck dumb. It was late in the afternoon and some of her colleagues who were on the early morning shift were preparing to leave the laboratory for the day.

She was sitting at her work station trying to make sense of data she had collected earlier in the day. She was so wrapped up in the complex calculations that she almost missed the flashing light on her phone which indicated an incoming call. She flicked her finger across the screen and was astonished to see the name 'Pablo Hernandez' on the screen as caller ID.

Being a self-confessed anorak, Samantha Frobisher always made sure that she logged information as soon as she got it, so she had naturally entered his number into her phone after he had given her his card. And now here he was calling her. She was gobsmacked!

'Hello?' She didn't know why she had intonated her greeting as a question but, in her confused state, she still couldn't quite grasp the fact that he was calling her.

'Hello, Samantha?' His smooth Hispanic accent was unmistakable. 'It's Pablo Hernandez – we met yesterday.'

As if she didn't remember!

'Oh, hi Pablo,' she replied, trying to sound matter-of-fact. 'How are you?'

'Yes, all good thanks. I just rang to thank you for making my visit so very interesting. It was great meeting you and seeing all your friends in the serpentarium.' He paused.

'It was good to meet you too,' she said, enthusiastically, 'and I'm really glad that you enjoyed your visit.'

'Good! Good!' he exclaimed. 'The reason for the call is that I am writing up my report and have a few more questions which I would like to ask you.'

'Oh, that's okay,' she replied, 'I'm not leaving just yet so fire away.'

There was a pause, and Samantha thought that perhaps they had been cut off. 'Are you still there?' she asked, expecting to get no answer.

'Yes, still here,' he replied. 'I was actually thinking if we could perhaps meet up to go through the questions. I much prefer it if we can do this face to face.'

'Oh… okay,' she stammered, wondering why he couldn't just go through them on the phone. I mean, it'd be nice to meet up but not really necessary, she thought.

'I know it's short notice but what about this evening?' he asked. 'I must get the report finished before I take on an assignment back in Spain and I'm running out of time.'

Wow! He was certainly keen to get this audit all tied up, she thought. Oh, God! What had she got to do this evening? No, she couldn't really spare the time. Or could she meet him for a quick drink on the way home? Aaargh! Decisions!

'Er,' she paused, finally coming to a decision, 'well I could possibly meet you for an hour or so if that'll be long enough.'

'Sure!' he replied immediately. 'Let's do that and see how we get on. Do you know The Moody Mare on Seven Mile Lane?'

'Yes, I know that,' she confirmed. 'I think it was called The

Beeches last time I was there. Must be a few years ago now.'

'That's the one!' he replied. She could almost hear him smiling. 'What time can you be there?'

She looked at the clock on the wall. 'Around 6.30 p.m. I should think.'

'Great, I'll look forward to seeing you then.' And that was it – he'd gone.

She stared at her phone. Not even a 'goodbye' or a 'see you later'. Was that rude, or presumptive – or had he prematurely cut himself off? Well, she had said one hour so at least she had a get-out there. Anyway, her hair really did need washing! She smiled to herself at that thought.

The car park at The Moody Mare was about a quarter full but she managed to park close to the door of the pub. Although it was a very cold evening, there were quite a few early-doors drinkers crowding around the small bar, lively chatter and banter filling the air.

Samantha Frobisher spotted Hernandez sitting at a table to her right as she entered the pub. He rose to greet her as she threaded her way around a small group of drinkers, and they shook hands rather formally.

'What can I get you to drink?' he asked. Samantha really fancied a large gin & tonic in a huge bowl glass but thought that she should, perhaps, stick to a non-alcoholic drink. In any event, she would need her wits about her later. So, she asked for a Diet Coke, slice of lemon, no ice.

She took her coat off and laid it over the back of the chair before sitting down. Hernandez was back almost immediately with two drinks which looked remarkably similar. Was he one of those boring people who always had what you were having? She hoped not.

'Cheers!' They clinked glasses and each took a sip of the cold drink.

'Thanks for stopping by on your way home at such short notice,' he began. 'Gemma's great to work with but she is also very demanding. I have to be in Madrid for another audit on Tuesday so she has insisted that I get your audit finished before I go. Doesn't give me much time.'

His hooded eyes locked on to her across the table, a broad smile showing off very white teeth. She busied herself by taking another sip of her drink, trying to remain calm and aloof. After all, she didn't know what sort of questions he wanted to ask her and, in any case, she didn't have to stay for long did she?

'Okay,' he went on, 'I just had some questions about your work which I hadn't thought to ask when we met on Tuesday.' He reached inside his jacket and pulled out a folded-up piece of paper and laid it on the table beside him.

To Samantha's relief, the questions were nearly all about the conditions in which she kept her snakes. Hernandez made a comment that she probably couldn't accommodate any more snakes in the space she had available to her. She agreed with this and told him that she had started to think of alternatives. He suggested that, if space was at a premium, she would always be able to sell some of them on. In fact, he knew of several collectors who might be interested. She promised to give this some thought.

They carried on talking generally about methods of keeping snakes in captivity, how important it was to keep their habitats clean and germ-free, and how difficult it was to do that given the time it took. Hernandez talked about his own small collection, and told some tales about how he had obtained some of his species. She found one tale about capturing a Saw-Scaled Viper in the jungles of Sri Lanka particularly hair-raising.

Some of the tables around them were beginning to fill up with people coming in for an evening meal, and Samantha suddenly became conscious of the time. She looked across at the watch on Hernandez's wrist and saw that it was now nearly 7.30 p.m. She really must be going soon.

Hernandez had sensed that she was looking at his watch. 'Sorry that we have gone over time, Samantha. Have you got just a few more minutes as I only have a couple more quick questions?'

'No, that's fine,' she lied. She really did need to get home soon.

'Good! Thank you,' he began. 'I wanted to just ask you about your snake milking activity.'

Shit! This was a subject she really didn't want to talk about. But Hernandez carried on.

'I know that you are milking the snakes for all your research work,' he said as his eyes once again locked on to Samantha's, 'and that you have to be careful to monitor the amounts of venom being taken from each snake and the regularity of the milking. But I am wondering if you are keeping other records which I didn't see on the day of the audit.'

'What exactly do you mean?' she asked, a cold shiver running down her spine. Surely, he couldn't have spotted anything untoward in her meticulous recording of milking activities. Could he?

Hernandez seemed to be choosing his words very carefully. 'What I'm trying to say is that an experienced herpetologist like yourself would be able to tell quite quickly if a snake was being over-milked. Wouldn't you?'

'Well, yes – I suppose so. But...' She was struggling to think how best to reply to his leading question.

'Do you agree that, if you gently caress the venom glands, you will at least get some idea of the amount of venom the snake has stored there?' he asked, his eyes now drilling into her head. She looked away.

'You see, Samantha, my problem is that some of the snakes I handled when I was in your serpentarium felt as if they had very little venom in their glands yet nothing had been recorded by you to say that you had milked the snakes recently.'

Samantha stared at him. She felt her face flushing and was immediately grateful for the dim lighting in the pub. 'Well, I'm afraid that I have no explanation for that,' she replied, frostily. 'All I know is that I fastidiously record everything I do with those snakes. Why would I not record all the milkings I had done?'

Hernandez shrugged his shoulders. 'I don't know the answer to that question. But, if you're happy that you are correctly recording everything you are doing, then I cannot really argue with that.'

She was incensed by his impertinence. 'In any case, just caressing venom glands is not a reliable indicator of how much venom a snake has stored. And, as you well know, some snakes do not manufacture venom so quickly after a milking.'

He couldn't argue with what she was saying. But, although he still had his doubts, he had clearly decided that this was not the time and certainly not the place to push Miss Frobisher further.

'Okay, that's really useful,' he said as he watched Samantha reach for her coat from the back of the chair. 'Thank you so much for taking the time to meet up this evening – it's been a great help for my report.'

'No problem,' she replied frostily, quickly buttoning up her coat. 'I'll look forward to reading it.' Hernandez didn't appear to have a coat so they both walked out into the cold night air. Samantha plipped the key fob for her car and the indicator lights lit up on her Audi Roadster.

'Nice car!' Hernandez purred.

'My other pet!' she said, mischievously while opening the driver's door. 'Pity it doesn't bite!'

She noticed Hernandez frowning. 'Sorry, I must be going. I hope that you have a successful audit in Madrid.'

She pulled the door shut, cutting off any response he might have made and immediately fired up the engine. Getting away from this man and getting home were now her top priorities. She swept out of the car park and into the pitch darkness of Seven Mile Lane.

42

Thursday 23 November

The Ops Room at Pembury Road had all but fallen silent as it often did at this time of the early evening. It was that sort of witching hour when those with families went home, and those without went to the pub.

Ted Selitto had joined one of the darts teams for the winter months, and they had gone off for an early supper at The Bell Inn at Kemsing before their match against the pub team later in the evening. By his own admission, Selitto was pretty rubbish at darts but he enjoyed the camaraderie of the team and those they played against – and tonight's fixture was almost local for him so he wouldn't have far to travel home.

Grace Kendall had unusually left on time as she was having dinner with one of her girlfriends this evening so wanted to get home for a quick shower and change of clothing before heading out to The Leicester Arms at Penshurst. On the menu would be a couple of plates of steak and chips, a glass or two of red and a whole evening's worth of chatting and catching up.

Sarah Hunter was sitting at one of the spare desks and had logged herself onto the computer in front of her. Although she was a DI, she didn't like having a desk assigned specifically for her use. That only meant people could leave papers and post-it notes whenever they were passing. But, with no office or nominated desk, there was nowhere to leave meaningless messages and bits of paper. If someone wanted to tell her something, they would have to speak to her in person or call her.

She put Google Maps up on the screen and typed in Bembridge Airport. She then played around with the mouse, zooming in and out of the area around the airport, trying to familiarise herself with the terrain. Situated on the north east corner of the island, she read that Bembridge was in fact classified as a village although it seemed to cover quite a wide area. In addition to the airfield, it boasted a harbour which looked as if it was a favourite for yachties and other sailors of small craft. The satellite pictures showed an interesting coastline with many interesting beach walks to enjoy, and there was a lifeboat station at the end of a long pier which jutted out into the Solent.

Clicking back on to the map of the area, she eventually found the road in which the Prospero Inks house was located and then clicked the satellite picture. This didn't really help as there were clearly a number of trees obscuring a view of the road so she manoeuvred the mouse until she got a view at street level. There weren't many houses along the road and she was pretty sure that she had identified the one she wanted by the high hedges in front of it. But she couldn't get a good view of the house itself.

She opened another browsing window and idly googled Prospero Inks. Nothing came up apart from the entry at Companies House. She recalled that the company sold materials for tattoo artists. As she didn't know anything about tattoos apart from how ghastly they looked, she googled to see if she could find out the ingredients for tattoo inks. She discovered that there was an extensive range of different inks and pigments and assumed that these were the sort of products that Prospero Inks sold.

Her mind turned to Reggie Lemon and his connection to the house. Did the car link him to the death of Jacqui Anderson? Or to Monroe? Her imagination was now in freefall. Were Lemon and Monroe associated with each other in the drugs world? Well, anything's possible, she told herself but that did seem to be a bit far-fetched. Anyway, what about the Lemon & Lime organisation? She googled it and got an all-singing-all-dancing website with lots of pages gushing about sleek modern building designs and unimaginably extravagant corporate entertainment.

How the hell did Prospero Inks fit in with Lemon & Lime Promotions? Or had it just been a passing fancy for Mrs Lemon before she got booted out in favour of Lulu Harrison. And who is Lulu Harrison? Is she part of Lemon & Lime? Was it she who lent the car to Anderson? Did she actually *know* Anderson? Bloody hell. Should they be looking more closely at Harrison?

Wrapped in her thoughts, she reached for her phone and scrolled through her list of contacts. Once she had found who she was looking for, she pressed the icon to connect the call. It was answered on the second ring.

'Hi Jack,' she said, trying to sound matter-of-fact but feeling a slight fluttering in her stomach.

'Sarah!' Pennington exclaimed. 'Great to hear from you? How're you keeping?'

'Oh, you know, the usual – not enough hours in the day, can't see the wood for the trees. That sort of thing.'

'Tell me about it!' he replied.

'Oh, and thanks again for the other evening – very

enjoyable.' Thank goodness she had remembered to thank him.

'No problem,' he replied. 'We must do it again sometime.'

There was a slight pause before Hunter continued.

'Anyway, have you got a minute as I just want to fire a name at you to see if you've got any intel because we've come up with a blank here.'

'Yeah, go ahead Sarah. Always good to find out what's going on in your world even if we do work for the same organisation.' He laughed.

'Remember I told you about the death of a snooker player in suspicious circumstances and we found that he was probably carrying drugs in specially adapted snooker cues?'

'Yes, you mentioned that.'

'Well, we've come up with the name of a potential associate. It's a rather convoluted path back to the snooker player but does the name Lulu Harrison mean anything to you?'

The silence on the line was palpable. In fact, Hunter was beginning to think that the call had been disconnected. She was just about to speak again when Pennington cleared his throat and spoke.

'Where have you got that name from?' he asked, his voice almost a whisper.

So, Sarah Hunter told him as much as she knew about all the connections that were going around in her head. And all the questions she kept asking herself in a vain attempt to get some answers to how it all fitted together.

'We know nothing about Lulu Harrison apart from the fact that she is a registered director – in fact, the only director

– of Prospero Inks, that company I told you about when we had dinner. That's it.'

'Hmm. I remember you saying that this house on the Isle of Wight is close to an airfield,' Pennington said.

'Yes. I've just looked it up on Google Maps. A mile or less. And it's got a tarmac runway – not grass.'

'That, Sarah, is a very useful piece of intel,' Pennington said after another pause, 'and it may or may not be relevant to your investigation. Remember I told you about some new guys on the block? Well, we are looking at the possibility that these guys are heavily reliant on the distribution of drugs by air. So, if your house is next to an airfield then it's possible that it is being used as a store or some sort of distribution centre.'

'So, are you thinking that this directly connects Lulu Harrison to the new guys on the block?' Sarah asked.

'Well, as you can imagine, we are feeding on scraps of disjointed intel but in one of the reports there was a reference to a *String Girl*. Before he disappeared, our man had said that he had heard someone referred to as *Looby*. One of the bright sparks on our team suggested that *String Girl* might be a reference to *Looby Lou* who was a puppet character in the *Andy Pandy* children's programmes which aired back in the mists of time.'

Hunter was getting slightly confused with all these names but she had heard of Looby Lou and she could see that someone with the name of Lulu might also get the nickname Looby Lou.

'I'm now just wondering if Looby Lou could, in fact, be Lulu Harrison,' Pennington surmised.

They talked for a bit longer before Pennington had to go.

But he was very keen to continue the exchange of information with Hunter because his team had got news of a huge shipment of Class A coming into Kent within the next ten days. He had suggested that they could perhaps meet up on Sunday around lunchtime for a bite to eat when he might be able to give her a further update on the case he was working on.

After the call, Sarah had remained at the desk, sitting in front of the computer screen which was still showing the satellite image of Bembridge airfield. It was abundantly clear that access to the house would be a lot easier if you came in by air. And flying drugs to various locations opened up a whole stack of other opportunities for distribution with the minimum of fuss.

She idly zoomed out from the satellite image of Bembridge until the screen was filled with the whole of the Isle of Wight and the coast of the mainland. It never ceased to amaze her how it looked as if the island would fit snugly into the Hampshire coast – Cowes plugging the neck of the Solent, Yarmouth becoming an extension of Lymington, Ryde snuggling up to Portsea Island.

She zoomed further out until, on the bottom of her screen, the island of Guernsey appeared. She sat back, just staring at the screen and the two islands. Was there really anything to tie Harrison to Lemon and Lime? The link with the Bembridge house was tenuous at best.

'You're getting ahead of yourself, girl,' she muttered as she closed down all the websites she had accessed and then logged out of the system. 'You don't even know for certain how the snooker player and his moll died yet!'

43

Friday 24 November

The motor driving the fan in the little heater clicked and clunked as it desperately tried to dispense some warmth into the small office adjoining the autopsy room at the Tunbridge Wells mortuary. Dr Toby Swartzman was sitting behind his desk, scrolling through a lengthy report on his laptop while Sarah Hunter and Ted Selitto looked on from their seats on the other side of the desk. The pathologist had called to say that the toxicology report on Davie Monroe was inconclusive so Hunter had decided to pay him a visit to find out exactly why they could not yet define the actual cause of death.

'The problem we have,' Swartzman was saying as he continued to scroll through the report, 'is that the usual practice of examining for prescription medicines and alcohol followed by screening for other organic drugs or poisons has detected the presence of at least one toxin. The scientists have, therefore, carried out quantitative testing to see how much of the substance is evident, but they haven't been able to identify the toxins involved.'

The detectives looked at each other, Hunter with a frown creasing her forehead.

'So, Monroe was definitely poisoned but we don't know the substance which was used by the killer or, indeed, its make up.' As she was speaking, Hunter realised that she was repeating exactly what Swartzman had just said, but she felt better for just summarising it again for her own benefit.

'That's basically it,' replied Swartzman. 'Forensic toxicology is required to establish what drugs were taken, and if an excessive intake of the drug occurred. If so, did this contribute to the death – or was it the root cause? In the case of Davie Monroe, his toxicology screening was positive which means that a drug or multiple drugs were present in the body. However, after more specific tests were applied, the scientists were unable to show exactly how much of the drug was present – or even what that drug was.'

'Bloody hell!' Selitto exclaimed. 'How can that happen with all the knowledge we must have of toxins these days?'

'Good question, Ted, and one for which you would have expected a straightforward answer. There are a lot of substances and toxins in our world today and, in post mortems, toxicology is mainly used to establish if an excessive intake of a drug contributed to the death. In poisoning cases, toxicologists still mainly expect to find traces of substances such as aconite, strychnine, oleander, mercury, arsenic – that sort of thing.'

'Okay, Toby,' Hunter said, getting up from her chair and shuffling over to the window which looked in on the autopsy tables. No bodies on them at the moment, she noted with a sense of relief. 'So, we suspect that Monroe died because he was poisoned although we don't know what he was poisoned with, and we clearly don't know who the poisoner is. Not sure that we'll be able to make much progress on that basis.'

'Well, that's not quite all, Sarah,' Swartzman replied, introducing a note of caution. She propped herself against the wall, waiting for him to continue.

'The tox guys have asked Porton Down scientists to take a

look, and I have to say that I reckon that they had no alternative but to do so.'

Hunter was non-plussed by this news, and just stared at the pathologist. How was this going to affect her investigation? Was she going to have to wait for months whilst layer upon layer of boffins did whatever it was they did to establish what was used to poison Monroe? And they hadn't even got to Jacqui Anderson yet!

'Christ, Toby,' she eventually muttered, 'what's the thinking behind that?'

Swartzman was now concentrating on his screen. 'Seems that they identified a cocktail of toxins in Monroe's body, some of which they have been unable to identify. The upshot is that they're now concerned that he was attacked with some sort of fast-acting nerve agent.'

'What, like the Skripals in Salisbury last year?' Selitto interrupted. He had taken a particular interest in this case and knew quite a lot of the detail.

'Well, it's highly doubtful that Novichok was used to kill Monroe but the method of delivery could have been similar,' Swartzman surmised.

Hunter pushed herself off the wall and re-took her seat in front of Swartzman's desk.

'We're pretty sure we know how the toxin or poison or whatever it is was delivered,' she stated, looking directly at Swartzman. 'That scrape on the back of Monroe's hand has to be the entry point.'

'Probably didn't even require that,' Swartzman replied, his eyes firmly on the screen in front of him. 'Nerve agents enter the body primarily through the respiratory tract, although they may be absorbed through the eyes or skin. In the liquid state, they're hazardous via skin or eye contact and through ingestion.'

'That's right,' Selitto interjected. 'In the Skripal case, they found the Novichok in a perfume bottle. That woman who died just sprayed one of her wrists with it and fell ill within fifteen minutes. If we're right about the scratch on the back of Monroe's hand, the time between him getting the scratch and the time of death was about ninety minutes. So, something fast-working.'

'Yes, Ted, that's why I was originally thinking that we were looking for evidence of a neurotoxin because of the speed with which the body seemed to have closed down. And the killer would have had to take great care not to get the agent on his own skin or even to breathe it in. The strike at The Prism would have needed very careful preparation.'

'Hold on a moment!' Hunter stood up again and returned to standing by the window. This time there was a body on one of the autopsy tables so she immediately turned away to face her two colleagues. 'Let's not get too far ahead of ourselves. We seem to have got into James Bond territory here with shady characters roaming the streets of Tonbridge assassinating snooker players with phials full of nerve agents! That's bonkers!'

Selitto and Swartzman looked at each other across the desk. They had to agree with Sarah Hunter that it sounded bonkers, but the reality was that there was a dead body in cold storage not far from where they were sitting which contained traces of yet unidentified toxins.

Swartzman went back to scrolling through the information

on his laptop. 'The other factor we must bear in mind is that symptoms of neurotoxins include nausea which might explain the fact that there was a patch of vomit beside each of the bodies. They also cause seizures which, in my own opinion, is what happened to Monroe. Those similarities point to the probability that both he and Anderson were killed by the same person if not by the same toxin.'

Hunter had been scrolling through her phone, looking for information on neurotoxins. As she read some of the snippets of information on the phone's small screen, a feeling of unease started festering inside her. What were they really dealing with here? Was there a killer on the loose using drugs of such high levels of toxicity that people were dying almost the instant that the drug had been administered?

She read out the information on her screen. 'It says here that UK authorities now know much more about toxicity, detection, and general behaviour of these neurotoxins. Well, that's a step in the right direction. The only problem seems to be that some of them are stable enough to be stored as an ultra-fine powder. This means that they can be hidden and stored much more easily which makes them more likely to end up on the black market. A frightening thought.'

Silence permeated the small office, only disturbed by the continuous hum of refrigeration equipment and the ever-present sound of trickling water.

'Right, this isn't really helping,' Hunter said, returning to her chair. She stood behind it with her hands gripping the top edge. 'We'll just have to progress on the basis that both Monroe and Anderson died as a result of being poisoned and that they have, therefore, been unlawfully killed. That means we've got a murder investigation on our hands.'

The others nodded in agreement.

44

Friday 24 November

A moderate northerly breeze was sweeping across Guernsey airport as the Dornier 228 gently rose into the sky on its short journey to Alderney, a neighbouring Channel Island. The journey only took fifteen minutes but Jasper Lime knew that it could be a most unpleasant fifteen minutes if the wind really took hold of the little aeroplane.

Seats were arranged one on each side of a short aisle, and Lime had folded his lanky frame into one at the back by the door. He felt the wind buffeting the aircraft as its two Honeywell TPE331 engines dragged it to its cruising altitude of 1,500 feet. But the flight was never going to be long-enough for the passengers to feel any long-term discomfort. The Dornier was soon descending on to Runway 08 on the cliff tops at the western end of Alderney. After a couple of bounces, the aircraft settled onto the runway and taxied round to the small airport terminal. Once the propellors had stopped rotating, the door was opened and the nine passengers on board disembarked and walked across the tarmac to the single storey terminal building.

On entering a small arrivals/departures area, Lime made for the Aviator Café which wasn't difficult to locate as, apart from a couple of check-in desks, the café was about the only other outlet in the building.

He spotted her standing next to a magazine rack aimlessly flicking through one of the glam mags. Today, her blonde hair looked more like a generous stick of candy floss than anything else and was streaked with shades of red and blue. She was wearing dark aviator shades under a black Nike baseball cap, a sheepskin flying jacket, ripped jeans and flying boots. Diamond cluster studs adorned each ear and she sported a gold nose stud. He couldn't imagine how this trendy go-getter could ever have fallen for Reggie!

She had already spotted him and, replacing the magazine in the rack, she nodded her head in the direction of the exit and made her way out of the building, Lime in hot pursuit. Once outside, she turned to him.

'We're going to take a cab to a little pub I know so that we can have a chat. No talking in the cab – cabbies have ears. If he starts a conversation, I'll do all the talking, right?' Lime nodded, and they headed off towards the taxi rank.

They sat at a table in a quiet corner of The Divers Inn with a good view across Braye Beach through the window behind them. The pub would have been a busy place in the summertime with an extensive decked area outside. But, in the cold November sunshine, there were few takers for traditional fish & chips and a pint or two of lager.

Lulu Harrison had bought the drinks – a mug of black coffee for herself and a glass of red wine for Lime. She now sat facing Jasper so that she could see exactly what was going on in the pub behind him and, more importantly, she could keep an eye on people as they came in or went out of the pub.

'Did you fly in on your broomstick?' Jasper asked, trying to think of something which might make Harrison smile.

'Ha! Ha!' she replied, trying to cool her coffee down by blowing on it. 'Piper Archer DX if you want to get technical.'

'Why the hell are we here on Alderney?' he wanted to know.

'Landing fees on Guernsey are a rip off and there are too many snoopers on the island. No doubt someone would recognise you and then want to know who I was. Can't have a nice quiet private conversation over there. And I'm sure you fancied a trip off the island even if it is only for a day.'

He could hear the door of the pub open, and he saw Harrison's facial muscles tense up as she scrutinised whoever had just come into the pub. She soon relaxed and had presumably reverted her gaze to him although he couldn't tell what was going on behind those aviator shades.

'OK,' she said, having another go at trying to cool her coffee down. 'So, what's so important that I've had to fly over here to talk to you? You should be coming to see me if you've got some sort of proposition to make.'

'Yeah, well,' he replied, 'there's a few things going on at the moment which means that I would prefer not to set foot on the mainland for the time being.'

He noticed one of her eyebrows poking out above the shades. Must have got her attention. He quickly went on.

'Reggie tells me that you bumped into each other recently.' She nodded. 'And you've been using the house as a little storage area.' She nodded again. 'And not just for gear.'

'That was a mistake,' she interrupted. 'I explained that to your mate. Any case, that's all taken care of now. Nothing more to worry about.'

Jasper Lime felt a cold knot in the pit of his stomach. This woman should come with a health warning, he thought.

'Reggie tells me you're into shifting some new stuff these

days - fentanyl is it?' Lime tried to make it sound more like a casual question than a statement of fact.

'We're looking at it,' Harrison replied. 'Lots of our heroin buyers are asking for the new China White. It's illegally manufactured and gets its name because it comes as a white or off-white powder. They then hide it in other drugs such as marijuana or cutting agents so that it's eventually sold as other drugs, especially heroin.'

'So, the dealers are dealing what the users think is heroin but it's really fentanyl plus a cutting agent?' Jasper asked. He was quickly coming to the realisation that Harrison was onto something here.

'That's pretty much it,' she replied. 'Some study in the States found that as many as 70% of people turning up at hospital with a supposed overdose of heroin instead found that they were testing positive for fentanyl, something they never knew they'd taken.'

'Blimey!' Lime exclaimed. 'Dealers must be queuing up for this.'

'Well, it's certainly being used to increase profit margins. And it absolutely increases the addictiveness of drugs which also increases profits. So, it's a win-win for the dealers.' Harrison was finally able to drink some of her coffee but didn't seem to like it so she pushed the mug to one side.

'I've got dealers who are able to use tiny amounts of fentanyl powder to make fake drugs or reduce the amount of mainline drug they put in their products,' she continued. 'You can also get it in tablet form so that it can be sold as a counterfeit pharmaceutical.'

'Sounds like you've done your homework on this, Lulu,'

Lime enthused although he was having difficulty in seeing how she would be interested in the proposition he had for her. 'Any downsides for your dealers?'

She gave this some thought, turning her gaze to the left and right, presumably making sure that they couldn't be overheard. She leant in towards Lime.

'One problem we have,' she said in a conspiratorial tone, 'is that, because fentanyl increases the addictiveness of drugs, it has a short shelf-life which means that users will want their next dose much sooner than with other drugs. This causes dealers a problem in that they are having to restock users more frequently. Users probably haven't got the cash to buy on an even more regular basis than usual which is then causing a collection problem. The result of this is more violence as the gangs impose their ruthless will on the hapless users.'

She suddenly put a hand inside her flying jacket and took out her phone. Looking at the screen, she poked it a few times and then put it back into whichever pocket it had come from.

'The real problem we're encountering,' she continued, 'is that small margins of error in the dosage can be fatal. We also know that poor mixing techniques when adding fentanyl to heroin can easily result in overdose. This is making some dealers a little wary of fentanyl so we're holding back a bit. Also, there's a new variant on the market known as carfentanyl which is around 100 times more potent than fentanyl. It's a drug never intended for human use, and dealers and mixers are understandably a little hesitant about getting into anything where there could be a high death toll.

Not good for business.'

Jasper heard the door of the pub open again but Harrison only gave it a cursory glance – presumably someone leaving.

'So, what's your MO at the moment and why are you telling me all this about fentanyl?' Lime thought he had better move things along before Harrison lost interest and headed back to the airport.

'I'm telling you about fentanyl because it's new to the market in the UK. There's lots of dealers falling over themselves to get it because all they can see is the pound signs. However, some of my dealers are a bit wary of how to use it to get maximum value.' She placed her hands on the table, fingers splayed, beautifully manicured nails. 'You saw the problem we had trying to get it cut right. That bloke was sentenced to death the first time we injected him. We made such a tiny mistake with the mixing but it ultimately proved fatal.'

Lime nodded knowingly. He could see exactly what her problem was but he wasn't here to talk about her problems. He needed to move her on to the proposition he had in mind.

'Yeah, I completely get the problem with fentanyl but it's here and it's now so we'll just have to take it on board,' he said, spreading his arms and shrugging his shoulders. 'But how are you operating at the moment?'

She leant forward again, arms resting on the table. 'For the last few years, I've been happy to freelance as a supplier. There are a couple of key people I work for and they like that I can get supplies and drop them in on some grassy airstrip in the middle of nowhere. Don't get me wrong, it's good business and gives me a good lifestyle but these guys are running a bit scared at the moment. They just aren't ordering the sort of stuff I can get them which, in turn, would make the big bucks for me.'

It wasn't difficult for Lime to see that she had a bit of a problem. 'Could that just play into my hands,' he wondered.

'Okay, here's what I'm thinking,' he said, resting his elbows on the table, staring at the black orbs of her aviators. 'We're in with a guy who needs someone to get his gear into his suppliers on the mainland. It's a big organisation and he already uses powerful launches to land gear on deserted beaches along the Kent and Sussex coasts. He's also got a couple of drones dropping gear off to sites along the south coast. But he needs someone who can oversee these operations and make sure his suppliers are supplied.'

Harrison thought about this.

'So, he's not UK-based?' she asked.

'Nope,' Lime confirmed.

'Ile de Bréhat by any chance?' A glimmer of a smile cracked her lips.

'Would it matter?' he asked, just hoping that she didn't have any previous with Hennenbont that would put her off doing business with him.

'Probably not,' she replied after giving his question some thought.

'He's got plans to take over quite a lot of the lowlife in Kent and Sussex so are you happy with operating down there?' Lime asked but he already sensed that Harrison was interested.

'Great potential there, and plenty of places to land. As long as I can get in and out quickly that's all that really matters.'

Just what Jasper wanted to hear.

'Where are you based at the moment?' Lime wanted to know so that he could tell Reggie that it wasn't at the Bembridge house.

'Depends!' An air of caution sounded in her voice. 'I have a few options.'

So that was the end of that line of questioning, Lime thought.

'Do you want me to meet the old bugger or are you the filling in the sandwich?' she asked.

'Depends what he wants when I tell him you're on board,' Jasper replied.

'Okay, count me in for the moment on the basis that I can bail out if his terms aren't good enough,' she said after a further moment's thought.

Jasper Lime was mightily relieved that she had indicated acceptance of his proposition. Now all he had to do was to get Hennenbont interested. Then presumably he would have to arrange for Looby Lou to go over and meet him.

'Can you land on that island fortress?' Lime asked.

'Fuck knows!' she replied.

45

Friday 24 November

'Looks like he completely missed the bend and went straight on taking the street furniture with him. The wooden fence and the oak tree must have brought him to a halt.'

DC Carolyn Pennant was summing up what they could see from the road whilst DS Ted Selitto took some pictures with his phone. The white-suited CSIs were already in attendance, and Selitto had just caught sight of the ambulance leaving the scene on its way to either A&E at Pembury Hospital or to the morgue.

They were on the Ide Hill Road about a mile and a half from the little village of Four Elms. The road sported a couple of ninety-degree bends in quite quick succession and the driver of an almost brand-new Mini Clubman Cooper S had failed to negotiate the second of these. The road had now been closed which was already causing a major headache for locals and others who used this busy little country road on a daily basis.

The CSIs had already got some of their cones and evidence markers set out on the ground, and one of the team was busily photographing the whole area. As Selitto and Pennant moved in for a closer look, they could see that the front of the car was stoved in. The nearside was also badly damaged, presumably after coming into contact with a couple of road signs before bouncing off a mature larch and careering across a pathway into the unforgiving arms of the oak tree.

Pennant recognised one of her colleagues from her days in Traffic Division so she went over to see if he could give her a bit more information. Selitto tagged along, rubbing his hands together to keep the circulation going. Why *had* he forgotten to bring his gloves? He scolded himself for being so stupid.

'Boss, this is Moby,' Pennant said, introducing her colleague.

'Hello, sir,' said Moby, offering his hand to Selitto, 'real name's Mike Whale but I've always been called Moby.'

'Moby escaped from Traffic before I did and went into Forensics,' Pennant enthused as Selitto shook the proffered hand, hoping it might provide a split-second's worth of warmth.

'Yes,' Moby confirmed, 'I'd attended so many fatal RTCs that I wanted to get more into the detail of the investigation. Certainly keeps me busy.'

'Okay, Moby, good to meet you,' Selitto took over. 'Anything significant to report so far?'

'Well, it seems that the driver managed to get out of the car after the crash and started walking back towards the road before he collapsed over there behind the car.' Moby pointed to where two red cones had been positioned inside a ring of evidence marker flags.

Selitto shuffled over the damp ground to get a better look at the exact spot Moby was pointing to. He noticed that one of the marker flags had been stuck into the ground next to what looked like a small pool of vomit. He frowned and instinctively squatted down to take a closer look. Pennant had now joined him and was bent over, peering down at the ground in front of her.

Selitto stood up. 'Is that a small patch of vomit?' he asked the CSI officer.

'Yes, we've got it down as that,' Moby replied. 'He was still alive when the medics got here but he died as they were getting him to the ambulance. By all accounts, he was unconscious when they arrived on the scene and he had been sick before that. The medics did work very hard to try and save the poor man but none of their efforts seemed to resuscitate him. Strangely, he didn't seem to have any sign of external injuries so presumably he had suffered some catastrophic internal damage.'

'What, not even a cut forehead or bloody nose?' Selitto would normally have expected at least some sort of visible facial injury in a collision like this.

'Nothing on his face, no,' Moby replied. 'But he did have quite a lot of blood on his right hand and that was also smeared on his coat. We've also found blood on the steering wheel which would perhaps indicate that he had sustained a hand injury prior to the crash. Perhaps it was even a contributory factor in the crash.'

'Hmm!' Selitto grunted. 'Who's the CSM today?'

'That'll be Julian French,' Moby replied, looking around to see if he could spot his boss. 'In fact, looks like he's on his way over. I'd better get back to what I was doing. Nice to meet you – and nice to see you again Carolyn.'

'Nice guy,' Selitto commented as Moby sidled off, giving the approaching CSM a wide berth.

'Afternoon, Ted,' French called over as he approached the detectives. He nodded at Pennant as if he couldn't recall if they had met before. 'Checking up on us again?' he added, smiling.

'You know me, Jools, always like to see how the Crime Scene team are getting on,' Selitto retorted. They had known each other for a number of years and had met at countless crime scenes. Each man was hugely respectful of the other, and they always enjoyed a little light-hearted banter.

'Well, we're getting on as quickly as we can – don't really want to still be here when darkness sets in as I'm not sure that we've got enough lighting with us. In any case, we'll need to get the car taken away as soon as possible so that we can get the road re-opened in time for the evening commute.'

Selitto surveyed the scene again. 'Is it as straightforward as it looks?' he asked.

'Pretty much as you see it – missed the bend and went straight on. Probably got knocked off course when he hit the furniture which bounced him into the fence and then the tree.'

'Your colleague drew attention to some blood on his hand,' Selitto continued. 'Seems a strange sort of injury to get if there are no other external injuries from the crash.'

'Certainly something for us to puzzle over,' French replied as he took a few paces towards the open driver's door. The detectives followed him. 'Seems to be blood on the steering wheel which would indicate that the injury happened before the crash. We have also found traces of blood on the door handle which would, again, indicate that he was bleeding when he got into the car. The blood on his clothes looked as if he had simply wiped his hand down his front.'

'And the paramedics couldn't revive him?' Pennant asked.

'Well, we were on the scene before the ambulance left. This is quite a busy road so it got called in quite quickly.' French stepped back from the car and went over to the area marked by the two red cones. 'They worked on him here to start with but the equipment they really needed was in the ambulance. I think they lost him as they were stretchering him over.'

'I see,' Selitto nodded, picturing the scene quite clearly in his mind. 'Moby was saying he thought that the man had got out of the car after the crash rather than that he had been thrown out following the impact.'

'Looks like that because of where he was found,' the CS manager replied. 'If he'd been thrown out of the car on impact, it's unlikely that he would have ended up directly behind it.'

Selitto was nodding again. 'True. Very true. And you said you're getting the car taken away?'

French nodded. 'Yep. Low loader's on its way.'

'That's good,' Selitto replied. 'Not sure I'd fancy the Mini's chances of remaining in one piece being left here with a bit of *Police Aware* tape stuck round it!'

'Good point, Ted,' French said, smiling at Selitto's pessimism about the integrity of the local population. 'I've got a couple from Beth's team taking a quick look at the man's house where we assume that he started his journey. Over Edenbridge way. Should have the basis of our report ready by Monday if you want to drop by.'

'Er, thanks, Jools.' Selitto looked puzzled. 'Did you just infer that you know who this man is?'

'Well, yes – didn't Moby say?' French asked. The detectives both shook their heads.

'There's some gear in the back of the vehicle which we've assumed is his,' French continued. 'We found a brief case with some papers and visiting cards which should do for a preliminary identification until the pathologists do their stuff. And we also found a couple of snooker cues.'

Both Selitto and Pennant froze, each staring at French.

'Yes,' French continued, noting the surprise in the detectives' faces. 'I'm afraid it's another player from that tournament last week. Looks like Gavin Staunton has just been delivered to the morgue.'

46

Friday 24 November

Galvanised by the news of Staunton's death, DI Sarah Hunter had taken over the spare office they had been using for some of their meetings. DCs Azzar Mishraz and Elaine Jennings had found a couple of spare desks and some chairs. Jennings had even managed to locate Stuart Crosby's crime wall which she had dusted down and propped up against one of the walls.

Mishraz had printed off photographs of both Monroe and Anderson, and these had been attached to the crime wall. He had been having difficulty getting hold of a photograph of Staunton until Hunter suggested he look at the online programme for The Prism snooker tournament.

DS Ted Selitto had been despatched to see whether DC Jed Crowther was available to join the team. He had found Crowther deep in conversation with DS Angie Marshall who Selitto knew well from various cases they had worked on when they were DCs.

Marshall was a little older than Selitto and had made it known that she didn't want to progress much further up the greasy pole of responsibility. Selitto admired her for her honesty which in other forces may have led to her being sidelined into somewhere like the Cold Case Unit. But the powers-that-be in Kent recognised a good copper when they saw one, and Marshall was invariably in the thick of many complex investigations.

Selitto knew that Marshall rated Jed Crowther and, after he

had explained the case that was rapidly developing, Marshall had no hesitation in suggesting that Crowther join the team.

'In any event,' she said, mischievously, 'working with Sarah Hunter will give him an experience he is unlikely to get anywhere else!' She tossed a theatrical wink in Selitto's direction as he led Crowther away across the Ops Room.

With the deaths in suspicious circumstances of two high profile players who had been taking part in the same prestige event and one of their managers, Hunter felt justified in declaring this a 'major incident room'. Her team was now responsible for receiving, reviewing and indexing all information and material gathered during their continuing investigations. In due course, she would plug into the HOLMES 2 investigation management system which would assist her team members in their management of the complex process of investigating serious crime.

Sarah Hunter had called for quiet while she announced that DC Jed Crowther would be joining them for their current investigation. Jennings already knew Crowther but, as Mishraz had only arrived at Pembury Road during the sex trafficking case, he only knew Crowther by sight. The two of them shook hands rather awkwardly but with a smile. After that, Jennings had taken Crowther under her wing and was now busily briefing him up on the three deaths.

Seeing that the team were all busily engaged in setting everything up and generally getting themselves organised, Hunter crossed the corridor to the Ops Room and sat down next to Grace Kendall. It was late Friday afternoon and the room was thinning out with people leaving to get home for the weekend or dashing away for a quick forty-eight-hour weekend break.

'Not rushing to get away, Grace?' Sarah asked, keen to know what Grace was going to be up to at the weekend but not keen for Grace to think that there was any hidden intent in her casual question.

'On call this weekend so might as well just plough on here,' she replied. On-call weekends came around every four or five weeks and meant that the duty DS should be available to cover any significant criminal activity which occurred between close of play on a Friday and the following Monday morning. 'In any event, I've got plenty to keep myself occupied. What about yourself?'

'Full on here, I imagine,' Sarah sighed. 'This case seems to be developing by the hour. Have you got any intel on Gavin Staunton yet?'

'Not much, I'm afraid,' Grace replied, piloting the cursor around one of the screens on her desk. 'Another of these nearly men of snooker – good enough to play with the big boys but not good enough to maintain a place in the top echelon of the sport. Moved into the area recently following an acrimonious marital dispute. His estranged wife is still living in the marital home in Bromley. Nothing on his record – a few debts but nothing major. Seems to make a good living from snooker but not able to survive on prize money alone. Does a lot of exhibition and coaching work.'

'Any connection to Anderson?' Hunter wanted to know.

'Not that I've found so far. In fact, it looks as if he might do all his own management – that probably cuts down on costs.'

A thought suddenly struck Hunter.

'Damn!' she exclaimed. 'Has anyone been in contact with that Westie bloke?'

'Elaine was trying to get hold of him,' Grace replied, putting a picture of Johnnie West up on her screen. 'Last I heard, she had tracked him down to Kinsale in Ireland. Seems he has an Irish girlfriend who lives there so he spends a good deal of his winnings on flights to Cork. Very pretty part of the world by all accounts. Anyway, he's not here in the UK at the moment.'

'Hmm. Good and bad,' Hunter observed. 'Good that he's probably a lot safer where he is and bad that we can't quiz him about taking bribes.'

'Assuming that he did!' Grace cut in.

'Always assuming that he did,' Hunter repeated, looking at Westie's picture on the screen. 'Okay, but he remains a person to be questioned in connection with the bribery investigation.'

Hunter was just about to return to the MIR when she remembered what else she was going to ask Grace. 'By the way, who's delivering the Staunton death message?'

'The Met's dealing with that thankfully,' she replied. 'No doubt the estranged Mrs Staunton might be pleased but the poor child will have lost her father.'

'Indeed,' Hunter commented. 'There are always losers.'

Late afternoon had turned into evening as the team settled into the MIR. Internet connections and telecommunications with the outside world had both been established and were working thanks mainly to Azzar Mishraz's knowledge of IT. Hunter was pleased that at least one of her team knew his jack plugs from his sockets and the functionality of connectors. She might know something about policing but anything to do with technology left her cold.

Selitto had sent new boy Jed Crowther up the High Street to get some pizzas from Pizza Express so that they didn't all go hungry, and Elaine Jennings continued to attach information to the crime wall. Everything seemed to be coming together nicely.

Sarah Hunter was just thinking that it was time for a warming mug of coffee when she felt her phone thrumming in her back pocket. Beth Dench's name was showing on the screen. What was the Crime Scenes Manager doing calling her at this time of the evening?

'Hello, Beth?'

'Hi Sarah. Are you good to talk for a minute?'

This sounded ominous. They usually enjoyed a bit of banter when they called each other. Straight to business this time. 'Yep! Go ahead.'

'I'm over here in Edenbridge at Gavin Staunton's house. We've got a bit of an issue with something we've found here so we're having to set up a small exclusion zone around Staunton's lock-up. If you're able to get over here now, it would be helpful rather than leaving it until tomorrow.'

'Yes, okay Beth, should be able to get to you within the hour. Is the lock-up near the address we have for Staunton?'

'Just round the corner – you won't be able to miss it with our vehicles and lights!' she laughed.

'Okay – on my way. See you soon.'

Hunter pocketed her phone just as Crowther returned with the pizzas. She caught Selitto's eye and nodded towards the door. They both exited the MIR and headed into the Ops Room.

'Just had a call from Beth,' Hunter informed him, her voice just above a whisper. 'They've got something for us out at Gavin Staunton's place. No details other than she thinks we should get over there pronto.'

'OK, boss,' Selitto replied, looking a bit forlorn.

'And bring the pizza with you!'

That cheered him up, and he returned to the MIR to let the others know that he and Hunter were going off to Edenbridge. He also collected a few slices of pizza and put them into one of the empty pizza boxes before suggesting that everyone should head for their respective homes once all the systems were up and running.

Meanwhile, Hunter had briefed Grace about Beth Dench's call and promised to update her in the morning. She then grabbed her coat and scarf, and met up with Selitto as they made their way to the car park, the box of pizza safely tucked under his arm.

47

Friday 24 November

S elitto had lost the toss in the car park and was now driving his precious Megane through Chiddingstone Causeway on route to Edenbridge. After crossing the little bridge at Bough Beech, he took a left and headed for Four Elms, passing the Four Elms Inn just before reaching the centre of the village. He turned left at the crossroads towards Edenbridge and, after a couple of minutes, they found themselves driving through the outskirts of the town. Fortunately, the lights were green at the little narrow railway bridge, and they started to keep a look out for the CSI wagons.

On the journey, Sarah Hunter had uncharacteristically laid into the pizza, suddenly realising that she was incredibly hungry. Selitto's stomach continued to rumble in protest at lack of sustenance, the aroma of the freshly cooked pizza driving his olfactory sensors wild.

It wasn't long before they came across a road block comprising a patrol car with its blue lights strobing the area around it. Two traffic officers were doing their best to keep the traffic flowing past the small cul-de-sac in front of which the CSI vans had parked.

Hunter zoomed her window down and showed her warrant card to one of the officers.

'Okay, ma'am, you can get parked over there,' he said, pointing to an area beyond the tape which covered a large area around the entrance to the cul-de-sac. 'You'll need to get a full set of protective gear from the CSI van which must be worn at all times while you're on site, including masks. When you leave, the gear must be disposed of in the bin at the back of the CSI vehicle. Do *not* take any of the protective gear home with you.'

He lifted the tape up and Selitto piloted the Megane into a space beside one of the CSI vehicles and switched off the engine.

'Sounds a bit sinister,' Hunter commented as Selitto made a grab for the box of pizza which had been sitting on Sarah's knees. He grunted an affirmative 'yeah' to her last comment as he rammed a slice of pizza into his mouth. He greedily picked up another slice and began eating it whilst still in the process of swallowing the first slice.

Hunter turned to look out of the passenger window, preferring not to watch the feeding frenzy going on next to her. Eventually, she decided to get moving and stepped out of the car. A cold wind was blowing around the cul-de-sac and there was sleety drizzle in the air.

Once they had got fully kitted up with the protective clothing, hair nets, hats, gloves, overshoes and masks, they made their way around the corner to where a small colony of lock-up garages was located. They had no trouble in spotting their destination although they were somewhat surprised to see that a PVC speed tent had been erected and attached to one of the garage doors. Arc lights had been arranged both inside and outside the tent, and a couple of white-suited investigation officers were combing the ground around the lock-ups.

Just as they reached the tent, a flap in the material opened and Beth Dench stepped out into the cold. She was slightly taken aback at seeing two figures dressed head to toe in white approaching but soon realised who they were.

'Ah, there you are!' she exclaimed, removing a pair of safety glasses. 'Glad you could make it as we've got a bit of a situation going on here. Sorry about all the PPE but it's really necessary and you'll also need the safety glasses when you're in the tent.'

They huddled together, trying to keep out of the icy breeze which was blowing through the cul-de-sac.

'Ted, were you at the scene of the RTC?' Dench asked. Selitto nodded. 'So, you would have noticed that the deceased didn't appear to have any external injuries apart from a bloody hand.'

Selitto nodded again. 'Yes – one of your boys said that he had wiped blood on the front of his clothes, and we were shown traces of blood on the steering wheel of the car.'

'Okay,' Dench continued. 'I've got a couple of my guys going over the apartment but this is probably where the action is. Glasses, masks and gloves on, then follow me.'

They all entered the tent which had been sealed onto the door to the lock-up. An arc lamp provided brilliant light, and two crime scene investigators were very carefully swabbing an area around the door's handle. Hunter was surprised to see that they were each wearing protective face shields as well as safety glasses and masks. What on earth was going on here, she wondered.

Beth Dench shuffled around the limited space within the tent and invited the detectives to take a closer look at the door. Switching on a powerful torch, she played the beam over an area around the handle.

'We have found some spots of blood on the door, mainly underneath the handle,' she pointed out. 'But there is more evidence of blood on the handle itself. We are assuming that this will probably be the deceased's blood as he is likely to be the last person to open this lock-up but we'll check it out after the post-mortem.'

Hunter and Selitto just stood there, watching and listening as Dench continued.

'Now, this is the interesting bit. Can you see that the natural symmetry of the handle on either side of the lock has been disturbed?'

The detectives craned their necks towards the handle, trying to see what Beth Dench was getting at. Eventually, Sarah Hunter noticed what appeared to be a sliver of fine metal hanging down from the back of the handle.

'So, what's that then?' she asked. 'Has someone cut away some of the handle to make a sharp surface?'

'A bit more intricate than that,' Dench replied. 'They have somehow attached slivers of razor blades to the back of the handle thus guaranteeing that anyone touching it would cut their hand – possibly quite badly.'

'That explains Staunton's cut hand then,' Selitto surmised.

'It explains the cut hand,' Dench repeated, 'but it doesn't explain why he died.' They all stared at the door handle.

'And the explanation of his death is?' Hunter asked.

Dench turned off her torch and faced the detectives. 'The reason we're wearing all this protective gear is that we have detected that some sort of substance has been applied to the handle. As there are also traces of it on the door behind the handle, we have assumed that it has been sprayed on. However, we have no idea how stable it is in its current form. That's why we've put up an exclusion zone around the lock-up.'

Hunter was subconsciously nodding. She was thinking back to the other two bodies lying in the morgue, both of which had been subjected to an unknown toxin or nerve agent. Was Staunton now the third person to die in similar circumstances?

Dench continued. 'So, current thinking is that our man goes to get his car out, cuts his hand on the razor blades which allows a deadly toxin to enter his blood stream. Within a matter of minutes, his body starts to shut down and he crashes the car as a result. A few minutes after that, he's dead. Looks like you've got the real Angel of Death stalking the streets of Kent, Sarah.'

Hunter and Selitto had spent a bit more time with Beth Dench discussing the referrals which had already been made to Porton Down. Dench had advised them that she would also be referring Staunton's lock-up to the government scientists straightaway due to her concerns about the level of toxicity of the substance on the door, and whether it was in a stable condition. She didn't want her team being exposed to anything that was going to put them at risk.

Hunter was in total agreement. She also wanted to have a quick look around Staunton's apartment whilst she was there so Dench called up the investigator who was handling the search.

'Donny's up at the apartment so you'll be able to catch up

with what he's found there,' Dench said as she bade them farewell and pulled back the flap of the tent to let them out.

They walked to the apartment block in silence, each lost in their own thoughts. Donny Campbell met them at the door of Staunton's apartment.

'No need for safety glasses and masks in here,' he said as he ushered them down a short hallway and through into a spacious lounge. The detectives had been so deep in thought that they hadn't even realised that they were still wearing the full set of PPE.

Putting her mask and glasses in her pocket, Hunter looked around the room noticing that it was sparsely furnished. There were a couple of comfortable lounge chairs with a small occasional table between them, a big screen TV propped on a table in front of the chairs and an ornate dresser on the far wall.

'The kitchen's through there,' Campbell was pointing through another doorway, 'and there are two bedrooms and a bathroom off the hall. Not much furniture, a few kitchen cabinets, built-in wardrobes – a real bachelor pad.'

'Or perhaps a pad he wasn't planning on spending too much time in,' Selitto suggested. 'Found any hollowed-out snooker cues?'

'There are a couple of cues in one of the bedrooms but they look as if they've seen better days; no tip on one of them. The team back at base have removed two cues from the car so I presume that those are the ones currently in use. We'll be taking a close look at those later.'

Hunter was eyeing up the dresser and thought that this one would go well in her little house. It looked a bit uncared for and definitely needed some ornaments on its shelves and perhaps a vase of flowers. Campbell saw her interest in it and came over to stand next to her.

'There's something you'll be interested in if you look in the bottom drawer,' he said, conspiratorially.

As she still had her gloves on, she squatted down and immediately felt a sharp needle of pain surge through her left leg. She grimaced but carried on with opening the drawer. Lying on top of a pile of *Private Eye* magazines was a bottle gift bag. Lifting it out of the drawer, she realised that its contents were certainly not bottle-shaped. She stood up and laid it on the middle shelf of the dresser so that she could examine the contents.

After emptying the bag, she stood back and feasted her eyes on the piles of bank notes.

'Fifteen grand,' Donny Campbell was saying. 'Counted it all myself. All used. All untraceable. We'll be doing more tests on the notes but it looks like it came through the letter box. All these ground floor flats are part of the street numbering system so have their own postal addresses. There's evidence to show that this bag was hand delivered but probably not by the postie. Can't find any outer envelope with Staunton's address on it.

Hunter looked across the room at Selitto. 'So, I'd say that our Mr Staunton was less than economical with the truth.'

Selitto nodded. 'Yep. A whole ten thousand pounds more than he was willing to tell us about.'

'Which is starting to make the bribe a bit more attractive,' Hunter continued with Selitto's train of thought.

'But why go to all the trouble of bribing him only to then

kill him?' Selitto asked, mainly to himself. 'And then to not make any attempt to get the bribe money back.'

'Well, that's for you guys to ponder,' Campbell said. 'I'll be in one of the bedrooms if you need me.' He started to move away from the dresser towards the hallway and then turned back to face the detectives.

'And don't worry about anything being hidden under the floorboards. There aren't any! Solid block flooring throughout.'

As Campbell left the room, Selitto moved round towards the dresser to take a closer look at the money.

'You know, boss, there's still one part of this that I just can't fathom out. It doesn't make sense to me to eliminate the guys who've been bribed *and* to waste the guy who ultimately benefitted from the bribes. Or is it to do with some sort of drugs war?'

'I can't see much evidence here of Staunton being involved in dealing or supplying,' Hunter replied. 'There must be something else that connects them. Something we're missing.'

48

Saturday 25 November

S he activated the screen on her phone. 02:47 in large white numbers lit up the bed around her. She reached out and switched the bedside light on. She turned her head back to look at the cherub-faced young man lying next to her. Stubble was randomly scattered over his cheeks and chin, and there was a clump of dark hair on the top of his head which made it look like the business end of a bog brush. The look on his face was one of contentment, and he snored gently.

Not bad, she thought to herself. I'd probably score him a seven out of ten. Extra point for stamina? She smiled at the thought.

She had treated herself to a night on the town to see who she could pick up. In many ways, it was her indulgence in self-flattery which spurred her on when she hit the town. Did she still have what it takes to attract men and would they be able to arouse her to the level of her exacting needs.

Darren or Drew or Damon – or was it Dick? No, she would have remembered that name. Anyway, whatever he was called, he had made it clear that he was interested in her almost as soon as she had walked through the door of the pub. She was deft at spotting people with an interest in her across a crowded room, and whatshisname was almost drooling by the time she had parked her pert little bum on one of the vacant bar stools. He was with a rowdy group which was predominately made up of men although there were a couple of young women who looked as if they were no more than arm candy considering the amount of attention they were being given.

She knew the pub had a microbrewery attached to it so decided to order a pint of their golden ale. She always found that drinking pints created more inspiring chat-up lines, and certainly got a woman noticed. In fact, an elderly man sitting further along the bar had raised his glass to her when she took the first mouthful of her beer.

But it was whatshisname who had his eyes locked onto her, and it wasn't long before he broke away from his gang and lurched over towards the bar. To start with, he positioned himself about five feet away from her, pretending to see if he could catch the bartender's attention. He kept turning and smiling at her, all the time shuffling closer until he was standing right next to her.

'Haven't seen you in here before,' was his opening gambit.

'That's probably because I haven't been in here before,' she replied with a smile.

'Very good,' he nodded. 'That's probably why. Yes – very good. Hadn't thought of that!'

At this rate, the conversation was unlikely to be scintillating so should she just cut to the chase and tell him to take her back to his place so that she could enjoy whatever he had to offer?

'Celebrating with your mates?' she asked, nodding her head in the direction of the group he had walked away from, none of whom seemed to be missing him.

'Nah, just a group of work mates. We've been working late so thought we'd have a few beers on the way home. Seem to have been here a bit longer than expected. What about you?'

'Fancied a drink, didn't I,' she replied with a coquettish smile. She was starting to give him the signals. How long would it take him to recognise them? She took another mouthful of her beer and seductively licked her lips to wipe away any lingering foam.

'You from round here, then?' he asked. Another question from the book of the world's worst chat-up lines.

She lowered her head and peered up at him from hooded eyes.

'Hey! Let's cut the crap. How're you getting home?' she asked.

He told her that he was going to leave his car where it was because he would be over the limit for driving, and he would be getting a cab. There was a rank just up the road by the bus station.

She knew that.

'Shall we get going then? I mean, there's not much point waiting around here is there?' This caught him slightly off guard but he recovered quickly and knocked back the rest of his beer. She pushed her glass away and slipped off the bar stool.

'You going to tell your mates you're leaving?' she asked, buttoning up her coat.

'Nah! I'll text them from the cab,' he said as they walked out into the fresh air, and the sleety drizzle borne in on a cold easterly from Siberia.

Once they reached his flat, she realised that there was no likelihood of an offer of another drink or a coffee as his sole intention seemed to be to get the clothes off her back as quickly as possible. It was also clear that he had little experience of gracefully undressing a woman so she had to give him a lot of help to ensure that nothing got ripped in his frantic attempt to get her naked.

After this rather frenetic beginning, she had been pleasantly surprised to discover that he was, in fact, a kind and considerate lover. He took time to delicately arouse her, expertly using his tongue and fingers to bring her to the edge of the abyss before plunging into her as wave after wave of sheer pleasure washed over her.

After a brief respite, he had resumed his exploration of her body, titillating erogenous zones which she had almost forgotten about, stroking here, licking there. She completely abandoned herself to the pleasures he was bestowing on the most intimate parts of her body as she shuddered with satisfied delight.

Eventually, he had slipped off her and gone to the kitchen to get a drink, returning with two glasses of fresh orange juice.

'All I've got in the fridge I'm afraid,' he said apologetically as he headed for the bathroom to get rid of some of the beer. She eyed the two glasses on the bedside table before reaching for her bag.

And now it was 02:47 in the early morning. She swung her legs out and sat on the edge of the bed. She knew that whatshisname wouldn't be waking up any time soon. He had unwittingly drained his tumbler of orange juice which had been laced with a concoction of psychoactive drugs. In fact, he'd be lucky to see the light of day until early afternoon, and his headache might be gone by the following morning.

She picked up her knickers and bra which were beside the bed and put them on. She then wandered around the room collecting the other items of her clothing which had been liberally flung to all corners.

Out of the corner of her eye, she noticed that her phone was flashing. She sat back on the bed and accessed her emails. There was one new message.

Ring me. Now.

What the hell did he want? Perhaps to congratulate her? Must be something important. His emails weren't normally this abrupt.

She got the burner phone out of her bag and dialled him up on the only number stored in the phone. It didn't take long for an answer.

'Hey, Tinx! How's it going?' Oh, that voice. Parts of her body started tingling again. Stop it! She admonished herself. It wouldn't take too much more to arouse her again, but then she'd be annoyed that she'd rendered whatshisname useless and totally unable to satisfy her needs.

'You there?' he growled.

'Yep – bright eyed and bushy tailed,' she replied facetiously.

'God! You Brits certainly have some quirky ways of saying things.' She could almost hear him smiling. 'Okay, listen up.'

She readied herself for news of a change of plan. He always said 'listen up' when things were about to change.

'By the way, good job on that snooker player. Got the cops in a right spin by all accounts. Money's all in. You should be counting it tomorrow.'

She smirked. Cheeky bastard!

'Anyway, that other job I've got planned for you. Looks like things are moving quicker than we expected. There's a meeting tomorrow which may lead to the opportunity for you to get the hit done in mid-week. This is a real important one, Tinx. We've got to get this right. But it's a changing landscape.'

Suddenly there was a noise behind her. She froze, holding her breath.

She counted to three before leaping off the bed and turning round all in one move. She let out a long sigh as she realised that sleeping beauty had simply turned over and was now facing the wall. Perhaps he had coughed – or farted.

'You okay, Tinx?' the voice sounded concerned.

'Yeah, yeah! No probs,' she said, mainly to reassure herself.

He continued. 'We'll know more tomorrow so I'll get intel to you. Keep looking at emails. There'll be a couple or three guys involved so make sure you've got enough dope. You might not have long to get it done either so you'll need to consider method of delivery. Quick and easy so you can get away fast. I'll send you all the details – maps and everything. Keep looking.'

A pause. Was there anything else he wanted to tell her? No? The lengthening silence signalled that he'd already disconnected the call. Fucking tosser!

49

Saturday 25 November

I t had been much later than planned when Sarah Hunter had eventually crawled into bed on Friday night. In fact, her bedside clock showed that it was already Saturday morning when she finally put the light out.

Ted Selitto had driven her back to Pembury Road after they had finished their examination of Staunton's Edenbridge apartment. Sarah had gone up to the MIR to get her notes written up in her case record book whilst they were fresh in her mind, and had suggested that Selitto should go home and get some rest. He, on the other hand, was keen to see if he could get any more information about the snooker player so he had joined her in the MIR.

They had eventually called it a day and gone their separate ways. It had been a bitterly cold night and, with the sleety drizzle trying its best to freeze on the roads, Sarah had taken it very carefully when she got onto the smaller country lanes on the way to her cottage.

Once indoors, she had ramped up the heating and made herself a scrambled egg on toast which she ate whilst aimlessly flicking through the TV channels. Finding nothing that took her attention, she reached into her back pocket for her phone and was annoyed to see that she had a missed call. She was even more annoyed to note that it had been recorded some four hours earlier. How had she missed that? Had the phone connection been lost for a time?

She dialled up voicemail and found a message from Grace

Kendall. There had been some developments on the Isle of Wight so she had set up another video meeting with DS Jones at 10.30 a.m. on Saturday morning. Curiouser and curiouser! Could a house on the island really be connected to the deaths of two snooker players in Kent? It was with this question running through her head that she wearily climbed the stairs and got herself ready for bed. After burrowing down under the thick winter duvet, she closed her eyes and allowed sleep to wrap its tentacles around her.

When Saturday eventually dawned, there was not a cloud in the sky and the low sun was casting long shadows over a countryside which had been whitened by frost.

Sarah had been up early and enjoyed a long hot shower, even deciding to wash her hair under the jets of pulsing water. Although she had then had to spend time with the hair drier in hand, the end product was worth it and she spent some time standing in front of the mirror simply brushing her hair – something she fondly remembered doing for long periods of time when she was a child. She was the envy of all her friends because she had the longest hair.

Although her journey to Tonbridge was blighted by the low sun which made driving difficult, she made it in good time and was sitting in the Ops Room with a steaming hot cup of coffee when Grace Kendall arrived. They exchanged pleasantries and were just about to prepare for the link up with DS Jones when the phone on Kendall's desk rang. She answered it and then looked across at Hunter.

'It's the front desk for you,' she said, passing the phone over.

Sarah took the call.

'Oh, hello ma'am, Constable Gamrasini here at the desk. Sorry to trouble you but we've got a young woman down here who desperately wants to speak to anyone who can help her find someone who she recently met. She thinks that this person comes from Kent but that's about all the information she has.'

Hunter looked at Kendall, a frown starting to crease her forehead.

'How on earth are we supposed to help with that, Constable, and why are you asking me anyway?' she asked rather gruffly.

'Well, I wouldn't normally refer these people to you ma'am, but she did mention that the person she is looking for is Billy Woons. That's why I thought you might be interested.'

Sarah Hunter almost stopped breathing. Billy Woons? The mastermind behind the biggest case of people trafficking in Kent. The man who had shamelessly exploited countless young women over many years right under the noses of the Kent Force. The man whose life was ended by a sniper's bullet on a rocky headland in Cornwall just a matter of a few short months ago. And now someone was downstairs trying to find him! This was a person she definitely had to meet.

'Okay, Constable, I'm on my way,' she said as she disconnected the call and walked straight out of the Ops Room. Kendall watched her go, a quizzical look on her face.

Once downstairs, she walked into the area behind the front desk and spoke to PC Gamrasini. He indicated a young woman sitting on one of the seats which was bolted to the floor along one side of the corridor in front of the reception desk.

'Says she won't leave until she's spoken to someone,' Gamrasini said. 'Pleasant enough but quite firm. Not from these parts – Eastern Europe I'd say.'

'Okay, I'll take her into IR3 if you can operate the door locks.'

Hunter went out through the door into the reception area and stood in front of the woman.

'I understand that you are looking for Billy Woons.' The woman nodded. 'And how do you know this Billy Woons?'

The woman looked up at her. 'I met him in Riga and he said I could visit him if I was in the UK.'

Sarah's mind was now racing. Riga! That was the one piece of the jigsaw about which they knew very little. Although they knew that Woons had been to Riga, they didn't know why or who he had met there. Was this a heaven-sent opportunity to clear up some of the unanswered questions from her investigation? Perhaps this woman had the answers.

'Okay, just wait there,' Hunter instructed. 'I'll get someone to show you to a room where we can have a chat.'

She went back into the area behind the reception desk and told Gamrasini to process the woman into IR3. Hunter would be back in a few minutes.

She then rushed upstairs to see Grace Kendall and found that Selitto had decided to come in for the video call with DS Jones. She quickly told them about the woman who was in reception so Selitto accompanied her back downstairs to IR3.

They sat facing an attractive young woman who had just taken off her woolly hat to reveal long dark hair which tumbled around her shoulders. She unwound a long woollen scarf but kept it loosely around her neck – it wasn't *that* warm in IR3. She stared across the table at the detectives, her dark eyes sparkling in the stark lighting, her youthful complexion giving the impression of a fun-loving, warm-hearted and caring individual.

'Right,' Hunter started, 'can you begin by telling us your name and where you are from.'

'My name is Eleanora Smirnova,' the woman replied, 'and I am from Riga which is the capital of Latvia.'

'And how long have you been in the UK?' Hunter continued.

'I came in September and stay with some friends in a place called Croydon. You know it?'

Both detectives nodded although they would probably have preferred not to have had to confess that they knew the place. Hunter in particular had bad memories of the Croydon riots of 2011 when she had been with the Metropolitan Police.

Eleanora continued. 'I have been seeing some of your country. London is my favourite city but I also like Brighton and I have been to Birmingham to a rock concert. Little Mix. They were fantastic! I will soon be staying in Hastings with some more friends.'

Hunter had no idea that there were so many Latvians in their midst and made a mental note to check the stats for Kent.

'Okay, Ms Smirnova... Eleanora.' Hunter couldn't decide what to call her. After all, she wasn't a suspect and, indeed, had only come into a police station because she was trying to find someone. Maybe that's what they did in Latvia if they were looking for someone. Perhaps 'Eleanora' would be more appropriate; certainly more friendly.

'You say you are trying to find Billy Woons.' It was more a statement than a question. 'Could I just ask how you know Mr Woons?'

'Oh, yes. A very nice man. I met him at Riga airport and helped him get a flight to London. I was only doing it as a favour for my grandfather. Mr Woons had some cuts and bruises on his face and I was just trying to take him to the right boarding gate.'

Her English was very good, Hunter thought. However, she was desperate to know how old Smirnova was and so asked to see her passport. Nineteen. No visas for travel anywhere else and nothing to show her entry into the UK because she was coming from another EU country.

'And when you were with Mr Woons, did he tell you anything? Like where he had come from. Why he was in Riga.'

Eleanora looked down at her hands which were clasped together in her lap. 'I knew that he had come from Tbilisi because that was the flight I met. But he didn't really tell me anything. He did make some good comments about me, that I would never know what a difference I had made to his life. He was crying at one point.'

The detectives looked at each other, frowning.

'He also told me never to do any more work for my grandfather. It was too dangerous. But he seemed to be a very upset man. I just wanted to see if I could find him in the UK to say hello again. Somebody suggested asking the police so I thought I would come here on my way to Hastings.'

'Okay, Eleanora,' Hunter said, engaging with the Latvian,

'I'm very sorry to have to tell you that Mr Woons died soon after he returned to the UK. He was killed in a shooting a long way from here.'

Eleanora immediately put her hand to her mouth, eyes wide in shock at the news of Woons' demise. 'That is terrible!' she exclaimed.

Hunter waited a moment before continuing. The young woman appeared genuinely upset by the news.

'Ideally, we would like to take a statement from you if you would like to help us.' Sarah could see the value of getting a statement from Eleanora so she was trying to sweet talk her into telling them all that she knew. She did, however, realise that they didn't have the manpower to do that today. 'How long are you going to be in Hastings?'

'Oh, for a few months,' came the reply. 'I am wanting to study performing arts in the UK. They have a good college there which I hope to get into.'

'Good, so you can come back here one day and we can have a longer chat about your meeting with Mr Woons.'

Eleanora smiled and then started to well up. 'Sorry,' she said looking down at her hands again as a teardrop gently splashed onto the table. 'It's just a shock hearing that he's dead. I really wanted to see him again.'

Hunter fiddled about in her pockets and eventually pulled out a card which she pushed across the table. 'This is how to contact me. Can we have your phone number so that we can call you?' Eleanora gave them all her contact details including her address in Hastings and then sat back in her chair, looking around the room.

'Is this where you meet bad people?' she asked, innocently.

'Not all bad,' Sarah smiled.

'Is it a good job to be a policeman?'

'Well, sometimes it's not good but mainly it's very rewarding.'

'Maybe I should become a policeman instead of being in showbusiness,' Eleanora replied, her eyes wide, her smile broad.

'Maybe!' Sarah was now laughing. 'Just let me know if you change your mind about acting.' They all laughed as Hunter got up to signify that the meeting was at an end.

Eleanora tucked her hair under her woolly hat and rewound her scarf around her neck as they left IR3 and headed back to the reception area. Sarah shook her warmly by the hand and said that she looked forward to seeing her again soon so that she could give them her statement. She then watched as the young woman made her way down the steps of the station and out into the cold morning sun.

Sarah Hunter was fairly buzzing after her meeting with Eleanora and was keen to share the news with Grace Kendall. Selitto stopped off at the kitchen area to get two cups of coffee while Hunter continued on to the Ops Room.

There, she was surprised to see Elaine Jennings in conversation with Kendall about the Tonbridge Angels match against St Albans City that afternoon. It was well known that Jennings was a great fan of the Angels, and she was trying to persuade Grace to go along to the match with her. When her invitation was politely declined, she went over to chat with Jed Crowther who had also sauntered in on his day off.

Selitto arrived with the coffees and placed Hunter's mug on

the desk in front of her, retreating to his favoured spot by the window. Kendall was keen to hear about what had been going on since Hunter had simply got up and left the room.

Hunter told her about Eleanora and how she had met Billy Woons at Riga airport, and how she was now in the UK and wanted to look him up. She had been saddened to hear that he had been killed because she felt that, in some small way, she had bonded with him when they had met.

'The most important thing,' Hunter was saying, 'is that this intel fills in the blank we have regarding what he was doing in Riga. Quite clearly, he was just changing planes – nothing more than that. And he didn't meet anyone apart from Eleanora. Anyway, she's going to come in again to give a statement.'

'Well, that's a bit of luck isn't it?' Kendall remarked. 'I always thought that Riga was something to do with an escape route so presumably they sent him back to the UK via Riga to prevent other parties from following him. I bet he was still on the airline manifest for the direct Tbilisi to Gatwick flight so they would have been tracking the wrong plane.'

'Hmm, you're probably right, Grace,' Hunter surmised, 'but that didn't delay his ultimate downfall by much.'

50

Saturday 25 November

Although the clock in the Ops Room steadfastly remained on 09.50, Sarah Hunter knew that the time was ticking up towards 10.30 a.m. which was the time set for their meeting with DS Jones from Ryde police station. It had been a busy morning and now she and Grace Kendall were sitting facing the webcam which was clipped onto the top of one of the monitors on the desk in front of them. Selitto stood by the window out of shot, and Elaine Jennings sat to one side of the desk, also out of shot. Hunter had invited Jed Crowther to listen in to the discussions.

DS Jack Jones suddenly materialised on the screen in front of them, and Grace made all the introductions. Jones looked even colder than he had done the last time they had spoken, and now seemed to be wearing a chunky winter coat in addition to his woolly scarf. He also introduced them to DC Fiona Robertson who was sitting next to him. She was wearing a bright red Musto jacket much favoured by the sailing fraternity. Hunter recalled that sailing was one of the main leisure activities on the Isle of Wight so presumed that Robertson probably spent some of her leisure time on the water. Her woolly scarf hung loosely round her neck and she had a notebook on the table in front of her.

'Good morning, DS Jones,' Hunter started. 'I hear that you've had a busy time since we last spoke. Perhaps you could just take us through what you've been up to.'

Jones had a large notebook in front of him and

immediately referred to it before responding.

'Yes, ma'am, it has been fairly busy round here. Following our last call, I went over to the house in Bembridge and took a walk around the grounds. As we already know, it appears to have been professionally boarded up. Wasn't really much to see but I did find an overturned water butt down one side of the house. The ground around it seemed to be wet which looked like the butt might have been recently emptied. And, unless I'm very much mistaken, it must have been the source of the smell which was reported by the officer who originally eyeballed the house.'

Hunter reached across in front of Kendall and grabbed a piece of paper. Grace handed her a pen when it was obvious that Sarah hadn't anything to write with and then looked on as her DI started writing herself a note, something she had hardly ever seen Hunter do before.

Jones was continuing. 'So, I returned to the extensive decking area at the back of the house and found that the door into the utility room wasn't locked.'

'I hope you used that as a good excuse to have a nose around,' Hunter interrupted, still furiously writing on the paper in front of her.

'Certainly did,' Jones continued. 'The whole place didn't look as if it had been lived in for a while although there were some hints that it might have been visited recently. There were a couple of sticky ring marks on the breakfast bar in the kitchen – mugs, bottles, cans, something like that. Looked quite recent.'

Jones looked down at his notes. 'There's a storage room which is jammed full of gear that you would probably expect to see in a tattoo parlour. Also, a considerable number of jars of all sizes containing powders and other substances. The powders are mainly white but also reds, blues and greens which may be something to do with pigmentation. There were also a number of jars of white powder in the kitchen cabinets – all labelled in some sort of scientific code. I did take a couple of samples which we've sent away for analysis.'

Hunter hadn't got the faintest idea about how inks for tattoos were manufactured or whether, indeed, they began as powders and then got mixed into an ink-like substance.

'Anything else?' she asked.

'Not really,' Jones replied, looking across at DC Robertson. 'Upstairs bedrooms were all empty, nothing in wardrobes and chests of drawers, and nothing in the bathroom cabinets. One bedroom had a peculiar odour in it like vomit mixed with disinfectant but I didn't have time to explore further.'

'Okay,' Hunter said, 'what are you going to do with it now?'

'Well, there's been a few developments here,' Jones was looking directly into the camera. 'We've got a body which was washed up on the shore at Whitecliff Bay. DC Robertson here has been dealing with that so I'll let her fill you in.'

Fiona Robertson gave her account of the discovery of the body of an IC-One male on the sands of the picturesque Whitecliff Bay less than a mile from the house. Early indications were that the man had drowned although it appeared that his neck had been broken. Robertson did not have enough information to speculate whether the neck could have been broken post mortem by waves pounding the body against a rocky outcrop at the corner of the bay. There had been a strong south-easterly blowing and the tide had been particularly high.

'Where's the body at the moment?' Hunter wanted to know how long it would be until they had a cause of death.

'The body's been taken to St Mary's Hospital at Newport for the post-mortem,' Robertson replied. 'They're normally pretty quick to give us a heads up on cause of death so I am expecting that later today.'

'Okay, that'll be good,' Hunter replied, sensing that her investigation may well be linked to this house on the Isle of Wight. But how? Why?

'There's one other piece of information for you, ma'am,' Jones said, leaning towards the camera to get Hunter's attention.

'One of my team did a bit of digging on your Lulu Harrison,' he continued. 'Not a name we've come across and, in any event, we obviously don't know everyone who's on the island. We don't, for example have passenger lists for all the ferries. But we do know the names of people who come in by air because, on landing, they have to provide certain flight information when paying landing fees. This normally includes name of pilot and any passengers as there is a fee per passenger. One of our DCs thought to take a look at these lists for Bembridge and Sandown airports, and it didn't take him long to find out that Lulu Harrison flew into Bembridge Airport on Wednesday and left on Thursday.'

That got Hunter's attention. A light went on in her head. There was a connection here. Something else was connecting the Isle of Wight house with her investigation.

'That, DS Jones, is an extremely interesting discovery!' she exclaimed, looking directly at him on the screen.

'You might also find this bit of information useful.' Jones clearly wasn't finished and Sarah wondered what else he had for her.

'She flew herself in and out of the airport,' he continued. 'Flies a Piper Apache registration G-LOOB. Small plane but big enough to take passengers. And she did have a passenger – noted on the information sheet as P. Deshvilli.'

This silenced Hunter. Her brain was thrumming inside her head. Harrison was not only a real person but she was also a qualified pilot, able to travel all over the country in a fraction of the time it would take her to drive from A to B. This should be a major breakthrough but how could Harrison be in the frame for killing Monroe and Anderson? Then a thought struck her.

'What about leaving Bembridge, does she have to report her destination before leaving?'

'Not as far as I'm aware,' came the reply. 'They report on landing in order to collect the landing fees, but they don't seem to have to submit flight plans when they leave. I should also advise you that Bembridge is without an air traffic unit at the moment so it is likely that she would just take off and then rely on her own onboard navigation systems. At some point, she might have contacted ATC but probably wouldn't have bothered if she was landing on a small private airstrip.'

'So, presumably I might be able to find out when she was airborne if I really wanted to. I mean, we've got the aircraft registration number and the date of the flight so someone at Air Traffic Control may have taken a call from her at some point during that day.'

'That's a possibility, ma'am, but I'm not really an expert on all the protocols for flying small planes,' Jones explained.

'Okay, Jack, don't worry. I'll probably need a bit of time to just work through all this information. But one thing's for dead certain, we need to know exactly what's in those containers in the house. Can you get a forensics report on that as a matter of great urgency?'

'I'll see what I can do. Our local forensics people should be able to give us a rough idea of what we're dealing with but otherwise most of our testing is done in Southampton. Just adds another layer of delay.'

'Okay, do what you can, and keep me informed about everything,' she stressed, wanting to make sure that Jones got the message that 'everything' meant *everything*!

Soon afterwards, Grace Kendall disconnected the call. The detectives just stared at the blank screen. Selitto was the first to break the silence.

'So, are we now saying that Lulu Harrison's a person of interest?' he asked, pushing himself away from the wall and taking up a position in front of the desk, arms folded.

'She's certainly someone we need to speak to,' Hunter replied, 'but is she our killer?'

'Well, she's a woman to start with,' Kendall cut in. 'We've so far identified the killer as a man. So, have we got that wrong?'

'Shit!' exclaimed Hunter, realising the implication of this statement. 'Looks like we're going to have to take another look at that CCTV footage, Grace.'

51

Saturday 25 November

D S Jones's revelation that Lulu Harrison was a qualified pilot and had her own aeroplane had galvanised the team, and they immediately set about trying to trace and track her movements.

Hunter had put Jed Crowther and Elaine Jennings onto this although she knew that they would both be leaving at around 2.15 p.m. so that they could get good seats in the stand at Longmead Stadium. Crowther had somehow been persuaded that it would be a good use of his time this afternoon, but Hunter wondered whether an afternoon out with Jennings and the hot pies at half-time might have been the real reasons.

Meanwhile, Grace Kendall was retrieving all the CCTV from The Prism so that they could have another look at their suspect.

Ted Selitto had taken on the task of identifying airfields where Harrison could land her plane. He quickly discovered that there were not only a number of registered airfields but there were also other landing sites where farmers kept a five or six hundred metre strip of cut grass with a windsock in the middle so that the pilots could judge wind direction when landing or taking off. A lot of the farmland airstrips were off the beaten track and it was unlikely that any register was kept of aircraft movements at these venues. Everyone was happy as long as the landing fees were deposited in the honesty box.

The main problem was that they had no idea where

Harrison came from. She wasn't on the PNC so it was difficult to focus on any particular area. If she travelled around by air then she could literally be living anywhere. Kent had a number of recognised airfields like Biggin Hill, Lydd, Headcorn and Rochester. There were also lesser-known airfields such as Old Hay near Paddock Wood and Farthing Corner near Rainham.

Selitto had also identified a couple of airfields over the county border in East Sussex – Deanland Airfield and Kittyhawk Aerodrome, both of which were close to the county town of Lewes. Further afield, there was a busy aerodrome at Redhill and the larger Fairoaks airport between Chobham and Chertsey.

But all this assumed that Harrison only operated in the south-east of England.

Before they left, Jennings and Crowther had established a contact with Air Traffic Control and had discovered that small aircraft were basically free to roam in uncontrolled airspace. They were not bound by law to make contact with ATC so there was a good chance that many of Harrison's flights went unrecorded. She could fly wherever she wanted as long as she didn't stray into airspace which was controlled by National Air Traffic Services.

Jennings had told Selitto that she had asked the contact at ATC if they had any information on the whereabouts of G-LOOB after the aircraft had left Bembridge a couple of days ago. If they could establish the destination of that flight, they might get some idea of her location.

Selitto was, however, wary of getting too excited about this avenue of investigation because he knew that some people kept planes on farms where they were stored in barns, far away from any prying eyes. Trying to find a Piper Apache without having a reasonable idea of where it might be would be like looking for the proverbial needle in a haystack.

Eventually, he tired of looking for more airstrips and joined Hunter and Kendall who were once again poring over the CCTV feed. They were now watching the suspect frame-by-frame as he made his way out of the auditorium and across the foyer before exiting the building.

Sarah was keen to see where the foyer desk had been located and if there was any sign of someone from security. It was soon evident that the desk had been placed next to the entrance on the Sunday evening but, despite using both cameras to survey the entrance to the theatre at the time the suspect left the building, she could see no sign of anyone else in the foyer.

She was becoming frustrated because, no matter how many times she viewed the CCTV, she just couldn't see that their suspect was anything other than a man. So, if Lulu Harrison really was a suspect, she was the wrong sex to start with.

Ted Selitto had been out to get some sandwiches from Greggs just up the High Street, and they were each sitting at separate desks in the Ops Room idly talking through the events of the last few days. Grace Kendall was in full flow regarding her dislike of tattoos when the phone on her desk suddenly sprang into life.

She took the call with the others looking on, munching their sandwiches. Grace seemed to be doing very little of the talking but was taking copious notes and soon the call had finished.

She took a quick look at the notes she had made and then looked up at her colleagues.

'That was a guy from ATC,' she began. 'Elaine spoke to him earlier today. He's had a quick look on their records for the South-East and noticed that an aircraft with the registration G-LOOB landed at Alderney airport yesterday late morning.' Hunter and Selitto exchanged glances across the room.

'Bloody hell,' Sarah exclaimed. 'What on earth was she doing there?'

But then it suddenly dawned on her. 'Wait a minute! That's not far from Guernsey is it?'

'Which could give us a connection with this Reggie Lemon guy,' Selitto added. 'But, if she was going to meet him, why not fly into Guernsey? It's got a commercial airport.'

'Perhaps she didn't want to be seen at a commercial airport. Perhaps the landing fees are too high. Could be anything.' Grace was staring intently at her screens, piloting the cursor through pages of information.

'Okay,' she eventually said, 'you can get from Guernsey to Alderney by air and by sea. Aurigny Airlines fly a few times a day between the islands. It looks like there's no regular ferry service at this time of the year but you could hire a boat to take you there if the weather's fair.'

'Thanks, Grace. That gives us something to go on.' Hunter was getting a little buzz of adrenalin as a new line of enquiry suddenly opened up in front of her. She looked over to where Selitto was picking up the last crumbs of his sandwich.

'Ted, get onto Alderney airport and find out if any Aurigny planes arrived from Guernsey mid-to-late morning yesterday.

See if Reggie Lemon was on the manifest. Might as well ask them if they knew where G-LOOB was headed when it left.'

'Will do, boss,' Selitto replied, leaving the Ops Room and crossing over the corridor to the MIR.

Hunter was now sitting in the chair next to Grace Kendall looking at an aerial view of Alderney airport.

'She can only have been there to meet Lemon, surely,' Sarah started as if she was trying to convince herself that Lulu Harrison wouldn't have flown to Alderney for any other reason. 'He must have something to do with that house and, as her name's on the deeds, they must at the very least know each other.'

'The only way I can link Lemon to the house is through the ownership details which I got from Land Registry,' replied Kendall, continuing her train of thought. 'His wife was the registered owner before Harrison took it over upon the finalisation of the Lemons' divorce.'

Silence descended on the room. Sarah's mind wandered back to the previous evening when they were standing in a cold tent looking at the booby-trapped handle on the garage door. She suddenly got up from her chair and wandered over to the window, deep in thought. She watched as a Southeastern train passed through Tonbridge on its way towards Ashford, its carriages glinting in what was left of the late afternoon sun. Grace looked up just as Hunter turned away from the window and started talking out loud to no one in particular.

'When do you think that trap at the Edenbridge lock-up could have been set?' she asked. 'Surely not in daylight hours – it would have taken time and care to attach those razor blades. So, probably set up during the night. Thursday night. In which case, Harrison must have been here in Kent on Thursday night before flying to Alderney on Friday.'

'Good point!' Kendall exclaimed. 'That means that there's a good chance that she might have started her journey to Alderney from a Kent airfield on Friday or, at least, landed somewhere in Kent on Thursday so that she could get to Edenbridge. Let me see if I can get hold of any of these airfields although we may have to wait until tomorrow as I doubt there's much flying still going on today – the light's already starting to fade.'

At that moment, Selitto burst through the door into the Ops Room.

'Boss, it looks like we might be barking up the wrong tree,' he reported. 'I got through to Alderney but they said I had to speak to Aurigny about the passenger list. Eventually, I managed to get hold of someone who I think was quite high up in the organisation. He was reluctant to give me any names but changed his tune when I warned him that he would be withholding vital information in a multiple murder investigation.'

Hunter and Kendall stole a glance at each other. They could just imagine Ted bending this poor man's ear.

'Anyway,' Selitto continued, looking down at his notebook, 'there was a flight at 11.30 a.m. yesterday to Alderney. But Reggie Lemon wasn't amongst the passengers.'

Hunter looked askance. 'Shit! Then what the fuck was Harrison doing on Alderney?'

'Don't worry, boss,' Selitto continued, 'there was another passenger on the flight who I think you'll be interested in.'

Hunter looked at Kendall who simply shrugged her shoulders. They both looked back at Selitto.

'Jasper Lime took that flight to Alderney.'

52

Saturday 25 November

I t was very quiet. The only sound was the gentle humming of small electrical motors as they drove specialist equipment which was required 24/7 to maintain life. Special screens across the windows diminished much of the natural daylight, and small units provided controlled lighting across selected parts of the room.

It was extremely rare that anyone needed to work in the laboratory over the weekend so Samantha Frobisher had been very careful not to attract attention to herself as she passed through all the security systems. Although she knew that they would record that she had come into the lab on a Saturday, she also knew that Alicia Gabriel, her manager, never checked the monthly security lists which showed details of everyone entering and leaving the premises.

She had crept across the lab and then unlocked the door to her serpentarium. She now flicked the switch on her little desk light and, after unlocking the bottom drawer, she took out the battered notebook.

Samantha was still seething at the comments made by Pablo Hernandez when they had met up on Thursday evening. She simply didn't believe that he could tell that she was falsifying records just by feeling the venom glands of a snake. She replayed the conversation in her head. He had virtually accused her of not recording the correct amount of venom extracted from the snakes in her care.

Her recollection of their conversation was that he reckoned

that she had been under-recording the quantity of venom which had actually been extracted. In other words, she had been falsifying the records to hide a suspected over-milking practice. She couldn't believe that he had had the nerve to cast doubt on the efficacy of her data input.

Samantha was meticulous at making accurate records of how much venom she had extracted. Had she somehow miscalculated the split between the official record and the amount she recorded in her battered notebook? She couldn't believe that she had done so, but perhaps it was now time to remove the notebook altogether just in case anyone instigated a search.

She opened the notebook and read through page after page of neatly written information about all her milking activities going back over time. This was the only really accurate record of the amount of venom extracted from each snake, and she was happy with the accuracy of her records. Was he trying to lay a trap for her? Was he frustrated that he couldn't find anything negative about her work which he could put into his report? Or was this some sort of weird and sophisticated way of getting into her knickers?

She sat at her desk for a few moments to consider these questions, but eventually concluded that her records and the data she had recorded would stand up to detailed scrutiny if required. She decided against going into the data system to make any changes to her records in case she left any footprint showing that she had been in the lab today.

In any case, Samantha Frobisher was principally here for another reason. Some of the venom she had taken on Tuesday had gone off during the journey home – one of the frost bags had not kept its contents at the correct temperature so, today, she needed an emergency supply of venom.

After carefully studying all her recent milking activities, she decided that the Tiger Snake would provide her with the quality of venom she needed – a potent mixture of neurotoxins, coagulants and myotoxins. She knew that the venom was fatal for humans if left untreated as, apart from anything else, it caused instantaneous paralysis leading to death due to diaphragmatic paralysis.

She pushed the notebook to one side and went about preparing the equipment. After stretching a piece of latex over the top of the glass beaker, she made sure that it was tightly secured. She then retrieved a retort stand from beside her desk and tightened the 3-prong clamp around the beaker.

Once everything was in place, she went over to the cupboard in the far corner of the room to put on her safety clothing, particularly the reinforced rubber knee-length boots. If, for any reason, she dropped the snake, she had to make sure that it couldn't bite any part of her lower legs.

The Tiger Snake looked to all the world as if it was asleep, its banded scales showing ragged stripes of pale yellow and black along its muscular body. Samantha carefully extracted the snake from its cabinet, feeling its body tense in her hands. As she had no one to help her, she would have to do the milking whilst wearing her protective gloves. But that held no concern for her.

Holding the snake's head over the beaker, she gently eased its jaws apart to expose the fangs. She then brought the head down on the latex covering, making sure that the fangs punctured the material before she expertly massaged the venom glands to optimise the secretion of the venom. She watched as a very acceptable amount of deadly liquid pooled in the bottom of the beaker.

Quickly returning the snake to its cabinet, she unclamped the beaker and sealed it before placing it in the fridge beside her desk. Removing her gloves, she wiped the back of her hand across her forehead and was surprised to feel it damp with perspiration. She hadn't realised how tense she had become.

Samantha updated the records in her notebook but made no attempt to update the information stored on the company's databank. They would never know about this milking.

She then took off all the protective gear and returned it to the cupboard. Finally, she removed the beaker from the fridge and placed it inside the special frost bag which she used for transporting venom and which was normally kept in the freezer cabinet.

She was desperate to get out of there. Stuffing the frost bag and her notebook into a small rucksack, she let herself out of the serpentarium and then out of the laboratory. If she was going to maximise the effectiveness of the venom she had just collected, she knew that she had to get home quickly. She would then have a long night ahead of her.

53

Saturday 25 November

After the news that it was Jasper Lime who had made a trip to Alderney, Grace Kendall swung into action to find out as much as she could about the man who had been Reggie Lemon's business partner for many successful years. She also checked with Guernsey Police to see if he had a criminal record on the island but the slate was clean.

Sarah Hunter had played devil's advocate in order to establish how certain they were that Lime had gone to Alderney specifically to meet Harrison, and that it was not simply a massive coincidence that they both happened to be on the island at the same time without meeting. But, in the end, they had to conclude that Lime and Harrison had both travelled to the island with the express intention of meeting each other. To have both been on the same tiny island at the same time as each other without meeting just didn't make sense.

Selitto had continued with his task of identifying airfields and airstrips in the counties of Kent, Sussex and Surrey. Hunter had suggested Essex as well but, after some discussion, they both agreed that they should concentrate on the three counties to the south of the Thames to start with. He had also been trying to get more information about recent flights made by G-LOOB but without much success. Either Harrison hadn't been flying or she simply wasn't logging her flights. This was an alien world for Selitto but he stuck manfully to the task and refused to be bowed by the complexity of Civil Aviation Authority and Air Traffic Control practices and procedures.

Hunter had taken a long call from Beth Dench who was also putting in a Saturday in order to get a further handle on Staunton's crash and their gruesome discovery at the lock-up. Dench had told her that that they had found some drugs at the apartment, hidden under an area of the block flooring. It seemed to have been all wrapped up ready for distribution which suggested that Staunton may have been in league with Monroe although the snooker cues they had so far discovered had not been hollowed out.

Darkness was falling as Grace Kendall stuck her head round the door into the MIR.

'Sorry to interrupt, Sarah, but I've got Jack Jones on another video link from Ryde. Says it's important.'

Hunter and Selitto stopped what they were each doing and headed for the Ops Room where they took up their customary positions around Kendall's desk.

DS Jones was on the screen and was once again accompanied by DC Fiona Robertson. Both of them still looked as if they were waiting for someone to come and fix the heating.

'Afternoon, Jack,' Hunter said, 'I hear you've got some more news for us.'

'Yes, ma'am,' he replied, not bothering to consult his notebook this time. 'We've had a call from the pathologist over in Newport where the PM's been done. She's pretty sure that the guy was dead before he went into the water. There was a little water in his lungs but it wasn't seawater – it was fresh water. She also said that it wasn't fresh as in tap water but, rather, it was fresh as in rain water or some other uncontaminated water – fresh water lake maybe.'

'Interesting,' Hunter commented. But she wondered where this was leading as Jones continued.

'His body shows signs of being fairly knocked about which fits with the area of coastline where he was found. Quite a few rocky outcrops there, and the easterly winds have been strong in the last couple of days. But the pathologist has also noted serious bruising to his wrists and ankles which would indicate that he had been tied up or manacled for some time before death. Some of the skin had also been scraped away leaving ugly sores. His neck had been broken but that could have been post mortem.'

The three Kent detectives glanced at each other, Selitto with a deep frown on his face.

'So, is your pathologist offering a cause of death if it's not drowning?' Hunter asked, also frowning as she stared at the image of DS Jones on the screen.

'Well, she found evidence of injected drug use and, although we'll have to await the tox reports, there are extensive needle marks in both elbow joints, and in other areas of the body. It's her view that he probably died of a drug overdose following which the body was disposed of.'

'But that doesn't explain the freshwater in the lungs,' Kendall interjected.

DC Robertson picked up on this point. 'We're testing another theory that the body was kept in the water butt at the house where some of the rain water got into the deceased's lungs. We've now asked the pathologists and the CSI's to see if the two can be linked together by DNA or whatever.'

There was a brief pause. Sarah hated pauses on video calls. Everyone just sitting staring at the screen, looking gormless. Thankfully, Jones got going again.

'We've also got an ID on the deceased,' he said. 'Bit of a drifter but known to a few in the Bembridge Harbour area. Name of Brad Jolley. Does, or did, crewing for some of the larger yachts when they're racing. Recognised by one of the morgue assistants who does crewing work in his spare time. Said that Jolley always seemed to be dossing on boats and bigger yachts. We've put him down as having no fixed abode.'

'Okay, that sounds like good progress,' Hunter summarised, 'although it looks as if you've now got a murder investigation on your hands.'

'It certainly looks that way,' Jones agreed. 'We also think that one of the powders in the house will test positive for cocaine. One of our colleagues is part of the HantsPol drug squad and I showed him the sample I took from the house. He's pretty sure it's cocaine but it'll have to get tested. We'll also have to now take a good look at that house.'

'Yes, keep us in the loop on that one.' Hunter could sense that she had got as much out of this call as she was going to get and, after a couple of final felicitations, the screen went blank. She sat back in her chair.

'Well, not sure if that gets *our* investigation much further,' she said to no one in particular, 'but they're obviously going to have plenty to do on the Isle of Wight.'

Although it was now past 5.00 p.m. there was still a good crowd of people strolling up and down Tonbridge High Street. The shop windows were jammed full of Christmas decorations and tempting yuletide offerings, and Sarah Hunter looked into some of these as she made her way up the road to Boots to get a fresh supply of tissues. For some reason, her nose had been running for a couple of days although she didn't feel as if she had a cold. Perhaps it was just the weather. In any case, she wanted to exercise her injured leg so the walk was doing her good.

Wandering back to the station on the other side of the road, she just managed to get into Chatfield Butchers before it closed. She had spotted some plump Lincolnshire sausages in the window and thought that they would make a nice meal for this evening, but ended up buying other bits and pieces so that she eventually had enough food to constitute a mixed grill for one person.

On her return to the station, she put the food into the fridge, made herself a cup of tea and wandered back into the Ops Room. Grace was still sitting at her desk scrolling through screen after screen of information, occasionally stopping to read something that had caught her eye.

Hunter took a seat at one of the empty workstations and got Google maps up on the screen. She wanted to have a good look at the area where the house was at Bembridge. She quickly found it and then got onto the satellite view. She could see that the house was about midway between the airfield and Whitecliff Bay where the body had been discovered. What she hadn't appreciated was the number of static caravans in the area, and she counted at least three holiday parks. However, she also realised that they would be closed at this time of the year so it was unlikely that anyone would have seen a body being dumped into the sea.

She manoeuvred the cursor around the screen, zooming in and zooming out, and managing to find some photographs which showed that there were some cliffs along parts of the bay. Surely, he hadn't just been pushed off one of those, she thought. In any case, it didn't look as if the tide got that far up the beach. So, had the body been tossed into the water elsewhere? Was it even connected to the house and its empty water butt? Oh well, that was HantsPol's problem – not hers.

She was still absent-mindedly staring at the screen when Ted Selitto barrelled into the room.

'Think I've got something here, boss,' he exclaimed. Hunter was all ears and Kendall had stopped her scrolling.

'Remember Jones told us that the car came over to the island on the ferry from Southampton?' The others nodded. 'Well, I thought back to that car which turned up at Meadowlands in the trafficking case, and recalled that it was stolen from Southampton airport. So, could our friend Jasper Lime have flown over from Guernsey to Southampton and then driven to meet Harrison at the Isle of Wight house?'

'Hmm! I like your thinking, Ted,' Hunter said enthusiastically, but then slightly tempered her reply. 'But where would he have got the Prospero Inks car from?'

'Well, I spent some time thinking about that,' Selitto continued.

'Long-stay car park at the airport?' Kendall interrupted.

'Yep, that's what I came up with, Grace. So, I've been on to the long-stay car park at Southampton and they do have cars which are parked there for quite lengthy periods of time. They could look the car up for us if we had the registration details so I'll have to get that from Jones.

'Good work, Ted,' Hunter said enthusiastically.

'There's more,' he continued. 'I rang the airport and they confirmed that there are flights each day to and from Guernsey with Aurigny Airlines. So, I rang that guy again. Can't say that he was very impressed by me interrupting his Saturday afternoon again but he understood the urgency and had a look at the manifests for Wednesday morning.'

Both Hunter and Kendall had eyes locked on Selitto.

'But no Jasper Lime, I'm afraid.'

The others looked a little deflated.

Selitto continued. 'I was just about to hang up when I suddenly remembered our old pal, Reggie Lemon and, hey presto, his name was on the passenger list for that flight.'

Sarah Hunter threw her head back and screamed!

54

Saturday 25 November

By 7.00 p.m. Hunter felt as if her brain was about to explode. Although she had three dead bodies in the morgue, all patiently waiting for her to discover why they were there, Sarah was all too aware that the real action was taking place outside her area of operation where she had no influence or control.

After Selitto's discovery that it was likely that Reggie Lemon had been at the house in Bembridge, he had to leave as he had been invited to attend a concert at St Nicholas Church in Sevenoaks. This was to be preceded by a meal at the Sun Do restaurant in Sevenoaks although he was already late for this.

Grace had emailed a photo of Lemon to DS Jones and asked him for an ID from the traffic officer. If they could get a positive ID then they could tie Lemon to Lulu Harrison and Prospero Inks.

Sarah now sat alone in the MIR and just stared at the satellite image of Alderney on the screen in front of her. Did Jasper Lime and Lulu Harrison meet on the island? Where did they meet? Why did they meet? What was Lime and his mate, Lemon, up to with Lulu Harrison? And how did it all tie in with Prospero Inks? There was another name they hadn't yet considered – Gustav Holmes. Should they be looking more closely at him?

The biggest problem she had was linking their activities with the deaths of two snooker players and one manager on her patch. The only connection they had was that Jacqui Anderson had been found in a car registered to Prospero Inks. They suspected that Davie Monroe was supplying drugs, and that Gavin Staunton was probably a dealer. It was now a distinct possibility that drugs had been found at a house owned by Harrison but which had previously been owned by Lemon's ex-wife.

Lemon and Lime both knew Harrison, or at least they had both met her independently of each other in the last seventy-two hours. Lemon had also been in Tonbridge on the night Monroe was killed. In fact, he had been in the same building. But Sarah couldn't see how he could possibly have killed Monroe. And he couldn't have set up the trap which killed Staunton. As far as she was aware, Lime hadn't even been on the mainland.

But they knew nothing of Harrison's movements. Could she have killed Monroe? They were certain that the killer was a man but could Harrison have disguised herself as a man? Did Harrison have time to booby trap Staunton's garage between meeting Lemon at Bembridge and meeting Lime on Alderney? She doubted this. Although it was technically possible, it would have probably meant her going without sleep for at least thirty-six hours – never a good idea for a pilot.

So, was there someone else who was the killer? Someone who was not yet even on their radar?

She stared at the crime wall. One of the team had helpfully stuck pictures of Lemon and Lime on it, probably printed off from their website. But they weren't linked to anything else. She let her imagination run wild. Were they, in fact, drug barons operating from a safe offshore location where they weren't under the same scrutiny as they would be on the mainland? And were people like Harrison and Monroe the chiefs on the ground in the UK with people like Staunton as the bottom feeders?

She rather liked this idea so started to let it develop in her head. Lemon and Lime could travel in and out of mainland UK via many different routes. They could even travel by private plane or boat. There would be very little record of their movements unless they travelled by scheduled flights. Harrison had the wherewithal to do the same and probably did most of her travelling by air. Again, it would seem that she could probably get around without anyone knowing where she was.

Hunter looked up as the door opened and Grace Kendall stepped into the room.

'How's it going?' Grace asked as she walked over to take a look at the crime wall.

'Doing my head in!' came the less than enthusiastic reply. Sarah was struggling, and she knew it.

'Well, I'm famished,' Grace said, turning to face Sarah. 'Fancy joining me for a plate of noodles at that Thai place up near the castle?'

Hunter remembered the components for her mixed grill which were still in the fridge. But it would be nice to sit and have a chat with Grace – it might just clear the log-jam in her head. The mixed grill could surely keep until tomorrow. And, in any case, she liked the infrequent occasions when she and Grace could have a decent girlie natter.

They both grabbed their coats, scarves and woolly hats

before leaving the station and wandering up the road to the restaurant.

55

Saturday 25 November

S arah Hunter had overlooked the fact that it was Saturday so was surprised to find the restaurant doing such good business. However, Grace seemed to know the woman who greeted them at the door, and they were shown to a small table for two which offered a degree of privacy being as it was situated on its own in a corner of the restaurant away from other diners. Perhaps Grace was a regular here and this table was kept for her.

'Have you got the phone with you?' Hunter asked as they finally sat down. The 'gold phone' was the mobile phone assigned to the person on-call from CID and had to be carried at all times either on or off the premises. Kendall now took it out of her bag and placed it on the table between them so that she could at least see it light up even if they couldn't hear when a call came in.

Grace's friend who had shown them to the table was soon back with a plate of Thai appetisers, saying that these were on the house. She handed out menus and took the drinks order – one large bottle of sparkling water between them. Sarah was glad that she had decided to accept the offer of eating out – it was nice to be with her friend and colleague in a social setting.

They were soon chatting, occasionally animatedly, about experiences in their lives and other little anecdotes about everyday living. Grace had recently moved into an apartment in Medway Wharf, a development on the banks of the River

Medway in the centre of Tonbridge, and had many amusing stories to tell about estate agents, solicitors, removal companies – and her new neighbours. Sarah Hunter had some amusing stories of her own to tell about her move to the Kent countryside a few years earlier, and they had a good laugh at how she had originally been viewed by some of her new neighbours.

Plates of Pad Thai came and went as did some indulgent bowls of coconut ice cream. There was much laughter and merriment at the tables around them which contributed to a generally enjoyable evening.

The arrival of two cups of coffee, however, prompted the conversation to return to their current investigation, and they each expressed their frustration with the lack of progress. Sarah was keen to hypothesise about what they knew and the leads they had, and Grace was an interested listener who occasionally tossed her own views into the pot. She was also keen to ensure that her friend didn't beat herself up too much about her perception that no progress was being made.

Their discussions ranged from The Prism to the Channel Islands, to the Isle of Wight, to flying private planes, and to the mystery surrounding the actual cause of death of the three bodies in the morgue. Lowering her voice, she told Grace about her call with DCI Pennington and the work he was involved in regarding a suspected huge shipment of drugs. And how he had also been very interested when she had mentioned the name Lulu Harrison. Especially as his intelligence sources hadn't uncovered the fact that she held a private pilot's licence.

Leaving many of their questions still unanswered, they

decided that it was time to make a move. They had already agreed to go Dutch, and Grace's friend quickly split the bill in half giving each of them their own receipt. They thanked her and wished her well as they walked out into the perishing cold of a November night.

Whilst they were paying the bill, Kendall had invited Sarah to drop by her apartment on the way back to collect her car from Pembury Road. Although she was very tired, Sarah had wanted to see Grace's apartment so they walked along the bank of the River Medway, marvelling at the view as the lights from the footpath danced on the fast-flowing waters of the river.

They took the lift to the top floor and Grace let them into a darkened hallway which was soon flooded with light at the flick of a switch. She carried on through to a kitchen area which opened out into a huge lounge and dining area at the end of which were patio doors leading out onto a small balcony overlooking the river.

'Hey! What a great pad,' Sarah enthused, as she made her way to the windows to look out on the river. Grace then showed her round the rest of the apartment before tempting her with a cup of jasmine tea to keep her warm on the journey home. Sarah sat back on the two-seater sofa as it was the only item of furniture in the lounge part of the room. Grace brought the mugs of tea over and sat next to her.

They sipped their tea and chatted about furnishings and the difficulty of getting the right colour paint for the walls in a room which got a good deal of sunlight during the day. And soon the tea was finished and the conversation had meandered to the point when Sarah thought it would be polite to leave.

Perhaps realising this, Grace suddenly turned towards Hunter.

'Do you mind if I ask you a personal question, Sarah?' she asked.

Sarah was slightly caught off guard but said that of course she had no objection.

'It's just that I wonder if you ever feel lonely?' Grace's big blue eyes searched Sarah's face for a reaction.

'I think we all feel lonely in this job,' she replied after taking time to reflect on the question. 'Although we work in a team, someone has to take ultimate responsibility. It's that position of responsibility which is a lonely place.'

She looked her friend in the eye. 'Why do you ask?'

Grace felt her cheeks starting to tingle with heat.

'Oh, I don't know. It's just that I have so much respect and admiration for you that I want you to be happy – and I want to see you happy. But sometimes I see a lonely person, burdened with self-criticism about not making progress. A person who gives so much to everyone around her and then goes home alone to an empty house with no one to share the angst of the day, no one to help you to at least gain some respite from the stress and complexity of the job you do.'

'Well, I suppose I've got used to it over time,' Sarah eventually replied. 'I admit that I don't find it easy to make friends – present company excepted – and I'm rubbish at relationships. But I often crave the isolation of living alone which gives me time to think and reflect on the sort of person I am, and the sort of person I want to be.'

On impulse, she took hold of Grace's hands and set them

on the sofa between them. 'You really don't need to worry about me. I have learnt to cope with loneliness.'

A tear suddenly cascaded down Grace's cheek.

Sarah was somewhat overwhelmed by the realisation that this woman, who was such an important part of her team, was genuinely concerned about her wellbeing. She went to pull Grace towards her.

'Come here,' she whispered softly. 'Come here.'

Grace moved her body so that her head was now resting on Sarah's shoulder. The two women looked deeply into each other's eyes. Sarah could feel her heart starting to pound, a tingling sensation raking through her body.

It was difficult to say who made the first move. As Sarah's lips lightly caressed the soft skin of her friend's cheeks, Grace pulled Sarah towards her. At the same time, she tilted her head slightly so that their lips clashed in a fury of expectation. Tongues darted and deftly explored, breathing became heavy and sonorous, hands started to gently caress bodies which were pitched together in a tight embrace.

The two women manoeuvred their bodies against each other, both becoming lost in the sexual tension which they were creating. Eyes were tightly shut, lips and tongues sending signals of delight to tired brains.

Suddenly, Sarah pulled back and stared wild-eyed at her friend.

'This is madness,' she whispered, trying to get her breathing back to something approaching normality. 'Pure madness!'

She squirmed out of Grace's lingering embrace and pushed herself off the sofa. Standing up, she looked around the room

– looking for what? She didn't know. Her mind was in turmoil.

Grace was now sitting on the edge of the sofa, bent over, arms wrapped around her legs, staring at the floor.

Sarah squatted down in front of her, a sharp searing pain shooting up her injured leg. She reached out a hand and cupped Grace's chin, gently raising her head. Tears were flowing freely from those gorgeous blue eyes. Sarah felt weak and ashamed. She had to get away, to be on her own, to referee the battle between her head and her heart.

'My dear Grace,' she spluttered, still unsure about what she should do but reluctantly deciding that she had to leave, 'I must go now. Don't ever regret this moment. I just need time to sort myself out. I treasure and value our friendship, but I don't think that I'm ready to take things further right at this moment. Give me some time.'

More tears escaped. 'Please don't cry,' she whispered, leaning over and gently wiping away a tear, her lips caressing Grace's perfect skin once more. The saltiness of the tear tasted divine.

Getting back on her feet, Sarah went across the room and shrugged herself into her coat, winding her scarf around her neck. She looked back at Grace who still sat with her arms now wrapped round her knees, staring mournfully at Sarah.

'I just need some time,' she sighed, feeling a lump forming in her throat. She turned and headed back down the little hallway and let herself out of the apartment.

Walking to the lift, Sarah was suddenly overcome with guilt. Should she have walked out on her friend as she had done or should she have stayed so that they could talk things through? She stopped in her tracks, turning back to face Grace's apartment. The temptation to retrace her steps and knock on the door was almost overwhelming. But something was holding her back. A little voice in her head was telling her that now was not the time.

As the lift clunked down to the ground floor, she felt the tears welling in her own eyes, and by the time she reached the road, she was gently sobbing. Her tears were freezing on her cheeks in the icy wind. All her thoughts centred on that moment of sheer bliss which she had just experienced not only with her friend, Grace Kendall, but, more worryingly, with her colleague Grace Kendall.

56

Sunday 26 November

I t had been a frustrating night. Sarah had spent much of it awake, racked with guilt about letting her emotions run away with her. Occasionally lapsing into tearful sobs as she recalled the events in Grace's apartment. She had broken her one golden rule – she was becoming emotionally involved with a member of her team. The urgent physicality of their brief embrace had frightened her at the time but the memory of it had left a warm feeling inside her.

And, as if that wasn't enough to keep her mind occupied, the continuing quest to find a link between all the disparate leads in her investigation kept putting itself centre-stage and demanding attention.

But it was thoughts of Grace which held sway. She eventually decided that she didn't regret her actions. She had feelings for the woman. They were of a similar age leading similar lives – both living alone and working nearly all the hours God made. She was, however, a little surprised at how much she had enjoyed the experience having never before had a physical relationship with a woman. Yes, there had been some fumbled cuddling with one or two of her girlfriends in her early teens but that was all.

She felt comfortable in Grace's company. There was no need to try to exert influence as there often was with others in the force, particularly the men. They worked well together, they had stimulating conversations, they did not have to prove anything to each other. They were comfortable in each other's company. Sarah found Grace physically attractive, and had enjoyed the warmth of their embrace. The difficulty was that she wanted more.

The sandman had eventually come along and sprinkled some of his magical dust into Sarah's eyes so she awoke with a start to the sound of her phone ringing. She grabbed it off the bedside table, noting that the time was 08.44 a.m. Caller ID – Beth Dench. Frowning, she swiped the screen to take the call.

'Morning, Sarah, hope this isn't too early for you on a Sunday!' As ever, Beth was obviously full of the joys and hard at work. Once the pleasantries were concluded, she got straight to the point.

'We've had an interim report from Porton Down which must have come in overnight. I thought I should contact you straightaway as their tests are showing up something that we haven't any experience of. I was, therefore, wondering if you would like to come over to the lab so that we can have a chat.'

Almost without thinking Sarah said she'd be there in an hour which was fine with Dench. She then called Selitto, apologising profusely for getting him on a Sunday morning. No problem there – he'd already been to the gym followed by an egg & cheese McMuffin for breakfast on his way home. Sarah couldn't quite see how the two were compatible with each other but they arranged to meet at the lab at 10.00 a.m. anyway.

Sarah was now in a rush. Thank goodness she had washed her hair the day before – that would have really delayed her. So, with her hair tightly tucked into a shower cap, she just stood in the shower letting the hot water cascade over her, memories of the previous evening still at the forefront of her mind as she gently lathered *savon douceur* all over her body, watching as the soapy foam dissipated in the onslaught from the jets of water.

She almost forgot to put on her smart jeans for her lunch with Pennington but, otherwise, the weather called for warm clothing at all times. She toasted a couple of slices of bread and slathered them with marmalade. She ate one whilst collecting keys and her bag from where they had been discarded the previous evening, and she stuffed her phone into her coat pocket. Holding the second slice of toast between her teeth, she locked up the cottage and headed for the car.

A further delay of five minutes to get rid of frost on the car windows and she was finally on the road, remarkably arriving at the lab at the same time as Selitto. She checked in the mirror to make sure that her mouth wasn't covered in marmalade and toast crumbs, and then hurried over to the entrance.

Beth Dench was waiting for them and showed them up to her area on the third floor. Once they were all sitting at the table in one of the small meeting rooms, mugs of coffee and notepads in front of them, Dench began.

'Hope you don't mind me suggesting that we meet this morning but I just think that it will be easier for you to press ahead if we can consider these preliminary findings together as they are rather unusual.' She opened a file in front of her.

'But, before I get onto the report from Porton Down,' she continued, 'remember that I mentioned that we had found a

342

couple of partials on the BMW which Anderson was in? They were detected on the driver's seat sliding mechanism. This initially led us to consider that whoever drove the car to the cemetery may have had to either adjust the seat so that it was closer to the steering wheel or, alternatively, so that it was further back.'

The detectives looked at each other, nodding.

'Well, you'll be pleased to know that we've got a match,' Dench continued, a twinkle in her eye, 'but I'm afraid that it might also cause you a further headache.'

Hunter looked quizzically at the CSI Manager.

'The partials are a match for Davie Monroe,' Dench announced.

'My God!' Sarah exclaimed. 'He can't possibly have driven it to the cemetery – dead men don't drive!'

Selitto was wondering whether this revelation did, in fact, make much difference to their investigation as his boss continued with her diatribe.

'Don't tell me it was his car all along and that Anderson didn't, in fact, have any link to Prospero Inks through the car? So, do we think he drove from Essex to stay with Anderson in Brasted, and then they shared the driving to and from The Prism for all his matches including the final? Did she then scarper, get into the car and drive away from The Prism before being found dead in it some ten hours later having been killed in between times? You couldn't make it up!'

Selitto knew better than to interrupt Hunter in full flow so, once she had calmed down, he offered his thoughts.

'The only difference this makes to our investigation is that the car now possibly links Monroe to Prospero Inks rather than Anderson. And, as we know that Monroe is into drugs, there must be a fair chance that drug-dealing is the link with Prospero. Which then brings back into focus the question of whether Lulu Harrison is the killer.'

The three of them sat there thinking about this turn of events. Eventually, Beth Dench returned her gaze to the file on her desk.

'Let's get through this report and then see if we are any nearer concluding that Harrison is the killer.'

There was an air of anticipation in the room as Dench continued.

'Now, the original pathology reports on Monroe and Anderson concluded that they were poisoned. This brought on an acute reaction which, in effect, closed their bodily functions down. However, the people in the lab were unable to identify the toxins involved so they forwarded the samples to Porton Down for further analysis. I understand that the scientists down there were initially concerned that they had some sort of nerve agent on their hands. Hence our extreme caution with Staunton's house out at Edenbridge the other night.'

She glanced down at her papers before continuing. 'Anyway, they're now of the view that we haven't got an emergency on our hands like they had in Salisbury with the Skripals. But they have concluded that the main ingredient in whatever it was that killed our two victims is snake venom.'

Hunter and Selitto shot each other a glance. 'Snake venom?' Hunter repeated, intonating the words as a question.

'That's what they've discovered,' Dench continued, 'and not just any old snake venom but venom from some of the most dangerous snakes in the world.'

'*Some!*' Hunter exclaimed.

'Yep,' Dench replied. 'Your guys were killed with a deadly cocktail of snake venom plus deadly poisons such as cyanide, arsenic and strychnine. They are also carrying out tests for botulinum toxin which is one of the most toxic substances known. Whoever wanted those people dead wanted them dead in a hurry. The combination of the venom and the toxins would have been super-fast acting.'

'Christ!' Selitto sighed, 'Staunton only managed to get about three miles from his apartment before he went off the road. The toxin got him that quickly.'

Dench again referred to her notes. 'Well, we haven't actually got their report on Staunton yet but the interim report from Porton Down on the other two advises that the scientists have mainly found evidence of a neurotoxic venom which tends to act more quickly. It attacks the nervous system and quickly stops nerve signals getting through to the muscles. This means paralysis which will result in the victim being unable to breathe. I think this fits in quite well with what Toby Swartzman found at the post-mortems.'

There was a moment's silence as the news from Porton Down sank in.

'Snake venom,' Hunter repeated. 'So, how do you get a quantity of snake venom then? Surely you can't just buy it in a shop or online.' She paused. 'Or can you?'

'Well, I'm not an expert on that, Sarah,' Dench replied, 'but I do know that extracting snake venom is a very delicate activity. It's known as snake milking and involves exposing the snake's fangs over a jar and then persuading the snake that it's biting its prey. The milker will massage the venom glands in order to extract the maximum amount of venom which is collected in the jar. I understand that it has to be frozen at around minus twenty Celsius within an hour of extraction, and it can then be kept for up to one month before it goes off.'

She looked at the two detectives. 'So, in answer to your question, I am not aware of venom being on sale in a shop but I have found it for sale online.'

Hunter and Selitto looked askance at this revelation.

'But,' she continued, 'the venom for sale online is unlikely to have the toxicity or deadly effect that has been detected by the scientists at Porton Down, mainly because it probably hasn't been kept in the prescribed conditions.'

'So, what are we looking for here?' Hunter asked, feeling that her investigation was stalling badly.

'My guess is that you're looking for a scientist who really knows snakes. Probably someone who either has their own serpentarium or who has access to one. Someone who has mastered the art of snake milking. Someone with a highly detailed knowledge of chemistry which enables them to mix snake venom with chemicals to create the sort of toxins that they've used to kill your victims.'

'Blimey!' Selitto sighed.

57

Sunday 26 November

J asper Lime was clapping his gloved hands together and jumping up and down on the spot, trying to keep warm in the icy wind which was blowing in off the English Channel. He had arrived early for his meeting with Pascal Hennenbont at his base on the Ile de Bréhat, a tiny island off the northern coast of Brittany in the Côtes d'Armor department of France.

The drug baron had stipulated that their meeting would be at the Rosédo Lighthouse, a 160-year-old stone structure at the northern end of the island about half a mile from the sea. Neatly manicured lawns surrounded the building, and there was a smart granite wall enclosing the grounds around the base of the lighthouse.

It had been an adventurous start to the day for Lime. Less than twenty-four hours earlier, he had been lunching with one of his property-developer mates who had been telling Jasper about a prototype of a brand-new ocean-going vessel that he had been developing. It was a mixture of a speed boat and a motor cruiser. He had told Lime that he needed to get some sea trials done, so Jasper offered up a journey over to the Ile de Bréhat as an opportunity for the craft to have a good run-out.

Lime had found the accommodation on board rather cramped and uncomfortable, and it was certainly not a smooth ride thanks in part to the state of the sea. But it had given him a fast crossing to the little island so there hadn't been too much time to think about being seasick.

Once they had arrived in the waters around Bréhat, they had been met by one of Hennenbont's henchmen in a powerful looking RIB. He had escorted them through the shallower waters until they reached a landing jetty where Lime thankfully stepped ashore. He had then been ushered into an ageing Citroen 2CV for the short journey to the lighthouse.

Although he always liked to try out his *Franglais* when he was in France, he decided it would be too complicated to explain to the driver that he had attempted to drive one of these cars when he was sixteen. But he'd had to give up because he couldn't understand the way the gears worked. In any case, he had been trying to steal it at the time so knowing how to drive the car would have been an advantage.

After being deposited at the lighthouse, Lime had another quick look at his watch which was showing 09.23 a.m. As he was now in France, he knew the time here was 10.23 a.m. so he still had a few minutes to wait.

He had just started to wander around the area of ground in front of the lighthouse when he became aware of the distant thwack thwack thwack of helicopter rotor blades. He turned to peer into the distance as a small spec on the horizon grew ever larger as it approached Rosédo. As it slowed on arrival at the lighthouse, the Robinson R44 hovered until the pilot had selected the best area of ground for a landing, the downdraught throwing up dust and other detritus. Lime turned away until he heard a dip in the pitch of the engine and the rotors began to slow.

Turning back, he was in time to see the door of the

helicopter swing open as the pilot jumped down to the ground and walked casually in his direction. Removing the flying helmet, Lime watched as the pilot shook a mane of blonde hair loose which, even at this distance, he could tell was streaked with colours. She tugged her fingers through the strands of hair on either side of her head.

'What kept you?' he called over.

'Ha! Ha!' Lulu Harrison replied. 'In case you hadn't noticed, I've had rather a long journey to get to this godforsaken place.'

She was now standing with Lime in the lee of the wall surrounding the lighthouse. 'Had to park the fixed-wing at Lannion on the mainland and then pick up this little beauty,' she said, pointing her thumb over her left shoulder. 'Just under twenty-five miles.'

'Didn't know you flew helicopters,' Lime responded, an air of surprise in his voice.

'There's a lot you don't know about me but don't let it worry your pretty little head,' she said, fiddling with the visor on the helmet whilst giving him a steely look. 'Anyway, where's the main man?'

Just as she said this, they heard a door opening behind them and turned in time to see a huge mountain of a man dressed head-to-toe in black making his way towards them with a perceptible limp. Black hair streaked with grey trailed out from under a classic black Breton cap, and most of his face was covered with a luxurious if unkempt black beard. Dark eyes full of menace peered at them from under the cap's peak, and he sported large diamond studs in each ear. As he drew closer, it was apparent that his nose had been rearranged on several occasions, and the lips on his large ugly mouth were cracked and bloody.

Pascal Hennenbont shook Lime's hand with a vice-like grip which had Jasper squirming. He then turned his attention to Harrison. Jasper quickly regained his composure and made the introductions as the Frenchman took hold of Harrison's right hand, looking her up and down before gazing over at the little Robinson which stood rather forlornly to the side of the lighthouse. Returning his gaze to Harrison, he looked deeply into her eyes before lifting her hand to his face and slathering his cracked lips over the back of her hand. He then turned and started off towards the lighthouse building. The visitors dutifully followed, Harrison vigorously wiping her hand on the back of her jeans.

Once inside, Hennenbont invited them to sit around a small table which had a map laid out in the centre of it. Rather alarmingly, Lime noticed that four other men had suddenly appeared from out of the shadows and now formed what could only be described as a guard around the table. He looked across at Harrison who looked completely unfazed by the whole experience.

Lime once again introduced Lulu Harrison to Hennenbont and then sat back in his chair, aghast, as Harrison started conversing with the drug baron in fluent French. Was there anything this woman couldn't do? There was much laughter between the two of them, the Frenchman's cracked lips parting to reveal several gold teeth as he grinned his way through a particularly long diatribe from Harrison.

Eventually, he reverted to his broken English and suggested

that they should get on with their discussions.

Over the next hour or so, Hennenbont told them about his plans to expand his drugs base in the UK and how he envisaged that they would be involved in running it.

He told them how he had developed a new sea-going vessel which would revolutionise the way drugs were transported to the UK. The vessel had been designed using 'stealth' technology to significantly reduce the chances of it being detected by radar or other infrared or radio frequency detectors. It was also quiet and fast.

On paper, Hennenbont's plan was simple. He would cram the vessel with small inflatable rafts and then recruit one rider for each inflatable. That person would be given a quantity of drugs specially wrapped in water-resistant material and using tamper-proof technology. The vessel would cross the Channel from France to the UK and, when just offshore the landing site in the UK, the inflatables would be deployed and driven ashore by their drivers who would then deliver their packages to a pre-arranged spot and disappear into the countryside.

Lime was impressed with this plan, and rather relieved that he had not been able to go through with the nomination of Monroe for this work. It seemed to be well out of his league. But he wanted to know where Hennenbont was going to get the drivers for the inflatables.

'That is the clever part of my plan,' the drug baron replied,' because these people are all here in France and desperate to get to the UK. We recruit from the migrant camps. We also take their money for the crossing. That is extra cash for us. And, when they get to the UK, they have more chance of not getting caught because no one knows they are coming.'

Lime had to concede that it was an ingenious plan, but where did he and Harrison fit in to all this?

'I know that your friend here drives helicopters so she will collect the drugs from the landings,' Hennenbont continued. 'And then you, my friend, will work with her to get the drugs into your supply and distribution chains.'

'What drugs are we talking about here?' Lime asked, still unclear as to what he might be getting himself into.

'Whatever you want! We can get whatever you want. You order – we supply.'

'Fentanyl?' Harrison asked.

Hennenbont stopped fiddling with the rings on his fingers and stared across the table at Harrison. Gradually a smile spread across his face, the bloody cracks on his lips widening even further.

'I see we have someone with great ambition,' he said, still smiling at Harrison. 'You and I know this is in great demand, and we know why.' He tapped what was left of his nose before continuing. 'So, yes we can get that. As I say, we can get *anything*!'

Harrison wanted to know how often these landings were envisaged and roughly where they would be. Hennenbont indicated that the landings would, to some extent, be weather-dependant but probably weekly. As to where, the coastline nearest to the French coast was favourite but it could be further west. It would depend on the time taken for a crossing as he had to take into consideration fresh air supply on the vessel.

The three of them sat looking at each other before Hennenbont looked down at the map and then turned it round so that Lime and Harrison were looking at the coastline between Hastings and Folkestone.

'We are going to run our first landings on Wednesday here,' he said, pointing to the map. A frisson of excitement flashed across Harrison's face; a feeling of dread fear clanged in Lime's heart. They listened on as the plan was explained in detail.

There were few questions at the end. There was very little that the drugs baron hadn't thought of. The ball was in Lime's court. He had to come up with a plan for the distribution and how he was going to involve Harrison. He felt slightly better in the knowledge that helicopters were involved which could quickly get the drugs to a safe destination, but distribution on this scale was going to be new to him.

The meeting didn't last much longer – Hennenbont had a lunchtime engagement at Paimpol, a small port on the coast of Brittany. Harrison asked if he wanted a lift but had to withdraw her offer when it was made clear that the four minders would have to travel as well. In any event, he wasn't very keen on flying in helicopters.

After another round of handshakes and a friendly slap on the back for Lime, they exited the lighthouse and wandered slowly towards the Robinson. Lime had spotted the 2CV parked away to his left, the driver looking as if he was wearing the car rather than sitting in it.

'What do you think, Lulu?' he asked, head down, watching her flying boots taking measured paces across the ground.

'Sounds interesting,' she replied. 'We can let it run this week, see how it goes, then decide if we want more.'

'What about the flying? You okay with that?'

She stopped in her tracks and turned to face him.

'Well, I'm assuming you're going to be supplying the flying equipment because my services don't come packaged with a helicopter. I only hire.'

Lime nodded weakly. He and Reggie had bought a helicopter a few years ago with the intention that one of them was going to learn how to fly the damn thing. But that had never come to pass so they now kept it at a heliport on the mainland where it was rented out. He just hoped that it had been maintained properly as neither he nor Reggie had used it for quite a few months.

'And it's still at that heliport you've stored it at before?'

Lime grunted an acknowledgement and then made a mental note to ring his contact at the maintenance hangar to check that it was still airworthy.

'Well, as long as it still flies it shouldn't be a problem,' Harrison continued. 'I mean, I'm assuming that the carriers will be told to get their packages to the helicopter and then disappear. If I'm sitting there with the lights on and the blades turning, they should be able to find me. Anyway, you'll be there so you can help get the packages on board.'

Lime nodded – although he wasn't so sure that he was going to be there. Or, indeed, anywhere near there. He needed to see if Hennenbont's plan worked before he put in an appearance. Although she didn't know it yet, Harrison was probably going to be on her own for this one.

'I need to look at the landing ground so let's talk tomorrow,' Harrison said, bunching her hair up on the top of her head before putting the helmet back on. She boarded the Robinson and then opened the pilot's side window. 'And you owe me seventy-five euros for the landing fees at Lannion!'

The sound of the engine starting drowned out his reply, and he scuttled away as the rotor blades began turning. Eventually, the little craft lifted off the ground and hovered before swooping into the air and away over the western part of the island. After banking to the south-west on its way back to Lannion, Lime watched until it became a speck on the horizon.

He looked down at the ground around him, and then cast a furtive glance towards the lighthouse before trudging over to the 2CV. He hoped the sea would be a bit calmer for his journey back to Guernsey.

58

Sunday 26 November

Sarah Hunter had arrived at The Tickled Trout about ten minutes early for her lunch date with Jack Pennington, and was relieved to find that there were a few parking spaces left. She knew that this was a popular local, and Sunday lunch would no doubt be a sell-out.

She sat in the car to reflect on her meeting with Beth Dench, and to try to make sense of the new information they had. One thing was clear – they were now looking for someone who had access to snake venom and who had the scientific know-how to mix it with other toxins to deadly effect. And, more importantly, someone with the wherewithal to deliver it.

They had been trying to fit the deaths to Lulu Harrison's movements but Sarah still thought that Harrison couldn't have killed Staunton. There was also still the question of whether Harrison could have disguised herself as a man to kill Monroe. Sarah was now even less convinced that Harrison was their killer as, from what little she knew of the woman, she really didn't see her as having the scientific background and knowledge which Dench had suggested would have been required to assemble the toxins used for the killings.

So, frustratingly, they seemed to be back at square one. Searching for someone with a specialist knowledge of snake venom was one thing but adding a thorough knowledge of chemical toxins and how to mix the two to deadly effect – that was something else. Just the thought of it sent a shudder down Sarah's spine.

Thankfully, Selitto had decided to go into the MIR at Pembury Road on his way home to get started on searching for what Dench had called herpetologists. Hunter didn't really know where one would start looking but, if Grace was also in, she hoped that the two of them would come up with something.

Suddenly, the thought of getting back to the station and walking into the Ops Room started butterflies fluttering in her stomach. What was it going to be like having to communicate with Grace as her superior when the two of them had been in each other's arms just a few hours earlier? She tried to wipe the thought from her mind and was relieved when she heard a tap on the car window.

Jack Pennington looked as if he had just got out of a hot shower. His cheeks were red and his hair was still wet, or was it the hair gel that modern man seemed to insist on wearing? Sarah was never sure. He rather clumsily kissed her on both cheeks, his designer stubble feeling rough against her face in comparison to the softness of Grace's skin. They exchanged pleasantries as they crossed the car park and entered the pub.

They were immediately hit by a wall of warmth which Sarah found most welcoming, and they were shown to a table for two in the corner of one of the dining areas. It seemed that Pennington had booked this particular table as he knew that it would give them some privacy.

Sarah had already decided that she was going to have the Sunday roast and all the trimmings, so Pennington followed suit. They said they'd delay a decision on the sticky toffee pudding until after they had finished the roast beef. They also ordered a couple of glasses of red wine and some water.

Once the waiter had departed, Pennington placed his forearms on the table and leaned in towards Hunter.

'How's your investigation going?' he asked.

'Round in circles if I'm really honest,' she said, smiling weakly. 'I've just come from a briefing with Beth Dench – do you know her?'

Pennington nodded. 'A class act by all accounts.'

'The tox samples for the snooker player and his manager were sent on to Porton Down who have now given an interim report that they contain snake venom mixed with extremely dangerous neurotoxins. Once that heady concoction gets into the bloodstream, you wouldn't stand a chance.'

'Jeez!' Pennington exclaimed. 'A real professional hit, then.'

'Well, yes, for want of a better description,' Hunter agreed. 'The problem is that I'm beginning to think there is a link between the killings here in Kent and suspected drug-related activities on the Isle of Wight.'

'Is this where Lulu Harrison comes into the equation?' he asked, leaning further in towards Hunter.

'Correct!' Hunter continued. 'It's a rather complex web of intrigue but we're looking at a man called Jasper Lime who designed the new Prism Theatre in Tonbridge and his business partner, Reggie Lemon, who was at the event on the night that the snooker player was killed. They both live and have their business headquarters on the Channel Island of Guernsey. The connection between our investigation and the Isle of Wight is that the car in which the snooker player's manager was found is registered to a company by the name of Prospero Inks. As you know, this company has its registered office at the house near Bembridge airport. We have also now discovered that the house was previously owned by Lemon's wife, Lucinda.'

'Okay, I'm with you so far,' Pennington said, and then pushed away from the table as two plates piled high with roast beef, Yorkshire puddings and all the trimmings was set in front of them. After bringing a bowl of horseradish sauce, the waiter wished them *bon appétit* and then retreated to the kitchen.

'Looks good,' Pennington commented, tucking in. 'So, what else have you found out?'

In between mouthfuls of delicious home-cooked food, Hunter told him about the discovery that Lulu Harrison had a private pilot's licence and that she had landed at Bembridge airport the previous Wednesday with one passenger aboard.

'Remember you mentioned that your intel had made reference to a *String Girl*, and someone else had thought of the character from *Andy Pandy*?' Sarah continued.

Pennington nodded, greedily helping himself to another dollop of horseradish sauce.

'Well, HantsPol have identified Harrison's aeroplane as having the registration G-LOOB which would pretty much identify her as being the *String Girl* also known as *Looby Lou* don't you think?'

Pennington had to agree with Sarah's conclusion that Lulu Harrison and Looby Lou were more than likely the same person.

Whilst they continued enjoying the excellent roast beef, Sarah also told him about the help they had been getting from the local CID who had made a quick search of the house.

'They've got to get the CSIs in there so no confirmation yet but our man took away some samples of white powder and showed them to a colleague in their drugs squad who said they were probably coke.'

She then went on to tell him about the body on the beach and the suspicion that it had been stored in the water butt at the house. Pennington looked up at that news, but Hunter allayed his fears that it was the missing Kent detective when she told him that it was a man known locally in the area.

'I told you that she had landed at Bembridge airport but there was no record of her plane leaving again. Well, the following day, we got a nod from ATC that the same plane had landed on the Channel Island of Alderney.'

'Alderney?' Pennington exclaimed.

Hunter proceeded to tell Pennington about their discovery that Lime had travelled to Alderney at the same time as Harrison had landed her plane there. She also told him that they had established that it was likely that Lemon had travelled to the Isle of Wight via Southampton airport, and that he had probably met Harrison at the house.

'So, you now reckon that Lemon and Lime are tied in with Harrison in some way?' Pennington asked before forking another brussels sprout up to his mouth.

'The circumstantial evidence is that they have each met independently with Harrison during the last seventy-two hours which just looks to me as if there's something going on.'

As they continued eating, Pennington went over the information which his team had managed to put together. They were principally relying on intel provided by their undercover agent – the guy who had been off-message for a week now. Although the concept of a drug baron building a sea-going vessel which couldn't be detected by radar seemed a bit far-fetched, Pennington's team had discovered that these vessels were available if you knew the right people and you had plenty of cash.

The idea of using migrants from the camps in northern France was something they hadn't thought of but it made sense. These people would be desperate and more likely to carry out any orders they were given if it meant getting safely to the UK. Because the undercover agent had not been in contact, they were lacking certain key pieces of information such as when a drop was going to be made and, more importantly, where. Pennington had forensically examined the information they had received from the agent, and he and his superiors were convinced that the plan was to come ashore between Hastings and Folkestone.

'We've studied that coastline in minute detail.' Pennington said. 'Our thinking is that they're not going to try and land around Dungeness for obvious reasons. It would probably also be tricky getting the tide right around Camber and Rye. So, if you discount the areas of the coastline which are built up, you are left with a stretch to the west of Winchelsea. It seems to offer good landing opportunities as well as a quick escape route across fields.'

Although she was really enjoying her meal, Hunter was also listening intently. This whole thing sounded bizarre yet, if their intelligence was correct, then her investigation was without doubt connected. And there had to be a common thread. Was that thread Lulu Harrison? Or was it the two in

361

Guernsey? Or was it another, as yet unidentified, person? It almost didn't matter who the drug baron was – they'd never catch him here in the UK. But the others were within UK jurisdiction.

Eventually, knives and forks were laid together on empty plates. The waiter arrived promptly to remove the plates and take the order for dessert. Reluctantly, neither Hunter nor Pennington had room for the sticky toffee pudding so they just ordered coffees.

'How does this all link up with your ongoing investigations here?' Pennington asked.

'Well, the only link is the car that Jacqui Anderson was found in which was registered to Prospero Inks. The discovery of drugs in Monroe's snooker cues doesn't seem to link to Lemon or Lime. At the same time, we have evidence of players being bribed to allow Monroe to win the tournament – why? And who by? We don't know the answer to those questions. And, in any event, our best witness to the bribing of snooker players is now in cold storage at the morgue.'

'What about Harrison?' Pennington asked.

'We only came across Harrison because she is down as the sole director of Prospero Inks which is registered at the Bembridge house. She is also the registered owner of the house having taken over ownership from Lucinda Lemon some four or five years ago. The discovery that she is a pilot and has her own plane was pure happenstance.'

Pennington raised both eyebrows – had he heard that word before? He'd file it for possible future use once he had established its meaning.

'We haven't found out anything of any note about Harrison,' Hunter continued. 'She's not on our radar and not on the PNC. As I said, I've been trying to fit her as our killer but the timings just don't work. Which leaves me with the continuing problem that I have three bodies and no idea who the killer is – or what the motive is for each killing.'

She felt her phone thrumming against her thigh and stretched out a leg so that she could extract it from the pocket of her jeans. Ted Selitto's name lit up the screen.

'I'll just take this,' she told Pennington as she swiped the screen. Pennington sat watching Hunter as she jammed the phone to her ear, eyes roaming the surface of the table in front of her. She twiddled a loose strand of hair around her fingers and occasionally tucked it behind her ear before retrieving it for another twiddle. Pennington watched her, fascinated by her every move. Whatever the call was about, it was the caller who was doing all the talking. Eventually, Hunter pulled the phone away from her ear, swiped the screen and placed the device on the table in front of her.

'Right, that was Ted,' she told Pennington. 'He's just had a nod from some contact he's made at Air Traffic Control who's told him that our friend, Lulu Harrison, made a flight this morning to somewhere called Lannion.'

Pennington looked blank and shrugged his shoulders to indicate that he'd never heard of the place.

'It's in northern Brittany – real Breton country apparently,' Hunter told him. 'Does that fit in with any of your intel?'

Pennington's face suddenly tensed up.

'Shit!' he exclaimed, his voice now low and conspiratorial. 'At one point, our man sent us a signal about having to make a journey to what he called the Breton peninsula but we think he meant the Brest peninsula. So, if Harrison's travelled to that area, there might just be some connection.'

Hunter watched Pennington as he tried to fit this information into the web of data that his people had already collected. He reached inside his jacket and took out his phone.

'Let's see exactly where Lannion is,' he said, poking the screen until he had a map of north-west France in front of him.

'Perhaps it's where the main man hangs out or where he has his base,' Hunter suggested. 'I doubt that he'd be based on the Normandy coast – far too close to the action.'

Pennington frowned at the image on the phone as he used his fingers to tease more detail out of the map.

'Bloody hell, Sarah!' he exclaimed under his breath. 'This Lannion place is really close to the Ile de Bréhat. That's definitely a place of interest for us. Did Ted find out anything else about her flight like where she started out from?'

'No. Apparently she checked in when she was leaving British airspace and crossing over to the French side.'

'Any flight plan for the journey back to the UK?'

'Not that Ted's been able to find out yet.'

Pennington sat in silence staring at the map on his phone.

'Dare I ask what the significance of the Ile de Bréhat is?' Sarah eventually enquired.

Pennington looked across the table at her. 'If Harrison's been to Bréhat she's likely to have been talking to one of the biggest and most dangerous drug barons in northern Europe. Remember the name, Sarah – Pascal Hennenbont. He is known to be a ruthless operator who has been involved in any number of grotesque murders but the French authorities have never been able to pin anything on him.'

Hunter looked suitably impressed at Pennington's description of the man but, in her own mind, she was wondering how the hell that was going to help with her investigation.

59

Sunday 26 November

There was a satisfying click as the wall panel sprang open in front of her. She hated changing the pin number which controlled the door mechanism in case she made a mistake and then couldn't access her secret room. But she knew that she had to go through this process every two to three weeks in order to maintain the highest level of security.

Once inside the room with the door safely locked, the LED lighting lit up the work surfaces and the two workstations that she had installed. There was the usual low hum of the refrigerators – and another noise.

Cocking her ear to catch the sound again, she made her way over to the sink and found that she must have left a tap dripping last time she had used the room. The strainer plug must have been mistakenly depressed after she had last been here, and about four inches of water had accumulated in the bottom of the sink. She also noticed a single Petri dish nestling under the water.

She was just about to reach out and pick the dish out of the water when she suddenly yanked her hand back and stood staring into the sink. A cloud of confusion tripped across her mind as she fought to remember what work she had done when she was last in this room. She never ever left equipment in the sink – that was one of her golden rules – so how did the Petri dish get there? She turned to look around the room, and then went over to the little refrigerator. Opening the door, she checked that everything was as she remembered it. She then quickly scanned the rest of her laboratory equipment, looking in drawers and cupboards, inspecting the contents of cabinets. But everything seemed to be in order.

Could it really be that she had forgotten to put this dish away? A cold shiver ran down her spine. Surely someone couldn't have gained entry to this room. No, it was impossible, and she cursed herself for being so careless in leaving the dish in the sink in the first place. Releasing the strainer plug and letting the water run away, she picked up the Petri dish and scolded it as if it was a small child. After venting her fury on this inanimate object, she put the offending item in the drier.

Rather nervously, she crossed the room and sat down at one of the work stations before opening the bag she had brought into the room with her. She needed something to calm herself down so she laid out the contents of the bag on the workbench and sat back looking at what she had accumulated.

In front of her were a couple of fine spray dispensers, a water spray bottle, a glass spray bottle, and a trigger spray dispenser. She now needed to test them out to see which one was most effective and which was the easiest to use. The amount of space it took up for carrying purposes was a major consideration as was the need to avoid degradation of the contents of the dispenser whilst in transit. Glass or plastic?

She took the dispensers over to the sink and filled them with water. Ideally, she wanted a misty spray but not one which was too gentle – she might need the spray to travel a distance of five or six feet. She also didn't want a dispenser which was just going to dispense a jet of liquid. That was far too risky and could end in disaster.

After a lot of water had been splashed and sprayed into the sink, she settled on one of the glass trigger spray dispensers. She felt that the trigger mechanism propelled the spray further than the other dispensers. It was also compact and easily controlled with one hand. She felt that it would fit snugly into the pocket of the jacket she would be wearing which was a prerequisite as she would not be carrying a bag at the time of use. As it was glass, there was no danger of the contents having a corrosive effect on the dispenser which had also been her worry about plastic dispensers.

Once she had dried the area around the sink, she put on her lab coat and went back to sit at her workstation. She put on a pair of nitrile gloves and a face mask before tucking long strands of her hair under the plain baseball cap she was already wearing. She stuffed a pair of safety glasses into the top pocket of the lab coat.

Over the next two hours, she carefully carried out a series of experiments – titrating, distilling, heating, cooling, crystallising, filtering, extracting. She was trying to see which agents reacted best with each other in a stable state. Whatever concoction she eventually decided on would have to remain in the dispensing bottle away from refrigeration for several hours. She had to make sure that it would not break down into its constituent parts during that time.

It was tiring work and required high levels of concentration. But eventually her work was done and she set about cleaning up the various pieces of equipment she had been using. She was pleased that she now knew how she was going to construct the toxin, and how she was going to deliver it.

All she now needed to know was when and where.

60

Sunday 26 November

The return journey to St Peter Port was even more uncomfortable than the trip over to Bréhat. The owner of the prototype vessel had wanted to open the engines up to see how they performed in a sea that wasn't exactly calm, so they bounced and crashed their way over the forty-five-mile passage back to Guernsey.

Staggering slightly as he gratefully stepped ashore at St Julian's Pier, Jasper Lime made his way back to the North Esplanade before crossing the road to The Thomas de la Rue pub where he had arranged to meet Reggie Lemon.

As soon as he entered the pub, he spotted Lemon who was disdainfully looking at his watch. Okay, Lime, thought, I'm a little late but not that much! He stopped by the bar to get himself a glass of the local Liberation ale and then joined Lemon.

'God! Never again!' he said as he flopped down onto the chair opposite Lemon. 'It might be quick but all comfort has been sacrificed for speed. A real boneshaker!' He took a long draught of the beer and then wiped his mouth, placing the glass on the table in front of him.

'Well?' Lemon looked enquiringly at his business partner. 'What did our friendly Frenchman have to say for himself today? Presumably Looby Lou got there?'

'She got there alright – turned up in a helicopter. Did you know she could fly choppers?'

Lemon shook his head. 'There's probably a lot we don't

know about her,' he said, sagely.

'Yeah, she said that as well,' Lime added, thoughtfully.

He took another glug of beer and then leant forward on the table. 'Anyway, our French pal is gearing up his operation in the UK. Reckons he's devised a devious way of getting stacks of stuff over there and Looby's now part of the plan to airlift it away after it lands on the shores.'

Lime then spent some time briefing Lemon about the meeting with Hennenbont and Harrison, answering the occasional question as he went. After he had finished, they lapsed into silence, each with their own thoughts about Hennenbont's plan.

'This is going to give us a lot of extra work,' Lime observed. 'There's no doubt there's the market but have we got all the lines set up to move this gear on in the quantities he's talking about?'

'That's why we needed that Davie Monroe,' Lemon sighed. 'I keep trying to work out who took him out – and why. I mean, he was doing quite a lot for us but, essentially, he was his own man transporting all his gear round in snooker cues. Interesting concept but gave him limited opportunities for expansion. Did you ask the Frenchman if he nobbled Monroe?'

'No, I did not!' Lime replied, an air of annoyance sounding in his voice. Bloody stupid question, he thought.

'Anyway, you're going to have to find quite a few more like him if we're going to be able to shift Hennenbont's stuff,' Lemon surmised. 'Presumably Looby's just doing the flying is she?'

'Well, yes – Looby's doing the flying but the problem with

her is that she's up to all sorts of other things,' Lime continued. 'She's well into all this new gear like fentanyl and its potential to make her a fortune. Unfortunately, it also has the potential to kill quite a lot of people although she doesn't appear to be too worried about that. She even started talking to Hennenbont about it.'

Lime then told him something of the discussions he had with Harrison when they met on Alderney. How she had been happy to freelance as a supplier, how she drops supplies into key customers on grassy airstrips, and how a lot of these guys are running a bit scared of the new drugs – preferring to stay with the tried and trusted rather than ordering the sort of stuff she can get them which makes the big bucks for her.

'I've read up about that fentanyl stuff,' Lemon interrupted, 'it's highly addictive and dealers are having to get stock much quicker than with, say, coke or crack or charlie. According to Looby, it's called China White on the market.' He paused to drain the last dregs of his beer. 'As far as I can see, it's only going to be of any benefit to us if Hennenbont can keep up a regular supply. Dealers will also need all the other gear to cut it with. Jeez! This could be a massive operation, Jas. Are we really sure we're up for it?'

'Course we are, Reggie,' Lime said, getting up from his chair. 'You having another one? Fancy a bowl of chips?'

'Okay – get some chicken wings as well.'

Lemon sat back in the lounge chair and watched Jasper Lime making his way to the bar. He never liked to get too involved in the drugs side of their business, and tended to leave it all to his business partner. He was, however, happy to be the contact with people like Monroe because he often travelled to different venues on the mainland, and could always set up meetings with dealers and suppliers. But this association with Hennenbont worried him. The guy was not only in a completely different league to them but, by all accounts, he was a very dangerous individual. There were plenty of stories of people going to meetings on Bréhat and never being seen again. Occasionally, he had heard about body parts being washed up on the shores of Brittany. Lemon always thought that he knew where they had come from. He just hoped that Lime wasn't signing their own death warrants.

Jasper returned with fresh glasses of beer and placed them on the table.

'Food's on its way,' he announced. 'Right! We do, of course, have one little problem and that is that Looby is expecting us to be there when the shipment comes in this week.'

Lemon almost choked on his beer. 'You have got to be joking,' he spluttered, replacing his glass on the table. 'You have *got* to be joking!' he repeated.

'Well, she's definitely expecting us,' Lime replied, 'but that doesn't mean we have to be there.'

'What's the plan for us, then?' Lemon asked.

'Hennenbont's expecting us to be on the ground when his ninjas arrive on the shore,' Lime explained. 'We're then supposed to guide them to the helicopter so they can dump their gear before making off into the night. Don't forget, this is going to be around two o'clock in the morning. We then climb aboard and swoop off into the night sky with Looby and God knows how many millions of pounds worth of toot.'

'Well, you can count me out of that one!' Lemon exclaimed.

'Yeah, I've pretty much counted myself out of it as well,' Lime replied, moving his glass to make way for the arrival of the chips and chicken wings.

They tucked into the chips and wings, taking the occasional mouthful of beer, maintaining a silence, deep in thought.

Reggie Lemon eventually looked across the table at Lime. 'You going to tell Looby, then?'

61

Sunday 26 November

The drive back to Tonbridge had been slow. Not because of Sunday afternoon traffic but because Sarah Hunter had been in contemplative mood and, if the truth be known, she hadn't really been concentrating on her driving. Fortunately, the traffic had been light and only one car had lost patience and overtaken her, the driver rather unnecessarily giving her the finger in the rear-view mirror. She always drew solace from such behaviour, happy in the knowledge that she was likely to live longer than that idiot.

She eventually arrived at the station and parked up. On the journey, Johnnie Walker had been on the radio playing seventies music, and she just had to hear the end of the Steely Dan classic '*Do It Again*' – so evocative of that era. But she had to get up to the MIR and face Grace Kendall for the first time since that fateful moment the previous evening. It had to be done – she simply couldn't avoid being in the same room as her. They worked together for God's sake!

On reaching the first floor, she spotted Ted Selitto sauntering into the kitchen area so she decided to join him.

'Hello, boss,' he greeted her. 'Good lunch?'

'Roast beef to die for – company not quite so good,' she joked. 'And you? How are you and Grace getting on?'

'Not that brilliantly,' he offered. 'It is a Sunday after all. Not many people around for us to call. Anyway, I'll let Grace tell you about that. I've been trying to track our friend, Lulu Harrison, which hasn't been very easy. My new best friend at

ATC may soon be removing my number from his favourites list.'

Hunter smiled at that. She knew that Selitto was like a dog with a bone when he really got on to something, and she could imagine the guy from ATC groaning when he saw Ted's number come up on his screen again.

'So, we've still not got any idea of where she went when she came back from France,' Hunter replied as they started to walk back towards the MIR.

'Well, we haven't drawn a complete blank,' Selitto said, with a measure of hope in his voice. 'We have been able to establish that she hasn't returned to any of the airfields in Kent, and she's not on the Isle of Wight. But, and this is a big but, there are 750 airfields in the UK many of which are in the south of England because they were needed for our defence against the Luftwaffe. Many of them are grass strips in the middle of nowhere with no one particularly interested in who lands there as long as the farmer cuts the grass and regularly empties the honesty box for the landing fees.'

Hunter pushed the door to the MIR open for Selitto who was carrying two cups of coffee, and they eased into the room. She spied Grace sitting at a desk in the corner by the window, and felt a frisson of heat around her neck. She just prayed to God that her cheeks hadn't turned pink.

'Hello, Sarah,' Kendall greeted her, looking up from her screen, 'good lunch?'

'I was just saying to Ted - roast beef to die for; company not quite so good! But that's being a bit unfair on my host!'

She moved across the room, removing her coat and scarf as she went, trying to avoid eye contact with Kendall for as long as possible. She made a fuss of draping her coat over a spare chair and then sitting at one of the work stations while Selitto had positioned himself by the window in front of Kendall's desk.

Sarah eventually looked across the room at Grace. Their eyes made contact and she felt a transfer of warm energy from her friend. The look Grace gave her somehow made everything seem right – and she knew instinctively that there was nothing to worry about. Their friendship was intact. It was business as usual. They had a killer to catch, and Grace was there for her. In fact, that's why they were all there on this cold and wintery Sunday afternoon.

'It's difficult to tell what these companies actually do,' Kendall was saying whilst, at the same time, updating Hunter about some of the research work she had been doing. 'They're listed as science-based organisations but the description is very broad. And, of course, there are many and varied sciences.'

'What about some of these so-called technology parks?' Selitto queried.

'Well, again, the word *technology* covers a multitude of different applications,' Kendall replied. 'It seems that we should be looking for a company that does research which probably involves animals – snakes and the like. But any company carrying out research using animals is probably going to be in deep cover to avoid the attention of animal rights activists and other eco-warrior organisations. Almost impossible to find them if we are just going to rely on our standard research techniques.'

'But not totally impossible?' Hunter asked, hoping that Kendall had some other suggestions.

'We're going to have to think outside the box on this one,' Kendall went on. 'One idea I've had is to get hold of some university professors and see if they know of any research facilities. We could possibly try some pharmaceutical companies, see if they have some contacts in the world of toxin research. A real off-the-wall thought is zoos – would they know where this sort of research is taking place?'

'Good idea,' Selitto interrupted. 'We could get in touch with that zoo down near Canterbury. I forget its name but I think Elaine might know someone there.'

'So, universities and pharma companies are certainly worth trying,' Hunter summarised. 'What about companies supplying equipment for keeping reptiles? They may be able to give us the names of some of their customers. Also, don't forget that our killer also has to have access to some dangerous chemicals so are we also looking at chemical suppliers?'

'Here's another idea,' Selitto offered. 'What about the Health & Safety Executive? Presumably, they'd have to check these places out on a regular basis, particularly if they're using live animals.'

'Yes, good thinking Ted.' Hunter was making a note of all these suggestions on a pad she had found in the desk drawer. Miraculously, she had also found a biro that worked and hadn't been chewed to within an inch of its life.

'Let's split up our research. Grace, you have a look through the technology parks, Ted, you see if you can identify any university professors and also have a look for any stand-alone pharma companies. I'll take a look at the HSE and chemical supplies companies. Let's leave zoos until Elaine gets in tomorrow.'

The others nodded their agreement to the plan. Selitto moved across to a vacant desk and fired up the computer.

'We're not going to be able to contact people at this hour on a Sunday but at least we can get a list of contacts ready for first thing tomorrow.' Hunter really wanted to get the research done quickly so that they wouldn't waste valuable time on Monday when the rest of her team would be there.

'Good idea,' Grace nodded her agreement, but was then distracted by the gold phone which had lit up on the desk in front of her. She answered it and then listened before telling the caller that she would be right there.

'Sorry but I'm going to have to leave you two for the moment,' she said, slipping her phone into her jeans' pocket as she got up from the desk. 'Looks like we've got a domestic which has got out of hand. Husband's kidnapped two of the children despite him being banned from the house. Usual fare for a Sunday afternoon, I'm afraid.'

'OK, Grace, hope to see you later,' Hunter said as Kendall left the room. She still had hopes of snatching a few moments with Grace just to clear the air after last night, but she also knew that these domestic call-outs had a nasty habit of rumbling on into the night.

After Grace had left, silence descended on the room. The only sound was the drone of traffic negotiating the roundabout below the window as weary Sunday afternoon shoppers made their way home from the retail delights of Tonbridge High Street.

Hunter wanted to know about the technology parks in Kent and had soon listed the Kent Science Park at Sittingbourne, Discovery Park at Sandwich and the London Science Park at Dartford. She also noted Kings Hill at West Malling. Each technology park had a number of science-based companies located within its campus, and Hunter soon realised that this was going to require a bit more research than she had originally envisaged.

Selitto decided to have a look through the register of professors and other specialists at Kent University in the hope of finding someone who might have an intricate knowledge of reptiles. Information was hard to come by, and he soon concluded that they would have to make direct contact with the university's various campuses in order to get much further with this line of enquiry.

He was just thinking of taking a look at how the Health & Safety Executive might help them when his phone started vibrating on the desk in front of him. A deep frown creased his forehead as he looked at caller ID.

'Boss, you'd better listen in to this.'

Hunter looked up as Selitto took the call, and listened intently as he communicated with the caller. Notes were furiously scribbled on the pad in front of him, and sincere gratitude was shown at the end of the call. Hunter wasn't sure what she had just listened to as Selitto had not actually said much.

'Well, that was my old mate from ATC,' Selitto smirked as he referred to the man as his old mate. 'He's found out that G-LOOB did come back to the UK this afternoon and probably landed at a tiny airstrip near Bideford.'

'What – Bideford, North Devon?' Hunter exclaimed before realising the stupidity of her question. How many other Bidefords were there?

'The very same!' Selitto replied, quickly googling a map of the area around Bideford. Hunter paddled her chair across the floor so that she was now sitting next to Selitto and looking at his screen. He was manipulating the cursor around the outskirts of the Devon town, zooming in and out of areas which appeared to be farmland.

He then switched to satellite mode and made a closer search of the areas to the south and west of the town.

'There!' Hunter said, excitedly pointing to an area on the screen which showed a farm with what appeared to be a mown track in the field near to some outbuildings. Selitto zoomed in further until they could not only clearly see the runway but there were also a couple of aircraft standing in front of one of the farm buildings.

He zoomed away from the airfield, trying to get his bearings in relation to Bideford. The airfield was, indeed, to the south and east of Bideford, probably not much more than five or six miles from the town. But that wasn't what had now caught his attention.

'Look,' he said, pointing to the screen.

Hunter leaned in for a closer look but could already see what Selitto was pointing to. As the image became clearer, she knew it was a large helipad.

They looked at each other.

'So, does she also fly helicopters?' Hunter asked no one in particular.

62

Monday 27 November

Sarah Hunter's index fingers tapped out the beat of the Stevie Nicks classic '*Rooms on Fire*' as she waited for a temporary set of traffic lights to turn green. She had come to a halt at yet another patch of roadworks which had no one working on it, and she wondered if there was anyone employed in the Kent Highways department at County Hall who actually co-ordinated the digging-up of roads around the county.

But the music on the radio was to her liking on this freezing cold November morning so she arrived at Pembury Road in good spirits.

By 07.30 a.m. the MIR was full to capacity now that DC Jed Crowther had joined the team so Hunter decided to get on with her morning briefing.

She called for order and moved over to the crime wall. Photographs of Davie Monroe, Jacqui Anderson and Gavin Staunton were spread across the top of the wall. Grainy photos of Reggie Lemon and Jasper Lime had also been stuck on the wall, and there was a blank square with the name Lulu Harrison underneath it. Someone had also drawn an outline of the coastline of southern England along with the Isle of Wight and the Channel Islands. Various lines and dotted lines went between the photographs and the specific points along the coast and on the islands.

'Okay, listen up! We're making progress but today I want all your efforts channelled into identifying our killer.'

She told them about the tox reports from Porton Down, and how they were looking for someone who had access to deadly snake venom. They also needed to track Lulu Harrison's movements after she landed her plane in Bideford – did she take a helicopter ride to somewhere else or perhaps she took off again and landed elsewhere?

But the hunt for the killer was Hunter's top priority so she delegated contact with university professors and local zoos to DC Elaine Jennings. DC Crowther was allocated contact with pharma research organisations, and DC Azzar Mishraz was assigned to the task of finding his way around the Health & Safety Executive.

The research that she and Selitto had done the previous afternoon was very superficial, and they had been distracted by the discovery of Harrison's landing at Bideford. So, she concluded that it would be best if the team started afresh. Let's see what they can come up with, she thought to herself.

'Grace, I want you to get back on to DS Jones on the Isle of Wight and see what other information he has come up with. Did his traffic cop ID Lemon from the photo we sent them? Can't remember if he ever got back to us on that. We should also be expecting the post-mortem report on the body found on the beach plus the CSI's report on the powders found in the house – and anything else they found there. Can you also get on to Bembridge Airport and find out how often Harrison has been there in the last year or so. And, while you're at it, you might as well ask for the same information from Sandown Airport – it's only a couple of miles down the road.'

Kendall nodded and wrote herself an extensive note before

turning back to her computer screen.

'Okay everyone, I want to know immediately you discover any useful information. If I'm not in here, call me. If I don't pick up, text me. We need to find this killer before he kills anyone else.'

She caught Selitto's eye and nodded towards the door. He followed her out of the room and down the corridor to the kitchen area where she busied herself making two mugs of coffee.

'I've had a call from Pennington. He wants us to go and take a look at an area on the coast where he thinks some big shipment of drugs is going to come ashore. He reckons that Lulu Harrison is tied in with it and that her involvement could lead us to those two who are based in the Channel Islands.'

'Well, we already know there's a connection through that house on the Isle of Wight,' Selitto said as they waited for the kettle to boil, 'and we must assume that she met one of them on Alderney. So, yeah, I reckon she's probably involved.'

'OK. I said we'd go down this afternoon.' Hunter had clearly already made up her mind so Selitto was happy to tag along. 'Let's leave soon after twelve so that we can get back in the light.'

She was just adding some milk to her coffee when DCI Iversen appeared in the doorway.

'Ah! There you are!' He nodded towards Selitto and then addressed Hunter. 'I know you're busy, Sarah, but I need an update. My office in five.' And, with that, he was gone.

'Hey, ho! Life wouldn't be the same without a briefing with the boss!' she said, turning to Selitto. 'Shouldn't take long so be ready for a prompt departure.'

The session with Iversen was shorter than she had expected. He was about to shoot off to a meeting with some of his counterparts in the Sussex force based at Lewes but wanted to hear how Hunter's investigation was proceeding.

'And you really think that Lemon and Lime are involved in all this?' he asked.

Hunter replied that she believed that they were part of a drugs cartel but she wasn't yet sure to what extent. Iversen had sounded a little disappointed about this news. 'They were a couple of young offenders in my days on the beat but I rather thought that they were now living on the other side of the tracks. Just shows how wrong you can be.'

'Well, it's only a line of enquiry, sir, although they are linked to this Harrison woman. But I've yet to be convinced that she's our killer. So, we've still got a number of strands which we're trying to tie together. Plus, I'm taking an interest in this drugs bust which Pennington's talking about.'

'Ah yes, I've heard about that,' Iversen replied. 'Coming ashore in some unmarked vessel which can't be seen on radar – or something like that. All sounds a bit far-fetched to me. Stick close to Pennington on that one and you shouldn't go wrong.'

Hunter wasn't sure what Iversen meant by that, and she was relieved when he announced that he had to leave. They both walked down the stairs together.

'One other thing, Sarah,' he said as they reached the first floor, 'don't forget to consider using the press to unlock some new lines of enquiry if you get stuck. That woman in

Maidstone's very good. You should give her a call.'

Hunter remained standing by the stairwell until she could no longer hear his feet clattering down the stairs.

'You have *got* to be joking,' she muttered under her breath before returning to the MIR.

Halfway through the morning, they got their first breakthrough. Jennings had been speaking to a professor at Kent University in Canterbury who had recommended that she contact someone at the local zoo. He had given Jennings the name and phone number of his contact who was the head keeper of reptiles.

After several attempts, Jennings had managed to make contact with the reptile house and had learnt that there were two or three companies in Kent which were carrying out toxin research using reptiles. The names she was given were Trelispe Industries which was based at Discovery Park in Sandwich and Marafrax Research which was based at Kings Hill, near Tonbridge. He couldn't remember the name of the other company but Jennings thought that two was better than none.

The next problem Jennings encountered was how to actually speak to a real person in any of these companies. The contact numbers shown on their websites were all linked to intricate voicemail connectors. She discussed this with Selitto after she found out that Crowther was having similar difficulty in contacting some of the pharma companies. It was eventually decided that Jennings and Crowther should pay a visit to the Kings Hill company that afternoon being as it was closer than the Sandwich-based company.

In the meantime, Selitto had a job for Carolyn Pennant.

'We're going to have to question those two Lemon and Lime characters but they are, of course, domiciled in the Channel Islands,' he told her. 'So, we're going to have to check if there's any protocol regarding how we make contact with them. I mean, I'm assuming that we can't just turn up on the island and arrest them. Suggest you get in contact with Guernsey Police and try to establish the ground rules as the boss seems to think that we should be talking to these guys sooner rather than later.'

Pennant was happy to take on this task and went back to her desk to start making calls.

On her return to the MIR, Sarah Hunter had sat with Grace Kendall who was having another virtual meeting with DS Jones. He reported that the PM on Brad Jolley had confirmed that cause of death was ultimately drowning in fresh water but that he would have probably been unconscious at the precise time of death due to the amount of fentanyl and heroin in his system. He had presumably been thrown into the sea to make it look like a swimming accident.

The CSIs had also found traces of his skin on manacles which were attached to one of the beds in the Bembridge house, and they had been able to link his body to the water butt. So, that theory had been proved right. The only thing they were still waiting on was the tox report on the powders found at the house – these had been delayed due to the sheer number of different samples that had been discovered.

Jones also mentioned that DC Robertson had followed up Selitto's suggestion that the car might have been stored in the long-term car park at Southampton Airport. She discovered that it had been kept there, on and off, for about two years. All parking fees were paid on time so there was no reason for the car park's owners to have been in contact with the registered owners of the car. Hunter assumed that Southampton was probably their entry point of choice to the UK – much less noticeable than if you kept arriving at Gatwick.

HantsPol was now treating Jolley's death as murder with Lulu Harrison and Pranvera Deshvilli high on their list of suspects. They were also now keen to interview Reggie Lemon as the traffic officer who saw the man in the car at the house had given a positive ID that it was Lemon, even from the grainy photo Kendall had emailed to them.

Jones asked Hunter to keep him informed of any sightings of Harrison which she was happy to do.

Once Jones had gone, Hunter sat with Mishraz to see how he was getting on. The people he had spoken to at the HSE had all been very helpful but he just felt as if he wasn't getting anywhere. It was difficult to work out how the organisation was structured, and which part of it was likely to provide him with the information he was looking for. Hunter could only offer encouragement as she would have probably lost patience with the HSE's bureaucracy a long time ago.

She eventually scanned the room and spotted Selitto in discussion with Jennings and Crowther. When he looked up, she beckoned him over. It was time to go.

63

Monday 27 November

Although the wind had shifted round to the west, it was still bitterly cold as Sarah Hunter hauled herself out of the Megane and closed the door behind her. She felt little pinpricks of moisture on her face and, licking her lips, she could taste the saltiness of the sea spray being carried on the wind.

Pulling her woollen bobble hat further down over her brow and the tops of her ears, she joined Selitto. They then walked up a concrete slope where they met the full force of the wind as they stepped onto the grassy path which ran along the edge of the beach. Menacing grey clouds rolled relentlessly across the sky and, with the sea looking equally as dark and uninviting, it was difficult to see any horizon in the distance.

Selitto caught sight of a cargo ship heading into the wind, making slow progress. It brought to mind the lines of a poem by John Masefield he had been forced to learn at school. Something about a dirty British coaster butting through the Channel – unfortunately, he now couldn't bring any of the other words to mind. But it was so evocative of the scene he was watching. The coaster was, indeed, butting through the Channel and, whether it was British or not, he didn't doubt that the crew were looking forward to being safely berthed within the confines of their next port of call.

They walked across the grassy path which, they now noticed, ran the length of the coastline as far as the eye could see. Stepping on to the shingle beach, their pace slowed as they adapted to the challenge of walking on pebbles. In front of them, the beach sloped down towards the incoming tide, and they could see the high-water mark running in each direction. Remnants of old groynes stood in the water like soldiers guarding the beach, their wooden hearts gradually being destroyed by years of erosion at the hands of the unrelenting tides.

A tall figure was walking towards them, well wrapped up against the elements in a long trench coat and a sailor's cap pulled tightly down on the top of his head.

'Hi, Sarah,' Pennington shouted as he came within earshot. 'Ted,' he said, nodding at Selitto, 'good to see you again. Thanks for coming down here. I thought it might be useful for you to take a look at the layout of the land where we think this drug delivery is going to take place.'

They had all hunched their shoulders in an effort to ward off the worst of the cold wind as it swept along the beach, and they were now looking at the panoramic view offered by this stretch of coastline.

Pennington turned and indicated that they should look at the area on the other side of the road, away from the beach.

'If our intel is correct,' Pennington continued, 'they'll come ashore somewhere along this beach and then make for the farmland that you can see across the road. Can you also see that there's a system of drainage ditches running through the fields? They're known locally as sewers. There's also a canal which borders the whole area.'

'So, what are they going to do with the gear once they get over there?' Hunter asked, stamping her feet to keep the circulation going.

'No idea, I'm afraid,' Pennington replied, apologetically. 'Still no news from our man so we're now flying blind on this one. In fact, if the truth be known, we only *think* that this is where the drop is going to be, we don't actually *know* for certain. Anyway, let's get off the beach and take a look at the fields. Follow me.'

Back on the grassy path, they soon found a set of concrete steps leading down to the road. Once they were in the lee of the wind, they could see that the area of farmland was quite extensive. Immediately in front of them was a seven-bar farm gate which gave access straight onto the farmland.

'It's a big area,' Selitto observed, 'and you can guarantee those drug mules, or whatever you want to call them, will be in and out of those ditches or sewers to throw everyone off the scent. Not much point getting dogs for this, I wouldn't have thought. And you say there's a canal at the top end of the fields? Navigable?'

'Well, it runs from Hythe and finishes near here,' Pennington vaguely pointed to their left. 'This last bit would probably not be fit for a motorised vessel – too much weed growing on the top of the water.'

'So, these guys aren't going to be picked up by boat on the canal and zoomed off to some safe house or anything like that?' Selitto continued with his questioning of Pennington.

'Judging by our previous experiences where these people get transported to the beach, they're just left to their own devices once ashore. They've all got mobiles so presumably they ring someone who then comes and collects them from wherever they're hiding.'

Hunter started to wander down the road. The others

followed and soon caught up with her.

'I looked at this area on the internet and thought I saw that there was a public path leading around one side of the grassland area which didn't have a gate.'

They kept walking until they came to an opening where a concrete path headed into the field.

'This looks like it,' she announced and set off down the path.

Fairly soon the path divided. Hunter instinctively took the righthand fork, quickly realising that there was a channel of water to their left.

'That must be the canal,' Pennington observed. 'It looks as if there's some weed floating on the top of it but not as much as I was led to believe. You could probably get a rowing boat on it or, perhaps, even some sort of motorised boat.'

They carried on walking for a further ten minutes until Hunter decided to stop and see where they were. In the distance, they could see the grassy slope leading up to the beach. Between the slope and where they stood were a series of fields dissected by the ditches. Behind them was the canal.

Selitto looked at the area of land between the beach and where they were standing, his eyes streaming as the cold wind bit into his very soul.

'These will be desperate people, adrenaline coursing through their veins,' he observed. 'They'll get across here quickly, no doubt – but where do they then go? And presumably they'll have to drop off the drugs. Is it possible that they'll have to get up to the canal to make the drop? They'd have to keep moving forward – no going back towards the sea. What's behind the canal?'

Pennington didn't know but suggested that it was probably more agricultural land.

'Looks more like scrubland from here so it may offer opportunities for hiding out until they get the signal to move on,' Selitto suggested.

'So, what's the plan, Jack?' Hunter was getting cold and badly wanted to be back at base in Tonbridge.

Pennington looked around the increasingly desolate landscape. 'I'm afraid that we haven't really got a plan because, right at this moment, we just don't know what we might be planning for, when it might happen, and how many insurgents there will be. Have we got the manpower? This will be a big operation. We don't know how much manpower we'll need or whether we've even got the strength in numbers. Will we have time to put it all together? God knows! And, we just don't have up-to-date intel from our guy. We can't have a crack squad of, say, fifty trained officers sitting waiting for something to happen twenty-four/seven. It's just not possible with all the uncertainty – quite apart from all the cuts in manpower that are going on at the moment.'

The three detectives stood in silence, each with their own thoughts, watery eyes roaming around the barren landscape surrounding them.

'Well, I don't know how you're going to organise anything unless you know a bit more about the extent of the threat,' Hunter commented as she turned to start the long trek back to the car.

'An idea of when the drop is going to take place would also be useful,' she added, rather sarcastically, although this comment seemed to get carried on the wind and never got as far as Pennington's ears.

To say that Sarah Hunter had misgivings about this whole scenario would be an understatement.

64

Monday 27 November

DC Elaine Jennings was annoyed that there were no unmarked pool cars available for their visit to Kings Hill. She and Crowther were, therefore, now sitting in a Vauxhall Astra which was emblazoned with the yellow and blue squares denoting '*Police*' and the Kent Constabulary.

'Shouldn't be too many questions at Reception about identity when we turn up in this,' Jennings quipped as they inched their way along Tonbridge High Street behind a No 7 bus on its way to Maidstone.

Crowther looked uncomfortable in the passenger seat, his knees jammed up against the dashboard. Despite his best efforts, he couldn't push the seat back any further so he had resigned himself to an uncomfortable twenty-minute journey to Kings Hill.

After they had managed to escape the clutches of Tonbridge, the traffic was light for a Monday afternoon and it wasn't long before they were turning into the tree-lined boulevard otherwise known as Kings Hill Avenue. Crowther consulted the map he had downloaded onto his phone and told Jennings that the address they wanted should be another two hundred yards on the left. Sure enough, they were soon pulling up to a bright red and white hooped security barrier. They showed their warrant cards to a guard who then raised the barrier, and they proceeded to the visitor's parking bay outside one of the modern low-level office buildings.

The sign to the left of the revolving doors read 'Marafrax

Research' so they knew that they had come to the right place. They introduced themselves at the reception desk and asked if they could have a word with whoever was in charge of the research company.

The receptionist made a close inspection of their warrant cards. 'I'm afraid all senior management are out this afternoon but the head of the laboratory is here. Shall I ask her to come down?'

Jennings said that would be fine, and they were politely asked to take a seat in the waiting area. A TV screen hung on the wall showing the BBC News Channel with subtitles as the sound had been muted. It always fascinated Jennings that the subtitles never seemed to be in sync, often showing the words spoken by someone who was no longer on the screen.

They didn't have long to wait before a door opened in the wall behind where they were standing, and a woman in a pristine white lab coat called over to them.

'Are you the police officers?' They turned and nodded whereupon the woman beckoned them towards her.

'My name's Alicia Gabriel,' she said, shaking hands with both detectives as she ushered them into a small windowless meeting room. Jennings noticed that there was another door in the opposite wall which their host had obviously used to access the room.

Gabriel invited them to sit at a round table which was positioned in the centre of the room, and she also took a seat at the table.

'I'm afraid that all my senior colleagues are out at a presentation this afternoon so you've got me instead!' Gabriel smiled before continuing. 'My colleague mentioned that you would like to talk about an ongoing investigation so how can I help?'

'Yes, thank you for agreeing to see us at such short notice,' Jennings replied. She then introduced herself and Crowther, and asked Gabriel if she could briefly explain her role at Marafrax.

'Certainly,' Gabriel started. 'I'm in charge of our research work on venoms carried by reptiles and arachnids. We study the biologically active ingredients in reptile venom to establish if they could be useful in the treatment of disease. Some of our experimentation involves the collection of venom so we keep a number of reptiles in-house. That's one of the reasons why you're down here and they're up there!' She laughed, pointing at the ceiling.

The two detectives smiled politely.

'All our work is completely above board,' she continued, 'and we work very closely with pharmaceutical companies. For example, one of our current projects is looking at scorpion venom which is essentially a neurotoxin that could kill you. However, it has been discovered that a compound of the venom may halt the progression of arthritis so we are now trying to assess exactly how this works.'

Jennings had always been interested in science, and it was fascinating listening to the work Gabriel and her team were involved with.

'So, these live reptiles and arachnids you keep on site,' Crowther was asking, 'how do you keep them? In cages or in boxes, or what?'

'Well, we keep the snakes in a serpentarium and the other reptiles and arachnids are kept in Perspex frames in a temperature-controlled room. All our storage facilities are very closely monitored by the HSE. In fact, it was only last week that we had a spot check from the blighters. Virtually no notice! A clean bill of health as usual, but they do keep us on our toes.'

At this news, the two detectives glanced at each other. If they weren't going to be allowed to see inside the laboratory, at least they could speak to someone who had seen the research work at close quarters.

'So, do you have individual scientists for each species?' Jennings wanted to know.

'Yes, each scientist is an expert in their own field,' Gabriel replied, suddenly looking very pleased with herself.

'So, you would have someone concentrating solely on snakes for example,' Jennings pushed on.

'Sure, that would be Frobes,' Gabriel gushed.

'Who?' Crowther asked, raising an eyebrow.

'Oh, that's our nickname for her. Samantha Frobisher. She's our herpetologist.'

The two detectives looked blankly at Gabriel.

'Sorry! That's the technical name for a snake expert,' she explained. 'Nothing our Frobes doesn't know about the slithery blighters. The best milker I've ever seen in all my years.'

Both detectives were now staring quizzically at Gabriel.

'Oh, sorry, another technical term. You have to milk a snake in order to get the venom. There's a particular technique to massaging the venom glands and dear old Samantha has the touch. She's a master at getting the most out of a snake.'

'And she has access to the snakes at any time?' Crowther asked.

'Well, yes, during working hours.' Jennings detected a note of doubt in Gabriel's reply but let it go.

'Sounds fascinating!' Jennings declared. She then looked over at Crowther before continuing.

'I think it might help us with our investigation if we could have a word with Ms Frobisher. Is she in today?' Jennings looked across the table at Gabriel.

'I'm afraid she's out at the moment,' Gabriel replied.

'That's okay, perhaps you could just give me her phone number so that I can give her a call sometime,' Jennings said, smiling at Gabriel and hoping that she wouldn't start preaching data protection at her.

But Gabriel didn't seem to have heard of data protection as she took out her phone and read off Frobisher's mobile number to the detectives.

'Thank you, Ms Gabriel, you've been a great help,' Jennings gushed.

Her platitudes clearly had the desired effect with Gabriel looking very pleased with herself as she steered the detectives back into the waiting area and asked them to check out at the reception desk before leaving the building.

Walking out into the car park, Jennings noticed a black Audi being manoeuvred into a parking space away to their right. Just as they got back to the patrol car, the Audi suddenly abandoned its attempt to park and accelerated away towards the exit and back onto Kings Hill Avenue.

'Was it something we said?' mused Jennings. Then she stopped in her tracks, thinking. 'On the other hand... wait here!' she commanded.

Crowther leaned against the patrol car and watched Jennings as she skipped over to the guardhouse which controlled entry and exit to the car park. She soon reappeared and strolled back to the car. They looked at each other across the roof of the vehicle.

'Samantha Frobisher by any chance?' Crowther asked.

'God! Were you always such a smart-arse party-pooper?' Jennings turned down the corners of her mouth and looked across at him. Then she smiled.

'Yes, that was our girl and she drives a nice black Audi TT Roadster. I've even got the number.'

Before they left, Crowther opened the rear door of the Astra and managed to release a badly mangled KFC box which had got caught up in the seat-sliding mechanism. After repositioning the passenger seat so that he had more leg room, Jennings started the engine.

'Come on,' she said, 'let's get away from these blighters and take this heap back to base.'

65

Monday 27 November

'You spoken to her yet?'

Reggie Lemon had just arrived at Jasper Lime's apartment and was keen to know whether his business partner had made any progress in his discussions with an increasingly irate Lulu Harrison.

The huge glass doors were firmly closed against an easterly gale which was battering the harbour at St Peter Port. Even with the doors closed, the two of them could still hear the sound of halyards thrashing against aluminium main masts on the boats lashed to the quayside.

Lime appeared to be in a reflective mood. He also appeared to be contemplating an enormous glass of gin and tonic. Reggie had seen smaller receptacles than that being used for flower arranging.

He walked over to the doors, and peered out through the rain-spattered glass. Time was running out, and they still hadn't got Looby Lou to fully commit to the audacious Hennenbont plan to get drugs and illegals ashore the following night. The sticking point was Harrison's insistence that they travel with her. Probably some sort of insurance policy to prove that the whole escapade was kosher and above board.

'I thought we'd agreed we weren't going,' Lime announced before taking a gulp of his drink. 'Can't we just tell her that she'll be flying solo on this one?'

'Well, you'd better tell her then,' Reggie replied. 'You're the main contact with her, not me. And, if she doesn't do it, we might as well sign our own death warrants because our ugly fat French friend will be coming for us.'

'Fuck him!' Lime exclaimed. 'I think I'd be more frightened of Looby Lou with her arsenal of drugs that no one's ever heard of and for which there are no known antidotes.'

Reggie plonked himself down on one of the chairs at the central island in the kitchen.

'Come on, Jas, time's running out. We need a plan.' Deep down, Reggie was starting to panic but he didn't dare let Lime see that he was weak in the face of adversity. Rather, he just sat there and hoped that Lime would grasp the nettle and come up with an idea that they could sell to Harrison.

The silence in the room was only interrupted by the rain crashing against the glass doors and the increasingly urgent thrashing of the halyards.

Another mouthful of mother's ruin and Lime swung off his barstool. Crossing the kitchen, he installed himself on the chair next to Reggie.

'I've got it,' he said, leaning in so close to Lemon that there could be no doubt that there was a large measure of gin in his drink.

'We'll tell her that Hennenbont wants us down on the beach to keep an eye on the landing. We'll then move up the field so that we can get a ride out of there on board Looby's chopper. We'll also tell her that we'll have fifty-grand for her as a thank you for a job well done. That should ensure her interest.'

Reggie Lemon stared at Lime, his brow deeply furrowed.

'And you really think that she'll buy that?'

'Course she will. The money'll get her – and it'll be all the sweeter if she thinks it's a payment from Hennenbont. I don't think she liked him very much although he seemed to be fairly struck on her.'

Reggie got up and walked round to the other side of the kitchen island. He leant on the marble top and fixed his eyes on Lime.

'There's only one thing wrong with your cunning little plan,' he said, trying to maintain eye contact with Lime who was now starting to avoid his friend's gaze. 'Where on earth is the fifty-grand coming from? That fucking Frenchman sure as hell isn't going to come across with that sort of money for Looby Lou even if he *was* struck on her.'

Lime shifted uncomfortably in his seat.

'Well, I didn't think we'd ever actually give her the money,' he replied, trying to sound a bit more bullish.

'Oh, terrific!' Reggie exclaimed. 'So, you'll tell her that Hennenbont's got a fifty-grand bung for her. However, when it doesn't materialise, she flies into Bréhat to confront him about something he knows nothing about! What the hell do you suppose would happen next? Well, I can tell you. We'd have both of them queuing up at the door, each of them waiting their turn to pick over what the other had left of our corpses.'

'Oh, come on Reggie,' Lime replied, trying to make light of the matter. 'After it's all done and we see that the plan works, we can just tell her that the fifty-grand was a mis-understanding. In any case, she's going to make much more than that by working with the French tosser so she'd be wise not to mention it to him – or us.'

There was a prolonged silence in the room. Reggie just couldn't believe that Jasper Lime could be so stupid – and so naïve.

'Well, you'd better pick up the phone to her and pray to God that she doesn't see through your subterfuge,' Reggie sneered as he stormed out of the apartment.

66

Monday 27 November

On arrival back at Pembury Road, Jed Crowther had quickly got on to the PNC and other databases to establish if they had any record of Samantha Frobisher.

Elaine Jennings had got straight on to the DVLA to establish ownership of the Audi and get details of the insurance cover. Carolyn Pennant had offered to establish ownership of the mobile phone number which they had been given by Alicia Gabriel.

But they soon discovered that it was not going to be straightforward tracking down Miss Frobisher.

Crowther was first to report no record of Frobisher on the PNC or any other database for that matter. Jennings quickly discovered that the Audi was registered to a Benjamin Mason at an address on Regent Street in London.

'Doubt that'll get us far,' Crowther observed. 'Sounds like one of those places where you just buy a mailbox. Something like 1,800 people and companies registered on each floor of the building.'

Pennant had finally got the phone company to divulge details of the mobile phone ownership. This time, Benjamin Mason was living in the centre of Shrewsbury. On checking the address, it was likely that the phone was registered to another mailbox.

Not to be deterred, Pennant then managed to arrange an immediate triangulation of the phone's signal to establish current location. She had been startled by the result.

'Bloody hell!' she exclaimed. 'Hey, guys, look at this.'

Crowther and Jennings studied the information on Pennant's computer screen. It showed that the phone had recently been in use less than a mile from the police station.

'Is that the best they can do?' Crowther asked.

'Pretty much,' Pennant responded. 'So, it looks like it's somewhere up The Drive or one of those roads round there.'

Jennings was reaching for her coat. 'Anyone fancy a walk?'

Carolyn Pennant was quick to volunteer, and the two detectives went off to see if they could find the black Audi.

The traffic was busy on the roundabout in front of the station as Jennings and Pennant headed off along Pembury Road. On the way down from the office, they had decided to take a walk up The Drive first to see if they could spot the Audi.

The road was reasonably well lit and had designated parking bays on both sides although parking was limited to residents only during certain hours of the day. Even in the dark, it was clear to see that there were different building styles with very little uniformity among the many houses.

Jennings and Pennant weren't going to dawdle as it was turning into another very cold evening so they picked up the pace as they proceeded up the incline to the top of the road. Just to make absolutely sure that they didn't miss anything, they split up - Jennings took the pavement to the left and Pennant the one on the right.

Eventually, they reached a road junction where The Drive gave way to Hilltop and was bisected by Baltic Road. The two detectives came together on the corner of the junction and compared notes.

'Presume you saw it?' Jennings asked.

'Yes, not too far down from here,' Pennant replied.

'It may not be parked outside Frobisher's house,' Jennings observed, 'but it's probably quite close. When we go back down, have a look at the houses with no lights on. She's probably lying low if she thinks we're looking for her.'

'Other thing I noticed was that there's no room to park on some driveways,' Pennant observed. 'Which may be why she's parked in the road.'

'Okay. Try to keep a note of house numbers,' said Jennings. 'Let's go!'

They walked back down the road, a little slower this time to make sure that they noted all the dark houses and those where there was no space for a car on the drive. Some houses already had two cars on the drive, there were at least two drives with skips on them and one which resembled a builder's yard with a pile of sand, unopened pallets of bricks and a huge rack of scaffolding poles.

When they got back onto Pembury Road, they compared notes again.

'Two prime candidates on my side,' Jennings reported. 'One which was pitch dark and one with a mass of stuff on the drive. No room for another car. But I thought I could see a faint light through the window. Not sure.'

'I had two dark houses and one full drive,' Pennant confirmed. 'I've got the numbers. It was the strangest feeling at one of the dark houses. Although I was walking slowly past, it just felt as if someone was watching me. Creepy!' She exaggerated a shiver.

'Okay, let's get back,' Jennings suggested. 'We've got some

possible addresses and we've found the car. Can't do more than that.'

Back at the MIR, Jed Crowther had been trying to put into practice his long-held belief that most if not all houses in the UK had a mobile phone registered to at least one person in the house. Azzar Mishraz wasn't so sure but agreed that this was a great opportunity to try the theory out.

Once Jennings and Pennant had returned with their information about the houses of interest, Crowther got to work on testing out his theory. If he could show that one of the houses of interest on The Drive had no mobile phone registered to it, then they may have narrowed down their search even more. However, making contact with the phone companies wasn't going to be easy so he probably had a long night ahead of him.

Hunter and Selitto had been closeted in a corner of the Ops Room with Grace Kendall since their return from the beach, and all three of them now made an appearance in the MIR.

'Right, listen up everyone,' Sarah commanded. 'We've had some interesting intel come in from the HSE so well done to you Azzar for getting us someone to talk to. And well done to whoever it was who suggested that we contact the HSE in the first place.'

They all looked at each other, no one really remembering who suggested the HSE but all mentally patting themselves on the back anyway for possibly having done so.

'Grace has been chasing around the HSE and finally found someone who was involved with inspections. It seems that companies using animals for research purposes tend to have more frequent inspections. They were aware of Marafrax because it has been very recently inspected. In fact, the report hasn't yet been completed. But the key bit of intel is that Samantha Frobisher is mentioned in the draft report.'

She looked round the room to make sure she had everyone's attention.

'It seems that our Ms Frobisher may not have been correctly recording the amount of snake venom she has been extracting from the snakes that are kept on the premises. Apparently, if she has been over-milking the snakes then she would be automatically endangering their health. This is a major concern for the HSE.'

Carolyn Pennant thought that this could be a turning point in the investigation, and wanted to know if her DI had any further information about Frobisher.

'Ted has been back on to Alicia Gabriel who Elaine and Jed visited today,' Hunter advised them.

'Yes, I spoke to Ms Gabriel,' Selitto said, consulting his notebook. 'She's always had Frobisher down as a bit of a loner – completely besotted by her snakes and interested in very little else. Been working there for a few years but never been any trouble. Reliable and thorough. The only problem we have is that Ms Gabriel's records show her living at an address in Reigate.'

'In a house owned by Benjamin Mason no doubt,' Crowther interrupted, a comment dripping with sarcasm.

'We haven't established that yet,' Hunter continued, 'but it is starting to look like Samantha Frobisher is not the real deal.'

67

Monday 27 November

The burner phone was vibrating on the dressing table. The one number in its memory was emblazoned on the screen. She swiped the screen to take the call.

'Hey, Tinx – it's time to go,' the voice growled. 'You ready?'

She was nearly always ready to go but she seemed to be flying blind on this one. She hadn't received anything recently regarding target or location.

'Ready for what exactly?' she replied.

'It's tomorrow night,' he continued. 'All the information's on its way to you. It's a big one, Tinx. Going to cause a big stink. So, my advice to you is to get your pretty little butt away from the location as soon as you've made the hit and disappear for a few weeks if not months. The cops are going to be all over it. Turn your email on – should all be there by now.'

She didn't even bother replying. She knew that he had already disconnected the call.

She sat at the dressing table and fired up her laptop. There was the email, just as he had said. She keyed in the password which allowed her to read the encrypted message, then scrolled through the pages of information. When she got to the end, she went back to the beginning and read it all again.

'This is some fucking hit,' she said, staring at her reflection in the mirror. She was pleased with herself for having already negotiated a much higher fee for this job, but she now had some organising to do. Not the least of which involved her escape from the hit followed by her immediate departure from the UK.

She stood between the two mirrored doors of the wardrobe. Her naked body glistened in the subtle floor-level lighting as did the blade of the knife she held in her right hand. She stared at her reflection in the mirrors in front of her. She felt statuesque, almost Amazonian.

She had stood in the shower for what felt like an eternity as the jets of warm water pummelled her body. She had let her hair hang loose, wanting to feel the water cascading through it. She had alternated between lifting her head towards the oncoming water, feeling the jets gently pricking her face, and then ducking so that the water hit the nape of her neck and her shoulders. Her damp hair now hung down her back, the occasional droplet of water splashing onto the carpet below.

She liked the feel of the knife in her hand. She would delicately wield it later to extract some of her blood. This was one of her rituals before a complex and dangerous mission. She couldn't remember how she had started self-harming but she gained huge solace from the sight of her own blood flowing out of her body before she faced adversity.

However, that was for later. Right now, it was me-time. She had been gradually working herself into a state of excitement and arousal. Backing away from the mirrors, she carefully laid the knife on the dressing table before crossing the room and folding her lithe body onto the bed.

68

Tuesday 28 November

It was another early start for Sarah Hunter as her investigation was now assuming some real urgency. She never slept well when there was so much going on, and last night had been no exception. Although she had fallen asleep almost as soon as her head hit the pillow, she was soon staring at the red dot on the bedside clock and wishing the time away.

The team had worked on into the night on Monday, fuelled by pizzas delivered by Dominos and an excellent curry from the Kathmandu Valley which had received high praise from Jed Crowther and Carolyn Pennant.

They had received a photograph of Samantha Frobisher from Alicia Gabriel which had been taken for her security pass. Although it was not of the best quality, Ms Gabriel had insisted that it was a good likeness so they had printed a copy and stuck it on the crime wall.

Much of the time had been devoted to trying to find information about Frobisher, and considering why she would have wanted to kill two snooker players and the hapless Jacqui Anderson.

Hunter was always in her element during these late sessions, letting her imagination have a free reign, hypothesising about what might or might not be the case, eagerly seeking out the opinions of those around her.

They reviewed all the CCTV and TV feed from The Prism again but couldn't match the photo of Frobisher with the killer. Pennant spent some time looking for the Audi on the ANPR records for that Sunday evening but to no avail.

Grace Kendall had been reviewing the activities of Reggie Lemon and Jasper Lime. In addition, she had been plotting the known journeys made by Lulu Harrison who seemed to have become inextricably linked to the two Guernsey-based businessmen.

She had also made what turned out to be a very useful call to an air traffic controller at Lannion airport in France. He was able to confirm that, not only had G-LOOB been at the airport on Sunday, but that the pilot had then transferred to a helicopter. Although the controller had no further information on this, it seemed to be further proof that Harrison flew helicopters.

Hunter thought back to her discussions with Jack Pennington and his identification of Ile de Bréhat as a place of interest. It was entirely possible that Harrison could have visited the island on Sunday and that she could have met with the drug baron Pascal Hennenbont. But this was pure speculation – they had no proof.

In any event, Sarah was still not convinced that Harrison was their killer so it made far more sense for her to now concentrate their efforts on Frobisher. However, Harrison was still in the mix – but what was she up to? In fact, what were Lemon and Lime up to? Was there now a link between the Ile de Bréhat and the Isle of Wight? And was Frobisher linked to any of these people or these locations?

They had eventually all gone home to their beds with different thoughts spinning around in their heads, knowing that the following day would be another draining day of sifting through all the information in an attempt to find the smallest clue in their hunt for a deadly killer.

Selitto had booked an early session with George at the Better Body Gym in Sevenoaks, and had thrown himself into the exercise routines his trainer had put him through. After a good long soak in the shower, he picked his way carefully along the A21 to Tonbridge in case there were any icy patches after another freezing night.

As he drove, he kept thinking about the photo of Samantha Frobisher which had come in from her boss at Marafrax the previous evening. There was something about Miss Frobisher which was starting to intrigue him. Had he met her before? Or had he just seen her somewhere? In a pub or a restaurant? Perhaps he'd seen her working out at the gym? Her face looked familiar. Even though it was only a security photo, he could tell that she was undoubtedly attractive but it was her eyes that had held his attention. 'Alluring' was one word which had sprung to mind. 'Cold' was another.

Sarah Hunter was already in the MIR when Selitto arrived, and pointed him towards a plate of *croissants* which she had brought in. 'You'll have to get your own coffee!' she added.

While he was out of the room, she took a call from Elaine Jennings.

'You're not going to believe this, ma'am, but it's gone – no sign of the Audi either in the road or on a drive. I've been up and down the road a couple of times and have driven around some of the adjoining streets but no sign of it.'

'Okay, Elaine, you'd better get back here.' Hunter disconnected the call and sat back in her chair just as Selitto re-entered the MIR with a steaming cup of coffee.

'Problem?' he asked, noticing a disconsolate look on Hunter's face.

'The Audi's gone,' she replied. 'I should have got someone to keep an eye on it overnight. Shit! Why didn't I think to do that?'

'I'll get Carolyn onto ANPR when she comes in,' Selitto said, 'see if she can find it or track it.'

'Yeah, but I should have had that covered,' she continued. 'Why wasn't I thinking straight?'

Selitto offered a few platitudes but they did little to help. Hunter felt as if she had let the team down, and was annoyed with herself for not reacting appropriately when she knew that the car, and possibly Samantha Frobisher, had been right under their noses.

The news that they had lost the Audi only seemed to spur the team on, and there was a high level of activity throughout the morning. DCI Alan Iversen had arrived in the MIR for an update on progress, and had the time to listen to contributions from each member of the team. As usual, Iversen was inherently interested in how his young detectives were making out – particularly those he had identified as having potential when they first started out in the force.

Hunter was pleased to have some of his time so that she could again run through all the strands of her investigation to see if there was anything she was missing. Iversen seemed pleased with what he had heard but had to get off to a meeting in Maidstone. Before leaving, he beckoned Hunter to join him in the corridor.

'Have you heard any more from Pennington,' he asked as they slowly inched towards the stairwell.

'Only about the possibility of a major drugs bust down on the coast,' Hunter replied. 'Ted and I took a trip out there yesterday and met up with him.'

'Problem is he's lost the intel, hasn't he?' Iversen commented.

'Seems that way,' Hunter agreed. 'Doesn't sound too promising for their undercover agent. Anyway, we had a look at the potential landing ground so I've got a picture of it in my mind. Have you actually spoken to Pennington?'

'Sorry, Sarah,' he replied rather sheepishly. 'I'm only relying on what I've picked up along the corridors of power at HQ.'

'Well, if you want my input, I'd say that those two from Guernsey need close scrutiny.'

'What, Lemon and Lime? How far do you think they are involved in all this drugs business?'

'Probably very involved, I'm afraid. Problem is they seem to be irrevocably linked to this Lulu Harrison woman who travels everywhere by air, often without checking in with ATC.'

'Thought that was illegal – and bloody risky!'

'She also seems to have had a right stash of high-quality gear at a house on the Isle of Wight. And, as you heard, we've also just found out that she's probably been over to a tiny island off the Brittany coast not far from Guernsey.'

'Yes, I can see the connection.' Iversen had to go. 'Keep me informed, and let me know if there's anything you need from me.'

Hunter returned to the MIR and was just about to sit at

one of the spare desks when Pennant called her over.

'I was asked to make contact with Guernsey Police,' Pennant told her, 'and it was suggested that we contact a Kristian de Carteret. Sounds like he might be a DCI. Anyway, the guy I spoke to seemed to know of Lemon and Lime. In fact, he said that the police knew most of the moneyed inhabitants of the island.'

'Probably like that old cop show based in Jersey,' Hunter replied. 'Bergerac was it? He was a police inspector and knew all the high rollers. Remember it?'

'Vaguely,' Pennant replied, although her facial expression gave lie to the fact that she had never heard of the programme.

Morning had turned into afternoon by the time Jed Crowther had finally established that there were three houses in The Drive with no record of having a mobile telephone. Cross-referencing this information with Pennant's list from the previous evening, they concluded that one of these properties matched one of the dark houses.

Hunter was not sure about the efficacy of this method of detection but she didn't want to dampen the enthusiasm of the team.

'As I understand it, your theory is that someone was using the phone in the area of The Drive. Because the Audi was parked on the road, it is a possibility that Frobisher was in the vicinity. As both the phone and car are registered to addresses out of area, you are suggesting that Frobisher could live in a house which has no phone registered to it.'

'That's pretty much it,' Crowther confirmed.

'Could I, therefore, suggest that two of you get round to these houses right now and see what you get from a knock on the door,' Hunter said, 'so that we can conclude this line of enquiry as quickly as possible.'

Jennings decided that she and Pennant should return to The Drive as they had been the ones to identify the houses. Meanwhile, Hunter dropped into the Ops Room to see how Selitto and Kendall were getting on.

'Think I'm going to go cross-eyed if I watch that CCTV from The Prism again,' Selitto said as Sarah slipped into a seat on the other side of Grace. She looked across at him, taking in Grace's profile. As she did so, she felt an involuntary ripple of excitement run through her body.

'There is just no way we can make that a woman!' Kendall sounded frustrated. 'All the CCTV is good for is to identify that there was a killer. We think it might be a woman but the pictures don't back that up. I suppose that there isn't any more intel on this Frobisher woman?'

Hunter shook her head.

'By the way,' Grace continued, 'I've had Jones back on the phone from the Isle of Wight. Their CSIs have managed to find a print in the kitchen at the house which matches a partial they found on one of the manacles. They also found the same print on the water butt. Of more significance, they have established ownership of these prints.'

'And?' Hunter wanted to know.

'Pranvera Deshvilli,' Grace replied. 'They also want to question Lulu Harrison so the hunt is now on for these two women.'

'Good! At least that's progress – well, for Jones anyway.'

Hunter sat back and stared at the clock on the wall. It still read 9.50. At least it was now more of a distraction from what was going on in her investigation.

Grace had been flicking through some pages of notes on her desk and now broke the silence.

'Let's say that Samantha Frobisher is our killer,' she suggested, 'do we think that she's in with Lemon and Lime, and did she kill Monroe on their orders?'

'And Staunton?' Selitto asked.

'And Staunton,' Grace repeated. 'Beth Dench and her boys found traces of drugs under some of the loose block flooring in his apartment, and they discovered a box of ready-to-go wraps in a cupboard under the kitchen sink.'

'Surely two snooker players can't have been a threat to Lemon and Lime!' Hunter exclaimed. 'And, by the way, here's another question for you. Why did Anderson run away after she discovered Monroe dead?'

'Yes, I've always thought that a bit strange,' Kendall commented.

'Was it because she knew he was going to die?' Selitto offered. 'In fact, did she know the killer? In fact…. did she run off to be with the killer?'

'Presumably unaware that the killer had the same plans for her!' Kendall finished off what they were all now thinking.

'So, if the killer had befriended Anderson in order to get to Monroe, did Anderson also have a reason for wanting to get rid of Monroe?' Hunter was busy twirling her hair through her fingers, deep in thought about this creative thinking that was going on around her.

'And, presumably, if she had befriended Anderson as a

means to an end, it would be logical to assume that the killer despatched her once she was of no further use.' Kendall sat back in her chair.

'No wonder we couldn't find the Audi on the ANPR for the night of Monroe's murder,' Selitto interjected. 'If Frobisher is the killer, she wouldn't have needed a car. She would have just walked between The Prism and The Drive.'

'Do you think that Anderson followed her?' Kendall asked.

'Must have done,' Selitto replied, 'otherwise I can't see how Frobisher could have killed her. But then, how did she get the body to the cemetery?'

'Well, remember when we took another look at the cemetery, Ted?' Hunter joined the discussion, 'We thought it looked like there were escape routes across fields. She probably drove Anderson in her own car, moved her into the driver's seat, and then left the engine running with the pipe leading from the exhaust. She then took off on a bicycle or scooter which she had hidden beforehand – or perhaps she had transported it in the boot of Anderson's car.'

Silence descended on the three of them again although it was far from quiet in the busy Ops Room. Eventually, Hunter decided to try out another theory.

'You know, I'm just not getting that Frobisher knows any of these people. We've established that Harrison knows the two in Guernsey but I highly doubt that she knew the snooker players or Anderson. And would Lemon and Lime have known them? That's a possible as far as I'm concerned, but would they have been bribing the players in their own tournament? Unless…' Her voice trailed off as the hair-twirling became more urgent.

'Let's look at the drugs connection again,' she eventually continued. 'If Lemon and Lime are a couple of drug lords running a small cartel then perhaps they were trying to do a deal with Monroe and Staunton, possibly even trying to recruit them as lieutenants on the mainland. But the deal fell through or something else went wrong so the Guernsey boys got rid of them. Did they get Harrison to do that? No, I don't think they did because the timelines don't fit with what we know about Harrison's movements. I also doubt she has the scientific knowledge or access to snakes.'

Selitto and Kendall had both turned to face Hunter, quizzical looks on their faces.

'Yes, it's now starting to make sense,' she continued, staring into the distance. 'No wonder we're having such difficulty in finding the killer. Because the killer was unknown to all of them – possibly apart from Anderson. Not even Lemon and Lime know the identity of the killer.'

She looked across at her trusted colleagues.

'It was a professional job carried out by a professional assassin!'

69

Tuesday 28 November

S arah Hunter crossed the corridor and made her way into the MIR. Although it was early evening, she was pleased to see that all the team were still there and actively engaged in sifting and re-sifting the information they had painstakingly managed to pull together. She noted that Jennings and Pennant had returned from their foray back up The Drive. Mishraz was updating the crime wall under instruction from Crowther who had obviously just unearthed some new information.

'Okay, guys, listen up!' she called out to get their attention. An eerie silence fell on the room as she told them about the review of the case that she had just undertaken with Selitto and Kendall. And that it was now her belief that Monroe, Staunton and Anderson had been killed by a hired assassin. She fielded occasional questions from the team but, otherwise, she had free rein to expand on her new theory.

When she had finished, the team looked around at each other and then back at Hunter. Jennings was first to speak.

'Just to let you know, ma'am, that we visited those three houses in The Drive. Two were occupied by elderly couples who still haven't embraced mobile technology. But, at the third house, there was not only no answer but there appeared to be little sign of life.'

'Okay,' Hunter replied. 'Do we know anything about ownership or the name of the occupier?'

'Not at the moment,' Jennings continued, 'we're waiting

for Land Registry who are having a few technical problems. Tonbridge and Malling Council have it down as unoccupied for council tax purposes but say they are having trouble tracing the owner.'

'Why's that?' Hunter asked.

'Seems the owner is one of those shell companies based in the Cayman Islands. All their efforts to make contact go unanswered. They've pretty much given up trying to collect the money.'

'Right! We need to get in there,' Hunter declared. 'Elaine, I'll leave you to get a search warrant as soon as possible. Get the magistrates out of bed if you need to. I also suggest you take Sammy the Lock with you. I don't want to draw attention to our visit by going in with the big red key although you should probably go in with some covert back-up just in case. If it is Frobisher's house, I reckon she's flown the nest by now so you should just be careful in case she's booby trapped the place.'

'What about her place of work?' Mishraz asked. 'Should we be taking a close look at that?'

'Good point, Azzar,' Hunter replied. 'Better get on to Ms Gabriel and take a trip over there first thing in the morning. Presumably she's had a no-show from Frobisher today so she should be interested in helping us.'

Hunter looked around the room. Who had spoken to Guernsey CID?

'Carolyn, was it you who contacted Guernsey?' she called over.

'Yes, ma'am,' came the reply. Hunter sidled over to Pennant's desk.

'Get in touch with the guy again and tell him about our investigation. Just the bare details at this stage but make sure he understands our belief that Lemon and Lime are part of a drugs cartel operating in the UK. Find out what the procedure is if we want to arrest them and take them in for questioning. Do they set them up for a video-link from their station to ours or do we have to go over there? Or, indeed, do they do the questioning on our behalf? That sort of thing. I think we'll probably have to get the two of them lifted sooner rather than later. All understood?'

'Yes, ma'am. I'm on it!' With that, Pennant immediately reached for the phone although Hunter didn't think she'd have much chance of talking to anyone at this time in the evening. But at least it showed that Pennant was keen.

Hunter got up and moved over to Crowther's desk.

'Are you chasing Harrison?' she asked him.

'Well, I'm trying to, ma'am,' he replied. 'I'm trying to get confirmation that she's still at Bideford – or at least that her plane's still there. I have been on to the Devon and Cornwall force who have said they'll try to do a drive-by at the airfield but they're short of manpower so we can't really push them.'

'Have you been on to ATC,' Hunter asked.

'Yes, but nothing to report,' he replied. 'They haven't heard from G-LOOB since the return from France. I've also been on to that helicopter place near Bideford. They're checking their records to see if Harrison landed or took off from there. They also do hires and they're checking that as well. So, I'm on it but those that I'm talking to seem to keep fairly normal hours. Unfortunately, darkness tends to bring forward the time to go home at this time of year.'

'Okay, keep on it,' Hunter encouraged him before pushing herself off the desk and going in search of Selitto. She eventually found that he had returned to the Ops Room and was sitting with Grace.

'Here, boss,' he said, waving her over. 'The ANPR's just pinged the Audi,' he told her as she approached the desk.

'Where?' she asked as she took the other seat.

'Just here,' Kendall said, pointing to a map on her screen. 'She was on the A299 Thanet Way past Herne Bay and on the way to the Saint Nicholas at Wade roundabout.'

'What the hell's she doing down there?' Hunter looked as if she was interrogating the computer screen.

'Well, you've got a good choice of destinations from there,' Kendall offered. 'Canterbury, Margate, Broadstairs, Ramsgate. Used to be a ferry to Ostend from Ramsgate but that closed. The only other potential destination of note in that neck of the woods is Manston Airport.'

At the mention of the word 'airport', Hunter's eyebrows shot up.

'Bloody hell, is she making a run for it from Manston? Fuck! I thought Manston had closed down.' Hunter was appalled to think that Frobisher might get away by simply taking a short flight across to continental Europe.

'I'll get on to the airport and see what their operational situation is,' Kendall volunteered. Then, looking at the clock at the bottom of the screen, she added that there may be no one there at this time of night if the airport was inactive.

'I think we'll have to go one better than that, Grace.' Hunter had decided that she had to try and get ahead of the game with Frobisher. 'Issue an All Ports Warning on her. She's got to be someone we need to interview as soon as she can be found. Put the car registration details in it as well. Let's get that out now.'

'At least she's still in Kent,' Selitto offered, hoping to somehow placate Hunter who was back to furiously twiddling her hair through her fingers, her whole persona giving a good impression of a tightly coiled spring.

This was going to be a long night, he thought.

70

Tuesday 28 November

'Hello, Jack… hello? Is that you, Jack?'

'Hi, Sarah. Can you hear me?'

'Yes, better now. Where the hell are you? Reception's really bad.'

'Down at the coast again. Signal's very weak on my phone.'

'Okay. What can I do for you?'

'We've finally got a message from our man. We think it's bona fide but very short on words or information. It seems they may be planning…'

Silence.

'Jack, you're cutting out again.'

'… I showed you yesterday. Did you get that?'

'No – please repeat.'

'Sorry – piss poor signal here. We think there's going to be a landing overnight tonight.'

'What? At the location we looked at yesterday?'

'Affirmative.'

'The beach with the fields and the canal running round it?'

Silence.

'Jack, are you still there?

'… yes… yes… sorry. The guy who monitors the calls says our man refers to it as something else but he's pretty sure it's the same place.'

'Do you think that your man's going to be coming ashore with the insurgents?'

'God knows! The guy who took the call reckons our man

has been rumbled. He seemed to only have a few seconds to send us what he could.'

'Doesn't sound good. Anything we can do to help?'

'Can you get down…'

'Hello, Jack – you still there? You've gone again, Jack! Jack?'

'Hi, Sarah – yes still here – keeps cutting out.'

'You were saying… what is it you want?'

'I was saying can you get down here?'

'To where we were yesterday?'

'Affirmative. We're a bit thin on the ground and need some…'

Silence.

'Sorry, you've broken up again. What do you need?'

'Back-up, that's what we need. This intel's literally just come in and we've got very little manpower available.'

'We'd like to help but there's just me and Ted here at the moment. Could possibly rustle up a couple more.'

'Whatever! Anything would be better than what we've got.'

'Okay. I'll see what we can do and then let you know.'

'As I say, no idea on timing so suggest that you don't plan on going to bed tonight. And it's bloody freezing. You'll need thermals and some hot flasks.'

'Right, got that. And, before you go – remember we talked about Harrison flying to Lannion in France?'

'Yes… yes, you mentioned it at lunch.'

'Well, we now have a French air traffic controller who says she hired a helicopter while she was there. Presume she could have been intending to take a look at the Ile de Bréhat.'

'Sorry, Sarah, you're breaking up a bit. Did you just say Ile de Bréhat?'

'Yes, Jack – it looks like Harrison could possibly have visited there.'

'My God, Sarah – if she's been there and she's been talking to this Hennenbont character, goodness only knows what we might be in for down here on the coast.'

'Well, it's only a possibility. She might have been scoping the place out. There's no evidence of her landing on the island so it's doubtful that she saw the man.'

'Yeah, but I don't like the idea that… talking to… trying to flood… new gear… dreadful consequences…'

'Jack, I'm not getting much of that.'

Silence.

'Jack… ?'

71

Wednesday 29 November

Detective Constable Jed Crowther closed the door of the Megane and sat back in the rear passenger seat. Condensation continued to form on the windows even after the occasional wipe of an elbow to brush away droplets of water for a clearer view of their surroundings. They had already finished their flasks of hot coffee which had not helped the condensation problem.

Selitto had parked in the lee of the grassy bank which tumbled down from the beach above. As the door of the car had opened, he had noticed that the time had already crept on to 01.15 a.m. with still no sign of any action.

'Nothing doing up there,' Crowther reported, referring to the last thirty minutes he had spent patrolling the beach. 'Tide's not far from being full, I'd say, so perhaps something's going to happen soon. Hardly any wind but fucking freezing!'

Sitting in the front passenger seat, Sarah Hunter grunted her acknowledgement of this embellished titbit of information. Selitto raised his eyebrows but kept his own counsel.

'Did you see Elaine?' Hunter asked.

'She's over in the field behind us talking to a couple of uniforms,' Crowther replied. 'Unless they've got some more manpower hidden away somewhere, we're very thin on the ground here,' he continued.

'Agreed!' said Hunter. 'This is either going to be a successful surveillance exercise or a monumental operational failure.' She adjusted her position in an effort to stop her body armour vest poking into her lower ribs – it really was the most uncomfortable piece of protective clothing but was deemed to be necessary in these circumstances.

'They've let us have a couple of these night vision glasses,' Crowther continued, passing the objects through the gap between Hunter and Selitto. 'Not bad, actually. Gives you a reasonable view in the dark.'

Hunter tried them out, looking out at the fields on the other side of the road. The glasses certainly improved the definition of the land, and enabled her to see quite a lot of detail. 'Hmm. Not bad,' she commented.

She was grateful that she had been able to have a daytime recce of the area just thirty-six hours earlier. It would have been impossible to have imagined the whole terrain if they had simply turned up in the dark. She had got Selitto to park by the track that they had walked up so that they could make a quick getaway if needed.

The Airwave radio burst into life on the dashboard in front of her.

'Gold Commander to Tango November Nine.'

Hunter picked up the radio and pressed the 'Talk' button. 'Tango November Nine.'

'Sarah,' Pennington's tinny voice crackled over the airwaves, 'we're thinking that this may have been a duff bit of intel. The tide's pretty much as high as it's going to get and we're not convinced that they're going to come in on the ebb. So, just to let you know that we're going to give it another hour and then call it a day. You okay with that? Over.'

She looked at Selitto who simply shrugged his shoulders. She pressed 'Talk' again.

'Tango November Nine. Roger. Understood. We'll stay to the end. Over.'

'Gold Commander. Thanks, Sarah. Out.'

The Airwave gave one last crackle as she replaced it on the dashboard.

'You weren't doing anything else were you, Ted?'

Selitto feigned a yawn. 'What, apart from getting some shut eye?'

They lapsed into silence.

Hunter poked the screen of her phone for a time-check. 01.52 a.m.

'I'm going for a walk,' she announced. 'You coming, Ted?'

She grabbed the Airwave and got out of the car. Wrapping her scarf tightly around her neck and jamming her reinforced police-issue cap onto her head, she set off for the flight of steps nearest to the car. This would take them up to the beach. Selitto followed her and they eventually stood together on the shingle looking out to sea.

In the pale moonlight, they could just make out the brilliant white of the foam crest on the waves as it snaked along the beach as far as the eye could see. The view was enhanced by the rhythmic sound of water lapping onto the beach just a few yards away from them. The tide was now either at its height or it had just started to ebb.

Hunter took a few steps along the shingle, picking her way carefully. She didn't want to aggravate her leg injuries but, at the same time, she felt that she had to keep moving to keep warm. She was about to turn and walk back to where Selitto had remained, marking their exit from the beach, when she thought she spotted a light on the water. She stared through the darkness, trying to gauge how far away it was.

Perhaps it was just some sort of reflection from what little moonlight there was. Or the light on one of the small inshore fishing boats which often came out in the dead of night along this stretch of coastline.

But, as she watched, the little light was joined by another. And then another. They looked like three tealights dancing on the water.

She turned and crunched her way across the shingle back to where Selitto was standing. 'Look, out there!' she exclaimed, pointing over her shoulder.

He couldn't really see where she was pointing but scanned the area behind the emerging figure of his DI and locked eyes on the little lights out to sea. The number seemed to be growing by the minute.

Hunter pulled out the Airwave. 'Tango November Nine to Gold Commander.' A crackle and then Pennington was on the line.

'Gold Commander. Go ahead, Tango November.'

Sarah hadn't the patience for all this formality so she just ploughed on.

'Jack, are you at beach level or below?'

'I'm in the field, why?'

'You'd better get up to the beach. It looks like your intel might be correct after all.'

'Christ! Are you sure, Sarah?'

She was staring out to sea as more and more little lights

became visible, all slowly but surely making their way to the shore.

'As sure as I'll ever be,' she said as the wave of little lights kept on coming.

'On my way. Gold Commander out!'

72

Wednesday 29 November

Hunter and Selitto stood watching the continuing proliferation of lights as they bobbed on the water, heading inexorably towards the beach. How many could they see now? Neither detective could be bothered to count. They both knew that numbers didn't matter - they simply didn't have the manpower to deal with something of this magnitude. And these people weren't going to surrender without a fight, particularly if they had consignments of drugs to deliver. They would have travelled halfway round the world for this moment, and would have been fleeced for every penny they had just to get here.

'Any bright ideas about what we can do?' Hunter asked as she manoeuvred herself back to the top of the steps.

'The only thought I've had is to let them get into the fields and then try to make them believe that they can't get back to the road,' Selitto replied, looking over towards the fields from his vantage point high up on the beach. 'If we were able to push them up to the canal, then they would have three options – surrender, fight or swim for it.'

'Yeah, sort of thing I had in mind. We really need to find Pennington. He's obviously not on the beach. Come on, let's get back to the road.'

They retreated back down the steps to the car. Hunter banged on the window and beckoned Crowther to get out of the car and follow them. 'And bring the night glasses,' she shouted as an afterthought.

She then went over the road and found DC Elaine Jennings still in conversation with a couple of Pennington's team. Hunter quickly briefed the three of them before telling Jennings to follow her. The other two officers scurried off to find their leader.

Standing in the middle of the road, Hunter wondered what on earth Pennington was planning on doing. She released the Airwave from the clip on her jacket. 'Tango November Nine to Gold Commander.'

Pennington replied almost immediately. Yes, Sarah – go ahead.'

'Have you got a plan for dealing with what's about to come ashore?' she asked. 'Like, what do you want us to do? Where do you want us to be located? Are we going to be arresting these guys or just watching to see what they do? And have you made a call for back-up yet?'

There was a pause. Hunter wasn't surprised. Pennington was way out of his comfort zone here. He was about to be overwhelmed by a completely unknown enemy. How many of them were there? Were they armed? If so, what with? If they started shooting, there was no tactical firearms team here. Knives? That would make close-armed combat virtually impossible.

'Sarah – you there?'

'Roger.'

'Our plan is to let them get off the beach into the field and then try to pen them in till back-up arrives. Now that there's a positive sighting, we're getting some more manpower down here including firearms and dogs.'

'Okay, that's good,' Hunter replied, chuckling to herself

that Pennington had come up with the same plan as they had. The extra manpower did, in fact, make it a much more viable plan, and she was pleased to hear that there was going to be some firearms cover – just in case. But she was still frustrated by the lack of planning.

'Where do you want us to be stationed?'

There was another pause – Hunter could hear some shouting in the distance. Pennington was back on the line.

'First landings are imminent. Can you guys get up that path – about where we were yesterday and then spread out. We're using torch beams to begin with to let them see that they're surrounded so if you could do the same that would be good. Got to go. Good luck!' There was a dying crackle from the Airwave as Hunter clipped it back into place.

They could hear some more shouting which seemed to be coming from the beach so Hunter presumed that the first of the insurgents had landed. She doubted that Pennington's men would be challenging them on the beach. Meanwhile, Selitto had dashed back to the car and was now dishing out the torches he had requisitioned earlier from a rather fusty sergeant at Pembury Road.

'Okay, let's get up this path,' Hunter commanded as they headed away from the beach. Trying to see the track by the very faintest of light from the moon, they soon realised that they now had the canal to their left so at least they were going in the right direction. Hunter stopped and looked back towards the beach.

'Here they come!' she blurted out. The others turned to see little lights appearing at the top of the beach although some were being extinguished as soon as they came into view.

Hunter wondered if they were headband torches. If they were discarding their lights off, were they planning to attempt to cross the fields in complete darkness? Or had they got night vision glasses? Doubtful, she thought, but not impossible. Nothing seemed to be impossible.

They continued their march along the track – Selitto leading, Crowther bringing up the rear. Individually, they kept looking back at the developing situation behind them. Hunter noted that the intended ring of light had not yet materialised to seal the entrance to the field so she presumed that not all the insurgents had left the beach. She did, however, feel that they were now far enough into the field and she called out to the others to stop and spread out.

Using one of the night glasses, she could vaguely see some of the insurgents starting to make their way across the field, tripping and falling on the uneven surface, but certainly making progress. She also noticed a line of police officers now assembled along the road and, as they started to enter the field with torches lit, she instructed the others to switch their torches on.

73

Wednesday 29 November

I t was Selitto who first heard it. A low hum which gradually built into the recognisable thwack thwack thwack of a helicopter. His initial thought was to congratulate Pennington on managing to get the force helicopter here so quickly bearing in mind it always seemed to be on patrol in Essex.

The lights of the aircraft appeared to his left, flying in low over the canal at the top end of the field. Just as it reached the grassland area, its powerful searchlight was switched on before it reduced height and hovered over the ground.

Even without the night glasses, Selitto now realised that this was not the Kent & Essex Police helicopter. It bore no markings, and wasn't even the right shape. And then everything suddenly fell into place. He knew exactly who was piloting the helicopter. He also knew who else was likely to be on board. And he knew he had to do something.

Just as his mind was processing all these thoughts, he spotted a movement behind the helicopter and away towards the canal. He grabbed the other night glasses from a rather startled Jennings and focused on a figure dressed all in black. He couldn't imagine what this person was doing running towards the helicopter from the canal but he did know that he had to find out. And then he was off.

Off across the long grass which bordered the field, and then tripping and slipping and sliding across the grassland towards the helicopter. He kept his eyes on the other figure which was probably going to reach the aircraft before him but he knew that he wasn't far behind. He had no idea whether he had been seen by the pilot or not but he didn't care – if he was right, this person needed to spend many years behind bars.

As he got closer, he realised that the rear doors of the helicopter were open and the insurgents that had already reached the aircraft were throwing packages across the rear seats before running off towards the canal. He could now see the outline of the pilot sitting in a little pool of blue light thrown up by the console panel in the front of the cockpit.

The noise was deafening as he reached the helicopter, the downdraught from the rotor blades also hampering his progress. Pulling himself up onto one of the landing skids, he wrenched the cockpit door open. Almost at the same time, the door on the other side of the cockpit opened and a figure dressed in black and wearing a balaclava swung into the cockpit.

One of the insurgents almost knocked Selitto off balance as he too climbed onto the landing skid and threw his white sack into the aircraft. But Selitto hung on grimly, never taking his eyes off the person who had entered the cockpit opposite him.

The pilot immediately turned to face the intruder and flashed a torch beam onto the balaclava. It was only for a split second but, in that tiny microcosm of time, Selitto had seen enough to know exactly who the intruder was. Even through the crudely cut holes of the balaclava, he recognised the eyes that stared back at him with fiery intent. He could never forget those eyes.

Quickly realising that there was no one else in the helicopter, he pulled himself into the cockpit just as the balaclava-clad figure produced what looked like an aerosol dispenser from her jacket pocket and started spraying a liquid into the face of the pilot.

Selitto shouted at the intruder, trying to make himself heard over the crashing din of the rotor blades. But his intervention only served to fully alert the intruder to his presence, and he felt a spray of cold liquid hit him full in the face. He jerked his head back and, as he did so, he sensed the pitch of the engine change.

His eyes were starting to stream and his vision was blurring but he could sense that the pilot was now manoeuvring the control stick and, at the same time, reaching down to grab the control lever in preparation for getting airborne.

He lost sight of the intruder as the helicopter suddenly lurched into the air, the downdraught scattering the insurgents who had made it across the field. Selitto was catapulted out of the cockpit and lost his footing on the landing skids before cartwheeling through the air and landing in an ungainly heap on the rough terrain. His left ankle had gone over sickeningly on impact, and he knew that that would be him in a boot for the next few months.

But, just as this thought was crossing his mind, he started to experience overwhelming nausea and he was having great difficulty breathing. Despite the cold, he was sweating profusely, and he was starting to shake violently. He quickly realised that the feeling in his hands had disappeared whilst, at the same time, he felt vomit rising up his throat. He started to turn his head to be sick but lapsed into unconsciousness before he could do so, the vomit splurging into his mouth with no means of escape.

74

Wednesday 29 November

Sarah Hunter couldn't believe what she had been watching through the night glasses, and shrieked when she saw Selitto tumble from the helicopter as it took to the air. Crowther was already on his way across the grassland to reach his stricken colleague, and Jennings had moved up closer to Hunter.

'There's something wrong with that helicopter!' Jennings shouted. 'The pitch of the engine's all wrong. The pilot hasn't got enough throttle for the take-off. I once had a boyfriend who flew these machines and this one doesn't sound as if it's going anywhere.'

They both watched, an increasing sense of dread etched on their faces, as the aircraft started to yaw violently from left to right. Jennings gasped as the craft then began rolling to the left before suddenly pitching skywards. It hung in the air for a few tantalising seconds, it's searchlight strobing across the dark clouds above. But it was now doomed and, as it continued to lose power, it finally flipped over and crashed to the ground. A huge explosion shook the pathway they were standing on, and an enormous fireball lit up the night sky.

Hunter's phone was thrumming in her pocket. It was Crowther.

'Not good here, ma'am,' he started. 'The DS is in a bad way. He's got a badly broken ankle but more of a concern is his face. It looks like he's been sprayed with something which has started to chew up his skin. He's vomited and passed out.

He was in danger of choking on his vomit but I managed to get his airways clear before he suffocated. He needs immediate treatment.'

Sarah Hunter was in shock. She knew she had to snap out of it. Her man needed her in his darkest hour. She wouldn't let him down.

She ripped the Airwave from her jacket and urgently called Pennington. She could only just hear him in amongst the cacophony of sound which was obviously surrounding him back at the roadside. He was, however, able to tell her that a full-scale emergency had been declared. There were many casualties from the helicopter crash site but he agreed to send a team of medics up the track to collect Selitto as soon as they arrived.

As she finished the call, she looked skywards at the sound of another helicopter approaching and was relieved when Jennings identified it as a Kent Air Ambulance. The two of them then left the path and stumbled across the field to where Selitto lay. By the time they reached him, Sarah was beside herself with pain caused by the unevenness of the terrain which was playing havoc with her weak legs.

Thankfully, the Air Ambulance had landed reasonably close to them so Hunter called across once a couple of medics had exited the aircraft. After a quick assessment, they decided that Selitto needed an immediate transfer to hospital so they loaded him into the helicopter and took off into the night sky.

Hunter, Jennings and Crowther slowly returned to the pathway, each wrapped up in their own thoughts about what they had just witnessed. They started the long trek back towards the beach just as another Air Ambulance landed in the field to their left. They were aware that some of the insurgents were still running across the field beside them, but Hunter presumed that Pennington now had some of his team located close to the canal so no doubt they would pick these stragglers up.

The helicopter was still burning furiously away to their left although they could see that the night sky was also reflecting the flashing blue lights from a number of fire engines. The air was redolent with the smell of kerosene. There was also a line of ambulances on the roadside in the lee of the beach wall, their blue lights bringing a hauntingly ethereal beauty to this desolate area of coastline.

Back at the road, they found Pennington giving orders to the increasing number of officers from the three main services. He was faced with the horrendous task of trying to prioritise the rounding up of the illegal insurgents and the urgent need to co-ordinate the rescue of those who had been injured in the helicopter crash.

Hunter didn't envy him one little bit having already heard that at least four insurgents and a police officer had been killed. Lights were starting to be erected and she looked back at the field leading away to the canal in the distance. White packages were dotted across the ground as far as the eye could see, discarded by the insurgents as they streaked across the field on their way to anticipated freedom. But no one was bothering to collect these up at the moment. They seemed so insignificant in light of what had just happened.

She felt numb as she allowed a despairing thought to invade her mind. Had her right-hand man, friend and trusted confidante been poisoned by the same evil concoction which had accounted for Monroe and the others? It was a gut-wrenching thought.

Jennings and Crowther had gone over to Pennington to see if they could offer any help or support but were now trudging back to where Hunter had remained alone.

The three of them stood together in silence. No one even felt the sub-zero temperatures on this tragic November night. They were already numb with cold.

75

Wednesday 29 November

As Ted Selitto had been taken off to hospital with the key fob to his trusty Megane in his pocket, Hunter and DCs Jennings and Crowther had had to rely on the kindness of others to get back to Tonbridge – which hadn't been easy. They eventually arrived back at Pembury Road feeling as if they had visited every corner of Kent on the way. Crowther was quickly despatched to Jimmy's Café to get two breakfast platters for himself and Jennings, and a mushroom omelette for Hunter. They made do with canteen coffee.

In the MIR, they shared the story of their night down at the beach whilst picking at their breakfasts. Grace Kendall was already chasing around to find out where Selitto had been taken. Mishraz was now dealing with ATC to find out where the helicopter had come from. He had managed to get its registration number from a contact he had in Kent Fire & Rescue who he had originally spoken to after a fire at a house in Hildenborough.

The mood was sombre. They were a man down, albeit temporarily they hoped. All their thoughts were with Selitto.

They returned to the question which had been bugging them – why had Selitto suddenly rushed the helicopter?

'He grabbed the night glasses from me,' Jennings was saying. 'He then swore and thrust them back at me before tearing off across the field. Perhaps he saw something – or someone?'

'Perhaps he saw someone,' Crowther offered. 'After all, how

did he get his face sprayed? Did the pilot do it? Supposing someone else entered the helicopter and sprayed both Ted and the pilot? Would that explain the crash?'

They sat and thought about this.

'Did you have a look through the glasses after he left, Elaine?' Hunter wanted to know if she had perhaps seen something which she hadn't classified as important.

'Well, I did have a quick look but there were an increasing number of people running around the helicopter as more of the insurgents got across the field. But now I come to think of it, there might have been someone making their way over from the canal *behind* the helicopter – meaning that they couldn't have been an insurgent because they were running towards the beach.'

'Degree of certainty?' Hunter asked.

'Can't be one hundred percent – but perhaps it was easier to see that person at the time Ted had the glasses.'

Mishraz's phone rang. Looking over at Hunter, she nodded for him to take the call. They watched as their colleague listened to information he was being given.

'Okay, thanks for that,' Mishraz eventually said as he ended the call. 'This may get us a bit further,' he said, turning to face the team, 'the helicopter was owned by Prospero Inks Limited.'

There was silence in the room.

'Fuck's sake!' Hunter exploded. 'I've had enough of hearing about this bloody company!'

'Perhaps Ted thought that Lulu Harrison was piloting the helicopter,' Kendall offered. 'Perhaps he hoped he could catch her red-handed. Perhaps he thought that there would be others in the chopper. Lemon and Lime, perhaps? It was a four-seater, after all.'

'And if he saw another person running from the canal, he thought that we could round up even more of them,' Jennings offered.

Hunter had quickly calmed down and was thinking more logically while Kendall continued with her forensic reasoning.

'So, if the pilot was Harrison, would she have sprayed whatever it was into Ted's face? Is she, in fact, the killer?'

'Or, if there was someone else who arrived from the canal, was it their intention to kill Harrison if she was, indeed, the pilot?' Jennings asked. 'If you like, Ted just got caught in the crossfire – he got sprayed just because he happened to be there at the same time, not because he was a target.'

Silence took over once again, the hum of the traffic the only distraction.

Sarah Hunter thrived on challenges, particularly when she was confronted with the need to prioritise a number of key actions, and her mind was now racing through everything that needed to be done.

'Okay,' she started, 'Elaine, where are we on the search warrant?'

'Carolyn's taken that over and should be on her way back from Sevenoaks court as we speak.'

'Good. You two had better organise a small search team and take Sammy the Lock with you. Better also take some tools in case you have to break any doors down once you're inside the house.'

'Grace, I want you to stick with Ted – find him for a start

and then find out how he is and when I can visit. It's vital that we know what it was that he saw.' Kendall nodded and then excused herself so that she could return to her desk in the Ops Room to start her search.

Hunter could feel the anger rising in her but she knew that she had to maintain her cool in front of her team. She looked around the room.

'Jed, get on to that Inspector in Guernsey and get him to arrest those fuckers, Lemon and Lime. If we have to, we can go over there to interview them. They're key players in all this. There's flights from Gatwick I think, but check that out as well.' Crowther started referring back to the case notes to find the identity of their contact in the Guernsey Police.

'Azzar, we need to know more about Harrison's flying activities and where she keeps these aircraft. Anything that you can get from ATC. Try and get some intel on the ground at Bideford. Try all the Kent and Sussex airfields. Contact the two airfields on the Isle of Wight again. Perhaps talk to DS Jones again. Tell him that he may need to end his search for Harrison although Deshvilli is presumably still at large.'

Once she knew that everyone was engaged on the tasks she had handed out, Hunter had gone down to the changing room on the ground floor where she freshened up at one of the large basins next to the shower cubicles.

She gripped the sides of the basin with both hands and stared at her gaunt face in the mirror. Without really understanding how, she realised that Ted Selitto had become an integral part of her life. And now he was fighting for his own life as a result of doing the only job that had ever interested him. She couldn't imagine solving complex cases without him by her side. Without his wise counsel at times when her investigations seemed to be stalling. Without their visits to the pub at the end of the day when they ruminated on the day's events. Without his sunny disposition which brightened up even her darkest days.

'Come on, Ted,' she implored her reflection in the mirror. 'You can do it. Don't leave me now.' A couple of tears rolled down her face and splashed into the basin. She felt so powerless. All she could do was wait and hope that Grace would soon track him down. She turned the tap on and splashed cold water on her face.

As she wandered back up the stairs, her phone vibrated in her back pocket. DCI Jack Pennington. She stopped at the top of the stairs listening to what he had to tell her.

The helicopter had crashed at the point where the strategy of penning the insurgents into the field was starting to work. Unfortunately, nine of the insurgents had been killed in the ensuing fireball along with one police officer. It would take days to identify the remains of the pilot but they were fairly sure that it would turn out to be Harrison.

Pennington expressed his deep concern about Selitto's health, and told her that he had a similar situation – three of his team were in hospital with severe burns.

'Remember I told you I thought that our man's cover might have been blown? Well, when we checked the beach long after the fireworks had died down, we found that one of the little inflatables which littered the shingle had a body strapped to it. It was our undercover agent with a bullet through his temple. He'd had his tongue cut out which had then been nailed to what was left of his forehead. Doubt that he knew much about it but just goes to prove my description of Hennenbont and his gang. These guys are seriously deranged.'

Agreeing to keep in touch, Hunter disconnected the call and sloped into the Ops Room where she sought solace in the company of Grace Kendall.

'Making progress,' Grace told her. 'They took him to St Thomas' Hospital in London so that he could be assessed and stabilised. Apparently, there was talk of taking him to The Hospital for Tropical Diseases but, for the moment, he's being kept at Tommy's.'

'OK, thanks Grace. I'd better get over there and chance my arm that they'll let me see him.'

76

Wednesday 29 November

The team gathered in the MIR for the 6.30 p.m. briefing. Crowther and Jennings looked dead on their feet, extremely fatigued, but they were still fully engaged in chasing up information. Hunter had taken a train to London where she had visited Selitto at St Thomas' Hospital. She had now returned on one of the many commuter trains coming out of London at this time of day, and was able to provide an update on his condition.

'He's in ITU so he's being well looked after,' Sarah told them. 'I was able to speak to the doctor who is supervising his care. He reckons that Ted has a reasonable chance of pulling through although it's too early to tell whether he will suffer any long-term effects. Looks like he was sprayed with another of these toxins although they are still carrying out tests. I mentioned snake venom so they'll be testing for that as well. He probably escaped certain death because the toxin seems to have only entered his body through his nose and mouth. That meant that it didn't go directly into his bloodstream. There's some disfigurement to the skin around his lower face and neck where the substance has had a burning effect, and he's suffering from blurred vision. The doctor said he thought it looked like a sulphuric acid burn but he wasn't sure. As I said, they've done all sorts of tests so we should know more about what he's been subjected to in a few days' time.'

She looked around the room. Everyone looked tense but relieved at the news that Selitto had a chance of pulling through.

'I did manage a few words with him,' she continued. 'He was a bit delirious even though he's quite sedated. He wasn't really making much sense but he's adamant that there was someone else in the helicopter. He kept talking about recognising the eyes. Those eyes, he kept saying.'

There was silence in the room, each member of the team hanging on every word of the report Hunter was giving them.

'I think I know what he was talking about!' Kendall broke the silence as she rose from her chair and moved towards the crime wall. She pointed to the photo on the security pass belonging to Samantha Frobisher.

'When he saw this photo, he talked about the eyes and his belief that he had seen them before. He was convinced that he'd seen Frobisher somewhere. It was the eyes that drew him in.'

'That's interesting, Grace,' Hunter replied, 'because those are about the only words he spoke. *Those eyes*, he kept saying. So, should we assume that Ted reckons he saw Frobisher in the helicopter? And, if so, was she flying it?'

'She could have been the figure running up from the canal,' Jennings butted in. 'If she entered the cockpit on the opposite side to Ted, then he would have been looking straight at her.'

They all stopped to think about this, trying to picture the desperate scene inside the cockpit of the helicopter. Eventually, Jennings interrupted the silence which had again draped itself over the team like some sort of invisible blanket.

'Speaking of Frobisher, there's evidence that she's been at that house on The Drive.'

Hunter was all ears. 'How did you get on there?'

Jennings told them how her team had made a quiet entry

into the property using Sammy as requested. It had all looked neat and tidy – and empty. No sign that anyone was living there, an almost sterile atmosphere inside the property. It was Carolyn Pennant who had spotted a small panel on one of the walls which looked as if it might control a secret door. Sammy couldn't work his magic on the panel as it was clearly driven by biometrics so one of the uniforms had applied the big red key. After smashing their way through the false wall, they had found themselves in a well-equipped laboratory. However, fearing that the room might be booby trapped in some way, they quickly decided not to venture any further and simply preserved the scene to await the arrival of the CSIs.

They had also carried out an external survey of the property and found a further entry panel at the back of the double garage. Having bludgeoned their way through another false wall, they had found themselves in a self-contained unit consisting of a small kitchen, a wet room and a huge luxury bedroom. Rather disturbingly, they had found a blood-soaked pillow on the bed and a trail of blood leading across the bedroom floor and into the kitchen before it ended abruptly at the external door. Then nothing. This was also being left to the CSIs.

'So, what do we make of that?' asked Hunter.

'I'd say that it could be where Frobisher operated from,' Jennings replied. 'We'll have to see what Beth Dench makes of the laboratory. She spent some time there late this afternoon. The blood's a bit left field. The puzzle is that the trail doesn't seem to continue after you get through the external door. We couldn't find any sign of blood in the garden or evidence of a body being dragged from the house. So, we're not even sure if we should be looking for another body or what?'

'Let's leave that to Beth and her crew.' Hunter didn't really want to deviate away from her own line of enquiry just now.

While Jennings had been talking, Crowther had taken a call and had left the room. He now returned and sat at his desk.

'Anything we should know about, Jed?' Hunter asked, detecting that he looked a little paler than when he had left the room.

'Yes, ma'am, that was DCI de Carteret from the Guernsey Police,' he started. 'It seems they visited Jasper Lime's apartment to take him in for questioning as we requested. They were able to make entry to the apartment because the door was ajar.'

Hunter could suddenly see where this was going.

'It seems that, once they got into the apartment, they were faced with a scene of utter carnage. The DCI's description was that Lime and his associate, Reggie Lemon, had been slaughtered in the kitchen. Various kitchen implements had been used to wreak havoc with the bodies of the two men, and the floor was awash with blood. He'll be filing a report for us as soon as he has a chance to get his own investigation up and running.'

There was silence in the room.

Hunter got up from her desk and walked over to the crime wall.

'What I haven't told you yet,' she said as she put a line through the photographs of Lemon and Lime, 'is that the body of the undercover agent working for Jack Pennington was found on the beach strapped to one of the inflatables. He had been shot in the head, and his tongue had been cut out and nailed to his forehead.'

There was an audible intake of breath as each of her team took in the grim details she had just given them.

'It seems that Pennington had discovered a connection between Lemon and Lime and a French drugs cartel run by Pascal Hennenbont. Last night's landings must be considered as a failure as, from early reports, Hennenbont would have got virtually none of his supply of drugs onto the streets of the UK. They were either left lying in the field or were destroyed in the helicopter crash. So, heads had to roll – quite literally it seems as far as Lemon and Lime are concerned.'

She wandered over to the window and looked out as another train made its lazy way across sets of points before entering Tonbridge station.

'So, this is how I see it,' she said, turning back to face the team. 'Lemon and Lime were in with Hennenbont, and they ran the UK for him. They probably relied on small suppliers and dealers such as Monroe and, possibly, Staunton to shift their gear. They also had some sort of association with Lulu Harrison through the medium of Prospero Inks but I really get the feeling that the tattoo supplies company was Harrison's baby.

Prospero Inks was a great cover and allowed her plenty of freedom to do whatever she wanted whilst using the house on the Isle of Wight as a base. It also allowed Lemon and Lime an opportunity to acquire goods and property in the UK which were not linked to their own business interests.'

'However, I'm not sure that she was a willing accomplice in their dealings with Hennenbont although it seems most likely that she met him last Sunday. Prior to that, she had individual meetings with both Lemon and Lime. Perhaps they were trying to entice her to join them in their association with Hennenbont, and the trip to Bréhat was her anointment on becoming part of the cartel. The greatest gift Harrison had was that she could fly. This solved so many problems for Lemon and Lime regarding distribution of their gear around the country.'

'But, and this is a bit of a leap of faith, someone didn't like what was going on and threw an enormous great monkey wrench into the mix by killing Monroe and Staunton. This after Lemon and Lime had probably sweet-talked Monroe into joining them in their association with Hennenbont by doing all they could to get him to win the snooker tournament, even bribing his opponents. However, having promised Monroe to Hennenbont, and then finding that he had been bumped off at The Prism, they had to find a replacement *post haste*. Step forward Lulu Harrison who just happened to be sitting around twiddling her thumbs on the Isle of Wight with her Albanian girlfriend.'

'Hennenbont clearly had some big master plan to flood the UK with choice gear which is what came on the intel to Pennington's unit. They managed to get an undercover man into the Frenchman's inner circle and just about stayed on top of what was going on. Without that man, we wouldn't have had any clue about last night's landings. But there is clearly someone else who is just as interested in what Hennenbont is doing – and who also has intimate knowledge of Lemon and

Lime's operation. However, I'm afraid that we haven't a clue who that person is at the moment.'

'What we do know is that, whoever this maverick is, he or she knew Samantha Frobisher and what she can do. Frobisher has been provided with such good intel that all she has to do is turn up somewhere and carry out the kill. She has easy access to snake venom, she is a top-class chemist, and she's probably got a laboratory full of deadly chemicals in her house. In short, she knows how to deliver death to order.'

Hunter looked around the room; she knew that she had everyone's full attention.

'Frobisher has the perfect cover. By day, she is the shy, retiring, nerdish scientist who likes nothing better than sitting in her serpentarium stroking snakes. By night, she turns into a deadly assassin with no scruples or thoughts for the people whose lives she is painfully erasing.'

'I think there's little doubt that Frobisher is our killer and, based on the evidence that we have found in the house on The Drive, we should be able to get a conviction. The only problem we now have is that we don't know where she is.'

Kendall's phone started to vibrate on the desk in front of her so she slipped out of the room to take the call.

'What about Jacqui Anderson, ma'am, where does she fit in?' Mishraz wanted to know.

'The jury's out on that one, Azzar,' Hunter replied. 'I had been thinking that she knew Lemon and Lime but I'm increasingly of the opinion that, although she may have known of them, she had probably never met them. I think that Frobisher used Anderson as a means of getting to Monroe. As we now know that Frobisher lived in The Drive,

I'm wondering if that is where Anderson went after she found Monroe's body. Had they arranged to meet up after the body had been discovered? Did Anderson even know that Frobisher had been planning to kill Monroe? Or had they become lovers? Who knows! All that we can deduce is that it is unlikely that Frobisher had intended that Anderson should remain alive to tell the tale.'

Grace returned to the room.

'They've found the Audi,' she informed the team. 'Top floor of the short-term car park at Gatwick Airport's South Terminal.'

'And?' Hunter asked.

'Timed in at 05.17 a.m. this morning. They've got a very slick information system at Gatwick so the officer I spoke to looked up Samantha Frobisher on the flight manifests for the day.'

'And?' Hunter asked again.

'No show,' Grace replied. 'She's not showing on any of the airline manifests. For today or tomorrow.'

'She could have left Gatwick by train,' Pennant offered.

'Could have done,' Hunter conceded, 'but my money's on her flying out of there as early as she could. New identity no doubt.'

'Shall I get a photo circulated to the check-ins and gate personnel?' Grace asked.

'Won't do any harm,' Hunter replied. 'If anyone does recognise her then we might at least know where she was travelling to. But I've come to the conclusion that Frobisher is far too clever to fall for that one. She will have completely changed her identity – and may even be travelling as a man!'

This time it was Hunter's phone which was vibrating on the desk where she had left it. She didn't recognise the number so stepped out of the room into the corridor. She swiped the screen to take the call.

'DI Hunter,' she growled.

'Oh, hello there. This is Doctor Engleman at St Thomas' Hospital. You remember we met earlier this afternoon?'

Hunter froze. Please God, no!

'I thought I should call you as there's been a development with Ted Selitto,' Engleman continued.

Sarah Hunter screwed her eyes tight shut. Was this her worst nightmare?

77

Thursday 30 November

The azure blue sea gently lapped onto the white sandy beach. A semi-circle of rocky outcrops jutted out of the water about two hundred yards from the shore looking like sentries protecting the beach. A couple walked past, hand in hand. Their footmarks leaving lazy imprints in the soft sand. Further out from the shore, the sea became the same deep shade of blue as the sky. Little clouds which were formed like wispy bits of cotton wool gave the only indication of the whereabouts of the horizon.

She watched as a small local fishing boat made its way across the bay to land its fresh catch at the quayside next to the club lounge. That would be her lunch arriving. Some fresh wahoo with oysters and shrimp – perhaps a couple of crab claws and a few mussels. A glass or two of Veuve Clicquot Rosé champagne. Plenty to look forward to.

She lay back on the blue and white sun lounger, lazily allowing one arm to hang over the side. She sifted fine grains of warm sand through her fingers as she continued to luxuriate in the view. There was a tiny zephyr of cooling breeze coming off the sea which made this the best time of the day for lying out in the sun.

After lunch, she would go for a stroll around the bay before pushing the sun lounger into the shade under her gazebo where she would probably enjoy a short afternoon siesta. Much later, in the early evening she would make her way to the club bar which was set on a promontory at the corner of the bay. The views from the terrace as the sun went down were to die for. There, she would drink a few cocktails and see what the rest of the evening had to offer in the way of entertainment. Perhaps she would listen to some jazz or maybe some steelpan music. Or she could take herself off to the Cubana Disco in the depths of the hotel if she fancied a sweaty liaison with a hunky medallion man or two.

The sound of her phone's discrete ring tone disturbed her reverie. She rummaged around in her beach bag and eventually located the device. She swiped the screen and held it to her ear.

Silence. But she knew he was there.

'Hey, Tinx, check you out!' he eventually drawled. 'You made it then!'

Silence again. How did he know where she was?

'By the way, I'm loving that bikini you're wearing today! Suits you!'

She leapt up from the sun lounger, the phone spilling out of her grasp onto the sand, her eyes swivelling maniacally around the small bay.

He couldn't be here – could he?

Acknowledgements

This second outing for Hunter & Selitto has been inspired by the wonderful response to my first book, *Danger*, so a big 'thank you' to everyone who read and commented so positively. Writing the second book wasn't as difficult as I expected although the complexity of the plot occasionally caused me many hours of anguish and self-doubt when I just couldn't get the continuity right.

One of the many comments about *Danger* was how readers could imagine themselves working alongside the main characters in the book. I hope that readers will, again, feel as if they are working with Sarah Hunter and her team as they track down a deadly enemy. The lovely countryside of Kent is still to the fore in this book and I hope that readers enjoy the other main locations – the Channel Island of Guernsey and the Isle of Wight.

As a little-known author, I have done all my own extensive research without being able to rely on the help of those with expert knowledge. Most of the locations mentioned in the book are real although the terrain of some may have been distorted in order to accommodate the storyline. The Prism is, of course, purely fictional although Tonbridge & Malling Council might like to consider something like it to promote the arts in Tonbridge. As always, all errors and inaccuracies are my own.

Thanks, as ever, go to my publisher, James Essinger, at The Conrad Press for his continuing belief and support. James is unfailingly enthusiastic about everything to do with writing, and I am very lucky to be part of his impressive and growing cohort of exciting authors.

I should also acknowledge the incredible support I have received from friends and family, some of whom are real afficionados of crime fiction. I am particularly grateful to Anne Eaves and Isobel Carver for their constructive comments on the early drafts of this book. I am also eternally grateful to my dear sister and sternest critic, Lindsay Crawford Jones, to whom this book is dedicated. Your support and encouragement have been invaluable throughout, and your lists of questions and corrections have always kept me on my toes.

I am finding that being an author requires a huge amount of patience from those who are nearest and dearest so thank you to all my closest family for your unfailing support – you know who you are. And a special hug and words of gratitude for Barbara who has had to put up with me spending hours at my desk trying to be creative. It is difficult to imagine how I would ever have been able to complete this book without your encouragement, wise counsel and support. Thank you.

Robin Nye, September 2021